SCHWERES WASSER

Heavy Water

*Merry Christmas Paul!
I hope you enjoy it.
John Alex Owen
12/19/17*

JOHN ALEX OWEN

outskirts press

Outskirts Press, Inc.
http://www.outskirtspress.com

Paperback ISBN: 978-1-4787-8907-9
Hardback ISBN: 978-1-4787-8908-6

Library of Congress Control Number: 2017906367

Cover Photo © 2017 thinkstockphotos.com. All rights reserved - used with permission.

Outskirts Press and the "OP" logo are trademarks belonging to Outskirts Press, Inc.

PRINTED IN THE UNITED STATES OF AMERICA

PROLOGUE

I returned to college for a reunion, after many years away. It was my pilgrimage back to Hanover, back to youthful overexuberance, trying to relive a time that probably never truly existed in the first place. By pure chance, I ran into my history professor, James Lockhardt, at the beer tent. He had been my major adviser back in the day, and I thought he was a very good guy. I was sad to learn that he was finally retiring after 40+ years of teaching, but I was glad to get to see him at the reunion. He asked how my career as an author was coming along, and for some reason, I proceeded to burden him with my quest to uncover a new story worth writing about.

As always, he listened intently and politely, and when I finished complaining about my lot in life, he smiled and weighed in. He suggested that I speak with a another retired professor, a friend of his, who was an elderly German immigrant and had a fascinating story about his exploits following the Second World War. The professor recalled my interest in the post-WWII era, and he was somehow sure this would make a suitable story. He also suggested that I do some research on some of the changes and interesting things that had surfaced after the reunification of East and West Germany, in the wake of the fall of the Berlin Wall, in 1989. In particular, he suggested a specific article in *Midlantic Monthly*, an international affairs magazine.

Then he laughed and reminded me that I should have spent more time in the library in college. Given the circumstances, and much like back in college, I did not pay great attention to his suggestion and after a few minutes further conversation and catching up, we parted and I continued to commune with long-lost classmates.

The next morning, after the hangover had started to wear off, I began to think about what Professor Lockhardt had offered. He knew me well and he had never steered me wrong. It would have been easy for him to have said nothing and just wished me luck in my search, but he had offered something for my consideration. Something I would have to explore if just to satisfy my curiosity. But, before I committed to speak to his friend, I thought that maybe I should also take his advice about doing some homework first. It might save a lot of wasted time. So, much as I had done back in college, I headed off to Baker Library to study history.

The library had changed a lot in thirty years. Computers had replaced file cards and this, along with some helpful staff, made finding the magazine issue the professor recommended a snap. There were several separate articles in this issue focused on the immediate years following reunification, and they covered the economic impact of reunification, and the social and political implications, as well as families reunited and valuables returned to rightful owners and the exposure of several ex-East German officials as crooks and ex-Nazis. It was interesting reading, but no great mysteries. Except that there was one story that was incomplete, and because it lacked closure, it was fascinating. Millions of dollars in Nazi gold had been found hidden in a wall in a small church in East Berlin. There was no explanation for how it got there, who put it there, or where it came from. What an interesting puzzle to research and solve, I thought--Nazi gold. But solving a sixty-year-old mystery involving Nazis in a foreign country I did not know well seemed a little daunting, to put it mildly. And what were the chances that this particular story related to the old German man the professor wanted me to see? Seemed like a long shot, but it was too interesting to let it drop.

To my surprise, Professor Lockhardt had known exactly which articles I would find interesting and he felt that his friend might be able to shed some light on the mystery. He also hinted that the article I "discovered" was only a small part of the complete story; interesting, but a sideshow to the main event. He said no more, but gave me a phone number and address in a nearby town across the river in Vermont. I was completely hooked at this point. I called, and after some introductions and explaining why I was calling, the elderly man invited me over to talk. He suggested that I bring lots of paper and thought we might spend a few hours over a couple of days together. I thought he was joking, but would find out once we met that he was quite serious. And of course, Professor Lockhardt had been correct; what I thought I knew was only a small part of the story.

This story would have been impossible to unravel before the fall of the Berlin Wall in 1989, the Freedom of Information Act, which allowed access to many documents sealed as "Classified, Top Secret" some sixty years ago, and of course, the internet. It was a lot of work, and yet a lot of fun. This book is dedicated to the professor and to the German whose story this really is, Herr Eric von Malloy, or should I say, my new friend, Rick Malloy.

CHAPTER ONE

It was a bright, early-spring day in northern Germany, without a cloud in the blue sky and only a light, cool wind coming down from the north. The small town of Faschgarten, about sixty kilometers northeast of Berlin, near the community of Gerswalde, was largely deserted, as its inhabitants had fled in anticipation of the Russian troops who would overrun the area within hours. It was not a large town to begin with, but today it was very quiet. The only sounds were the boom of distant artillery, a dog barking--left behind by a family in their hurry to get out of the Red Army's path--and the noise from the trucks and men at the local forschung werk, or research factory, who strangely had not yet vacated the area.

The old converted factory building was full of activity. Men in white lab coats were being directed by German soldiers as they packed boxes of papers and equipment to put into a truck. These soldiers were easily recognizable with their black uniforms, two sig rune lightning-bolt emblems on their collars, and the death's head symbol on their caps. They were from the elite and ruthless Schutzstaffel, the SS. The men in lab coats were directed to create a pile of documents in the middle of the loading area, just inside the building. Boxes taped shut

1

and marked with a blue Reich's eagle emblem (the Reichsadler, the state emblem used in Germany since the early 1870s) were thrown in the pile. Boxes sealed and stamped with a bright red Reich's eagle and swastika were carefully loaded onto the truck. In a secured area, back toward the rear of the building, a few scientists were carefully unloading file cabinets and the safe that was kept inside the window-less room. These were not the most senior scientists, as they had been ushered away a day earlier to avoid any possibility of capture by the impending Russian advance, but they were knowledgeable assistants who had been told to remain behind to finish up small projects and pack up the final documentation.

These mid-level scientists were proud to be at the "factory" in Faschgarten. They knew that they were lucky to be a part of this effort and were excited about the progress their research teams had made. These white-lab-coated men back in the secure area were apprehensive about what might happen to them if captured by the Russians, but they were also eager to get relocated to the promised new facility and to continue their work, and so their emotions were a mix of fear and great excitement. As a group, they acted nervous and meek. When they finished emptying the files and sorting the papers, a small bundle of the most sensitive papers, taken from the safe, was carefully wrapped in a yellow canvas cloth, stamped with the red Reich's eagle and swastika, and held aside. The remaining important technical papers from this area were finally placed in boxes, also marked with the red Nazi eagle and swastika, and carted out to where the other soldiers and technicians were working. A group of three SS soldiers, having surveyed the building and grounds, had begun unpacking explosives for the demolition of this facility. It would not be left for the Russians.

Dieter Von Hessler, a captain in the Nazi SS, stood by his staff car outside the entrance to the building. He was flanked by two other SS troopers, both carrying automatic weapons. They had made sure that they stood next to him, as if they were his bodyguards, although there was no apparent reason to need such protection. Dieter was the senior officer in charge. He had been given this simple assignment, which consisted of gathering up papers and lab equipment to avoid seizure by the Russians. He wondered to himself: *Doesn't the War Ministry have more important things to be concerned with than this deserted, no-place factory and a bunch of papers?* Either the papers were more important than he could imagine, or he was an insignificant officer who was no longer valued by his superiors. This did not look like the sort of facility that held secret papers valuable to the Reich. He had been to Peenemunde, the primary secret weapons research facility of the Reich up on the Baltic Sea, and he knew that this small place lacked everything Peenemunde had. There was no railroad access, no airfield, no port, and no decent roadway anywhere near here, compared to what was available further north. Peenemunde was purposely built with new laboratories, and test and production facilities, not at all like this old factory. Peenemunde had hundreds of researchers, mechanics, and engineering staff, with barracks and guards and multiple levels of security. It was not a small pool of men in lab coats working in an old converted wagon factory. In fact, the only thing this location had going for it was that it appeared insignificant. It was small and secluded, and private. It just seemed out of place for anything of value to the war effort.

As he stood there watching the scene unfold in front of him, Von Hessler wondered about what this secret mission meant for his future. He had not been told what the contents of this factory were, or what work was conducted here. He had not once thought to question his orders, but it was clear from a brief look at the facilities that this was not a place that was critical to the development or supply of weapons or aircraft, or parts, or anything he could imagine. It was small and lacked access to bring in raw materials or take out significant weaponry. Unlike most of the manufacturing locations in the Fatherland, this location was remote, not near any major cities or any raw materials supply. There were also no signs that there had been significant traffic in or out of the town recently. Most interesting of all to von Hessler, the buildings lacked all the typical symbols of the Third Reich — no swastikas, flags, signs, or bright-red paint. Just a bland, small, run-down factory compound that had housed some type of sophisticated equipment, all out in the middle of nowhere. Although most of the workers as well as the heavy equipment had left the previous day, Dieter could not help but notice those men in white lab coats, who he knew surely were not factory workers. Whatever kind of research the War Ministry had been conducting here, they had wanted to keep it very low-profile.

He had never been in this town before and did not know any of the men here, including the SS troopers standing beside him. Was that a coincidence, or had he been selected for that reason? It was uncomfortable, but he was a low-level man on a brief mission. He also wondered if he had been selected because he was trusted, or because his name was Von Hessler, nephew of a senior member of the high command. It was not too far-fetched that a superior in the SS felt he could gain favor by sending the Field Marshal's nephew out on a routine mission and then giving him medals for great bravery and success. It would not be the first time this had occurred and certainly not the last. He could understand that.

Given the nature of this assignment, at least as he knew it, he was surprised that his superiors had considered the need for a back-up team. Another small group of SS men were stationed at a crossroads a few miles away, in case he needed assistance. As he thought about it, he wondered why an inconsequential job like this should be thought to require such back-up. Additionally, his final orders had been sealed, and were not to be opened until after all the boxes were packed and the final preparations made for destroying the factory. This was a common practice for classified matters, but this seemed most unusual for such an apparently innocuous assignment. And as many times before, he had been told that failure to carry out those orders would be considered treason against the Reich. It was all very unusual, but then these were very unusual times. He stopped and listened for a second. *Were the Russian guns getting louder?* he wondered to himself.

The last of the red sealed boxes were brought out and loaded into the truck, thirty-six boxes in all. Several dozen blue sealed boxes had been piled in the middle of the building, and there was the separate large packet of documents carried to the staff car. These had been wrapped in the yellow cloth that also bore the red swastika and eagle, and the bundle was tied with black ribbon before being placed in a metal lockbox. The box was sealed and locked and put on the back seat of the car. Then the SS men went back to their tasks of wiring the building for demolition.

Von Hessler looked at his watch, then at the factory and the loaded truck, and seeing that the mission was on schedule and that it was finally time, he opened his orders and read them. As he read, he began to realize that this could not be an ordinary factory and these could not be ordinary papers being destroyed or taken away only to avoid embarrassing the Reich if discovered. The gravity of his orders was such that it was clear this mission had been conceived at the highest levels of the SS, maybe by Himmler himself. He was torn between the disgust he felt for the order he was about to give and the exhilaration he felt knowing that he had been chosen to lead this very important mission. As instructed, he waited until the demolition men had completed their work, then turned to the troopers on either side and gave them the orders he had received. They seemed more prepared to carry out these orders than he was to give them, for they acted without hesitation. The SS troopers turned toward the white-coated factory men and the other soldiers in the factory and opened fire with their MP-43 assault rifles. Each gun used a clip holding thirty bullets, and the troopers methodically used their weapons, replacing the empty clips with full ones and continuing until their job was completed. It was over in a few seconds, although Von Hessler thought to himself that it seemed like it took much longer. Eighteen men, fathers and sons, workers and soldiers, all dead, murdered so some apparently important papers could be kept secret. Three workers had tried to run and been shot in the back. One soldier had tried to return fire in vain, only to be cut down in his tracks. It was not clean like he had hoped, but messy and cruel. But it had been his orders, and he had loyally obeyed.

As directed in his orders, he and one of the two remaining SS men got into his large Mercedes and backed it out, away from the building. The other SS man backed the truck out and went back to start the fire and detonate the explosives set to destroy the building. He handled the explosive material, the igniters, the wiring, and the detonator with precision, indicating a comfort level gained from experience. Von Hessler watched as this SS man expertly doused the boxes with gasoline and lit them and then moved on to the final wiring for the detonation of the charges placed around the building. This demolition man was not a random choice for this mission, but hand picked by Von Hessler's superiors. And though it made perfect sense that the man would be an expert at arson and demolition, it still was unexpected. Von Hessler also noted that the explosive being used was the expensive newer plastic type explosive, made with Hexogen, a compound similar to the Allies' sophisticated RDX Composition B. Someone wanted to make sure that the job got done right and had provided the very best materials to do it.

There had been too many surprises so far, and Dieter did not like it. What would be next?

After a few minutes, the soldier emerged with the detonator and looked to Von Hessler for the signal. Von Hessler nodded and the man turned the handle to activate the detonator and pushed the plunger. The explosives did their job. First the loud noise and then a "whoosh" of air, then the hurtling of wood beams and roof and walls through the air, followed by the dust created by the building's collapse. As the dust began to settle, the fire engulfed the remaining mass. There would be no papers found and probably none of the eighteen bodies would be found, either. And if they were, it would fall on the Russians to explain. No, there would be no tracing the cause of this minor incident. Anyone looking into this fire would have bigger issues to contend with than what looked like the Russians killing a few German soldiers and the burning of a barn.

It was starting to get late. The staff car turned around and led the truck out of the town. As directed, they headed south toward a predetermined Weinstube in Eberswalde on the outskirts of Berlin, where they would be met by a new team who would relieve them of their cargo. As they drove, Von Hessler again began to wonder what his fate in this mission would be. He had done his job and was no longer needed. And there was another team taking over. He started to worry, but frankly he had few alternatives. If they wanted to kill him, he was as good as dead.

The back-up team of three more SS men had been waiting all day. They were stationed at an intersection 10 kilometers south of the factory and had been told to stay there until further orders were received. They did not know what their purpose was or might have been, or even why they needed to drive up north for 50 kilometers to sit all day by the side of the road. *Didn't the SS have better uses for its men than this? Especially at this time in the war*, they thought. But there they sat. They smoked cheap cigarettes and talked about their families and what they would do after the war, but mostly they just sat. At 6 p.m., after nearly nine hours of waiting, the SS staff car carrying Von Hessler and the truck loaded with boxes stopped and gave orders to the waiting men to follow them back toward Berlin. *What a wasted day*, they surely must have thought.

The now three-vehicle convoy continued south along the predetermined route, chosen largely because it would not encounter either the Russians or German army or civilian personnel fleeing the

Russians. It was not the most direct route, but knowing that not being captured by the enemy or being detained or delayed by the army was important, it was a very wise choice of roads. And Von Hessler understood that whoever had chosen these roads also knew which roads the retreating Wehrmacht would be on, and which they would not be on. He was beginning to feel a bit better about being assigned to this mission, this apparently very important mission.

By nine o'clock, they had reached the rendezvous at the Weinstube just north of central Berlin where they had been directed to stop. They arrived on time and so had their replacements. They were greeted cordially by two new SS men waiting at the restaurant, men even more eager and dedicated, thought Von Hessler. He wondered if they were his executioners as well. They relieved him of command of the truck and took the lockbox from his car, and they conveyed congratulations from his superiors for successful completion of his part in the mission. He was to stay and have dinner at the Weinstube and then he could drive himself back to his barracks near Pottsdam, without mentioning a word of the day's activities to any one, of course. The remaining men were to get into the two trucks and continue with the new SS men. Their jobs were not over yet. They secured the lockbox in the lead truck with the new SS men and prepared to leave. Within ten minutes of arriving at the meeting place, the trucks were back on the road and Von Hessler was standing alone with his staff car in front of the Weinstube. He would have to drive himself home, but that was a small issue, he thought. He felt relieved, and a little proud.

As he stood and watched the trucks disappear out of sight, Von Hessler wondered whether these young, eager SS men knew anything of the day's events, or for that matter, the contents of the lockbox or other boxes in the truck. It was not his place to inform them and he realized that he too did not know what the papers in these boxes contained. What he did know was that someone high in the ministry had gone to considerable trouble to keep it a secret. He turned to go in to dinner, and as did, he thought he heard the trucks backfire several times, but it was of no matter to him. He had done his job. He was tired and hungry and wanted to go home. He went into the Weinstube and shut the door behind himself.

It had not been a backfire that Von Hessler had heard. The trucks had hardly gone two kilometers before they stopped. The new SS men said they heard a noise from the engine and they must stop and tell the second truck about the engine trouble, in case it got worse. But this had not been the reason for stopping. It was their orders that caused them to stop there. Orders that came from very high in the SS, so high that they certainly would have been issued or approved by the High Command. Orders that were brief and direct: "All members of the original team, except Von Hessler, must be eliminated within five minutes from leaving the meeting point." No one associated with the original trip was to be left alive.

The first of the two new SS men walked back to the second truck casually, pulled out his pistol and shot the back-up team, one, two, three--each once in the head. The second of the new SS men similarly disposed of the remaining two original troopers riding in the back of the front truck, who had themselves done the killing of the scientists back at the factory, in front of Von Hessler. The empty truck was loaded with the five bodies and driven off into the woods out of sight. No one would find this truck for days and by then, the Russians would surely get credit for this. The two new SS men returned to their vehicle, the truck carrying the boxes and the lockbox with the yellow packet of secret papers.

The now lone remaining truck headed southwest to its appointed destination. Von Hessler had been right about one thing. The two new men did, in fact, know little about the contents of the truck they drove and they had been hand-picked for their dedication to the Reich and the knowledge that they were not very inquisitive types. They were killers with a cruel streak, like many of their SS brethren. They had been recruited out of prison by the brownshirts to do what they did best--stir up trouble. They were intimidators, thugs, and completely lacking conscience. They knew of each other, but there were no ties to anyone, except the Nazi party who had gotten them out of prison. They did their job, no questions asked. They knew neither where the boxes came from, nor what was in them. They did not know who issued the original orders for this mission or what happened at the research factory 60 kilometers north earlier in the day. They only knew to meet a truck, dispose of its occupants quickly and discretely, and deliver the contents of that truck as directed. Their orders were sequential, to be opened only after the completion of the one before it. The importance of this mission impressed the men, and they were not the sort to disobey orders from the top.

The truck arrived at its first destination in the East Berlin suburb of Friedrichshain. The orders seemed somewhat strange at this point, but they would do as they were directed. The lockbox that was being carried up front between the two men was to go to an address on Gartnerstrasse, to a stonemason who lived there. The senior of the two SS men was to deliver the lockbox while the junior man stayed with the truck. To avoid undue attention he was to walk the half-mile to the stonemason's house. In the middle of the night, at precisely midnight, he would knock on the door. As directed, they parked the truck in the center of the town and the senior man left to deliver the lockbox. Much to this senior officer's surprise, he was greeted at the door as he approached. With little more than a brief exchange of words to identify the receiver of the lockbox, the SS man handed the box to the man described as a stonemason and returned to his truck to continue with the remaining 36 boxes.

The man known only as a stonemason, named Rudolph Werner, was, of course, much more than a simple carver of granite and marble, for he had held a different job for the past seven years and was now a high-ranking member of the SS. He had given up his work in the construction trades and moved up to serve the Führer and the Reich. Himmler himself had actually chosen him personally for this mission and he knew the seriousness of the job. In the early morning he would take the contents of the lockbox to its final resting place nearby and he would be responsible for documenting its location so that subsequent followers of the Reich could find the lockbox in the future. Herr Werner had an understanding not of the specific documents inside the box, but of the importance of the contents of this lockbox. He also understood that when he had finished his mission he would never make mention of it again. What he did not know was that Himmler's plan did not include his living long enough to tell anyone. Orders had been put in place to eliminate Werner and his family in the following week, using the pretense of being traitors to the Reich. However, the Russians closed in too fast and Werner was killed in the street fighting several days later, and the orders to kill his family were never able to be carried out. With his death, and then Himmler's death, the location of the secret documents was known by no one.

The older SS man returned to the truck and as instructed they opened their last sealed order. It gave them specific directions to deliver the remaining contents of the truck to a secluded facility northwest of their current location, away from the city. Neither of the two men spoke, but it was understood that they were pleased to be nearing the end of this assignment and would have some time for rest and relaxation. It had been a strange night already and although they did not much care, they also did not know what this mission had been all about. They started the truck and drove on as ordered, silent in the late night. As dawn began to break, the truck was close to its last stop, an underground mine which had been converted when the Allied bombing began. It was an old salt mine, burrowed into the hill by hand before the turn of the century and nearly 45 kilometers northwest of Berlin.

Its location was ideal, near the center of power, yet not close to any military targets which would cause the Allies to pay attention to this area. It had been used as a storage facility earlier in the war; later it was a major field headquarters where business could be conducted without fear of interruption from the constant Allied bombing raids. Now it was to be a repository, a vault where valuable and important items of the Third Reich would be packed away until they were needed again. Hans, the younger soldier in the truck, noting that they were a few minutes ahead of the assigned schedule, asked his senior comrade to pull over so he could relieve himself before they arrived. The two men stood by the road, pissing into the bushes as the sun began to come up. They lit and smoked a cigarette and then, after a few minutes they resumed the last few kilometers of their trip. They wanted to arrive on time.

The truck arrived at the secure underground repository right on schedule with its cargo in the back and the two SS men up front. They were waived through the hastily made gate area and directed to back up to the loading area at the entrance to the mine and then to stay in the truck. The boxes would be unloaded and they would return to their station post, back in Berlin. What the two SS thugs could not see and did not know was that as the last of the boxes was being removed, a small box containing explosives and a timer, set to go off in ten minutes, was put up toward the front, next to the back side of the cab area, just a foot or so behind the seats of the SS senior driver and his younger partner. The driver was signaled that the unloading was complete and again told that he should return to his post without stopping in route. They headed off, back down the road, toward Berlin, mission complete and nearly over. They were tired. It had been a long night and both men wanted to return to their barracks and sleep for the rest of this day.

Approximately 5 kilometers out from the mine repository, there was a large explosion. The truck virtually erupted as it was torn apart.

The front cab section, with its windows blown out, veered off the road and slammed into a tree, bursting into flames. The rear of the truck had been blown into small pieces. No survivors were possible and none would be found.

The delivered cargo, back at the mine, would continue into a secure underground bunker where the thirty-six boxes, each marked with the red Reich eagle and swastika, were labeled, logged in, and filed away, safe from Allied bombing missions. The intent was that they remain safely hidden until the Reich could turn the war around and was ready to continue its research. In the meantime, the bunker would be guarded by the army and if necessary, they would collapse the entrance, sealing the cave, so that no Allied soldiers would be able to get in. At least that was the plan. In practice, the Allied advance was so swift and the German retreat so uncoordinated that the Wehrmacht soldiers fled their posts as the American 7th Armored division closed in on the area only several days later. These boxes of documents would be discovered by the Americans, along with countless art treasures and museum pieces also stored by the Nazis in this old salt mine.

The mission was over, and it had gone exactly as conceived and planned.

Later that morning it was reported with great regret to Field Marshal Von Hessler that his youngest nephew, Dieter, had suffered a fatal heart attack while eating dinner at a Weinstube just north of Berlin. He had been a splendid officer in the SS and would receive a full military funeral, of course. It was so sad. The Führer and Herr Himmler had both sent their condolences, personally.

Chapter Two

The European war was finally over. The madness that was the Third Reich had finally capitulated in early May and the dust of war was beginning to settle. In America and England, France and the Soviet Union, there was great joy and celebration. In Germany, it was the final conclusion of a decade-long catastrophic nightmare. It was not surrender so much as the culmination of complete and total defeat. The Allies had completely conquered the German republic in a way that few previous wars had ended anywhere. This was not like the negotiated peace that ended the First World War, or like the brokered peace accords that ended the Spanish-American war or The Crimean War, or anything like the negotiated terms that ended the War of 1812 or the American War for Independence. Germany had been conquered, occupied, and turned to ashes.

It was tragically sad how little remained of a once mighty nation. Government, industry, society and cultural systems were in ruin. Major cities such as Berlin, Frankfurt, Dresden, and Cologne had largely been reduced to rubble and millions of the civilian occupants either killed or left homeless. The population of Berlin alone had dropped from over five million to under three and a half million between 1940 and 1945. The currency was virtually worthless, there were few paying jobs to return to, and nearly everyone had suffered a personal loss during the conflict--a son, a brother, a father. Maybe the house was destroyed, or all possessions confiscated or destroyed, or all of the above. There were very few people in Germany who were not devastated by the insanity of the Third Reich.

The once-mighty Wehrmacht--what was left of it--had surrendered, but not until the very end. Those that were captured by the Russians were marched off to Siberia to work in labor camps or died trying to get there. Less than one in ten would ever see home again. The western Allies had captured over two million German soldiers during the war, and by the very end the German soldiers that remained were a rag-tag lot who were often hungry and poorly equipped to continue fighting. The tanks, artillery, and support vehicles that had not been destroyed by the advancing armies were often found abandoned in retreat, out of fuel or ammunition.

The Luftwaffe had been rendered powerless by the vast numerical superiority of the Allies. By the war's end, Allied bombing raids were meeting token resistance from German fighter planes. There were a few isolated planes that had not been shot down, or bombed while still on the ground, but for all practical purposes, the German air force was destroyed and the factories that could replace the planes were in rubble. All but the youngest pilots were dead, or injured so as to be not able to fly, or had deserted. The airfields were bombed out so much that after capture the Allies had to rebuild them in order to land their own planes.

The Kriegsmarine had been annihilated. Vastly outnumbered in surface vessels by the British Navy from the start of the war, almost every one of its mighty ships got sent to the bottom of the sea. What was not sunk was scuttled in port to keep the Allies from gaining use of them. The submarine force, once the terror of the Atlantic, had been forced to run for cover by enhanced radar, airplane spotters, and better Allied convoy support. As a result, subs had to scavenge off the high seas for supplies after the Allies began bombing the ports at Bremerhaven and Hamburg around the clock, and captured the re-fueling stations off the coast of France and Spain. Of the over 700 submarines launched by the Nazis, only a small percentage survived to surrender. The remainder had been sunk, scuttled, or lost at sea. The survival rate in this branch of the service was horrendous, with over 75% losses at sea. What had initially been considered an elite honor had turned out to be virtually suicidal.

Many of the High Command, realizing their complicity in war crimes of the worst sort, had taken their own lives as the end approached. Others, such as Field Marshal Hermann Goering, had surrendered peacefully, apparently believing that they would be treated only as soldiers doing their government's bidding, not as madmen, murderers, or war criminals. There were rumors that Hitler was dead and other rumors that he was hiding out in a bunker or had fled the country. But, at least he was nowhere to be found and his reign of terror was over.

In deference to the Russians who had suffered so severely at the Germans' hands, the western Allies stopped short of Berlin and allowed the Russians to enter the city first. Their hatred of the Germans and desire for revenge for the destruction they had experienced created a frenzy in which the largely destroyed city was further pillaged and plundered. This time it was by ground troops, not from bombers overhead. It was an ugly scene and not a safe place for any German to be. The men were rounded up and many were imprisoned or shot; the women were often raped and beaten. Children were left to go hungry on the streets. Berlin in June of 1945 was a hellhole--a terrible place to be.

As the dust settled on this utter devastation, and in an attempt to stabilize and manage the conquered area, Germany had been divided into four sectors by the Allies. The Russians took the eastern part of the country, the French took the southwestern part along their borders, the English took a slice to the northwest, and the Americans took on the southern and east central sector. By late June, Berlin itself was also broken into four parts as well, with the Russians taking the largest portion, including the city centre, named Mitte. It was clear at the start that the three western Allies would work together to start to get the country back on its feet. But the Russians had no plans for cooperating with the West. They had been invaded and nearly overrun by these Germans, and their casualties had been enormous. Over twenty million Russians were dead as a result of this war, and Stalin was not about to forgive and forget. Many Russian military leaders also believed that the western Allies had done as little as possible to assist in defeating the Germans and let the Russians shoulder the cost in human lives. They would not be trusting of the western Allies.

It was in this atmosphere of destruction, division, and mistrust that the Allies each began sifting through the rubble that was Germany in mid-1945. One of the many tasks was a process called de-Nazification. It included the cataloguing of nearly every remaining German citizen and their participation (or lack of participation) in the Third Reich. In the US zone alone it included registering approximately 13.5 million citizens. Of course, the Allies were looking for war criminals primarily, but they interviewed bankers and lawyers, accountants and factory workers, as well as those who had actually served in the armies or the SS. To turn oneself in to the Americans was considered first choice by most German military, as they understood the hatred the French and English felt after the war and they knew full well that the Russians would treat them worst of all. As a result, the American sector was flooded with ex-soldiers and SS trying to avoid the retributions of their conquerors. Wealthier Nazis had fled Europe and had found that several countries in South America would allow them entry and had no law under which they could be extradited and brought back to stand trial. Others, who had neither the means nor the will to flee, had

17

changed their appearance and their names in an attempt to conceal their part in the horrors that had occurred. In France, the Nazi collaborators were dealt with harshly and quickly, often without the benefit of trial or fair hearing. On more than one occasion it was learned too late that the person shot or hung was the wrong person, a case of mistaken identity.

The Americans wanted no part of this lynch mob revenge mentality. All of the Allies, as a result of the Yalta conference in early 1945, and then the Pottsdam conference after the surrender, had agreed long before the war ended that there would be a war crimes court and significant war criminals would be brought to justice. Exactly when and how that would be accomplished was just being laid out, but the Americans recognized that gathering evidence and using rules of law in the days immediately following the end of the war was important to the eventual success of those war trials. This fact led to the setting up of strict guidelines and rules about evidence and interrogation, and rules about the handling of German citizens to avoid ugly situations later on. It was an inefficient bureaucracy, but a necessary one.

Assigned to this tedious detail in the newly created American sector in Berlin was American Captain William (Bill) Smith, intelligence officer attached to the Army First Division. He came to Europe as a part of the Office of Strategic Services, the OSS. He had been reassigned to Army US Group Council, a part of the US occupations forces acting under the Allied Control Council. Smith was tasked with heading up one of several units of about 125 men who would conduct the short interviews with soldiers, individuals, and families and compile dossiers on all citizens without clear background or record. The German soldiers were lined up for inspection and they removed their shirts to see if they had the SS blood-type tattoo. If so, they were under automatic arrest as SS accomplices and were to be held as prisoners of war pending further investigation. If an SS man were also an officer, he would be held for investigation of war crimes as well.

After inspection, a German doctor gave them a brief physical exam to identify really ill people for treatment. They filled out a brief counter-intelligence questionnaire and finally were interviewed to determine whether they should be further detained or had technical skills related to intelligence or military interest. Their orders were to be thorough, but orders also called for each unit to get 25,000 people processed each week. The identified dossiers and lists would be completed in 6-8 months.

These were not typical interviews. The objective was not to determine guilt or innocence or qualifications for some position. It was to find liars--people with something to hide, which usually meant hiding their past association with the Nazis. For the most part, it was routine--questions about where you lived and worked during the war, education, family, languages spoken, prior arrest record, employment or skills, need for financial assistance to feed a family, etc. This was not the Great Inquisition, and the Allies knew that an elaborate effort to fool them might succeed. But this would catch 99% of the remaining war criminals, and it might also help catch any other criminals the Nazis had let loose from prison during the final days of the war.

Captain Smith had been given his detailed orders. Aside from the obvious SS men, he was not to waste time with low-level military and quickly refer ranking officers to the appropriate unit for determination as to whether their division was involved in any war crimes and if so, whether they were personally involved. All civilians were to be quickly catalogued and released immediately--no detaining them more than a few hours at most. However, he was instructed to pay particular attention to German scientists who worked for the Nazis. The United States had a keen desire to acquire the scientific knowledge gained from the experiments conducted by the Nazis, whether it was for jet aircraft, rocket technology, medical research, or bomb production.

Smith saw a little of everything. During the course of his assignment he would catalogue and review files of numerous minor scientists and a few doctors. No mad scientists or evil human experimenters, but typically laboratory workers who had a minor role in developing a part of a device which never saw fruition but was aimed at significant technological advances in its area. Often their descriptions were so fantastic that he dismissed them as Nazi fantasy. He read the documentation on each of these people and passed all interesting files on to the War Department for further review. He had heard from another team of interviewers that there was a V5 rocket program which was determined to create a missile that would go all the way around the earth at an altitude that was so high it made no sense. The word they used, "umlaufbahn," translated to mean "orbit" the earth. He was astounded when the response to his query about the fuel for such a rocket was "It runs on oxygen, of course, like in the air." It was so preposterous that the team leader felt he had to forward the report to Washington. Their immediate interest came as somewhat of a surprise to everyone and led staff to wonder about the sanity of the men back in Washington. Further, several of these so-called rocket scientists were reportedly even brought back to the US. It all seemed very odd.

There were assorted senior-management-level industrialists involved in the automotive, railroad, and construction industries, whom the government wanted to use to get the infrastructure and the economy rebuilt. Typically these men received visits from the State Department, and some even took jobs working for the occupation forces redesigning and rebuilding Germany.

Then there were several otherwise typical doctors and nurses who had worked as assistants in the concentration camps and who had observed or even conducted genetic or other medical research on live prisoners to learn how to create a more perfect people. These were rare but created quite a stir when one was identified. Washington had indicated that while it absolutely wanted any and all research in this area, it wanted nothing to do with these people. Hands off as far as any kind of special treatment for them. They would never be allowed to practice medicine again, and some would be charged with serious war crimes. The government did not want to be associated and ordered that these files be turned over to the war crimes tribunal for further research as appropriate--after copies were typed up and sent to Washington, of course.

And then there were the munitions manufacturers. Captain Smith read the files of several of these manufacturing executives, engineers, and scientists, all trying to create a bigger, better way of destroying things through explosives. They could quickly be separated into the money-grubbers who saw profit in war, and the eccentric scientists who only seemed to want to improve on the existing technology. Whether it was dropped from a plane, put in the nose of a V2 rocket, placed under a bridge, thrown, or shot at the enemy on the ground, they all wanted about the same thing. He had sent the first few files of various production managers on to headquarters for review, and the message that came back was "Don't waste a lot of time on these people--leave it alone."

The scientists were another matter. The US army and government were very interested in their activities, and Smith was encouraged to send any interesting files along for review. He had continued to forward numerous files of inventors/scientists in the gun and ammunition manufacturing area, and even the file of a low-level assistant who had worked on the design of the V2 rocket. But after sending nearly forty files that he thought showed promise of being able to assist the US military in weapons development, he had heard little or nothing--no official encouragement, and there was no feedback that the files were even being reviewed.

Captain Smith continued commanding the team as usual, referring suspicious files to authorities and cataloguing the remainder. His work life had become a monotonous, boring desk job, and he was ready for a change. He had settled into a rhythm of living for the nights and weekends. Each night had a designated dining location or a date with friends. Sunday and Wednesday was always the officers' mess, Mondays and Thursdays he and two other officers usually went to a nearby Bauhaus for schnitzel and beers. Tuesday was poker night and rotated around various locations. Saturday night was typically a USO dance--a time to think about home and talk to and maybe dance with a woman who spoke English the same way he did. Friday was the night out on the town with buddies.

Berlin was a mess, and it was a wild town in these immediate post-war days; sophisticated entertainment was nowhere to be found, but fun for a bunch of US army guys with money was not hard to locate. Beer and wine were plentiful and easy to acquire, by both legal and black market means. And although it was technically forbidden for the soldiers to partake, the fact that there were so many young women with no money and no prospects meant that there was an abundance of sleaze and prostitution easily available. Smith was not interested in this and went out of his way to avoid this part of the city, but it was a reality of post-war Berlin.

By the end of July 1945, just a few months after the end of the war in Europe, the US army, supervised by army intelligence, which would replace the OSS in September of the year, was beginning to get weary of hunting for Nazis, and the main war trials at Nuremberg along with minor trials in other cities were finally getting organized and underway. Most of the obvious citizens had been interviewed and cleared or detained. Only a few specific areas in Germany had any potential Nazis unaccounted for, and the interrogations in the American sector were nearing completion. It was time to begin to fold up the operation in Berlin and cease the interrogation process. Captain Smith received orders to begin dismantling the offices and packing up the documentation of his efforts. It would not take long--a few weeks--and he would be reassigned to another post, maybe in Paris, London, or back to Washington, he hoped. It had been an innocuous assignment, really. It was not very difficult and certainly not dangerous. He had met some wonderful people as well as a few real scumbags. He had seen the ravages of war in the faces of mothers and fathers who had lost family members and their homes, and he had seen the hope and despair on the faces of the young children who did not understand at all. He had come across many good stories that would be interesting to tell to friends back home and a few he could never divulge for security reasons. As he thought about the many files and the fascinating stories many of them held, he grinned at remembering one of his all-time favorites. The entire group had joked for days about the "water bombers," as they came to be called.

This favorite story had been brought in by two Hungarians who were taken prisoner at the end of the war in the area north and west of Berlin near an old salt mine which had been converted for storage. They were released after several days' confinement and interrogation, but they told an interesting story. They claimed to be scientists working on a secret bomb weapon so powerful that it could completely destroy several square miles. They were very adamant when talking about their research and the results they said they had achieved, but they admitted that the bomb was never actually built or even tested. It sounded ridiculous, of course, but they were insistent and thus it was real enough to probe a bit deeper. As had been suspected, there was little to take very seriously. The two Hungarians both said that the bomb's explosive material was a combination of radioactive material, with the use of some special water. They called it "heavy water" or Schweres Wasser in German – it sounded like a child's play toy. They claimed that they had worked in a small laboratory in a factory in the town of Faschgarten, but army intelligence had no records of any factories in this pastoral farm town capable of bomb production, and the Russians confirmed that there was no sign of any factories there now. There were no documents, the scientists had no supporting materials to substantiate their claims, and none of the co-workers they named seemed to exist. Besides, the men lacked credibility, seeming very academic and more than a little scatter-brained. It was too fantastic to give much credibility, yet these two separate scientists had given very similar reports. Strange, but not at all credible.

The entire group of GI's under Captain Smith's command talked about these two nutty Hungarians trying to pass as serious scientists for several days. It was assumed that they were just further evidence of the madness that comes out of war, and they were dismissed as crackpots, possibly even escapees from an institution, like several before them and a few that came after. It would not be unique, except that their story stood out as being one of the most absurd. Hitler was planning to hurl water bombs at his enemies. Smith decided to hold these files and not send them to Washington, where he might be ridiculed. They would be interesting to remember about how insane war can make people, even scientists. Water bombs, indeed. No, these files were sealed and packed away with the other thousands of files, boxed and stored in a warehouse.

CHAPTER THREE

When his next assignment came, it was not the reassignment Smith had wished for. He had set his sights at least on Heidelberg, or better yet, London or Paris, and he thought he deserved a promotion and maybe even a commendation and an interesting assignment. He had served nearly three years and he had come ashore just after Normandy and crossed the Rhine at Remagen in support of the 1st Division. He had seen good friends and complete strangers killed standing next to him. He had fulfilled his orders after peace was declared and had faithfully administered the screenings of thousands of German citizens. He believed that he deserved a good post.

Instead, he was assigned to be the adjutant senior army intelligence officer in the American sector in the western part of Berlin, where he would act as the local intelligence officer until a suitable replacement could be found. It was a comfortable schedule and it was better than being shot at, as Smith had experienced only nine months earlier, but it was not why he joined army intelligence. He stayed in the same barracks, kept his friends, and continued his monotonous lifestyle.

On Tuesday morning, August 7, 1945, Captain Smith's world began to change. The night before, while at a bar with friends, having

25

drinks and reading newspapers from back home, there had been an announcement that the US had bombed the Japanese mainland, the city of Hiroshima, on Monday, August 6th. That alone was not unexpected, for everyone knew that the marines and army were gearing up for an invasion of Japan and had been bombing the Japanese for months in preparation for the attack. What was unexpected was the description of the air raid and the results of the mission. A single bomber, carrying one single bomb, had completely devastated the entire city. It was called an atomic bomb, and the United States had dropped this Atomic Bomb on Japan.

It hadn't immediately occurred to the captain that night, but as the dawn came on Tuesday morning he started to realize that there were two Hungarian scientists that he and others had dismissed as crackpots who had described something a lot like this atomic bomb thing. Their story was still full of holes, but he could not ignore the feeling that there was more truth to their story than he had imagined possible. Maybe he should do a little digging around to see if there was any further substance to their tale--and if he could find any, he would pass their files on to Washington and ask for guidance as to how to proceed.

On the following Thursday, August 9th, the world was again shocked by the detonation of a second atomic bomb over Nagasaki, Japan. It had been smaller than the first bomb but had produced even greater destruction. Reports told of tens of thousands of people dead, even more badly injured, dozens of city blocks evaporated and the entire city reduced to rubble from a single bomb.

That same week in early August, Captain William Smith was assigned to lead a detail of thirty-five men to empty out the equipment stored in an old, abandoned salt mine west of the city. The Germans had evidently used the mine to continue their propaganda machine without interruption from Allied bombing late in the war, and as the end came near, they stored valuables and printing machinery, along with hundreds of boxes of papers, some marked with a red Nazi eagle and swastika. Because he had demonstrated significant skills in his previous assignment in cataloguing items, he was given the job of emptying the mine and sealing it--it was not safe to keep it open without any guards, and the Allies were not about to post guards at this abandoned hole. *Another thankless but necessary task*, Smith thought as he accepted the assignment. At least he would get out of the city for a few days.

The art and valuables had long since been removed from the mine. Captain Smith was not sure whether they had been officially removed or stolen by Allied soldiers or starving Germans. But the stuff was long gone. His team first set about removing the various pieces of equipment and placing them on large trucks for use back in Berlin. Other machinery--such as generators, printing presses, and office equipment--was also removed and taken away. The remaining boxes, over a thousand file cases, were to be reviewed, catalogued, and stored away with the prior civilian files for future use if needed.

The immediate task was labeling and cataloguing the sealed boxes. It would take months to sift through the materials inside each box, and Smith no longer had a staff of 125 men to assist him. He could see that his military intelligence career was turning into a career as a file clerk, and he did not care for it. Each box had been labeled by the Germans to show the place of origin of the box and the date on which it was sealed and placed in the mine. It also had a space for an authorized signature level required for removal of the boxes, which appeared to show three different levels of approval. Most of the boxes were designated level one or level two priority by the Germans--only thirty-six of the boxes marked with a red eagle and swastika were also marked with a level-three signature required for removal. Smith noted that there were not very many of these boxes and ordered that they be kept separate from the rest, but he did not see any need to look at them after noting that they were full of letters, papers, and diagrams written in German. It would take several weeks to translate and figure out that there was nothing really important in any of them, anyway. Maybe it was detail of some officer's personal life or plans for a new eastern front, or architectural drawings for a house for the Führer. Whatever it was, Smith could not imagine it was very important, months after the end of the war.

Over the next ten days all of the boxes removed were relabelled and each assigned a new number. Along with the Germans' labeling description of the contents, the information was written both on the outside of the boxes, and this information was recorded in a ledger before the boxes were carted away for safekeeping. By the end of August, all of the items once stored in the old salt mine were removed and either returned to owners, impounded as confiscated Nazi property, or placed in warehouse storage. The mine was temporarily sealed with a dirt mound built in front with bulldozers until it could be permanently sealed with explosives.

The weeks and then months came and went, and little changed in Berlin. The Russians had become more belligerent, but that was hardly a surprise. The fall and winter in Berlin were strangely quiet as the whole world watched and read about the Nuremberg Tribunal, which had started in late November and would drag on for most of 1946. It was now April of 1946, and Captain William Smith was only three months from his discharge papers. He was already counting the days to leave Berlin and Europe--forever.

Captain Smith was awakened at 4 o'clock in the morning on Sunday, April 14th by two men pounding on the door. When he answered the door, he was surprised to find that they were an MP escort. It seemed that the warehouse that contained most of the American and British civilian papers was on fire, and his presence was requested at headquarters, now. When he arrived it was clear that the authorities did not believe this was a run-of-the-mill accidental fire. *So some ex-Nazis wanted to destroy their records*, he thought. *What does that have to do with me? And why can't it wait until later in the day? Unless they want me to help fight the fire, I don't know why they couldn't wait until the morning.* He was approached by Major James Whitcombe of the US Army Intelligence unit, who asked him to come into a nearby office. This had been Smith's old command before he had been asisgned to desk duty in Berlin.

"Please be seated, Captain," Whitcombe started. " I understand that you are the resident authority on the materials and papers that were in that warehouse? Is that correct?"

"I do not know about much in the warehouse other than the civilian papers and the boxes recently placed there, but if that is your concern, then I suppose I am the man, sir," answered Smith. "If I may ask, sir, why is the army all of a sudden interested in papers which have been sitting for over seven months and are scheduled for destruction next year, anyway?"

"Captain, we have good reason to believe that this warehouse was set on fire deliberately and we want to understand why. We hope that you can help us."

"Well, sir," responded Smith, "it does not take too much imagination to guess that some ex-Nazis wanted to cover their past by destroying their files. But surely you have thought of that."

"Yes," said Whitcombe. "I'm sorry, I failed to mention that the methods and the materials used to start that fire lead us to believe that the Russians set this fire."

"The Russians? But why would…?" thought the captain out loud.

"Let's cut to the chase here, Captain," barked the major. "You maintained a master file detailing all interesting, out of the ordinary, sensitive, or other findings. Is that correct?"

"Yes, sir, of course. It would be in the Headquarters file room-- some 2,000 or so pages of exceptions and 100 pages describing the labeled contents we brought from that salt mine which were also stored in that warehouse."

"The salt mine papers were in there, too? "asked the major, as if he knew exactly what papers were once in that old mine. "Damn Ruskies, what the hell are they up to? What do they know that we don't? Captain, I am ordering you to personally review the files and report to me anything that in your opinion would merit the Russians burning the damn building down. Anything. Understood?"

"Yes, sir, Major."

"Dismissed," barked the major.

Captain Smith went back to his barracks and got back in bed. It was still only 5 a.m. *Why me?* he wondered. *Can't I ever get away from those damn papers? Thank God they burned up.* He went back to sleep for a few more hours. At 8 a.m. there was another, more urgent, knock on the door, and when Smith finally got up and answered it, he was greeted by the same MPs who had knocked on his door earlier that morning.

"Excuse me, sir, but we were sent back by Major Whitcombe with a message, although it seems more like an order." The MP began to read: "To Captain William Smith, recently reassigned from his prior army intelligence post to serve under my personal command: Dammit, soldier. When we agreed that you would review the files, I meant now, today. Not next week or at your convenience. In case you did not hear and understand, you have been transferred to my command, effective immediately, and I expect to see your report as soon as it is humanly possible. Please indicate to the MP that you do understand. Major J. T. Whitcombe, United States Army Intelligence Unit, 1ˢᵗ Division, US Army."

Smith understood only too well. He had been hijacked by an eager GI Joe who was out to make a name for himself. This was just great. And coming only three months before mustering out for good. At least he would not be in this mess for long, he thought. Smith acknowledged the orders and got up, dressed, and went over to the headquarters offices to begin pulling the folders.

It was going to take some time, if he really was to go through the summary of every civilian file and the content lists for all of the boxes. But he could short cut the effort by looking at the log and reviewing only the interesting civilian files and the description of contents for the highest-level boxes from the mine--the thirty-six red- labeled boxes. It was now about 8 o'clock on Sunday morning. Out of over 123,000 files reviewed and written up, representing nearly a one and a half million citizens, only a few hundred or so files were still open and considered abnormal. The remainder were routine citizens or low-level military who suffered through the war, or they were identified war criminals whose names were passed on to the war crimes tribunals. Neither would have any reason to want to destroy the files, nor was there anything he could think of in those files that the Russians would care about. But he had orders, and he had to start somewhere, so he decided to begin with the files his own group had created. Smith pulled out the first page of each of the file summaries marked "open status--resolution undefined." At about 3-4 minutes per summary to review the facts and pass a quick judgment, he could do nearly 15-20 an hour. He estimated that it would take him about 14 hours to review all these summaries.

For the remainder of the day, he continued to pore over file summaries. During the process, he took notes to justify his thinking about what was pertinent to the issue at hand and what was not. By the time he had finished, he had identified exactly twenty-three cases that might potentially be interesting to the Russians, and each of these contained stories that did not check out. In that group were eleven scientists, including the two crazy men who said they had built a water bomb. Smith smiled as he thought about that story, but there was nothing in any of the file summaries that would warrant burning down a warehouse. After his 9-10 hours of reviewing the civilian and individual military files, he turned his attention to the papers from the salt mine. He had not eaten since breakfast, but he had now become intrigued by the quest and was actually not all that hungry even though it was nearly 7 p.m. already. He thought, *When I am finished, I will eat. The sooner I am done with this, the better.*

He had reasoned that for his review of the inventory of the outside descriptions of the boxes that had been brought from the salt mine that he would start with the seemingly most important and work his way down to the lesser files as time permitted. Smith began to review the labels and recorded data from the red eagle and swastika-emblazoned boxes first, the ones that required three signatures for removal authorization, and his first observation surprised him a lot. The boxes, all thirty-six, were listed as coming from a munitions laboratory (Reich Forschunglabor) in the town of Faschgarten, north of Berlin, now in the Russian sector. He immediately recalled that it was the town cited by the two Hungarian scientists who described their "schwerwasser bombe" which might be a lot like the atom bombs dropped on Japan. And it was the same town that he remembered that the Russians had declared had no factory or laboratory in it. There had been no markings on the boxes to indicate what work had been done at this laboratory; nor had the contents ever been inspected. The logs made no mention of either. It was only by coincidence that Captain William Smith had been involved in both cases and had remembered the scientists and their outrageous claims. If the connection was real, it was not personal history that was being covered up in the fire; it was the Russians trying to keep the Americans from learning the details about Germany's secret program to build an atomic bomb. Smith continued through the files looking for another clue or explanation but found none. It was now nearly midnight, but he was wide awake and alert and needed to talk with someone.

Captain Smith called for Major Whitcombe to meet with him immediately. Whitcombe wasted no time in arriving at the base file area where the back-up files and summaries were kept. Smith proceeded to walk through his review of materials lost in the fire, detailing the process of having duplicate record summaries kept on the base, not in the warehouse, and then his procedures for reviewing and going through the files as he had over the past twelve hours. He then laid out the entire sequence of events related to his months of questioning potential Nazis in the previous year, and ended with the facts and coincidences that brought him to his conclusions. He then told Major Whitcombe that based on his assessment, the Russians were most probably trying to gain information the Germans had on atomic bomb development while at the same time trying to keep the Americans from discovering what they were up to. The only thing that puzzled him was the scientists' talk about heavy water.

At the end of the explanation of his findings and conclusions, it was Whitcombe's turn to tell Smith what was going on. He looked around the office area and, satisfied that no one was within earshot, he turned to Smith and began to shed some light on the situation. Major James T. (Jimmie) Whitcombe explained that although he had indeed been stationed in Berlin at the time of the fire, he was actually not really career army proper. He had also been, in fact, previously a member of the OSS himself, who was reassigned to army intelligence when the OSS was disbanded by President Truman, in late 1945. That sounded familiar to Smith, as that was how he came into army intelligence as well. But Whitcombe then went on to describe how he had been part of the Allied raid on Haigerlock, a small town in southern Germany where atomic bomb testing and manufacturing equipment, along with the remains of an atomic reactor (and nearly two tons of uranium), had been found in a cellar underneath a baroque Schlosskirche (castle church).

Whitcombe had been serving as part of the Army Intelligence (G2) section assigned to the special ALSOS Mission, under Colonel Boris Pash (ALSOS was the Greek word for groves (as in olive groves), which happened to be the last name of the leader of the Manhattan project, Brigadier General Lesley Groves. Based on his experience at

Haigerlock, Whitcombe was promoted and stationed in Berlin specifically to be on the lookout for evidence of any Nazi atomic secrets. He was not making a big deal of his search, but was working under the cover of being an army major in the intelligence section. Up until now, he had found little to worry about. With this new information, he felt that things might be starting to heat up.

Major Whitcombe would make his report to a Colonel Charles Farston, the London-based commander of the US sector in Berlin, as soon as possible. The matter was declared "Top Secret" and all of the materials Smith and Whitcombe produced were placed in a dossier labelled "Confidential: Army Intelligence – Eyes Only." Based on the evidence and coincidence in the story told by Smith, Whitcombe filed a local report of "potential arson, no known reason or cause and suspects not identified." The case was officially closed in Berlin. It would be up to London to take action if it felt it appropriate. The dossier would be carried by courier on a special military plane that would stop only at Le Bourget, outside Paris, for refueling before continuing on to London.

CHAPTER FOUR

It was mid-day in London and Intelligence Officer-in-Charge Colonel Charles Farston was leaving for lunch at about the same time he did every Thursday. Even though he was hungry, he knew that the English luncheon he would attend with the top brass today would satisfy neither his stomach nor his brain. He was to report on the recent activities in Berlin and any unusual dealings with the Russians and any other issues that required immediate attention in the American-occupied sector. It had been exciting to attend these meetings for the first few months after the end of the war. Top ranking OSS and US Army Intelligence, MI-6's SOE, and French Occupation Police would detail fascinating and complex accounts about the goings-on in occupied and divided Germany. Escaping Nazis pulled off trains in the night with their families; black market operations trading stolen military equipment for gasoline or food; graft and corruption schemes; and the usual domestic crimes – theft, murder, assault, and the like. At the beginning, the issues were large, the problems were real, and the power that could be wielded was intoxicating. That was nine months ago. As things settled down, so had the thrill of being an intelligence officer for the occupied sector for the United States, stationed back in

London. Recently, it had been all about inconsequential matters which should be local police issues--not the business of conquering armies, and certainly not the problems Colonel Farston cared to deal with.

There had been little news to report again this week: a fight between American and Russian soldiers in a wursthaus bar over some women, which had resulted in the serious injury of one of the US Army Air Corps men; a stolen truck believed to have been taken for parts and the barrels of gasoline it had on board; and a warehouse fire in Berlin, which was believed to have destroyed some Nazi papers. The warehouse had caused a mild stir only because it was near a US supply depot that stockpiled used weapons and ammo after the war, so Farston had assigned an OSS retread that was already stationed in Berlin, old Jimmie Whitcombe, to look into it and see what the fuss was all about. These things usually turned out to be dead ends, but with senior brass involved and Whitcombe sitting around and available, it was easy to act like it might be important and assign Major Whitcombe to look deeper into it. Besides, if anyone could get to the bottom of it and make it stick, Jimmy Whitcombe would do it. In fact, thought Colonel Farston, Whitcombe's report was due today, at any time.

Farston got up and put on his coat to go out. It was mid-April and the cold, damp wind was biting in London that time of year. As he reached the door, his assistant caught up with him and handed him a sealed envelope. "This is the report from Major Whitcombe you were expecting, sir," his assistant called out, as he ran up. "It just came from the courier a few minutes ago and I have not read it yet, but he indicated that it may be important."

"Thanks," replied Colonel Charles Farston. "I'll read it during our lunch meeting if it gets too boring." The colonel went out of the door, leaving for his weekly staff meeting.

The meeting was held every Thursday in a back room at the small Boar's Inn outside Bletchley Park, the home for Britain's Government

Communications Headquarters (GCHQ), north of London. There were the official invitees, from each branch of the service, and their advisers, and the staff people who took notes and actually made things happen. For months, Farston had brought his assistant as well, but in recent weeks the issues had become so mundane that he did not feel it was a good use of his time. Similarly, only a little over half of the expected attendees were present when the meeting was called to order at 1:30 p.m. on April 18th, 1946. Lunch was served promptly, and the colonel was at least pleased by that. He had not had a bite to eat since lunch the previous day, and he did not like missing a dinner. His stomach rumbled and he became easily agitated. He was not at his peak when he was hungry, and so even those silly little cucumber sandwiches looked good to him at this point.

He put his papers down in front of his seat and immediately went to the side buffet table to get food. The group started the usual reporting around the table with readouts from the various occupying forces groups responsible for designated areas across Germany and Europe as a whole, each detailing their issues for the week. It was mostly the same old crap and would be mildly entertaining if he had not been through this meeting dozens of times before. He listened politely as his friend, Colonel André Pollack, in the western French sector, described the traffic problems the occupying armies were causing in the small villages and towns west of Paris. He described how the French, the people that we had liberated and whom had hailed us as heroes last year, now wanted us out of their towns as soon as possible. He listened as some other colonel, responsible for supply logistics, droned on for nearly ten minutes about the various problems related to soldiers stealing livestock in eastern France because they were tired of K-rations.

It was exhausting to sit through, Farston thought to himself as he opened the envelope containing the report from Major Whitcombe. He expected very little information and was surprised to see that

Whitcombe had felt it necessary to label the report "top secret--eyes only." Maybe Whitcombe was getting a bit melodramatic in his old age? Farston thought, *I'll have to have a talk with him later.*

By now an MI-6 officer, part of SOE, the Special Operations Executive branch, was giving his report. He began by detailing the progress in tracking unaccounted for high-level Nazis over the past week—frankly, they had done a lot of running around and had found very little--not one arrest in the past week. The report moved on to Russian activities in the Berlin sector, and although this was the area in which Farston was personally most interested, he was sure that the report would be as boring as the others had been up until that point. He noted hearing that the Russians appear to be up to something in Berlin and the area to the north of the city in their sector, but as yet neither MI-6 nor the US army intelligence had a good fix on what it was. They had observed a group of Russian civilian types questioning various prominent Germans in the sector and had been tipped off that these were Russian agents, most likely NKVD secret police.

The officer's report went on to say that our own intelligence sources had learned that they had been inquiring about a munitions factory in a small town north of Berlin. This was only odd because German records on such subjects were routinely very good and easy to obtain and these showed no records of there having ever been a munitions factory in the stated town. They also were searching for men who might have worked in that area during the last days of the war. It was all very curious, but made no great sense at this time. The town itself was very small and was considered unimportant, etc., etc.

Colonel Farston had begun reading the Whitcombe report:

> "On the morning of April 14th, a Sunday, at approximately 0300 local time, a fire was detected burning in four locations in a warehouse located at #17 Kirtnerstrasse where the American-led Allied Occupation Forces had stored a variety of

papers, documents, and dossiers. There were no munitions or armaments stored in the building, and most of the contents of the building had been in the building stored and undisturbed for some time, at least several months. The building was locked and secure, but was not guarded at the time of the fire. There was no loss of life. There were no specific suspects at this time although the fire was, according to the local fire marshals, of suspicious origin. However, the official determination has not yet been made. Our official position will be recorded as arson and it will likely be attributed to ex-Nazis attempting to destroy records, to avoid any political issues (as noted below).

The bulk of the documents destroyed were indeed interview notes from the war crimes de-Nazification records. But the fire was clearly not accidental. Upon further review by the military police fire squads at the nearby base it was determined that the type of incendiary used to start the fire and the method employed was more likely Russian, and it was probably carried out by the East German secret police or the Russian NKVD. No immediate motive for the fire was obvious; however, Captain William Smith was ordered to review the log books kept offsite to see if there was anything in this warehouse that the Russians might want to destroy. Fortunately, Captain Smith was not only the custodian for these records, but had led the teams who originally compiled a significant portion of these records and logged all of the materials into the warehouse.

As a matter of standard procedure, I interviewed Captain Smith approximately twenty hours after the warehouse fire and immediately after he had reviewed the logbooks and offsite records and a summary of his observations are as follows:

"The warehouse contained only two sets of relevant materials other than office supplies, equipment and so forth. First, there were detailed files on some 125,640 German families which were seen as potentially linkable to Nazi war crimes based on the age of men in the family, military service, known associations, etc. Secondly, there were 1,284 boxes of sealed papers that had been taken out of an abandoned salt mine just outside Berlin which the German high command had apparently used for storage. Of these boxes there were several apparent levels of security associated. The highest level was marked with a red swastika and eagle and required three signatures for authorized removal (whose signatures were required is unknown).

Based upon a review of all files which were not referred to the war crimes tribunal for determination but were still suspicious (approximately 268 files had been marked "extraordinary" but were not passed on to London for further review due to a lack of evidence or relevance) there were 17 which could either potentially relate to serious war crimes or were marked "still open, under review." None had specific evidence which would by itself support an arrest. Included are summaries of the nine scientists and four businessmen and four others who make up this group (see attached). These files have sat dormant for over eight months and there were no plans to reopen any of these files. In my opinion, it is very unlikely that any single civilian could have understood that these files still existed, known where they were located, and had the means to destroy them that were used. The four further files in this group do not meet the test of having war crimes potential, but are labelled most interesting and have been included in the appendix of my report for your review. These files include 1) a man who appeared to be involved in a black market business, including embezzlement and extortion; 2) a fraudulent doctor; 3) a couple whom we believe had illegally taken a baby from its mother in exchange for money; and 4) a pair of Hungarian scientists who claimed to have been working on an explosive device, a bomb, which was powerful enough for one bomb to completely destroy an entire city, more powerful than our recent atomic bomb (whose existence was unknown at the time of these interviews)--their claim preceded the Hiroshima explosion by two months.

Following up on these four leads, Captain Smith also quickly and efficiently obtained local police information to detail the current status of these four most interesting files as follows:

The suspected black marketer was stabbed to death in an apparent business altercation several months ago. The fraudulent doctor had disappeared (but is at least not practicing medicine in or near Berlin anymore) and the couple formally applied for custody of the child and upon being denied custody left Berlin for parts unknown.

Finally, the two scientists' outrageous claims appear less preposterous in light of the deployment of our own atomic weapon. Neither scientist was found in our search, and the only location they referred to in their statements was a munitions laboratory in a small town north of Berlin, which has not been located or confirmed.

The only other significant contents of the warehouse were the thirty-six boxes marked with the red eagle and swastika, which we now understand means top secret. The markings were similar to those used on scientific materials found in the Wehrmacht headquarters at the end of the war, which contained information on the V2 rocket program. Markings reserved for very important information. These boxes were part of a much larger group of boxes taken to the warehouse and all were destroyed in the fire. They were never opened and catalogued, but the writing on the outside of each was recorded. Besides a series of numbers, there was the source location name of a small town north of Berlin: Faschgarten.

Colonel Farston stopped reading the report at this point. His eyes were suddenly open wide, and his pulse quickened. He had just heard the report from MI-6 and the US army intelligence officer detailing Russian activity in a town north of Berlin and had read of a very real connection between that intelligence and the fire in Berlin. The logic of his conclusion seemed virtually inescapable: The Russians were seeking to obtain top-secret German research, and based on who they were pursuing and where they were looking, it most certainly was aimed at gaining the Nazis' research in order to build an atomic bomb, and they did not want the Americans to get that information or stop them. They surely had burned the warehouse and the records in it to hide their efforts.

Farston waited nervously until it was his turn, and then he delivered a mild and relatively boring account of the prior week's activities. There had been a brawl and it looked like the Russians started it, but this could not be proven; there was a case of theft which was still being investigated; and the case of a suspicious fire, which he flatly indicated was probably accidentally started by homeless people, but was still under investigation. He was not about to blurt out his theory--which might lead to ridicule--nor would he let all the people of various levels in that room have knowledge of the potential enormity of the situation. He would, however, cancel all his appointments for the rest of the day and call on the most senior US army intelligence officer he could find with this information at once.

General Henry Grimes was now the American commander based in London, responsible for US army intelligence in post-war Europe, and he was a serious and dedicated man who had learned the hard way to distrust everyone--Russians, Germans, French, English, and even some of the American military. Like most of the current army intelligence officers, he had been in the OSS during the war. Unlike Colonel Farston, however, he was a member of the top-secret weapons intelligence group, labelled X-2, and he knew exactly what was up with America's atomic bomb program. He had been consulted by the "Interim Committee" prior to the decision to drop the atom bomb on Japan, and he was well connected to top brass in the atomic weapons program. When he got a late afternoon call from a Colonel Charles Farston who said he needed to see him that day on an urgent matter, Grimes distrusted him as well. Before returning the call, he contacted army intelligence headquarters and inquired about Farston's current position, his recent assignments, and his record in the military. Deciding that Colonel Farston was neither a crackpot nor an alarmist, he had his assistant schedule dinner with Farston that evening in London. Based on Farston's cryptic description over the telephone, he decided to have it in private quarters in case it was half as important as Farston had made it out to be.

Farston arrived at precisely 6 p.m. at the Dorchester Hotel, as agreed, and the two men introduced themselves and went upstairs into a small private dining area, which was often set aside for foreign military use, usually for the American top brass. The room had no windows and had a large thick wooden door, which would make it very difficult for listening in on a normal-toned conversation. Colonel Farston took the extra precaution of having his driver sit by the door and asked the general to have his aide secure the area in a similar manner. General Grimes was annoyed by this cloak-and-dagger stuff, but until he heard Farston out, he agreed to go along. The two men quickly ordered drinks and dinner and then closed the doors to discuss this dossier which Colonel Farston had brought with him.

As he opened the files and began to organize the materials for Henry Grimes to review, Farston laid the groundwork for comprehending what the Russians were up to. It was common knowledge that the Russians had been employing any and all means to get access to our atomic bomb secrets. Already a half dozen spies had been arrested in the US for espionage and treason. Some were high profile, but most were very quietly put in prison without a lot of fuss or due process of law. When the end of the war had been near, a directive had gone out to all US troop commanders to be on the lookout for German scientists who could aid our military effort. It was equally understood that if we did not capture and control these men, then the Russians would. There had even been rumors of Nazi missile scientists being taken captive by the Russians and being held in the USSR against their will to design and build rockets and maybe even atomic weapons at a secret location in Sarov, the closed, top-secret military research facility in Nizhny Novgorod. Although unconfirmed, no one doubted for a second that Stalin was both terrified of the US atomic threat and fanatical in his desire to obtain atomic parity if not superiority.

Upon this base of information and supposition came the contents of the dossier: The burned-out warehouse building containing nothing of apparent significance except files about Nazis; the stand-out files were about scientists who talked of atomic type weapons in a place called Faschgarten. There was the activity in the Russian sector and reports of the Russians questioning anyone who might know where certain scientists could be found and focusing on work which might have been done in the small town of Fachgarten. And finally, the boxes from the mine marked with the swastika and red eagle--top secret, and each labelled with the named location: Faschgarten. In Colonel Farston's mind, the inescapable conclusion was that the Russians knew something we did not about the Nazis' atomic bomb program and were scurrying to get at that information and at the same time keep the Western Allies from finding out about it. After presenting his case to General Grimes, he finally stated what he had been holding inside since noon: "General, I believe that the Russians have stumbled onto a secret Nazi effort in the town of Faschgarten which has the potential to be equal or superior to our atomic weapons program. They may already have the information required to put them years ahead of us at this point."

General Grimes was more circumspect and less easily convinced. Because he sat on the US War Department's top-secret council and had X-2 clearance, he had access to information few others possessed. He received briefings from GCHQ at Bletchley Park, the British cryptographers who had moved from reading Nazi code to intercepting and reading Russian coded messages. He was aware of most of the current atomic bomb efforts and knew about the research already underway to build a more powerful bomb than the current weapons-grade uranium and plutonium bombs used last year on Japan. Based on the ideas and research of Edward Teller, a Hungarian physicist who had emigrated to the United States, the "super," as he called it at the time, was to be 1000 times more potent than the current atom bomb and use fusion, not fission, as its source of energy. Although it would surely be several years until perfected, Grimes knew that the advent of the "super" or hydrogen bomb would render current atomic weapons to antiquity.

The hydrogen bomb, or H-Bomb, got its name because it used an unstable hydrogen isotope called deuterium inside a fission bomb to create the chain reaction and release energy. Most commonly available as di-deuterium oxide (D_2O), it looked and acted much like common water, H2O, but with the heavier hydrogen isotope's atoms replacing the normal hydrogen atoms, it was often referred to as "heavy water." The isotope had been discovered at Princeton University in 1931 and won its discoverer, Harold Clayton Urey, a Nobel prize in chemistry. It was, of course, all theory at this point. But Grimes also knew that much of the theory of atomic weapons came from the Germans. They were among the first to postulate back in 1938 that a critical mass of Uranium238 could potentially be used to set off a chain reaction and an explosion many times more powerful than conventional TNT.

Grimes knew that it was due to a combination of mathematical errors and defections of their top scientists that Germany had not been able to create and use a functional atomic weapon during the war. He was also aware that the Germans had seized a large stockpile of uranium from Belgium early in the war and had gone to great trouble to capture the only significant production source of heavy water, a plant in Rjukan, Norway, about 75 miles west of Oslo. They had begun shipping heavy water back to Germany for testing and experiments. And the General knew that the US Air Force and RAF had tried to bomb the plant in November of 1943 and it had finally been sabotaged by Norwegian freedom fighters, supported by the British Special Operations Executive, SOE. What he did not know, what no one knew, was the nature and extent of the research done or the amount of progress that the German scientists had actually made, or exactly how close they had come to creating an atomic weapon, or what their designs would look like, or how they would perform technically. But Grimes knew that our top scientists, working with some of the recently joined German defectors, expected this new hydrogen- based weapon to be 1000 times more lethal than the current atom bomb, if it could be developed. Finally, Grimes was well aware that Leo Szillard was the Hungarian physicist who first patented the idea of the nuclear reactor, and he actually wrote the letter that Albert Einstein sent to President Roosevelt in 1939 recommending that the Allies needed to get ahead of the Axis powers in developing an atomic weapon. However, even if Colonel Farston's conclusion was on the mark, Grimes's appraisal of the situation was that this was a case of the

Russians once again being a day late and a dollar short.

However, Harold Grimes also saw himself as a good leader and mentor of his men and did not want to send this officer away without any encouragement, and he could hardly give a detailed explanation for his thinking. He saw little to this matter, if in fact it was real in the first place, but he would not lord it over his subordinate. "Farston, you know I am not able to discuss or divulge top secret atomic weapons issues with you," the general began. Farston was beginning to realize that if he did not convince the general that he had discovered something, that he would be viewed by Grimes as an alarmist and not someone to be trusted. He had a fine line to walk and his career depended upon it. Grimes responded quickly, realizing the predicament Farston was getting himself into.

"Colonel Farston--Charles, if I can call you that--I understand your desire to help and your belief in this matter. I have read your record and you are a valuable soldier and good leader. I cannot discuss details with you, but based on what you have told me, what I've been able to glean from these materials, and my understanding of our capabilities in the area, I cannot find a lot to get too excited about or to consider a priority at this time. I would like a continued report on a weekly basis in case the situation take a turn or develops more fully, but for now it is not a priority. Thanks for getting me out for a good meal, though."

Colonel Farston was visibly disappointed. "Sir, if I have not presented the materials to you well enough, I apologize, but I assure you that this matter is not a wild goose chase."

Grimes interrupted him, "Sir, you have an excellent record and a fine career ahead of you. Do not put all of that up for grabs over an issue about which you have not got the inside track." General Grimes got up and picked up his hat to leave. "It was a pleasure meeting you, Colonel Farston, and I hope our paths cross again in the near future." The senior intelligence leader turned to leave the room.

Colonel Farston realized he had been dismissed and that he had made a serious career blunder in scheduling this dinner so quickly. Damn, he had been too eager. He had needed more facts and proof at his fingertips. He had squandered what might be his only opportunity by being bull-headed and not dotting the i's and crossing the t's, something he was proud of being known for. As the army intelligence two-star general opened the door to leave, Farston--in a clear attempt to avoid further embarrassment--was wracking his brain for anything that would salvage this dinner meeting. He was a career man who had just seriously injured his career. It was damage control time, and he needed not to let the general leave thinking that Charles Farston was obsessed or had exercised poor judgment.

He quickly sucked it up, saluted his superior, and said, "Sir, I appreciate your indulging me on this matter. You are certainly right, sir; this is a waste of time and effort. Besides, the report says that the two Hungarian scientists interviewed were a bit crazy, saying they were building a water bomb, they called it schwerwasser bombe. It must all be a--"

General Grimes wheeled around back into the room, cutting off Colonel Farston before he could label his own effort a coincidence. "What did they call it?" he asked, with not just mild interest, but actual fear in his voice. "They were Hungarian scientists, you say, and they actually used the words 'heavy water' in their description? Good God, man. How many people have seen this report, and how many copies of it are there? Shut the damn door and let me look at that file again."

CHAPTER FIVE

Spring in New England is typically mud season. So it was in Cambridge, Massachusetts in the year after the end of the Second World War. At the Massachusetts Institute of Technology, the business of education had started to return to normal, and most of the top-secret war research efforts that had been conducted on or near campus had by now been scaled back to a trickle. Rick Malloy was back into the grind of working on his doctoral thesis in physics, having spent nearly three years on a leave of absence, first as a soldier and then assisting with war research. When the war came to the United States at the end of 1941, Rick, like so many other young men, rushed to join the armed forces. And the military was only too eager to take him. He went into the army, and based on his education and athletic ability was put into training to be a paratrooper in the 1st Battalion, 507th regiment. When it was learned he was a talented physicist and that senior government officials felt that his contribution would be far greater as a researcher at MIT, the war department washed him out of paratrooper training and sent him back to Cambridge. He had spent six months training and had nearly completed the entire program, but it was not to be; he was needed somewhere else. He consoled himself with the

49

knowledge that what he was doing was important to winning the war, but he was eager to play a more active part.

His research specialty was atmospheric-pressure-sensing devices, and although he was not able to talk about it to anyone, through his efforts during 1943, 1944, and early 1945 he made a significant contribution to the success of the Manhattan Project, the atomic bomb program. Without the pressure-sensing switch detonators, the atomic bomb might have been forced to use impact detonation, essentially going off when it hit the ground. This would have reduced the effectiveness of the atomic bomb by nearly 30%. But thanks to the team that Rick worked on, their detailed attention to research and the design, manufacture, and testing of the detonation sensors, the bomb could be set to explode at any selected altitude, and was in fact set at approximately 2,000 feet above sea level over Hiroshima and 1,800 feet above Nagasaki. But that was history.

Rick Malloy was back at the university, preparing to teach undergraduate classes to keep his mind sharp while he completed his doctoral degree. He had completed the required courses in metallurgy, mathematics, and physics and now needed only to finish his long-awaited thesis. At twenty-six years old, he was at his peak, physically and intellectually. He was in top condition due to his daily three-mile run along the Charles River and his playing racquetball twice a week. He had a small one-bedroom apartment on Marlborough Street in Back Bay that allowed him to participate in Boston's nightlife--a little older crowd than the student hangouts and campus scene in Cambridge.

Rick was a fairly handsome man, tall with wavy blond hair, with a decidedly Teutonic and regal bearing. This was not such a surprise if you knew Rick Malloy well, as all of his friends understood that he came from a wealthy German family who had sent him to the United States in the early 1930s to avoid the National Socialist movement of Hitler. Rick never dwelled on the fact that his family was old-world nobility or that his dad had been a captain of industry in Germany prior to the war. Rick was not a materialistic person and was content to let the bankers manage his money and rest on their assurances that he had more than enough to support his way of life. What he especially did not discuss with his friends or anyone was his homeland, which had become East Germany, or the fate that befell his family.

Born in Prenzlauer Berg, a suburb of Berlin, now in what became Russian- occupied Eastern Germany, in the fall of 1920, Eric von Malloy was the only child of Heinrich von Malloy, a baron and wealthy industrialist. His empire was created just before the turn of the 20th century, as the industrial might of a unified Germany began to take shape. His holdings included steel mills and lumber mills, and even an auto assembly plant which was a sub-contracter for work with Steyr and Daimler. He had reinvested much of his wealth in growth and expansion. The elder von Malloy was highly respected in political circles and although a young man at the time, was often consulted by the Prussian administration prior to the Great War. After the First World War, there was little to be proud of except heritage, and the von Malloy factories ran to keep people busy, not because there any were buyers of their goods. The Weimar government's failure and the rise of National Socialism--the Nazis--created an environment wherein industrialists like Heinrich von Malloy were forced to choose sides between communism and fascism. It was a no-win situation, and von Malloy refused to get involved with either. He would often say, "Let others get rich doing the Nazis' bidding, I will have no part of their tyranny."

This was both his honor and his downfall. The Nazis branded him an enemy of the state and as the people began to rally around the brownshirt movement, the future for all those who thought differently became increasingly dark. By early 1933, the baron had seen that he was in a bad position with Hitler now appointed chancellor, and after long discussions and soul-searching, he had sent his wife and son to America to get away from the coming storm. He was nobility and he owed his life to the fatherland, and so he would stay, but he knew that his future was not to be bright.

In August of 1934, following the death of President von Hindenburg, Hitler became leader (Führer) of all of Germany and soon after began the systematic taking control of key industries "for the good of the German people." One of the very first to be forced to join the "cartels," as they were called, was the industrial empire of von Malloy Geschellshaft. To make an example of the matter for other industrialists to heed, and because von Malloy did not graciously hand over control of his businesses to the Nazi administrators, he was arrested and accused of treason and high crimes against the state. No trial was ever scheduled and Heinrich von Malloy was simply held in jail with no hope of ever getting out. He would later be transferred to one of Himmler's work camps, east of Berlin, called Hohenschoenhausen, with hundreds of other political prisoners. If he did not die from malnutrition or exposure, he was intended to rot away into oblivion. And no one escaped from these hellholes. There was no news on his health, and frequent reports of random executions from the community in the surrounding area, but no official word was ever given.

His wife and son came to Milwaukee, Wisconsin, where there was a large German community for them to meld in to. In 1940, three years after hearing from Red Cross inspectors that her husband had been executed, Eric von Malloy's mother, Frida, remarried and started to get on with her life. She adopted the name of her new husband, Miller, and never again talked about her prior life in Germany or her German husband. This new life was never really accepted by her son, Eric, and the two grew somewhat distant from each other. They spoke frequently, but it was never deep or meaningful conversation. It was duty and respect, but the mother-son relationship was forever fractured.

Eric von Malloy had changed his name to Rick and dropped the "von" part of his name. He did this first because he did not want to be associated with being German in the 1940s and secondly because Rick was his father's nickname for him. He had heard through official sources that his father had died in prison, and although he held out hope through the end of the war, he felt deep down that it was so. When the war ended and the prisons revealed no Heinrich von Malloy, Rick Malloy finally accepted that his father had been murdered by the Nazis, one of millions to die senselessly.

Rick was an excellent student and studied hard. He already spoke perfect English and could read French, Italian, and Latin when he arrived in the US, because he was expected to do this based on his social position in Germany. When he graduated from high school in 1937, he and his mother agreed that he should go east to college and he was enrolled at the Massachusetts Institute of Technology in the fall of 1937. He was an exceptional student and athlete. He graduated in the spring of 1941 with honors and was offered a teaching job and admission to the graduate doctoral program. It was not all altruism on the university's behalf, for they wanted to use the mind of Rick Malloy for their own benefit as well. And the war research preparations were already well underway.

When war came to the United States, like millions of American men, Rick Malloy wanted to join the army. Rick was a bit too old to be drafted, so he joined the army, seeking to become a ranger, under false pretense by lying about his age, a common occurrence for those too young but rare for those too old. He completed basic training before his deception was discovered, but when his identity and skills were better understood by the war department, he was considered more valuable to the war effort by being at MIT and was therefore removed from overseas assignment. He studied physics related to barometric pressures during the day and assisted in experiments and research at night for much of the war. By 1943 he had completed all of the class part of the doctoral program except for his thesis, and with the war in doubt he put his life on hold as many others did and threw himself completely into the war research effort. He became a small but integral part of the Manhattan project.

He would recollect later that he never was actually fully aware that he was building a detonation mechanism for an atomic bomb--it was just intended to be a more adjustable and reliable detonator that might be used on any number of explosive devices. Besides, the words "atom bomb" had little meaning before Hiroshima. He was not privy to any atomic secrets and read about the dropping of the bomb in the newspapers like everyone else. It was not until much later that he understood that his contribution had been significant and that without it, the project might not have worked as well as it did. As did many of his friends who had worked on the project, he was conflicted by the pride of being part of this momentous achievement and the horror of the resulting devastation it created.

In mid-1946, as Rick Malloy's life was becoming normal again, he had also just recently met a woman. She was a wonderful person whom he had met at a night club and she shared many of the same interests that he had. She too was of German descent and also loved jazz music. Her parents were both dead from the war and she was working to get into Harvard, as a graduate student, seeking a master's degree in history. And she was beautiful. She had long auburn hair and blue eyes and was tall, over 5'9." She was also very athletic and in great shape and condition. With her long legs, she could keep up with Rick's running with almost no effort at all, and could often outrun him. She had a good sense of humor, and although her English was not as perfect as Rick's, she was clearly well educated and intellectually inclined. In short, she was about perfect for Rick Malloy. Her name was Anna Sturm.

They had only dated casually, and it was not really serious yet, but Rick could see that they had so much in common and seemed to get along so well that this relationship might become very serious over time. He was eager to let her become more involved in his life, and during the spring of that year he did just that. They met almost daily and retold stories to each other about their experiences since last being together. They dined and went to movies and spent the weekend together. And it was pretty good, Rick thought. *No, it was perfect.*

On the afternoon of June 5th, as he had done nearly every clear day this year, Rick went for a run along the esplanade on the banks of the Charles River. He was running at his usual pace when another runner came up alongside him and, calling him by name, asked if he could run and talk with him for a mile or so. Rick agreed somewhat reluctantly, although he was a little nervous that this man knew who he was and where he could be found. But then, it was a well-known routine of his, and most of his friends at MIT knew where he could be found at this time every day, so maybe it wasn't so strange.

The next half-hour must have seemed like a decade, for the information that was shared with Rick Malloy by the stranger and the requests the stranger made of Malloy were extraordinary, to say the least.

Captain William Smith, recently reassigned to active duty in army intelligence, stationed in Berlin, ran alongside Rick Malloy and began to unfold an incredible story, bit by bit. He told of German citizen interrogations after the war, the scientists whose stories were so preposterous until the Hiroshima explosion, the boxes marked with the red swastika and eagle, the warehouse fire of suspicious origin and likely set by the Russians, the storage cave and the town of Faschgarten. And he brought it back to Boston, Massachusetts, and his not-so-accidental run along the Charles River that afternoon.

Two months earlier, in London, as a result of the meeting between a Colonel Farston and General Grimes, a team of army intelligence field agents was assembled and assigned to devise a plan to beat the Russians in finding the Nazi atomic weapons program information. Their assignment was to verify that the issues were real, and either recover the research for the United States or destroy it such that no other nation could use it. The initial work was assembling all known information to help develop and track down leads — field-based research in Berlin combined with London Intelligence obtained from detained Nazi scientists and known research. Building on this information, they would develop and execute a recovery plan. Captain Smith had been assigned to lead the actual recovery part of the second team, and his first task was to locate the right person(s) to assist in the effort.

That individual would be a unique human being, one in fifty million. They would need to know the geography and customs of East Germany north of Berlin. They would need to speak the language like a native, with all of the idioms and expressions a local inhabitant might use. They would need to be loyal to the United States beyond question. They needed to be able to take care of themselves and if need be, to react violently without hesitation. They should be an excellent shot with both a rifle and pistol. The person chosen had to be in top shape and physical condition, able to move quickly, think keenly under pressure, and act accordingly. And they needed to be able to decipher technical documents written in German, understand complex physics and mathematical equations, and spot forgeries and false information quickly and without the help of a laboratory or research facilities. As was made clear by Captain Smith, after reviewing literally thousands of files and war records, they came to the conclusion that they needed one man: Rick Malloy.

This was a serious mission, and it was vital to America, said Captain Smith, and he made it clear that army intelligence would teach Malloy how to be an operative. He appeared to have most of the skills already and in a few weeks would have them all.

It had taken nearly twenty minutes for Smith to lay out the story as they ran along the Charles. They had started at the Hatch Memorial Shell in Back Bay and were now nearly up to the Harvard footbridge, along side the Business School and across the river from the crew boathouse. *It was such a beautiful day until this guy came along*, thought

Rick Malloy. *He has to be kidding, but obviously he is not.*

Malloy turned to Captain Smith as they continued up towards the football stadium: "I am not your guy, Captain. I am probably not as well qualified as you think, and more importantly, I do not want to do it. My life is finally starting to turn around and I am trying to put my past behind me. You come along and want me to relive the past, returning to a place I have not seen in thirteen years, where I surely know no one. Based on the pictures I have seen of Berlin, I would not recognize much of what is left. Assuming that the crisis is real, and who the hell knows about that, certainly not me, then there must be better qualified people."

Captain Smith spoke slowly and clearly. "I understand your concerns, and I can only assure you that the problem is real, and that having conducted a thorough search, we believe that you are indeed the most qualified candidate. I was supposed to show you this letter only if you refused to cooperate, but as I would prefer that that we develop a good working relationship and possibly even a friendship, I want to share this with you up front and let you know where I'm coming from."

He handed an envelope with a folded one page letter in it to Malloy and waited for him to open and read it. As Malloy opened it and looked and the official words and the letterhead and seal on the page, he stopped running, stopped dead in his tracks. The letter was an executive order from the President of the United States, on presidential stationery, with the official seal of the Oval Office, and personally signed in blue ink. The substance of the page seemed less important, referring to presidential authority in national security matters, etc. It concluded that:

"Based on a very real perceived threat to the national security of these United States, Captain William Smith, under the command of General Henry Grimes, US army intelligence unit based in London and assigned to the occupied areas in the American Sector of the former German republic, shall act with the full authority of my office in these matters. Any requests made by Captain Smith shall be construed as requests by my office and should be treated as directives from the Commander in Chief as described under Executive Order No. 9734B, dated June 3, 1946. Failure to comply shall be a Federal offence and under the circumstances, deemed to be Treason and treated as such."

And there at the bottom of the page was the signature of the President of the United States, Harry S. Truman.

Like it or not, Rick Malloy had just joined the army...again.

CHAPTER SIX

Rick Malloy was given a brief four days to close out his life in Cambridge, Massachusetts, before he would begin his journey to London or wherever he was going to be briefed and trained. He sublet his apartment to a friend who would keep it the remainder of the year, by which time either Rick would return, or the lease would run out. He had put the furniture he wanted to keep in storage in another friend's basement and he gave the rest to a local homeless shelter, and he lent his bicycle to another doctoral student who had long admired it. His story to each had been that he had a family emergency back home in Wisconsin, and his mother needed him there for an extended period of time. He would write them in advance of his return or call them in a few weeks, but he had to leave immediately. The story was credible and was easily accepted by all. Other than offering assistance and sympathy, as well as being genuinely concerned, all his friends and acquaintances bought the story easily. With all of his worldly matters taken care of, there were yet two more major things to be taken care of. First, he had to relieve himself of his teaching and class obligations at the university, and second, he had to tell Anna. As hard as leaving MIT might be, that would be the easy one.

Rick was beginning to understand the power of the people who had recruited him through his visit to the MIT dean's office to withdraw from classes "for personal reasons." He realized that he could not use his mother as an excuse with the university, as she could know nothing about this. His story that he needed to go help his mother was a flimsy non-excuse that, in light of his having spent almost a decade as a student to get this far, and his being within months of completing his doctoral degree requirements, he felt sure would be questioned severely by the university. A week or two was one thing; an indeterminate leave of absence without good explanation was another. There was no good story he could concoct which would explain his need to leave the university for an extended period of time at this point in his academic career. None he could use, at least.

Rick had wanted to see Dean Ames, a mentor and friend who had guided him through his academic career during the war and a man he hoped would understand and maybe not ask too many questions. He had had to wait outside the dean's office for nearly two hours for the dean to return from prior scheduled appointments and was pleased to see the usual compassionate smile on the dean's face when he arrived. They went into his office, and Rick started to explain his need to withdraw from MIT. To his astonishment Dean Ames was not only not surprised to hear that Rick Malloy, honor student and respected teaching assistant, was leaving on extremely short notice, but he was perfectly understanding of the request. He interrupted Rick as if to save him from further lies about his need to withdraw from the university on short notice, and then proceeded to surprise Rick even further.

Harold Ames, Dean of Graduate Students, said that he understood Rick's need to leave and admired his decision, and that in his opinion Malloy had earned and should receive his degree anyway. He would recommend this to the doctoral committee and when approved (not if approved) Dean Ames would send the degree to Rick's home in Wisconsin if he liked. It was not what Rick expected or was prepared for, but it confirmed for Malloy that the university and the government must be closer relatives than anyone might have thought. Whatever the dean had been told by army intelligence was of sufficient importance to make Rick Malloy a VIP in the eyes of university administrators. That, and little else, was certain. The other compelling thought Rick had was that whatever story the dean was told, he drew from it the conclusion that Rick Malloy most likely would not be returning to MIT ever again. And that was very disconcerting.

Rick had not seen Anna in three days, and with only 24 hours left he was getting concerned that he would not get to speak to her. It was very unusual not to hear from her at least every other day, although it was mid-week and she had her own work and obligations to take care of up river near Harvard Square. He had initially avoided calling her because he did not know exactly what to say. He knew he would have to lie to her because he had sworn to keep his real actions a secret, but he hated the thought. How could they build a strong relationship if he was willing and able to lie about something so important? It was troubling, and he had no time to sort it out. He picked up the phone and called her. She was in, and they made a date to meet for dinner at their favorite local hangout. Rick wanted it to be a special night, but knew that might signal something other than his needing to return to Wisconsin for a few weeks to help his mother.

They met outside Brandy Pete's, a local gathering place for drinks and a restaurant in the financial district of downtown Boston, easily accessible by Red Line Subway from Harvard. It was not a glamorous place, more of a family diner atmosphere, with good food at reasonable prices. It was a novelty for the city of Boston, and known primarily to local clientele. After ordering drinks and food, Rick began to tell Anna about his family crisis. She was very understanding, and although sad at the thought that they would be apart for at least several weeks, she was wonderful in making him feel better about the whole mess than he felt earlier in the day. She offered to go with him, but then recanted based on her work schedule and applications due at Harvard. He did not relay the stories about subletting his apartment, or about the furniture, etc., for it did not help his story about being gone just a few weeks. After dinner they walked along the waterfront of Boston Harbor, past the run-down wharves and then back up through the North End and through Scollay Square to Back Bay and to his apartment. They had an agreement that they did not stay over at each other's apartment on weeknights, but this one was special. It was his last night in Boston, and so they broke the rule and spent most of the night in each other's arms. In the morning, Anna kissed him a teary goodbye and left for her work. He had said he would write as soon as he arrived and would call as soon as he was able. It was not true, but it made parting a bit easier and he was lying to himself as much as lying to Anna.

The last tie to his old life was now severed. He packed the few clothes Captain Smith told him to bring, and hailed a cab to South Station. It seemed silly to take a train out of Boston headed west toward Albany, but the army intelligence man had made it clear that it was imperative that anyone who might be watching his actions believe he was bound for Wisconsin. So Rick picked up the ticket at the reservations window that had been held for him and boarded the train at the platform at the designated time. He found the assigned Pullman car and entered. As instructed, he had handed his one-way ticket to Milwaukee, with a change in Chicago, to the conductor and took his seat in the half-full coach compartment. The Chicago Limited left on time, belching smoke and steam, headed west through the Boston suburbs, bound for Springfield, Albany, Utica, Rochester, Buffalo, Cleveland, Detroit, and on to Chicago. Twenty-five minutes later, at the first stop at the Framingham Depot, as passengers got on the train, Rick Malloy nonchalantly slipped off the Chicago Limited and walked through the station to a waiting black Ford sedan. He got in and took a seat next to Captain Smith before the car rushed off, aimed for Hanscom Field, the military air base nearby.

Smith was smiling as he got in the car. "How did it go? Anybody seem to be following or too interested in your business?"

Malloy settled back in the car for the one-hour ride and relayed the events of the past four days. Rick was also interested in hearing from Captain Smith what the dean had been told, but Captain Smith was interested in Anna. He asked just exactly what information and lies she had been told, about how Anna took the news, her reaction, and what she said she would do while he was gone. His questions seemed to focus way too much on Anna, thought Rick, but she was the closest person to him, so maybe it was not so odd. And if she bought it--well, everyone else would fall into place.

The car moved along the road on Route 126 toward Concord, and soon was at the gates of the airfield at Hanscom Air Base. They were only briefly detained at the gate and when it was recognized that it was Captain Smith, the guards were told to step aside and an escort was provided to guide them directly out to the airstrip and the waiting plane. It was very efficient and seemed like overkill for this mission, but it was consistent with how Smith had overplayed this thing from the beginning, thought Rick Malloy. When they got out onto the field there were two similar planes lined up, far away from any buildings, and they were protected by armed guards. As they approached, Malloy could see a few Army Air Corps personnel--probably pilot, co-pilot, navigator, and crew-- standing around waiting for the car and Captain Smith to arrive. They looked tired and angry. The senior pilot, named Dunn, who must have been a colonel according to his uniform, approached Smith as he got out of the car.

"Are you the SOB who got us out here four hours ago to stand around for a damn routine flight to Washington?" he asked.

"I am," replied Smith, "and I insist that we have no further discussion of any kind until we are in the air." Smith looked briefly at each of the planes and then pointed to the far plane and turned to the ground crew and said, "We will take that one, so let's get it ready for takeoff in fifteen minutes."

The colonel piped up again. "The hell with no discussion. We are going nowhere and we damn well will discuss it right here and now, Captain."

The condescending tone in his voice was impossible to mistake. Captain Smith wheeled around and replied, "Fine, then follow me and we shall talk." He took the pilot, a superior officer by rank, by the arm and they walked out away from everyone else for a lengthy and what appeared to be a one-way lecture by Colonel Dunn to Captain Smith.

The co-pilot, standing next to Rick Malloy, seemed to be enjoying watching the discussion enormously. He proudly said, "I don't know who this captain of yours is or who the hell you are, mister, but my man Colonel Dunn out there is well connected in Washington, has two war decorations for bravery, and is the senior pilot at this air base. Nobody with any brains messes with him. When he's finished with your captain, I would not be surprised if you guys don't run with your tails between your legs to avoid being arrested."

Rick Malloy did not reply to the co-pilot, but smiled to himself. The discussion went on and was indeed most animated. After several minutes of politely enduring the pilot's tirade, Malloy watched Captain Smith pull the now-familiar envelope out of his inside jacket pocket, remove the letter, and hand it to the pilot. Although no one else could understand what was happening, Rick understood all too well. And so he was the only one not surprised by what happened next. The pilot, Colonel Dunn, stepped back, looked up at Smith, looked over in the direction of Rick Malloy, shook his head, and then came to attention and saluted Captain Smith. The effect that watching this encounter had on the co-pilot and other flight support staff back near the plane was no less of a shock than getting a bucket of ice water in the face unexpectedly. They all stood for a few seconds in shock, and then as it started to sink in, they began running to get the plane ready for takeoff.

Malloy was, however, surprised to hear that the pilot had thought they were bound for Washington. Malloy was sure that he remembered being told that they would fly to Bermuda, on to the Azores, and up to London from there. There was no need to pass through Washington.

Both of the planes were identical C-47 cargo planes, the military version of the DC-3. They were fueled and mostly ready to go before Captain Smith had arrived. Final preparations were made, they loaded the gear onto the plane Smith had requested, sealed it up and taxied down the runway. By noon they were in the air.

The bench seats on the plane were not very comfortable, and Rick Malloy sat at an angle to be able to look out of the window and to keep his butt from going numb. As soon as the plane was off the ground, Captain Smith went up into the cockpit and pulled some papers and maps out of his bag for the pilot and copilot to use. After a few minutes digesting the information, the pilot banked the plane and turned north, toward Saint John, Newfoundland, not south toward Bermuda, or Washington, DC. It appeared that Captain Smith was full of surprises. They were not taking the southern route to Europe, but the northern route instead. "Why?" thought Malloy out loud.

He would not have to wonder for long, as Captain Smith returned to the cabin and sat next to Rick and began to explain. "I have had to withhold some information from you and in fact mislead you a bit to protect you, me, and this assignment," he began. "When you asked me on the first day we met if there weren't any better candidates, I was not fully truthful. In fact, you were one of three possible candidates. It would not be fair to say one of you was more or less qualified than the other two, so, in fact, you are our best chance at success on this mission. We do not have time to start over if things do not go as planned, so we decided to have alternatives--a back-up plan, if you will. That has already turned out to be wise, as there was an accident--at least, I believe it was an accident--and one of the other candidates was killed before he ever left the US. I was not going to take a chance with you only to find out that it was not an accident and that we would then have lost two good men. Now that we are in the air, I can tell you that our destination is just south of Paris, not London, and we will stop in Newfoundland and Ireland for refueling en route. London has been scrubbed, because we suspect a leak in our security there, and there would be too many people involved with the operation in London to keep it a secret. In France, we will not inform the local intelligence people we normally work with of our intentions or who we are, and very few people will know exactly what is going on."

Malloy interrupted to ask, "What happened to the first guy?"

The captain looked at Malloy, thought for a second, and replied, "Let's just say that we have a safety parachute for everyone on board this plane, just in case." Then he got up and went to speak with one of the two crew members also on board.

At an airspeed of approximately 185 miles an hour and with a slight tailwind helping out, the C-47 reached St. John in a little over 4 uneventful hours. The plane landed at a Canadian military airfield and taxied to a hangar, where they were met by a small group of ground crew and a Canadian Air Force major who was eager to help and have it known that he had been helpful. Only the two ground crew members got out of the plane; they supervised the refueling and guarded the plane from any potential tampering. Whatever Captain Smith had said to them, they were taking it dead serious and examining every one and everything that came near the plane. As unsettling as the need to do this was, it was reassuring that they were doing a good job of it, thought Rick as he sat in the plane.

After about two hours the plane was ready, started, and taxied back out for takeoff. As they lifted into the air, Rick Malloy thought, *Next stop, Ireland—eight long hours away.*

It was another uneventful leg of the journey, and it was starting to look like Captain Smith had been unnecessarily cautious, until they were about an hour out of Belfast. At the instruction of Captain Smith, the pilot had declined to explain to the Northern Irish Airfield Tower Command the nature of the unscheduled US military flight, or who was on the plane, or its final destination. Although it was standard procedure to allow American military planes to land, something had changed. The tower in Belfast refused to allow landing unless the plane provided complete information, above what was typically required. The reason was not explained by the tower, but Smith suspected that they were extremely sensitive to and wary of the IRA threats of terror. And so the tower refused to grant landing privileges and requested that the aircraft seek an alternate airfield. Smith and the pilot had tried to convince the authorities that the plane was legitimate and had re-quested that they contact MI-6 or even Whitehall for clearance, but this just scared the ground managers even more. After midnight, they were not calling anyone. After more than ten minutes of haggling, the senior officer at the airport came on the radio and pronounced, "I do not care if you've got Churchill himself on the damn plane, you can-not land here without my permission. I am responsible for this facility and I do not, repeat, I do not give you permission to land." He went on to suggest two alternate locations, including Glasgow, Scotland and Manchester, England. He strongly recommended Glasgow, the closest location.

Smith looked at the map, conferred with the pilot and co-pilot about remaining fuel, and following a short discussion on the denial of landing privileges in Ireland selected Preston Airfield in England, just south of Blackpool. It was a small military field where they would be allowed to land, and they had been lucky to have a tailwind and so had conserved fuel in crossing the Atlantic. Smith did not tell Rick Malloy, but he knew that with Belfast out as a landing area, they should not have had enough fuel to reach but one other airfield, and they would have to be diverted to Glasgow, the nearest field. Other than Glasgow, they would normally be very lucky not to have had an emergency land-ing somewhere between Ireland and England. That troubled Captain

Smith, and so he chose not to go with the obvious and seemingly only safe choice. He and the pilot spoke again and the pilot informed the Belfast tower that they were proceeding on toward Scotland as recommended – "Thanks for nothing"!

It may have been luck or experience, but it was a good thing Smith had been cautious. He could not have known that a call had in fact been placed to the Belfast Tower earlier that evening warning of a potential IRA attack, possibly coming in from the air and disguised as Americans. He also did not know about the two black sedans, parked one each at the ends of the runway in Glasgow, with automatic weapons aimed to see that the American plane would not have a successful refueling in Glasgow. And the people that contacted the tower in Belfast knew that Glascow was the only other logical location to refuel.

Smith waited until they were only fifteen minutes out of Preston airfield before contacting them. The pilot knew the old code words from the war that indicated that this was a diplomatic flight, and although those codes had surely been changed for the major airports, at well after 2 a.m., for a trans-Atlantic flight running very low on fuel, they were accepted at Preston right away. The runway lights had been turned on and the ground crews awakened to service the plane. It was nearly 3 a.m. when the plane touched down on the far west coast of England, north of Liverpool. Everyone was tired and a little nervous about what they would find. Inside the plane they wondered about the reception they would get and from whom, and outside the ground crew clearly were interested in who would request landing at nearly 3 a.m. using a diplomatic code, and why?

Both were relieved by the innocuous nature of the other. Pleasantries were exchanged and a story told about failing to adequately fuel up on the flight down to London that caused this unexpected stop. Apologies accepted--the ground crew still remembered the night missions from the war and knew what to do. Because this field was a British airfield and was not used by the Americans, there were no US forces stationed there and no aircraft fuel readily available to refuel the plane. This meant waiting until dawn to reach proper authorities for permission, and that was unacceptable to Captain Smith. Waiting on the plane might make them an easy target, while leaving the plane might be even riskier. Smith took the senior officer on the ground aside and they had a short conversation. Rick Malloy could not see them clearly, but he was curious whether the "letter" would be pulled out again, and whether it would work in England. When Captain Smith returned, he found out.

"They will sell us the fuel at an obscene price, but we have few good alternatives. To avoid further suspicion, I have come back to the plane to make it look like I need to take up a collection. In fact, I am carrying enough pounds sterling to buy all the fuel we need, but I do not want them to know that," stated Smith.

"Sir," asked one of the flight crew who was thinking quickly, "I am glad you can get us aircraft fuel, but why are you carrying English money if you believed we were not stopping in England?"

Smith opened his flight jacket and said, "Fair question--would you care for Canadian dollars, French francs, Irish punts, Dutch guilders, or German marks, anyone?" With that said, he revealed several packets of money of different currencies. "Success depends on preparation, my friends."

Less than two hours after landing, long before the sun started to come up over northern England, the plane was taxiing toward take-off with enough fuel to reach Rome, never mind Paris. They would be safely on the ground at their destination in less than another two hours. *Maybe I was being a bit overly cautious*, thought Captain Smith as they safely took off and headed across England for the Channel and France.

At 7 a.m., two black sedans pulled into the Preston airfield carrying four men dressed in dark clothes and looking very foreign to the area. They had driven for four hours down from Glasgow to meet the plane, but they were too late. One of the drivers got out and found a few members of the ground crew who had serviced the US plane that made the unexpected landing. He questioned them about who was on the plane, how much fuel it took on, and where it might be heading. When he returned, his face was tight, and it was easy to see that he was concerned about the change in events. As he got back in the car he muttered several times under his breath "scheiss, damm Amerikaners, scheiss." He sat in the driver's seat for a second and stared straight out through the windshield, and then pounded his fist on the dashboard. The information he obtained was not very useful and clearly not what he wanted to hear. He knew that the plane could be anywhere in Europe by now. They had adequate fuel, a several-hour head start, and left no indication of where they were headed.

Russian moles in the US and British intelligence networks had learned of this mission and provided ample advance notice back to Moscow to stop it. Teams had been assigned to all the air routes into Europe, and men had been stationed to take action when the Americans were located. These agents had lost their best chance to stop the Americans from reaching Europe. Now it would be up to the East German secret police and the Russian NKVD to stop Rick Malloy.

CHAPTER SEVEN

A rrival of a US military plane at the small civilian airfield near Melun, 45 kilometers south of Paris, was only a minor surprise. This was not the large commercial airport, Le Bourget, near Paris, and it was not an emergency landing. Under any normal circumstances, this would be odd, and there would be questions about such a landing. But because it was officially cleared to land, the tower and ground crew were at least ready and waiting, if not courteous and helpful. The surprise came in part because the field staff seldom saw foreign government aircraft after the war, and in part because the plane landed, refuelled, and then took off for parts unknown without logging any flight plan with the tower. No one got out of the plane, with the exception of two civilian-looking passengers who got off with virtually no luggage and were met and escorted into the terminal quickly.

The landing had been cleared in vague terms through the French government to three different airfields near Paris, so as not to generate any undue attention, and in fact, only the plane's call numbers had been provided to the tower with instructions to let the aircraft land, so no one even knew that this was an American plane until it touched down. Instructions had been provided to the airport managers in person by a member of the Deuxième, the French secret police organization, that very morning, and they were very specific. The two arriving passengers were not to go through customs or immigration, but to be escorted directly to the terminal to meet with unspecified "French officials." These officials would have military identification. And although this was odd when compared to standard procedures; based on what many had seen over the prior eight years, not much came as a surprise here. The ground crew had seen this sort of thing enough for it not to cause too much of a stir. The request did not specify who was on the plane or even that it was a US plane that would be landing. It was merely listed as a routine VIP landing, and all courtesies were to be extended to the crew and the arriving passengers. It appeared that the French airport had no information at all about this landing, and what little they did appear to know would not be given out under any circumstances. In actuality, the senior French officials had long been a part of the planning of this mission and both the Deuxième and the Quai d'Orsay, equivalents to the MI-6 and the Foreign Service, were aware of the importance of who was on the plane and of their mission.

Prior to arrival, Captain Smith had changed from his military uniform into civilian clothes that would not seem out of place walking in any major city. Rick Malloy was still in his civilian clothes, the same ones he had left Cambridge with some eighteen hours ago. As they walked away from the plane, Captain Smith looked back to the plane to wave a "thanks" to the pilot and crew and it was then that Rick Malloy noticed that the numbers and markings on the plane had been changed at some point since they departed the United States. Smith confessed that in England he had taken the opportunity to use the large decals he had brought with him on the plane to change the numbers and put the words "London-Paris Air Courier" below the new numbers and on top of the US Air Force emblem. He could not hide the plane's green color or the fact that it was a US plane, but it was clear that he did not want to make it easy for anyone to follow their tracks. Malloy was impressed at his efficiency, but why was it necessary?

Once in the terminal, they were met by two French men, who, although dressed in civilian clothes, were clearly not civilians. These men spoke in broken English and motioned for the American pair to follow them. Smith had recognized them, and they exchanged a few words which satisfied him that these were the correct contacts, before leaving the terminal to go get into the waiting car.

Once in the car they sped off southeast, away from Paris, past Nemours and the little towns of Montargis and Amilly. They turned due east after about fifty kilometers, and then south again onto a winding back road. After nearly three hours they turned into a tree-lined lane and pulled up to a gate which was manned by a guard who looked like a farmer, except that most farmers do not carry automatic pistols in their pants. Acknowledged by the guard, the gate was opened and the sedan continued on down the lane and around a bend about a half-mile to a large Mansion House at the end. This was to be Rick Malloy's home and training ground for the next two weeks.

It had been a long trip, and so after a brief tour around the facility, introductions to the staff and trainers, and a quick meal, Rick Malloy had gone to bed to rest up and prepare for the training he would need if he were to have any chance of completing his assignment successfully.

Captain Smith sat down with the two men he had met at the airport and they began to review the training that would begin in the morning for Rick Malloy. The Frenchmen were in fact experienced Deuxième Bureaux operatives, or technically agents of the SDECE, the French Counter Espionage Service organized after the liberation of France, to replace the Deuxième, who had been disbanded by Hitler. They were on loan to the Allied command and at the disposal of US army intelligence for the next two weeks. Whatever else one might say about the French Army's fighting ability, the Resistance had had years of learning the art of underground survival and knew how to think like and deal with the Germans. They had devised the two-week training program to maximize Rick Malloy's chances of success and survival, and they would be integral in appraising whether he was ready to go or needed more training. The time would be spent in six areas: strength and conditioning, hand-to-hand combat, pistol marksmanship, an East German dialect speech refresher course, memorizing the new identity and thinking like an operative, and deciphering atomic scientific documents/plans quickly to determine their relevance and authenticity. The mornings would be devoted to the first three lessons, which were more physical in nature, and the afternoons and early evenings were dedicated to the more mental pursuits. There were to be fourteen days of twelve hours each day, with little or no time off. Only the nights were free for a stroll or reading a newspaper (in German, of course) prior to bedtime.

The two Deuxième men had assembled the trainers and the curriculum. Captain Smith would handle the strength training first thing each morning, focusing on running and stamina, not bulking up the upper body--there just was no time for that. The purpose was to provide the ability to literally outrun an enemy or to move more quickly than a lesser adversary. Smith was confident that Malloy was in good condition and that this goal would be fairly easy. In addition to this Smith wanted to teach some evasionary tactics to not only help with quick movement and strength, but stealth and quiet as well. This would be more technique than muscle and would take practice and time to master. A few good moves were all he could hope for Malloy to learn.

Marcel, the shorter of two Frenchmen, was a martial arts master and would endeavor to teach some basic hand-to-hand combat techniques over the brief period. Nothing fancy, but focusing mainly on how to use a knife effectively as a lethal weapon and how to defend oneself in unarmed combat. He knew that Malloy had been through basic training as an army ranger, but also that he never used these skills in combat and that at best they were rusty, and at worst, never really learned.

François, the other French operative, was a marksman. He would focus on making Rick Malloy not only a proficient shot at close range with the Swiss made SIG-Sauer pistol, but try to make Rick comfortable with the gun as an extension of himself. Rick would carry the SIG-Sauer with an attachable silencer in part because it would not link him back to the Americans, and therefore would brand him more of a freelance mercenary if apprehended. And the other reason was practical. Carrying the standard- issue American Colt was out. He would not have access to ammo for a US Army pistol in occupied East Germany, but he would be able to acquire ammo for German weapons like the Mauser and Luger. They had considered using several guns, including the Steyr and the Mauser and the Russian Tokarev TT, but the SIG-Sauer 210 was smaller, lighter, more reliable, and was chambered to use the ammo of the German Luger. It would be easier to conceal and less likely to fail at a critical moment. It was the obvious choice of a professional, and Rick Malloy was being trained to be a professional.

For the dialect refresher, the team had brought in an East German native named Alan Mannstein, who now lived in Paris. He became a trusted ally during the war as a key member of the Resistance and demonstrated his abilities on several occasions. He had been a German language teacher, but because his ancestry was Jewish, he lost his position at the university in Berlin and he had been barely able to escape Germany into France with his family. Just as it seemed that they would be safe, France fell and his life and that of his family were in danger again. He went into hiding and found himself in the Resistance. He knew most of the recent idiomatic expressions used in East Berlin and the speech mannerisms which would identify you as either a native or an outsider. He understood that Eric Malloy was of near nobility by birth and that his command of the language would be flawless, but sound very stilted to the common worker or shopkeeper. He would have to learn to speak like a more common man, including the use of swearing and the common use of his hands in making gestures--a thing upper-class Germans just did not do. He would have to abandon habits created as a child, such as always looking directly at the person you were addressing--an admirable trait, but one that few average people employed, and one which might raise suspicion about his background.

The fifth area--changing and memorizing a new identity and thinking like a spy-- would be relatively easy for Rick because he had already changed his name from von Malloy, which often indicated high social status, to Malloy. Still, with the potential that East German agents might be looking for him, he would have to look, act, and be someone other than Rick Malloy. In addition to using a false identity, everything else would need to change. His assumed background had been carefully chosen to maximize credibility and allow mobility. He would be provided with excellent forged documents that would indicate he was cleared by the East German police to search for his father, who had been missing since the war. He was to be on holiday while the factory he had been working in was being rebuilt, and he had been given several weeks to look for his father. It was not an uncommon story in the years after the war, and he would be one of many people trying to reunite a separated family. He would, however, need to memorize a lot of information about his new identity, the father he was searching for, his job, the town he lived in, etc. Two weeks of training was a short time. Besides this, he had to learn how to change his hair color from dark blond to gray and black; he would have to let his hair grow out a bit and grow his sideburns longer. After all, he could shorten longer hair to change his looks, but it took time to grow hair--time he might not have. He would be taught to alter his appearance to avoid being easily recognized. As a final touch, he was to be tutored in walking with poor posture, which combined with the right clothes and hair, gave the appearance of a much older, more tired, working man who would not draw anyone's attention.

The final area of his training was being able to authenticate and decipher technical documents written in German. Rick had become an excellent physicist in America, but he would be working in an area with which he was only partially familiar, one that was top secret, and in a language which he did not use regularly. He would undoubtedly encounter technical terms he would never have seen as a boy and which would not be easy translations to English. To accomplish this would require a two-pronged approach. For the first ten days, he would read up on German physics textbooks and white papers written and published before the war, in German, about their atomic program, to gain proficiency with the terminology. For the last four days, he would be assisted by Herr Doktor Franz Baumgartner, a sixty-five-year-old former German physicist who had defected to America early in the war and been part of the Manhattan Project.

Baumgartner had been assigned to the Kaiser Wilhelm Institute in Berlin where he had met both Werner Heisenberg and Walther Gerlach, two primary technical leaders of the Nazi effort to build atomic weapons. He was now doing research in England but would come to the Mansion House for a few days to convey a basic level of top-secret atomic and hydrogen weapon theory, mechanical construction requirements, and what to look for to identify and authenticate documents. He had been privy to many top-secret scientific documents of the Third Reich before defecting and knew of the levels of security, the stamping and signature levels required, and the relative importance of each level. With his help, Eric Malloy would not waste time reading irrelevant or falsified documentation. At least, that was the plan.

As the days progressed, the team conferred at the end of each day about the progress made during that day. By the time the instructors convened at 9 p.m., Eric Malloy was typically in bed asleep, exhausted from the physical and mental workout he was getting each day. By the end of the first week, the reports started to gain consistency. Eric was in fine physical shape and could easily run ten miles if he needed to. He was an excellent shot with a pistol when given time, and was getting faster at preparing and aiming his gun. His language proficiency was remarkable, and he had an excellent memory, which made learning a great number of details about his new life easy. Until Dr. Baumgartner arrived, there would be no reliable understanding of his technical abilities. The major weakness was in the area of hand-to-hand combat. Eric was quick and agile and strong. He was eager to learn and he understood the importance of self-defense. But he seemed to lack the killer instinct he would surely need to succeed. His momentary hesitation in harming another human was not an asset on this assignment, and he was currently considered unable to kill, even in self-defense. For the second week, the other sessions were cut a bit shorter and more time was spent on the hand-to-hand combat. Emphasis was placed on developing reaction times, being more aggressive in hostile situations, and developing an "it's me or you" survival instinct. Progress was made and Eric was a quick study, but at heart he was a pacifist; he had no desire to be a killer.

As the last day approached, the instructors gathered on the final night and gave their appraisals of the training, fitness, capabilities, and readiness of Eric Malloy for the mission. The consensus opinion had changed little over the past week and had only been borne out in session after session of hand-to-hand combat. Eric Malloy did not appear to have the first-strike killer instinct essential for this mission. He had not been seasoned in real combat or tested in battle, and lacked real-world experience. Two weeks was just too little time to indoctrinate him. He did not hate or fear his enemy and had no strong feelings for the mission that could be played upon to increase his aggressiveness. The recommendation of the two French trainers was that sending him in would be suicide and that the operation should be delayed or shut down. Captain Smith reluctantly agreed that under the circumstances it might be unwise to proceed, but he also reminded the team that it was London in cooperation with the US army intelligence who would make the final determination.

Smith retired from the meeting and went directly to the

communication room in the mansion. He knew it was late at night, but he wanted to provide his superiors with a status report. Ten o'clock at night in France meant nine o'clock in London. Late, but still working hours for the people he reported to. He went down into the basement to contact London using the wireless setup that he had already used several times during the past two weeks to keep the brass informed. The set was then linked by ground line from Paris to London on a more secure land line. This was an older unit, with no encryption, but the communications were given in code words, so it would make little sense to anyone else intercepting the signal. Not a perfect system, but as long as no names were used it would be hard for an eavesdropper to understand the content of anything tranmitted. And besides, obtaining a more secure means of communication might raise its own set of suspicions.

To his surprise, Colonel Farston was in his office and replied immediately. Rather than start with the bad news, Captain Smith unfolded the preceding two weeks of training for Rick Malloy and then apprised the colonel of the unanimous conclusions of the instructors. There was a long period of silence, after which Colonel Farston sent a short return message as follows: "Acknowledged. We are in a bind. First choice not available due to accident as is known. Third choice recently in hospital with appendicitis, no longer viable option. Leaves only second choice, your man, Malloy. Will brief superiors and return orders at 0600 hours. Over and out."

The transmission stopped and left Captain Smith staring at the receiver. He knew that under the circumstances, he would get an order in the morning that would effectively send Eric Malloy into a potentially deadly situation, which he was probably not prepared to handle. He also knew that Colonel Farston had used Malloy's name in the communication accidentally. He did it only once, but it was a mistake. It was a slip that should not mean anything, but Captain Smith was a professional who did not like slip-ups, even little ones by superior officers. Those were the facts, and there was little that he could do to change them. He retired to his room for bed. As much as he needed to rest, he would not sleep that night, not knowing what he was going to have to do and how it would likely turn out.

While almost all of the population of France slept, Celeste, an East German agent of Slavic descent who was stationed in Paris, was very much awake. She knew that they were running out of time to find the American named Malloy and neutralize him before he got involved. They had completely lost the trail after the American military plane disappeared from England fifteen days earlier. No planes matching the description of that aircraft had landed anywhere in Europe. Not in England, although they had searched the records of every possible airfield imaginable and discreetly interviewed ground personnel at most locations reporting anything unusual. They had similarly scoured France, Belgium, Holland, and Germany and found nothing. The damn thing had just vanished. The plane had been spotted in the Azores the following day, refueling, but with only the pilot, co-pilot, and navigator on board, that meant that they had dropped their passengers off somewhere and were returning to the US. The Russian operatives across Europe were pulling out all of the stops in trying to locate Rick Malloy. They were covering all military radio frequencies for a transmission, monitoring the mail and courier services from Paris to London, tracking the source of diplomatic pouches, all in hopes of getting a lead on the whereabouts of the American. Knowing that MI-6 and US Intelligence operated out of north London, and that the American was now somewhere in Europe, Celeste had begun calling in favors from various wireless radio operators in Europe. She asked for information on any interesting messages overheard and/or coming from strange places, and then she waited for the information to come in. It was a long shot, but her alternative was to sit and do nothing until Malloy resurfaced.

In ten days she had nearly 100 messages and calls reported to her of all types, but of all of these calls, one interested her the most. It was a wireless message that had been made three times during the period, and based on frequency triangulation, it seemed to come from an area about 80 kilometers southeast of Paris. Importantly, the transmission had been in English, not in French. After the third time, she contacted the operative who had reported these messages and asked that she listen in on the next call and relay as much of what was being said as possible, especially listening for the name Malloy, or any military names, dates, etc. At 22:30 hours she had gotten a call from the Le Bourget-based independent operative, who had reported the prior transmissions and dearly needed the money being offered for assistance. She relayed the substance of the transmission and the fact that the name Malloy was used once. Most importantly, she was able to locate the origin of the signal to the town of Gien, some 80 kilometers southeast of Paris. Celeste was ecstatic at this news. She immediately coded and relayed the information to her superiors in East Berlin, including in the message that she believed that she had found the location of Rick Malloy. She knew it might take as much as a day to find the exact location, but also that the Russians would have agents in that area in the morning. She had done her job and had found the missing American when no one else could do it. If all went as planned, she should get a nice promotion out of this.

At 0600 hours, a knock came on the door of Captain Smith's room. There was a message for him in the communications room in the basement. Smith was already dressed and had been for over an hour. He went to the communications room and read the coded message. It was brief and to the point: "No alternatives available, proceed as planned. Depart immediately for destination. Good Luck." His fear confirmed, Smith knew this meant the mission was a "Go"!

CHAPTER EIGHT

JULY, 1946

Rick Malloy had also gotten up early on this last day of training. He met Captain Smith for breakfast and they had a serious discussion about the training and the judgment of the French operatives. Malloy knew it would be useless to argue, but pointed out first that under the right circumstances he knew that he could be very aggressive--for example, if his life or that of someone he loved was threatened. But that was not the case, at least not to his knowledge. And secondly, he had been drafted into this "job"--he was not an eager volunteer. If there were someone deemed more competent, he would gladly step aside and return to his life in Cambridge.

"Rick, I like you. You're a good man, and I appreciate your honesty," said Smith. "So, I want to be completely honest with you and let you know where I am coming from. Although it may not have seemed like it so far, this is a dangerous assignment, and I insist you be the best prepared for it we can make you. I am confident in your abilities and have admiration for your courage and convictions in taking on this assignment. And, yes, you are the most-qualified person for this assignment. Besides, we do have orders to proceed today--actually, this morning--on to Germany, where you will be provided the most up-to-date information available and really get started. So, you are our man. Agreed?"

"If I'm the one, let's get it over with," agreed Malloy.

They had developed their plan to get into Berlin undetected, with alternatives, backups, and contingencies. It was not an obvious or direct route and was meant to deceive pursuers. Once in Berlin, Rick would cross over into the east to run down the various clues and follow leads provided to him by MI-6, army intelligence, and the research team working on the project. Smith would stay in Berlin to assist as possible and feed intelligence to Rick as it was available and possible. There was not much in the way of a professional or personal belongings to pack, as neither Rick Malloy nor Captain Smith had brought much with them. An hour later, Smith quickly thanked the French staff at the Mansion House as he got into the car and shouted to the two French operatives: "We will follow you back to Paris, okay?"

"Oui, m'sieur," came the reply.

The staff had loaded two sedans for the trip. *Just like the decoy airplane back in the US*, thought Rick Malloy. The French operatives took one car, and Smith and Malloy got into the other at about 7:30 a.m. and drove out of the gate and down the dirt road to the highway.

They drove together for several miles before they met up with another black sedan with two other men in it--apparently French operatives as well. They stopped for just a few seconds to exchange thanks, and the two cars carrying the now four French operatives sped off toward Paris. *Another decoy*, thought Malloy. He was beginning to learn a lot from the careful Captain Smith. He also noticed that they were headed northeast, toward Dijon and Germany, not northwest to Paris. As they drove the dusty roads northwest up toward Dijon, they passed through wine country and the famous vineyards Rick had read about and collected bottles from back in Cambridge. Another time, and he would love to spend a few days touring famous vineyards and sampling the various Burgundy wines. But today, that was just a dream as they drove on through the region.

Three hours later, at approximately 11 a.m., the black sedan carrying the two Americans pulled onto a side street a few blocks from the train station at Dijon. Over the last hour of the trip, they had discussed the path they would take into Germany and on to Berlin. Captain Smith had instructed Rick Malloy about his tactics during the training sessions over the past two weeks. Essentially, it came down to clear thought, thorough preparation, and attention to detail. Rick was sure he was observing a master at work. He did not know that Smith was not a formally trained field operative, but an intelligence officer. He had no way of knowing that Smith had really been drafted into this spy business just six months earlier and although indeed very good at what he did, he had only textbook training before embarking on this mission himself.

Based on the plan, it was clear that there was a desire to not leave any path to be followed, or at least have the path so difficult to follow that any adversary would fall further behind in their pursuit. Leaving the car behind, Smith would buy a ticket to Geneva, while separately Malloy would buy a ticket to Lausanne. It would be for the same train, and Smith would also get off in Lausanne. No one would be able to report two Americans traveling together, because again, Captain Smith was being cautious. At 11:35 the Capitole Express pulled out of Dijon, headed southeast into Switzerland with the two Americans aboard. Normally it might be unwise to get on a major cross-country train like the French Capitole, and in fact it would have been very ill conceived to have gotten on in Paris. Captain Smith knew that if the Russians or East Germans were looking for them, they would surely cover the obvious first. But getting on separately in Dijon, when the enemy, if they had any clue, thought the team was en route to Paris, and getting off in Lausanne, another smaller city, was wise and cautious. They would neither board nor depart in a major city, and there would be no memory of two men traveling together or even purchasing tickets for the same destination. The plan was to crisscross Germany, finally entering Berlin from the northwest, a less-likely direction for them to come from. They would be very hard to track or locate, and that was a good thing.

Back at the Mansion House, most of the trainers had departed soon after the Americans left. The entire staff of sixteen had been on constant duty and high alert for the entire two weeks of Rick Malloy's training. With his departure, they had quickly shut the kitchens, re-lieved guards, and nearly all had left for families or some time off. The two remaining staff had nearly finished cleaning up for the morning when a knock on the front door drew their attention. Opening the door, the maid was greeted by a man in dark clothes carrying a pis-tol with a silencer and speaking very broken French. "Where is the American named Malloy?" the leader demanded. He pushed past the maid into the room as the older house staff man tried to run away. On the other side of the room stood two more men, dressed similarly, and also holding guns. They had slipped in quietly through the back to join the man at the door. The older butler stopped, turned, and started to run up the stairs--and as he did, the East German leader shot him twice in the back. The gun had spit out two bullets, but it had made little noise, the large silencer being very effective. The maid screamed and ran to his side, but it was of no use. He was fatally wounded and in a few seconds would be dead. The two intruders who entered from the back confirmed that they had searched the house thoroughly and returned to report that this was clearly the right house, judging by the communications room in the basement, but no one was inside.

"Verdammt," muttered the leader, and for effect he pounded his fist on a nearby table. "Sit her down--she must tell us where he went. Tie her to that chair!" he said, pointing to an old wooden hall chair.

Over the next ten minutes, these men questioned the maid, now firmly tied to a chair, while the third searched the house and the trash, seeking more information. He found an article of clothing with an American label and a map with a route marked to Paris, but not much else. There was not a lot of time for these men to carefully coax information out of the maid. They were sure that the American named Malloy had been in the house earlier in the day and needed to quickly get in pursuit of him, to stop him dead. Every minute lost made that harder to do. As a result, the torture being applied to the maid by the East Germans was not subtle at all. This maid had been a member of the Resistance only two years earlier and knew what was in store for her. She would try to tell them little. She screamed when her arm was broken and cried as they debased her body in an attempt to get her to talk, but she knew that no matter what she said or did not say, they were going to kill her. And so mostly, she just cried. She told little, but they did beat her into divulging that two black sedans had left, headed north toward Paris just before 8 a.m. She was neither willing nor able to say much more before she collapsed into unconsciousness.

The East German leader determined that it was a waste of time to continue to pursue interrogation with the maid and that wherever the American had gone he was getting farther away every minute. Taking the map with a route marked to Paris and some other bits of information gleaned from a search of the house he went down to the communications room and sent a message using the wireless transmitter in the house to his superiors:

> "Found and searched American Malloy location. He is on the move, apparently headed for Paris this a.m. in black sedan with escort of two men in second black sedan. Suggest posting lookouts on the main roads entering from the South, at train stations and at airfields to intercept. Awaiting instructions."

He stopped and waited for an answer. After several minutes, the message came back and he was told to evacuate the area, to return to Paris and leave no trace of their visit.

Having decided that they had done all they could in the area and having gained all they were going to get from the maid and a search of the mansion house, these men quickly and silently left. They exited through woods at the back of the house in the same manner as they came--only this time, they were dragging two dead bodies to hide in the woods: the older staff man and the maid, both having been shot in the back of the head. They would not be found for days, maybe even weeks, and no one would ever know what actually happened.

Back in Paris, there was a rush of activity as both Russian and East German agents raced for the most-likely locations to spot the two approaching sedans. They stationed cars at the three most-likely roads entering Paris from the south and began the search. Men were sent to observe the entrances to the Gare Lazare and Gare de L'Est, the two train stations most likely to be used to get into Germany. The other stations would take passengers into Switzerland, Spain, or Monaco in the south, or Belgium and Holland to the north. Agents had already been watching Le Bourget airport as well as the smaller airfields surrounding Paris since they learned Malloy was in France. They were not eager to let him slip away again, and the fact that they had come so close and missed at the Mansion house earlier in the day spurred them in their chase. Unfortunately, it might be too late to spot and stop the sedans before they got to the city; too much time had passed. And if they got into Paris by car, the Russians were betting that they would leave by train or plane.

At 2 p.m. the Capitole Express pulled in to Lausanne, Switzerland, and the two Americans got off separately and entered the main station, the HauptBahnhof. Each separately bought a 2nd-class seat on a local train up to Basel, a two-hour trip, and were pleased that the Swiss border control stop had not been as issue. Upon arriving, they purchased, separately again, tickets on another three-hour local train up to Karlsruhe in West Germany. Going through German customs in the American zone would not present a problem and was prudent and less likely to draw any undue attention. This would get them into Germany by dark and they would stop there for the night. Captain Smith thought it very unwise to take a long express train or an overnight train. It would be too easy to trace the passenger manifests while they were on a long trip or to just wait for the arrival of the obvious trains coming into Berlin.

The trip up to Karlsruhe was uneventful, and the pair of Americans, Captain Smith and Rick Malloy, stepped off the train in this working-class German city in the American occupation zone near the Rhine and the Ruhr Valley, just before dark. They walked down the Bahnhofstrasse to a small Gasthaus that had several small rooms and secured two rooms for the evening. Smith badly wanted to check in with London and get any updates prior to going into Berlin, but he also knew that to make contact on an open line was dangerous, and so he would wait until the morning and call from a more secure location just before departing. In that way, even if traced, they would be gone by the time anyone could arrive. The pair went downstairs dressed in American army uniforms that Smith had obtained while they were training in France. With the occupation forces all over the western part of Germany, this was probably the most plausible explanation for two Americans traveling together. Anyone looking for them would not likely think twice about uniformed soldiers.

They had a mediocre dinner in the small dining room in the hotel and discussed the overall plan again before retiring for the evening. Tomorrow they would continue to wind their way into Berlin, and then Malloy would cross over into the eastern sector alone to follow clues provided by MI-6 and US army intelligence, posing as someone looking for his lost father. The only solid clue they had given him to date was actually an intercept from a Russian wire, which indicated that the East Germans were searching for a stonemason named Rudolph Werner. They had an address, but apparently had not found him yet.

In the morning they met for breakfast at 6 a.m. to discuss the travel plan for the day. After a light breakfast, they checked out of the hotel and returned to the train station. They had agreed that while Captain Smith went to a nearby large hotel, often used by businessmen and the military to place calls to London, that Malloy would go buy tickets for the journey. Smith called in to army intelligence headquarters on the agreed number and after being put on hold for a minute or so, was greeted by a voice he instantly recognized as General Grimes himself. Grimes decided to use first names for this open line communication and addressed Captain Smith without rank as "Bill," and indicated that he would like to be called Hank. Captain Smith was not even aware that Henry Grimes ever went by "Hank," but that was another matter. Hank it would be.

"Bill, we must consider the possibility that we are entertaining guests this morning," said "Hank" Grimes. "Do you understand?" Smith immediately acknowledged that he understood, and recognized that he was being told that there might be listeners on the line or that the line was tapped, or... *God only knows*, he thought.

"Hank" continued: "The recent visit to Paris did not go well and concerns us. I would suggest that you alter your own vacation itinerary and that you play things close to the vest." Smith recognized that he was being told that there might be a leak in the intelligence groups involved in his mission and that he should develop a new plan and not tell his superiors. "Close to the vest" would not mean much to someone who did not know English expressions, and this type of phrasing was often used for when there was a chance that someone who would have to translate the message was listening. It might not make sense in a direct translation, and the fact that it was used was a message in itself.

Prior to starting this assignment, Smith had been given a set of intelligence code guidelines to follow. One of the simplest was using unique phrases that only a native would understand to convey direction. This was not complex code, and with a little time could easily be figured out by the enemy. However, combined with the use of common American idiomatic expressions and the use of personal information that only the intended receiver would understand, this method of communication was very effective over the telephone or telegraph. The complex codes used during the war by the OSS, Nazis, Russian NKVD, MI-6 and the like were difficult to use on the fly and often required significant time and equipment to decode. These simple code guidelines were far more practical under the circumstances.

Smith thought quickly. Only a few in London knew his intended route. Was there a security leak, or was it just so obvious to any pursuers that they might go through Paris before heading for Berlin? He had to know. After a few seconds of silence, Captain Smith said: "I ate schnitzel this morning and have plans for a more substantive lunch. Wanted to know if the sink will hold water?"

Hank laughed but got the meaning instantly. "Be careful where you eat, and yes, the plumbing may be faulty. I am concerned that food poisoning may spread east." He knew that the original plan was to have spent the night in Karlrsuhe, therefore the reference to schnitzel indicated that they had gotten in to Germany and that they would be moving on that morning, as planned, toward Berlin. He also now knew that there might be a leak in London or Berlin that could jeopardize this entire operation. Hank's final comment was: "I would try some new cuisine if I were you. Maybe someplace different for a change, and surprise me. Good luck--over and out."

Smith met up with Rick Malloy on the train platform. As a result of his call to London, he had decided that it was too risky to continue on their previously planned path into Berlin directly. Rick Malloy greeted him with an ashen face and a newspaper in hand. On the front page of the *Alsatian Gazette,* a French newspaper published in German and read by many in this part of Germany, was a headline in German about apparent underworld killings in Paris yesterday. The story told of the firing of machine guns on two black Peugeot sedans at about noon as they approached the city on the Rue des Anglais from the south. One sedan hit a tree, burst into flames, and exploded. The other went out of control and plunged over a retaining wall into the river Seine. There were no survivors.

Witnesses stated that the assassins were waiting for the cars and had staked out the intersection in preparation for this attack. They fled immediately after and no good descriptions were available. The identities of the killed men had not been ascertained yet. Captain Smith grabbed the paper, looked at the article intently for a second, then asked Malloy to read it to him carefully, in English, for he could not read German very well himself. Malloy could tell that he was also disturbed by this latest information.

The two Americans reconvened in a café across from the train station and found a quiet and secluded corner to plan their next moves. Malloy translated the article first and then Smith recounted his call to London. They now felt a bit conspicuous in their army uniforms, although less so in the café than out in the open. The plan for the day had been to take a series of local trains, eventually getting into Berlin, and then to meet briefly with Allied intelligence and have Rick Malloy cross over into East Berlin before midnight. The army uniforms were expected to provide a bit of anonymity and shelter them from being hassled as many civilians were by the various occupation forces' police units, but now these uniforms might be a liability, and traveling together in the uniforms would make them easy to spot. Whoever had gunned down the two cars in Paris must have had access to the tactical plans made only yesterday back at the mansion house. They knew enough to look for two cars in Paris, but not enough to know it was a diversion. This, combined with the concern in London that there was a leak in security, was confusing and inconsistent. After all, London knew they were not headed to Paris, but they did not know of the diversion. And it also explained why London was so happy to hear from Captain Smith--they were not positive he was alive. Smith now was forced to believe that the Russians and East Germans knew way too much about what they were up to and that whoever was after them was deadly serious, had a lot of manpower, and was well informed. A more subtle approach into Berlin would be prudent. And they were on their own now; it would be too dangerous to use their arranged contacts for assistance in case of the obvious, that there really was a leak. The original plan was out the window, and they would be making it up as they went along.

CHAPTER NINE

Rick Malloy was fascinated as he watched and listened to Captain William Smith review their circumstances, the events of the last 24 hours, and then translate that into an action plan. The two Americans did not know about the East German infiltration of the Mansion House back in France, and that led them to believe that someone had informed the enemy that they were returning by car to Paris.

Smith reasoned, "The informant must have been local to the Mansion House and must have heard my words 'See you back in Paris,' which I shouted just before departing, and taken this at face value. London, of course, knew we were headed for Dijon but did not know about my planned diversion, so the leak could not have come from there. And the informant also must have assumed that the two black cars that left the Mansion House were the two cars that continued on to Paris. They did not fully know about the diversion either. Very strange. Hmmm. What it also says is that given these circumstances, and even if the East Germans or Russians have good contacts in the French police, it will be a day at least before they realize that we were not in either car. Right now, we should be assumed to be dead and this will continue unless there is a leak in London to report my call this morning."

"There should be no reason to continue to search for us right now," continued Smith. "But London had said that all ways into Berlin from the west were being watched. If there is also a leak in London, then my call will soon alert the Russians that we are still alive. That may also explain why the general himself was on the line. We must move fast. There is a narrow window of opportunity to get straight into Berlin while there is confusion in the mind of our pursuers about our status and location. If we miss that window, it will be far more difficult and dangerous to get there."

The fact that the real informant had been a maid who had told what little she knew under extreme torture before she was killed did not change the fact that the East Germans did believe that Rick Malloy was killed in one of the cars in Paris and it would be several hours before they learned differently. Over the next hour, a plan was drawn up by Captain Bill Smith to take advantage of this logic and use this advantage to be in Berlin before the Russians could figure out what happened.

The first part of the new plan was to change the appearance of the group traveling to Berlin. Even with the Paris diversion, East German operatives might still be on the lookout for two American men traveling together, so Malloy would not travel with Captain Smith on this journey, and both of them would have to significantly change their appearance. Entering the washroom at the train station, Rick Malloy would emerge a different-looking person only thirty minutes later. He had not shaved since leaving the Mansion House and used this to his advantage in creating a slight goatee beard that significantly altered his look. He combed his hair straight back instead of to one side, and he removed his army uniform and put on his civilian clothes again. He hunched one shoulder a bit and made sure he did not stand straight as a military man might. He would acquire a pair of eyeglasses at his next stop that would help complete the illusion. He looked at least fifteen years older, and he would look like a typical German civilian who had suffered through the war.

The next step was to further accentuate his look as an older businessman. Using monies provided by Captain Smith, he purchased a used leather business case and eyeglasses at a second-hand store nearby and then went to a store near the station and bought a work shirt, a pair of comfortable shoes, and one cheap black coat. He put these clothes on and wore them out of the shop, looking very much like an average factory or shop manager.

For the final part of the change, Rick Malloy, following the agreed plan, went down to the older section of Karlsruhe, the part that had been largely destroyed by Allied bombing during the war, to find a traveling companion. It was really too early in the day for this kind of endeavor; there would be more available women in the bars later in the day and that night, but he could not spare the time to wait. He spent a couple of hours looking in several of the bars and wursthausen before coming across a young woman who was willing to be his escort for the next day or so. She was waiting tables in a dive and Rick felt comfortable from sizing her up that she might be willing to accompany him for a fee. He had no experience in these matters, but common sense told him that if the money was right, she would be willing to assist him. In exchange for traveling with him to Berlin as his girlfriend for the trip, she would get a return ticket and $500 in German marks, a near fortune to her in these hard times. She was confused but relieved to hear that the job did not involve having sex with this man, as that was what most of her customers in the bar seemed to be interested in--only they did not have that kind of money, and she was not that kind of girl. She was just a working-class barmaid trying to survive. Rick had explained that he was searching for his father in Berlin and that he did not like traveling alone and often sought a travel companion on his trips to Berlin. He simply wanted to have someone traveling with him. He asked her to pack a small overnight bag and meet him outside the Hauptbahnhof in two hours, at 1pm in the afternoon. They would take the 1:30 p.m. Berliner Express and be in Berlin by 8:00 that evening. She could return whenever she wished.

Malloy thought the story about wanting a traveling companion was a bit lame, and he could see in the woman's face that she did not believe him for an instant. But for $500 she did not care what the story might be and did not ask too many questions about getting three months' pay for one day's work. Her name was Gerti, probably shortened from Gertrude, but she did not say. She had asked Rick's name and at first it threw him. Gaining his composure, he chose his mother's new married name Miller, and even used her husband's first name, Franz. This was not one of the identities he might need to assume once in East Germany, so it worked well. It also pointed out again to Rick how important it was be to be prepared for the unexpected. And he should have known that whomever he found to go with him would want to know his name. *Captain Smith would have been prepared*, he thought. Before leaving the woman at the bar, he reminded her that this was a private matter and she should tell no one what she was doing. She would be back by early morning, $500 richer, but she should not mention this to anyone. As Rick, aka Franz Miller, left, he gave her $50 in German marks as a good faith payment. Her eyes lit up and she gave him a quick kiss on the cheek.

Captain Smith was going to arrive in Berlin in a different manner. He was going to obtain a seat on a military convoy and enter the city as one of several hundred Allied soldiers being rotated in or out of the city. This was easy to set up, for he knew many of the right US Army people in Berlin. He had been stationed there for over a year and it had been only three months since he had been called to London by the Intelligence Services.

A couple of calls from the US army base nearby had secured him a seat on a military train that would leave Frankfurt late that evening.

All he had to do was be in the right place on time and he would be able to get on the train.

He met up with Malloy about noon back at the little café across from the train station and they exchanged stories about their mornings. Smith was impressed with Malloy's resourcefulness in obtaining a companion and teased him a bit about it. Smith had previously selected and rented an apartment in Berlin that would be the safe house in the Western sector for both himself and Rick Malloy. He had not cleared this through normal channels, and no one else had knowledge that this rented apartment existed, much less of its location. He had not wanted to use the standard safe houses, and he was now glad that he had taken the extra precaution. He gave Rick the address and they set a time when they would rendezvous there. It was near the East/West dividing line and just down the street from an intersection used for passing back and forth from East to West Berlin. The area was working class and a bit run-down, but there was always foot traffic and a casual passerby would not be noticed at all. If all went well they would meet there the following day. Malloy would most likely arrive ahead of Smith, and he would wait there. They were originally scheduled to get a briefing from London, but under the circumstances, that would have to wait until they got a better understanding of the things alluded to on the telephone with "Hank," General Grimes. Besides giving Rick the address, Captain Smith handed Rick Malloy the SIG-Sauer pistol with silencer he had been training on for the last two weeks and two clips loaded with ammunition.

"This is not likely to be required, but just in case," Smith said as he handed Rick the gun wrapped in a cloth to conceal it from any prying eyes. Rick slipped it into his inside coat pocket.

At half past noon, Malloy shook Captain Smith's hand and they parted company, each to find his way into Berlin. Smith took a train north to Frankfurt where he would meet up with men from the 104th military police unit who were being rotated into Berlin for a tour of duty on a late-night train. He arrived in Frankfurt without any problems and noticed no one paying any close attention to him at all. Still in his military uniform, he sought out the military coordinator at the station to check-in for the trip into Berlin as a Captain Ernie Sawyer, military police, his pre-agreed cover/alias. The arrangements had already been made, and he was checked in and told to go sit in the military embarkation area until advised on the time to board the train. At 8:30 p.m., about half an hour before the waiting MPs were scheduled to board, an enlisted man entered the waiting area, inquired about a Captain Sawyer, and was directed over to Smith's seat. Approaching Smith/Sawyer he introduced himself as Corporal Phil Hunter, sent with a package and sealed orders from the local Army unit stationed at Weissbaden, just outside of the city, to the east. He had been instructed to deliver it to Captain Ernie Sawyer prior to his departure. He was not privy to the contents and also had no clue who Smith/Sawyer was and did not ask. After handing the package a letter to Smith he saluted and left, having completed his delivery.

Smith first read the orders, which were sealed with tape and stamped with the official seal of US army intelligence. The orders inside read:

"Memorandum to Ernie Sawyer,
After contact earlier today I received a message from Berlin who said he was contacting me per your request. He informed me generally about your plans. Do not know all, but approve. Beware, path may be watched and you may be followed. Use the accompanying materials as you see fit. We will attempt to have a briefing package delivered to destination drop-off within two days for your use. Don't call us, we'll call you.
Regards,
"Hank"

The letter was obviously from General Grimes, who had to order the uniform and authorize his transport. There was not much to the message, except that London now knew he had new plans and seemed to approve. And that the final briefing would happen on schedule, but would not be done in person as had been originally planned. Other than that, the obvious possibility was that he might be recognized and used to get to Rick Malloy.

Smith went into the rest room, found a stall, and opened the package. Inside there was an MP armband, a white belt and brace, a matching cap, a baton or nightstick, and official military documents indicating that Captain Ernie Sawyer was indeed an MP recently attached to the 104th regiment and traveling to Berlin with this group of replacements. He would be able to blend into the group easily if needed. He hoped it would not be needed.

The train was a civilian train frequently used by the military to transport troops into and out of Berlin. It departed on time and chugged slowly east toward Berlin. It stopped frequently until it reached the East German border, and after being detained and checked out by the border guards, they continued non-stop into West Berlin. There were no surprise stops, no interruptions, and no one paid any special attention to Captain Ernie Sawyer. The train arrived late into the night, pulling in at nearly 3 a.m., and Smith did not want to risk going directly to the safe house in case he was being watched. He hitched a ride back to the barracks with some of the MP's that he had met on the train, and he sacked out on an empty bunk until morning. He had made it into Berlin easily, but in the front of his thoughts, he wondered whether Rick Malloy had made it and how the trip had gone. He had grown to like the guy. Time would tell.

Rick Malloy had left the little café ten minutes after Smith's train departed for Frankfurt. He purchased two sets of tickets on the

Berliner Express, a fast train connecting Geneva and Berlin, which passed through Karhlsruhe. He went to the bar area in the station and waited for Gerti to show up. *If she shows up*, he mused. He ordered a scotch and soda, a dreadful drink he did not like, but he remembered Captain William Smith and noted that anyone who knew Rick Malloy would also know he did not drink much, and that he truly disliked hard liquor. He was starting to get used to this spy stuff when Gerti walked up and sat down.

"Hi there, Franz," she said to Rick Malloy in a true working-class German accent. He got up, greeted her, and they sat and talked for a few minutes about the weather and her fascination with trains and travel. Gerti told him about her visits to Paris before the war and her trips into Belgium with her parents as a child. "Someday, I'd like to see London or even America," she said and Rick Malloy winced at the lie he was about to tell. He agreed that they sounded like places that would be interesting to see someday. Malloy was worried that Gerti might pry into his past, asking what he had done during the war--a question for which he had no planned or acceptable answer. But he also knew that many Germans did not wish to revisit the past. It was painful to think about their loss, and many were either ashamed of their passive participation or actually had something to hide. In any case, Rick was very relieved that Gerti did not bring that subject up. The conversation stayed quite light and superficial, much like a first date, he thought.

At the appropriate time they got up, gathered their small amount of luggage and went to the platform to board the train. This was just a whistle stop for the great train and Rick did not dare miss it. As they stood on the platform, Rick Malloy surveyed the crowd around him, carefully sizing up the other passengers and those standing nearby. *Could any of them be Russian agents?* he wondered. In fact, he saw two men standing strategically at the end of the platform holding what looked like a newspaper and occasionally looking up and surveying the crowd. *Could they be enemy agents?* he pondered? He would know soon enough if they were looking for him and if so, were they going to be fooled by his disguise and traveling companion?

The train pulled into the station on schedule and Malloy and Gerti boarded with the rest of the travelers and took their seats. The two men stayed on the platform. They did not seem to be boarding the train themselves. Rick did not care to let Gerti see that he was apprehensive about being followed, so he did not stare out the window at the men, but occasionally glanced in their direction as the train started to move. They did not get on; either they did not recognize Rick Malloy, or they were innocent bystanders. Gerti had brought a book to read and Rick Malloy was glad to see that he would not have to sit and talk to her all the way to Berlin, some eight hours hence.

The trip started out most uneventfully for Rick Malloy. The train chugged up through the Rhineland, stopping very briefly at Heidelberg, Mannheim, and Darmstadt, before a major stop in Frankfurt after nearly three hours. Rick and Gerti got off for a few minutes and stretched their legs and got a bite to eat before boarding the train again. The second-class coaches were far less comfortable than the first-class compartments, but they were much less conspicuous, and he did not want to give Gerti the wrong idea. Once out of Frankfurt the train picked up speed. They passed through smaller stations without slowing down on this inter-city train, and after another two hours had arrived in Hanover, where they made a final change onto the train that would take them east into Berlin. Less than an hour later, they reached the border crossing into East Germany at Helmstedt-Marienborn. This was the main rail route into Berlin from the west, named Checkpoint Alpha by the Western Allies.

Soviet troops stood solemn guard on their side of the crossing. The train stopped, and the porter and conductors came through the train and informed everyone that there would be no further stops until the train reached Berlin. All passengers not intending to proceed to

Berlin should exit the train now. The conductors were working their way through the second-class compartment, checking tickets and passports or government papers, when Rick spotted two more men outside the train talking, occasionally looking at a newspaper and then looking up at passersby. They were dressed much like the men back in Karlsruhe, thought Rick. They must be looking for him! They probably had a picture of him hidden in the paper that they were using to try to identify him. His mind raced and his body tensed up as he wondered if he was being overly paranoid or had really spotted his pursuers.

He sat back deep into his seat and waited for the conductors to come by. Looking at his and Gerti's tickets, then her travel papers, and finally his fake passport, the conductor only took a second before he moved on to the next row. He had to work a bit to keep Gerti from seeing the name on the passport, which was not Franz Miller. After an interminable few minutes, the train's whistle blew twice and the train began to move. The two men looked up and down the platform and then at the last instant, they jumped on the moving train. Rick Malloy's eyes widened and his heart began to pound. If they were agents, they had nearly three more hours to search for Rick Malloy on the train. Rick excused himself from Gerti for a trip to the toilet on the train and in the washroom he opened his bag and pulled out the Swiss pistol given to him by Captain Smith and loaded the clip of bullets into it. He checked the safety and then put it in his pocket. He splashed some water on his face and returned to his seat next to Gerti.

The train continued through Russian-occupied East Germany, past Madgeburg without stopping, toward Potsdam and on to Berlin. Gerti was asleep on Rick's shoulder, and he too was tired and a bit drained from the tension of this secret agent business. The two men Rick Malloy thought were agents had taken seats in another compartment several cars ahead of him, and they had appeared to not come out since they had entered. A nap was just what Rick Malloy needed. Just as Rick was beginning to think he had been a little too jumpy and his eyes were getting heavy, he saw one of the two men come through the door into his car and slowly walk down the aisle. He was definitely looking at the faces of the people as if he were searching for someone. Rick Malloy pretended to be asleep and scrunched up his face in a little contorted fashion to alter his appearance a bit more as the man approached. This man in a dark coat stopped at their seat, stared at Rick, and looked hard at Gerti. He opened his paper and looked at something inside, and slowly moved on to the next seat.

Malloy kept his composure, his eyes nearly shut, his heart racing, and he wondered whether the man had failed to recognize him—or, having found him, would wait for a better opportunity to confront him. Rick Malloy decided that he could not take the chance that he had been recognized, and he could not sit and wait to see what happened next. He had been instructed over and over back at the Mansion House: "You choose the terms of engagement, not the enemy," the French instructor had said in broken English. "If they choose, you lose," He thought about that agent who was now likely dead, killed in the car in Paris. Rick's entire body shuddered just thinking about it.

Rick waited until the man was nearly to the back of the train before he got up from his seat, leaving Gerti sleeping. He carefully followed the man in the dark leather coat into the last car and acted as if he were looking for the toilet and was a little bit drunk and woozy. As the man reached the end of the car Rick stepped up next to him as if to pass him. He pressed his pistol into the man's side and whispered into his ear with an East German accent, "Let's step outside and discuss why you were staring at my wife back there." The man was not prepared for this and started to struggle. Malloy pushed the pistol harder into the man's side and told him that unless they had a talk on the platform outside, he would shoot him dead on the spot.

The man clearly did not grasp whom he was speaking with and retorted, "I am just a rail police officer, sir. I meant no offense, and I advise you not to shoot me. I am not armed. My job is to patrol this train, looking for criminals and fugitives. I meant no harm."

Malloy pushed the man through the doorway at the end of the car, and they stood in the vestibule at the back end of the train. Still holding the gun on the man's back, Malloy shouted, "Where are your papers, show me your papers!" over the din of the train wheels going down the tracks.

"I have papers in my pocket," pleaded the man, and he started to reach for something under his jacket. But Malloy had already decided what he must do. He quickly lifted the revolver up, away from the man's back, and brought it down swiftly, butt first, on the back of the man's skull. The man stumbled and fell, knocked out cold. Rick Malloy caught him and propped him up. He searched his pockets and person and found a nightstick, handcuffs, and a set of Deutche Reichesbahn Police papers indicating that this man was indeed a West German rail policeman, probably hired by the occupying forces to patrol the train. He probably really was just looking for suspicious characters that he would report to the authorities when the train arrived in Berlin...a harmless policeman that Rick had just knocked senseless. Rick also realized that he could not now just leave the man on the train, as he would surely regain consciousness and recall Rick Malloy's face. He would have to either kill the man or throw him off the train. He was not about to kill an innocent man, so he chose throwing him off the train. He said a quick prayer that the fall would not kill the man, and pushed him off into a grassy area alongside the track.

Returning to his seat, he found Gerti still asleep. Rick wondered how long it would be before the other man, also probably a policeman, would come looking for his compatriot. Sure enough, half an hour later, after the train had passed through Potsdam and was starting to enter the Berlin city area, the second man came down through the car obviously searching for his fellow officer. Again, Rick pretended to be asleep, and this man paid little attention to the couple, instead looking intently for his friend. He did not find him and returned to the front of the train, no doubt thinking that he must have overlooked a car or something.

The train pulled into the Berlin Zoo Rail Station right on schedule. Because the East Germans controlled the railroads and many of the rail stations were either destroyed or now in East Berlin, this rail station was now the main station in post-war West Berlin, and where incoming passengers from the West would get off. The train whistled its stop and passengers began filing for the doors at each end of the car. Rick and Gerti were also standing, looking for the door, when Rick saw the second policeman race past the car blowing his whistle, looking for help from the military police in the station, no doubt for his lost friend. By the time a group of officials had been gathered, most of the passengers had departed the train and exited the platform, including Rick and his traveling companion, Gerti. They would find no clues as to the other policeman's disappearance, and it would be several hours before he would be discovered down an embankment near the tracks, having broken his leg and hit his shoulder hard when he landed after being pushed off the train. Although it was not exactly what he had prayed for, Rick Malloy's prayers had been answered--he was in Berlin without being detected, and he had not had to kill anyone to do it.

CHAPTER TEN

AUGUST, 1946

Rick was trying to be careful, and so he took nearly an hour to reach the apartment. Along the way he continued to ask himself, "What would Captain Smith do?" and then add a new wrinkle to the serpentine route he took. He had thanked Gerti for her company on the trip and had given her the remaining German marks. She hugged him, gave him a big kiss on the cheek, and he left her at the platform with a return ticket. He could tell from her eyes that she would like to go with him. Her life was an empty one, and her future was uncertain. She had no place she needed to be, and this sudden interruption was an exciting break in her routine. It was a hard life for a young woman in post-war Germany, and the allure of a handsome man with seemingly unlimited money who was not interested in abusing her was enormous. Malloy looked back at her as he exited the train station, and she was also looking at him. They smiled and she waved as he rounded the corner out of sight.

Rick was very conscious of the fact that someone, maybe even Gerti, might try to follow him. He had moved across the street from the train station, stood in the shadows, and watched for anything suspicious. He saw nothing. A part of him said: "This is foolish, get in a taxi and go to the apartment." But he also knew that Captain Smith would not be so cavalier and that he was probably still alive because of this care. So Malloy thought of an easy trap to see if he had any followers; he walked down the main strasse in front of the station and abruptly crossed the street and went back into the station through the western entryway. He made his way back through the front section of the station, making sure he stayed away from Gerti but also staying inside the main station area. He walked past the north portal exit and then turned back and quickly went out and hailed a taxi. He asked to be taken to the Brandenburg Gate area and looked back to see if any people ran out of the station to jump in a taxi or if a car pulled out after him. Neither seemed to happen.

When Malloy exited the taxi a few blocks from the demarcation line between east and west in Berlin, it was nearly midnight. He was also nearly a half-mile walk from the safe house apartment. He was beginning to remember Berlin a little bit from his youth, but the combination of being so young back then and the current state of destruction in the city caused him to study things intently in order to orient himself. Knowing he wanted to go north to get to the apartment, he headed west, then north, then east, then north again, in a zigzag pattern. Anyone following him would be easy to spot, and unless they knew where he was going, they could not anticipate or get ahead of him. Any casual observer would assume that he was a lost soul trying to find his way home.

He arrived at his destination--a run-down apartment building on a block that had not been destroyed by the bombings, and based on its appearance, would normally not be a candidate for an American staying in Berlin. It was an excellent choice as a safe house. Rick entered the building carefully and went up to the third floor to the room whose number matched the key he had been given. He looked at the lock and doorjamb to make sure no one had forcefully entered the apartment, then he put the key in the lock, turned it, and opened the door. He wondered what would be waiting for him on the other side. Inside it was dark, but the shadows cast by street lighting let him know this was an average meager one-bedroom that a factory worker might have. Rather than turn on the lights and let anyone who might have followed him to the building know which room he was in, he let his eyes adjust to the darkness and shadows. He found a small kitchen area, the sitting area, and a small bedroom with one single bed in it. He returned and locked the door shut, set his bag down, and got undressed. For the next few hours he could relax and get some sleep.

At seven in the morning, Rick was startled by the faint sound of the door lock being turned, followed by the door slowly opening. He quickly got out of bed and stood behind the bedroom door so as not to be seen from a distance. He stood in his underwear, barefoot, and as his eyes started to adjust and focus, he realized that his SIG-Sauer was out on the table, in clear sight and not in a place he could easily access unnoticed. *Damn*, he thought. His heart was pounding and his adrenalin was going when he heard: "Hey Malloy, are you hiding behind the door?"

It was Captain Smith, who had arrived the prior night and spent the night at a barracks. He was dressed as a civilian--a German-looking civilian, at that. After a brief greeting, Rick asked Captain Smith how he knew he was in the room. Smith showed him that he had placed a small piece of a matchbook cover in the doorjamb when he had left the room over a month ago. If anyone had opened the door--and only he and Malloy had a key--then the piece of cardboard would be displaced. There it was on the floor outside the door when he arrived at the apartment. Malloy was impressed by the simple trick.

Smith had brought some pastries and milk for Malloy. Juice or meat was hard to come by in Berlin after the war, and buying it while dressed as a German worker might attract attention. They sat at a small table in the kitchen area and talked about each of their trips into Berlin. Captain Smith was amazed to hear that Rick Malloy had actually thrown a policeman off the train, and he was relieved that it appeared that they had not been noticed entering the city. Malloy was impressed that he had been able to take command of the situation as well. He would need that kind of confidence and capability if he was to succeed.

Captain William Smith had been briefed at the US army base, earlier in the morning, on a secure line to London, and had learned that the East Germans now knew that Rick Malloy was still alive. This surely meant that the search was back on. As a precaution, Smith had drawn up new plans and integrated the existing intelligence and various bits of information the western Allies had about the possible secret bomb laboratory in Faschgarten and the two Hungarian scientists who seemed to have been working on a "heavy water" device, or atomic bomb. Over the past several months army intelligence and MI-6 had pieced together the special teams, organizations, and responsibilities of the Luftwaffe and Wehrmacht relative to the V2 rockets and secret munitions programs and had found that one SS colonel's name, Rudolph Werner, came up repeatedly in questioning of surviving soldiers. He was presumed dead, but he had lived in Berlin and had evidently been one of Himmler's close and trusted associates and an emissary in matters related to the secret weapons of this sort. He was not a scientist, but was reported to have been a stonemason before joining the Nazi party in the 1930s. With no skills other than his passion for the Führer and a strong will to further the Nazi cause, he had risen through the ranks to colonel in the SS by carrying out orders, no matter what they were. According to several sources, he had promised Himmler that his teams would develop weapons that would win the war on several occasions. As the Allies pushed toward Berlin and his credibility was further diminished, he was reported to have met with Reichsmarshall Himmler and received specific instructions related to these war secrets. According to family members interviewed by the Russians at the end of the war, several days after meeting with his leader, just weeks before the city of Berlin fell into Russian hands, he disappeared. Beyond this anecdotal information, there was the town of Faschgarten and relatives of the men who had worked there.

Interestingly, having a close relative who might have worked in a secret munitions lab near Faschgarten was so dangerous that those still alive had changed their names and moved, likely to avoid being associated with anything of the sort. This was easy to understand when the statistics of apparent suicides and heart attacks and fatal accidents of these relatives was reviewed. Nearly all of the close relatives had died during or since the end of the war, often under suspicious circumstances. The local police were not interested, or had been directed to not get involved. The Allied occupation forces had better things to worry about as well. As a result, almost anyone who could shed any light on what was going on at one of these secret munitions labs had been silenced permanently, or scared out of their homes and sent running for their lives. Whether it was Russians or ex-Nazis was not clear and really did not matter.

Bits of information that brought credibility to this story and sealed the desire in the Allied intelligence community to move forward with the mission that included Rick Malloy, came from the weapons manufacturers themselves. Records and materials seized at the Koenig Metal Works indicated that specialty metals, including titanium and platinum and various stainless steels vessels, were shipped to a small factory in the vicinity of the town of Faschgarten, presumably for bomb research, including development of bomb casings and internal detonation mechanisms. Orders for other exotic metal parts for devices that looked a lot like particle accelerators were found at another major equipment and materials supplier. These invoices matched up with those found in the only known Nazi atomic development lab, discovered by the Americans in Haigerloch, in the Black Forest. When that lab was overrun by American GI's, they found parts for a reactor, and atomic material, but the heavy water, the deuterium oxide, was long gone. This small lab held more than enough evidence to scare Allied intelligence, but no proof of any completed weapons and no documentation was found. It looked like these had been removed months prior to the end of the war. No one knew where they had been taken. Although the Nazis had been very thorough in trying to hide every shred of evidence, little pieces had surfaced, which led to the conclusion that there was potential for a larger-scale effort to design and build atomic weapons when the Third Reich collapsed. A final puzzle piece that the Allies knew little about was the Nazi development site at Peenemunde, a small town up on the North Sea, where the V-2 rockets had been developed. Unfortunately, the Russians overran this area and had not been willing to share any information on what was found there.

The hypothesis developed by combined Allied intelligence was that when the Nazis saw the end coming, they decided to hide this research for use at another time — whenever that might be. The information was not destroyed, but carefully put away for future use. Therefore, somewhere, most likely in the Berlin area, and certainly in a secure place, there was documentary evidence that could assist a group of competent scientists in developing a functional atomic bomb. Coming to this conclusion made finding these documents ahead of the Russians a US national security priority.

Malloy and Smith discussed the plan and their tactics, and they agreed to stay with most of the original plan that had Malloy going into East Berlin alone. Smith may have been able to provide some protection, but his lack of German language fluency and his American mannerisms would be a far greater liability. He would wait in West Berlin and be ready to assist from there. Malloy was given two reliable contacts in East Berlin who could get information out to the West easily. He memorized these and prepared for the upcoming job.

It was understood that the papers Malloy had would get him into the East, but if the Russians were seriously looking for him, those papers would likely not get him back out. Those types of papers would have to be obtained once inside, or another way out would need to be devised. This was especially true once it was known that Rick Malloy was in East Berlin.

At 5 p.m., after final preparations and a "good luck" handshake from Smith, Rick Malloy set out on his mission. While other workers were also returning to the East to their families, Rick Malloy passed through Checkpoint Charlie and entered East Germany, alone. His instructions were simple: Follow the lead(s) until you reach a dead end or find the information. The primary lead was provided by the Russians, and overheard by London. It confirmed that the East Germans and Russians were searching for, and may have come close to finding Nazi atomic secrets. Hopefully it would lead to more information, if not to the actual plans. Beyond this, he was to check in every few days, but not take unnecessary risks to do so. Although the border between the East and West had become harder to cross in recent months, passing through this checkpoint heading into East Berlin was relatively simple. No one was trying to break into East Germany, although many were trying to get out--and measures taken by the East Germans made escape harder and more dangerous every day. A single person with no belongings could pass in and out daily, but a family, or those with their life's belongings, were not going to easily move to the West. By now, most of those who could get out had gone. Rick entered the checkpoint and after presenting his papers, the guard asked Rick where he was coming from and where he was going, and upon getting an acceptable answer and having a line of others waiting to get through, Rick was waved through and into the East.

His first job was to find a place to stay. He knew this part of Berlin fairly well from his youth, but so much had changed and had been destroyed. He had been given a name of a small Gasthaus several miles away, convenient because this was headed in the right direction for his first destination. Rick walked at a brisk pace, but was careful not to look so athletic or healthy as to attract undue attention. He arrived just before dark and went in to find a room. The night clerk was just coming on duty and was surprised to see a new face looking for a room. Rick explained his travels in search of this father and with an understanding nod that was more of a "yeah, we all have problems, mister" acknowledgment, the night clerk pulled a key off of the pegs on the wall and gave it to Rick Malloy.

At secret police headquarters in Eastern Germany, the search for the missing two Americans had escalated into a full-scale manhunt. The fact that the Americans had been able to evade capture on several occasions led subordinates to exaggerate the capabilities of these two spies. They were reported to be highly trained in espionage, the most experienced senior operatives in the United States Intelligence Corps, masters of disguise who spoke several languages fluently and could disappear into thin air at a moment's notice. With every bungled attempt to apprehend them, the excuses, the myths, and the stories had grown.

In fact, the secret police senior officers were not at all sure what they were dealing with or where to look next. They did not know if the two Americans were even in East Germany yet, but they assumed the worst. What they did know was that if the Allies' mission was to find information about the atom bomb, sooner or later the Americans would show up in Faschgarten and in East Berlin. They would not be able to stay away, and the questions they would have to ask would give them away, no matter how they disguised themselves.

So a trap would be set that could not be anticipated, and from which the Americans would not be so lucky as to escape. In the town of Faschgarten itself, the secret police would place their own people and they would pay others to report any suspicious behavior. They would identify the person asking questions and follow them unseen, through a series of handoffs. They were not hoping to merely catch an American spy. That was necessary, but once eliminated, another would merely replace him. Their objective was to follow and engage the Americans. They wanted to learn what the Allies knew, to build on their information. At the right time, they would deal with Rick Malloy.

To accomplish this assignment, the secret police undertook a number of measures. In addition to the trap in the town of Faschgarten, they placed spotters along the roads leading north out of Berlin and towns surrounding Faschgarten. A picture of Malloy, taken back in Cambridge, Massachusetts, was circulated to operatives and police, to make sure that the American was identified. They then recalled one of their own top spies from foreign duty to help lead the investigation and make contact with Rick Malloy once he had been identified. As a matter of national security and national pride, they must not fail when the American arrived in East Berlin. The plans were completed and the trap was set. All the East Germans and Russians could do was wait until a report of a sighting of Rick Malloy came in.

In the early morning of August 8th, 1946, Rick Malloy woke up in a small Gasthaus on the outskirts of East Berlin. He and Captain Smith had planned his first couple of days, and he knew what he had to accomplish each day in chasing down clues. Today, he would visit the relatives of the Nazi colonel who had died late in the war under mysterious circumstances. It was not clear why the Russians had sought to find this man's family, and maybe they knew nothing, but then maybe they knew more than they themselves realized. Malloy, keeping his disguise intact, combed his hair back and left his beard a bit shabby to look like a tired worker. He left the Gasthaus and walked the three miles to the row house on #4 Gartnerstrasse and knocked on the door.

No one answered, and it looked as if no one was home, so Rick walked back up the street to an open area which had a couple of benches and sat and watched and waited. There was not too much traffic in this residential suburb of East Berlin and Malloy looked like a local sitting reading the newspaper. He sat for nearly three hours in that small park area until he noticed an older woman carrying groceries and holding the hand of a young boy go down the street and enter the row house at #4 Gartnerstrasse. Malloy approached cautiously and knocked on the door.

Rick was greeted by the young boy and then the older woman came to the door. Rick began to tell the story that he and Captain Smith had created for the occasion. He explained that his father had been in the army during the war and had disappeared. He had mentioned this address in a letter as one he had visited and Rick was desperately trying to find his dad, even to find out if he was still alive. It was a story Rick Malloy could deliver in convincing fashion for in fact his father had disappeared and he was interested to find out any information about what happened.

The older woman was very leery of Rick. She was not interested in recounting the death of her husband to a stranger--a person who may not be who he said he was. She asked Rick to step inside the house, but did not offer him a seat or any refreshment. She politely told him that her husband had been killed during the last days of the war and she did not think she could be of much help. The young boy, standing at her side, blurted out, "My father was a great colonel in the SS and he knew the ReichFührer personally." The older woman turned and slapped the boy hard on the cheek and told him to go into his room and shut his door. He began crying and ran off to the back portion of the house.

"He has a vivid imagination, as you can see," she said. "My husband was an average soldier, killed doing his job for the Fatherland. As I told the Police several weeks ago, he had no significant role in the war effort, and the only thing he left us was a few meager Reichsmarks in a bank safe-deposit box, nothing more."

Rick thought fast and created a look of concern and fear on his own face. "The Gestapo came here last month to question you?" he asked, now looking a bit more like a scared young man who had been beaten by the Nazis for being weak. "They came here?" he repeated.

The elderly woman, thinking she had terrorized the young man, pulled him inside and shut the door. "No, no," she said. "Not the Gestapo--the East German police came here. What is the matter with you? Sit down."

She took Rick by the arm and led him to a soft chair and sat him down. Rick's ploy had worked, and he had gained her sympathy and maybe some measure of trust at the same time. "What did the police want to know about your husband?" he asked innocently.

"They wanted to know about the safe-deposit box," she replied. "I gave them the numbers to open it, and they searched the house and then they left without a word. They were much like the Gestapo, now that you mention it."

"If the box was full of personal belongings, a little money and no important papers, why would they want to look into it?" Rick wondered aloud, as much thinking it to himself as really asking the old woman.

"I do not know, but they were very interested. That is all I can tell you. You must leave now, or I will call the police." She motioned for Rick to move to the door, as her discomfort with the conversation had reached too high a level.

Rick, recognizing that he had lost her, pulled out two one hundred East German marks out of his pocket and gave them to the woman. "You have been most kind to speak with me. Here, take this. I know you can use it for your son," he said as he handed the woman the money and stepped toward the door. The older woman looked stunned, and her gaze went from being offended by the offer to reaching out and accepting the money suspiciously, to being somewhat grateful, all in a few seconds.

"I am sorry to be so rude," she said, "but I am afraid for my son, and nothing good can come out of my talking to you. I hope you understand." With that exchange, Rick moved to the door and the woman shut it behind him.

As he walked away from the house, back up to the square where he had sat that morning, he thought about what he should do. Rick Malloy had a problem. He needed to see the contents of the safe-deposit box, but the woman was not going to tell him any more about it. "Nor should she," he said to himself. The box was the only clue he had, and though he was sure that the East Germans had gone through it, he must have a look as well. The realization sunk in that he was going to have to break into the house and find the information, assuming it was even still in the house. And as he thought about how he would undertake this task, he realized that unless he gave the woman and her son an excuse for helping him, they were in serious danger from the Russians. He also knew that he needed to leave enough time so that he could get to the box before the East German secret police figured out what he was doing. If they knew he was looking for the box, he would be easy to trap and catch. He returned to his Gasthaus to make plans for a burglary, and maybe a kidnapping as well.

Over a meager dinner of bread and cheese eaten in his room, Rick thought out what he would do. The next morning, early, he would return to the neighborhood and watch the woman and boy leave. He would then break in through a window and search the house while he waited for their return. To protect them from being accused of being accomplices, he would have to wait for them and tie them up and make a bit of a mess of the house. If he could not find the information himself, he would have to convince the woman to tell where to look by threatening the boy. Ugly, but it was likely to work. Then he would leave her more money to compensate for his behavior.

At 7 a.m., Rick Malloy was stationed behind a wall, in a spot where he was largely hidden from view himself, but where he could observe anyone coming or going from the house of the woman and boy on Gartnerstrasse. At 8:15 the woman and boy left the house and walked off past the square in the direction Malloy had seen them return from the prior day. He estimated that he had about 2 and a half hours before they would return.

The breaking and entering went like clockwork, with a ground-floor rear window easily opened by removing the caulk around the glass, removing the pane of glass, and reaching in and unlocking the window. He did not want to hurt the woman's house--and he was a scientist, not a burglar, after all. He climbed in and set to work methodically. Using what he thought was common sense, he assumed that the information was written on a sheet of paper and put in a safe place. Not the bathroom or living room or kitchen, but a bedroom or closet. He started with the main bedroom area and after fifteen minutes was satisfied that it was not there. He checked the closet--and likewise, no luck. After nearly two hours, he had searched all of the likely places and found nothing. He stood in the living room thinking about places he might continue to look, when he heard voices outside. It was the woman and boy returning early.

Rick pulled out his pistol and quickly positioned himself behind the door. The door opened and the pair walked in and gasp at the sight of the mess of their house. Rick quickly stepped behind them, shut the door, and raised his pistol. "Please do not make me shoot you," he said carefully. "I do not intend to harm you, but I will if I must. Please sit down over there." He motioned toward the couch. "Do not speak out unless I ask you to," he said matter-of-factly. When he had bound and gagged both the woman and the boy, he turned to the woman and said, "Tell me where the information about the safe-deposit box is, and you and the boy will not get hurt. Nod if you understand." The older woman nodded that she understood and started crying.

"Please stop that," said Malloy. "You are in no danger, and in fact I have tied you up for your own benefit." The woman looked at him as if she did not understand. "I need to see the contents of the safe-deposit box you mentioned yesterday, and if you point me in the right direction, I will leave you alone and the police will see that you did not help me. Is that understood?" Rick asked. The woman clearly was confused, but she nodded agreement. "So, show me where to look by staring at the place I should go." The woman looked down at the floor and avoided Rick's stare, but the boy looked up toward the fireplace mantel briefly, as if to see if something was still in its place. Rick Malloy noticed his glance and went to the mantel and took the items off the mantel one by one to inspect them.

He looked carefully at a watch, then a brass candlestick, and a photograph. The fourth item was a Bible. It was not a large or expensive Bible, but was a smaller home version and appeared to have been put to use a lot, at least judging by its condition. *Interesting for someone who was married to a Nazi*, he thought. Rick shook the book to see if any papers dropped out, but there were none. He sat down on the arm of the sofa when he noticed that the woman was staring intently at him, and he began to page through the entire book. In five minutes he had almost finished paging through the Old Testament and as he paged through the Psalms he noticed written in ink at the top of the page, above the 100th Psalm:

Kaiser Volksbank. #408-265-311.

CHAPTER ELEVEN

AUGUST, 1946

The Kaiser Volksbank was a smaller private bank that catered to the small group of wealthy clientele in Germany prior to the war. Founded in the 1870s after ther creation of Germany as a bank for the wealthy, it fell on hard times after the kaiser's abdication in 1918. The bank never recovered and was not in favor with the Nazis due to its old associations with the emperor. However, as it had neither Jewish owners nor significant clients, it had been left alone to survive the Third Reich. The building was an ornate, comfortable, and quiet establishment in an old-world kind of way. It had been a beautiful building prior to the war, signaling the status of the institution and its clientele. Today, while it was still impressive based on its size and location in the financial district of old Berlin, it was run down and slightly dilapidated. It had not received any direct hits from bombing during the war, but nearby bomb blasts had shattered beautiful windows, which had been replaced by ordinary plain glass, and the ornate stone carving on the front of the building was pock-marked and chipped from nearby explosions and gunfire. The new management obviously was not interested in spending monies on refurbishing the looks of a once-powerful private institution that surely would be handed over to the East German government. In all, as he looked at the building, Rick thought that this was an unlikely place for a mid-level Nazi SS officer to have an account.

Rick Malloy arrived on foot at the bank at 2:15 p.m. from his earlier break-in on Gartnerstrasse, forty-five minutes before closing for the day. He entered through the massive doors of the building and approached the main desk, where a small man with thick glasses sat waiting for customers to direct. Rick approached and asked whom he must see to gain access to a safe-deposit box. He was directed to a set of stairs that led to the basement vault area. He saw a sign with an arrow that further directed him down a hall to the entrance to the vault area. There was an older woman sitting behind a small but ornate wooden desk, who greeted him and asked what it was that he needed.

Rick had decided on the way to the bank that his story would be a close variation on the one used back at the widow's house. He was looking for his father, and a close friend (the woman he had just robbed) had volunteered that he was welcome to look in the box if he thought it would be helpful. She had provided the needed information to access the box. It seemed innocent enough to work. He carefully explained this to the woman and awaited her response. She looked through her paperwork to verify that the box was indeed registered to the people mentioned, reviewed the notes next to the data, and looked up at Rick Malloy.

"I am sorry, sir, but the box's contents have been emptied and there is nothing in the box at all. You are too late. The box has been empty for several weeks now," she said, without emotion of any kind. Rick wondered if she was telling the truth. "I have come so far--I would like to assure myself that this is another dead end," Malloy said.

"I assure you that I am correct, sir," the attendant replied, becoming a little testy. "However, the box has not been rented by anyone else; it is close to closing time, and as I am not likely to get any further visitors today, I will let you see for yourself. But it is a waste of your time and more importantly, of mine."

Her sarcasm was not wasted on Rick. He could not push this woman much more, so he thanked her for her helpfulness.

Rick had provided her with the appropriate account name and the numeric access code, but he did not tell her anything about the contact being an ex-SS officer. He was pretty sure that this would not be helpful and might cause her to get others involved. The attendant asked Rick for identification and he produced his fake East German passport. She recorded the name and numbers dutifully in her register. Then she took out her keys and opened the polished stainless steel vault access door that led into the main vault area. To the right were the cash, coin, and bullion vaults, guarded by two armed guards. To the left was another heavy door, which was open during business hours and allowed access into the safe-deposit box area. Rick was even more sure that a minor officer in the SS would not keep a box in this type of bank for himself.

Malloy was directed to the box and the process of opening the box began. First the bank's key, corresponding to the first three digits of the access code he had given, was inserted and turned clockwise one-half turn and removed, then, also based on the pass code provided by Rick, a second key corresponding to that code was placed in the door to the box and turned counterclockwise one-half turn and removed. The box's door was opened, and the attendant carefully removed the box and set it on a nearby table. The box was an oversized safe-deposit box, capable of holding large bundles of papers, or a fur coat, or several smaller boxes of materials. The attending woman opened the lid to the box and motioned to Malloy to look inside.

Sure enough, there was nothing in the box at all. It had been not only emptied, but cleaned out and even dusted such that there was nothing at all to see. The walls and bottom of the box shimmered, and in the bottom corner the only marks at all were those of the manufacturer, engraved into the metal of the box. As if to rub it in that she had been correct, the attendant tilted the box toward Rick and said, "You see, I told you that this box has been emptied, and here you see that it is so."

She started to shut the lid and Rick stopped her briefly, saying, "You are correct, and I apologize for not wanting to believe you, but seeing this confirms that this part of my search for my father is finished. I thank you."

As if to be simple-minded about it, Rick stuck his head down over the open box and looked closely at the walls and the manufacturer's mark in the corner. He quickly noted the name and address of the manufacturer, the box location in the vault, its size, and anything else he could imagine might be a clue, although he had no idea why he did so. It was about all he could think to do, for there was nothing else there to see, and he had no other clues to follow.

He thanked the attendant and apologized again, and after waiting for the box to be replaced and the attendant to close up the area and return to her station outside of the vault area, Rick Malloy went back down the hall up the stairs and out of the bank. It seemed to have been a wasted day, and his first and best lead was a dead end.

The call came in to the East Berlin secret police bureau about 3:15 p.m., and the alarm and confusion caused by that call might have made someone think an international incident had occurred. And maybe it had. The call, from a senior director at the Kaiser Volksbank, Herr Rolf Schwimmer, confirmed that a man vaguely matching the description of the American named Malloy, had come into the bank and asked about and been shown the empty safe-deposit box which had been emptied by the secret police only three weeks earlier.

Herr Schwimmer, as a part of his duties as the bank's managing director, was making his routine final pass through the various departments prior to the 3 p.m. closing of the bank for the day and had gone down to the vault area and asked the attendant, Jeanne, about her day. It had been a quiet and boring day except for this last customer who insisted on seeing a box she knew was empty. He had insisted, and since he had the required access codes and seemed legitimate, she showed him the box. She reminded her boss that this was the same box that the police had emptied a while back. Herr Schwimmer's surprise, when he had confirmed that it was indeed the box that had had its contents removed by the secret police, was such that he rushed to the telephone and called the police to notify them of what had occurred.

The police had arrived at the bank within minutes after the call and taken copious notes about the look and dress and demeanor of the man who had visited the safe-deposit box earlier in the afternoon. The chief field agent assigned specifically to this case arrived an hour later and she reviewed the notes, spoke with Herr Schwimmer and the attendant and the doorman. Based on what was observed, it was absolutely conclusive that the American, Rick Malloy, was in East Berlin and had been at the Kaiser Volksbank that afternoon. Based on the bank staff's description, the senior agent confirmed that it was him. A different haircut, different facial hair and clothes, but all the mannerisms and the specific characteristics indicated that it was Malloy. And, even more perplexing, the fact that Malloy was interested in that safe-deposit box.

"But why?" Herr Schwimmer asked. "It was empty, and it had nothing significant in it when you searched it the first time. Correct? How did he know about it, how could he know the access numbers, and in knowing about it, why is an empty box of interest?"

These were the questions the secret police could not answer, and it troubled them as well. Yet there were many more. How did Malloy get into East Germany completely unnoticed, and how could he hide out in East Berlin without a trace? His legend was growing by the minute as an experienced über-agent.

The secret police were both in panic and slightly in awe. Maybe it was to cover their failure to catch him, but they began to consider that this secret agent, Rick Malloy, the elusive American, might be a very talented spy. After all, he had now reached his destination, in spite of numerous serious attempts to stop him. His disguise had altered his appearance, and it was now known that he could speak German like a native, in a local and convincing fashion. He seemed to move freely with no visible trail and he surely must be well funded by the Western Allies. He was undoubtedly a small firearms expert, an excellent shot and trained killer in hand-to-hand combat. And finally, he showed up in the Kaiser Volksbank with information he should not have, and asking about a safe-deposit box he should not have known about. It terrified the mid-level agents. Even the more senior female field agent who was able to positively identify that it had been Malloy seemed surprised at his abilities and his actions. Were the other two American agents who had not reached Berlin merely a diversion for this master operative? It was to be the beginning of several very long nights at the East German secret police headquarters.

After leaving the bank, Rick Malloy had walked over to a small café diagonally across the street and sat down outside to have a cup of coffee. He had learned very little today, he thought. The day was a waste of several miles of walking, and the risk that he might randomly be stopped and in the process be exposed was weighing on him. He sat and thought about the safe-deposit box and he wrote down all that he could remember about the location, construction, materials, account codes, and the manufacturer whose name and address were engraved on the inside of the box. This last detail had been so small a thing he nearly put it out of his mind, but because the box was completely empty, it was also all that he had. So he wrote it down on the slip of paper:

Kellerproduktionsgesellshaft

143 Grunestrasse

Weissensee-Berlin

He remembered that there was a postal code below the address, but he could not remember it. Besides, he thought, he was not likely to send them a letter.

As he thought about the address, he began to remember his father and the many times he would accompany his father on local business trips to visit customers. It was good business to be a family man; customers liked the fact that Eric von Malloy loved to go along with his father when he was allowed. Rick thought about the vast empire of iron, steel, and glass manufacturing and assembly plants that his father had built by hard work and honest dealings. And he thought about the safe-deposit box he had just seen. It was stainless steel, and it was of a very high quality. Not very many fabricators could have made a product of that quality, and the raw material would have had to have been bought from a company like his father's. Even if it had been manufactured before the turn of the century, Rick was surprised that he did not recognize the name of the producer, who would have had to be a customer of his father's company or one of his competitors. The name meant little, as Keller was likely the name of the company or the family name of the business and produktionsgeschellschaft merely meant manufacturing company in German. It was not much of a clue. But, Rick also realized that Weissensee was on the northeast side of Berlin proper, and that it was a suburban area with little or no manufacturing or heavy industry. It did not make a lot of sense. To produce the quality and number of safe-deposit boxes he saw in the bank would require a large, well-equipped manufacturing facility.

Just as he was sipping his coffee and pondering this inconsistency, the sirens of police cars in the distance caught his attention. They grew louder and louder as they approached. He paid for his coffee and moved down the street to watch from a bit more distance as the three cars came to a stop in front of the Kaiser Volksbank and plainclothes policemen rushed inside. He wasn't sure how they knew or how they got there so fast, but he was positive that he was who they were looking for and that staying in the area was a big mistake. He walked briskly away from the bank, turned the corner, and ran down the street.

After several blocks, he turned in a different direction and went several more. After fifteen to twenty minutes he stopped, evaluated where he was, and took stock. He realized that somehow he had been recognized at the bank and that soon half of East Berlin would know what he looked like and be on the lookout for him. His small Gasthaus would not be safe for long, so he must clear out and seek a different place to sleep. He made his way back across the city carefully to the Gasthaus, and gathered his belongings. He did not check out of his prepaid room, and he left a few non-essential items behind to make it look like he would return. Checking out would raise too many questions--and besides, if they thought he would return, they might waste time waiting around for him there. He was thinking like Captain Smith, he mused. He thought for a minute longer and went back into the Gasthaus and asked the front desk clerk for directions to Treptow, a suburb Southeast of Berlin, the opposite direction from where he would be heading. Now, he thought, now he was acting like Captain Smith.

Malloy left the Gasthaus and walked down the street to an inter-section where he could get on a trolley car. He took the trolley across the city to the north. He would find another small inn where he could spend a few days and plan what his next moves would be. At least he was headed in the direction of Weissensee.

In West Berlin and in London that evening, US army intelligence and MI-6 were also on high alert. They had been monitoring all reports coming out of the east to get any information on Malloy's second day. Although they really did not expect to hear from him for a day or two more, the news they were getting made not hearing from him unbearable. In the past hour, US intelligence headquarters had gotten several reports that the secret police had conducted a raid in the center of East Berlin in the early afternoon. One report indicated that in this raid they had captured an American agent and taken him away. Other reports were vague and inconclusive. And a last report indicated that it was nothing at all. It was impossible to know what had actually happened, but all concerned feared the worst--Rick Malloy had been found and captured, possibly killed.

Chapter Twelve

Rick Malloy got off the aboveground trolley at the last stop on the northeastern side of Berlin in the Prenzlauer Berg district of the city. It was an area of row houses and small businesses that had been ransacked and pillaged by the Russians as they entered the city from the north and east. On the nearly hour-long ride, he had realized that his description would be out everywhere, and soon it would not be safe to be out in the open. He needed to change his appearance. Malloy walked about the shopping district in this section north of central Berlin until he found a Weinstube that had some traffic, as this was several hours before the prime time for this type of business. He wanted a bit of a crowd so that a new face would not draw a lot of attention. But he also wanted to be sure that inside the wine bar was not so crowded that he could not slip into the bathroom and lock himself in for a few minutes without causing a scene.

After surveying several alternatives, he chose a larger wine bar and went in. Once he had secured himself in the small restroom facility, which had only a sink and stand- over toilet, he got to work. Pulling out the small toiletry kit given him by Captain Smith, he opened it and got out scissors and a straight-edge razor and hair color of various shades. He had been combing his dirty-blond dyed hair over to one side, wearing it a bit long, as he had back in Cambridge. He quickly cut it shorter, and mixing the dye in the sink, proceeded to change his hair to dark brown. He trimmed his sideburns shorter as well, and now combed his hair straight back over his head, with a part down the middle. Also, with the razor he altered his hairline, slightly changing his look and making his face look much wider than before. The combined set of changes would not fool his mother, but to a casual observer, this would not look at all like the man described by the bank vault manager and sought by the secret police. He also took the first of four false sets of papers provided to him by Captain Smith, the ones used at the Gasthaus and the bank he had just left, and tore them up and flushed them down the toilet. Then he went out into the wine bar and had a glass of wine. He mingled and tried to relax a bit, soaking up the scene around him, the mannerisms of the people, the dress, their posture and expressions. To hide in broad daylight, he would need to seem just like these people.

He left the wine bar and continued walking around for a half hour, looking for a cheap hotel that would be a good place to make his base for the next few days. The Zum Holdstrum fit the need well enough. It was a small inn that was neither very cheap nor very clean, but it was on a main street with several entry and exit points, in case a quick departure was needed. After explaining that he had just gotten into the city from the northeast and was planning on surprising some friends but knew that they did not have enough space for him to stay with them, he was checked in to a room for a few days. Oh, and he paid in advance, which always seemed to buy a favor or two from the innkeeper. He took a room on the second floor and made sure that he could get out through the back stairway if a hasty exit was required. He would lay low for a while and plan his next move. He was very tired and went to sleep.

Back in East German secret police headquarters, there was excitement. Word spread that the American had made a mistake and would soon be apprehended. After twenty hours of showing a sketch of Malloy to hotel clerks and innkeepers, the search had finally paid off. They had been notified by the innkeeper of a small Gasthaus only a mile or so inside the Brandenburg Gate that a man matching Malloy's description had checked in a few days earlier, and he had not checked out. His clothes appeared to still be in his room. A search of the room confirmed that it was indeed the American Malloy who was staying there. The secret police put agents on round-the-clock watch for his return. When he showed up next, they would have him. At about the same time, the mystery about how he had known about the safe-deposit box had also been solved when a report came in detailing how a woman and her son had been tied up in their house. They said that they had been robbed at gunpoint and the man had forced them to give up information about the bank and the box. A neighbor had found them after several hours of being tied up. The robber perfectly matched the description given by the bank safe-deposit box manager. It must have also been Rick Malloy.

The stakeout in Fachgarten was virtually abandoned, except for one agent left there just in case. The plan to follow Malloy was now deemed too dangerous and was abandoned as well. He would be apprehended and they would use drugs to get information from him, and then he would be secretly tried, convicted, and sentenced for being a spy. There would be no press coverage or announcement that might require explaining what this mission was all about. This was East Berlin, in the Russian sector. People disappeared all the time and legal rights just did not exist, especially not for an American spy caught red-handed.

For those who had built up the American as being so competent, it was an embarrassing letdown. A professional would not have made such a foolish and amateurish mistake. Renewed confidence was back with the senior East Germans and Russian NKVD seeking the information about the German atomic bomb program. Their frantic efforts to obtain related information before the Americans could beat them to it took on a more normal pace, as they were more confident that the most recent American attempt would soon be stopped cold. The senior East German field agent informed her superiors that, based on this recent information, the American would probably be apprehended in a matter of hours, a day or two at most. And she was confident that she was correct. She had the hotel staked out and was relieved that her assessment of Malloy as being far from a trained and experienced agent had not been wrong. He would walk right up to them, like the neophyte he was!

The day dragged on and American Rick Malloy did not return to the little hotel near the Brandenburg Gate. As night approached, some of the comfort taken early in the day was dissipating. The absence of an arrest was painfully obvious to all at secret police headquarters. It was also noted and equally painful in Moscow.

For a while, the senior field agent assigned to track and apprehend Malloy had seriously wondered if he had fooled them all and was much more dangerous than originally believed, but this latest move had confirmed the American "super-spy" as a foolish amateur. "Or had it?" she wondered out loud. "Maybe he wanted us to think he was an amateur and then lead us astray while he was moving in another direction altogether." She found this line of reasoning very disturbing and unlikely, but if nothing else, she was a professional and was trained to be very thorough. She had to be. The number of women in the East German secret police was very low and none had attained her rank or the privileges she was allowed. She had not gotten where she was by assuming anything, or by sitting around and waiting for things to happen. She preferred to make them happen.

"Call the bank and arrange for the vault woman and the manager to meet me there in a half hour," she called out to one of her officers. "I want them to show me every move this Malloy made, his gestures, what he said, how he looked and acted. We must not assume the obvious when the answer may be more complex." She got up and sent for a car to be brought around. Sitting and waiting for the enemy to move was indeed not her style.

Malloy slept in late the next morning. He was tired from the training and the travel, and he was more than a bit taken back by being pursued so vigorously by the East Germans and Russians. It had caused restless sleep and he had needed to recharge his batteries. He missed being at home in Cambridge, and he especially missed Anna. He wondered if she missed him as well. He cautiously went out and got some groceries and brought them back to the room to eat in seclusion. He sat down to draw up his plan. He knew that the secret police would eventually figure out that he was not coming back, and he probably had a day, maybe two before they started to close in on him again. He would have to stay one step ahead and keep moving, but he would also have to make progress toward finding out whether there was any truth to this Nazi heavy water bomb thing. Clearly, the East Germans and Russians thought there was enough to kill and get people killed pursuing the matter. He would head to the address he found on the inside of the safe-deposit box to see if his suspicions about the box were accurate. It did not make a lot of sense, that someone would engrave a clue in the corner of a safe-deposit box, but it was all he had to go on. If this proved to be a dead end, he would have to go to Faschgarten, probably walk into a trap, and certainly be watched at his every turn. He decided that in the morning, early before anyone else was up, he would set out for the suburb of Weissensee and the house on Grunestrasse. Hopefully, the picture would become clearer there.

Captain Smith had made contact with Major Whitcombe after sending Rick Malloy into East Germany, and he had earlier in the week moved in at the command center in West Berlin. It was getting late, and they were monitoring Rick Malloy's progress in hopes of providing assistance, if possible. The team was in contact with London on an almost hourly basis, comparing information with MI-6 and trying to understand what was happening in East Germany, and what was happening to Rick Malloy. They had been informed that the East German police had rushed a bank, The Kaiser Volksbank, earlier in the day, and that talk about an American being apprehended was picked up on by informers. However, there was no proof that it was indeed Malloy, and no indication that if it had been Malloy, that he had been captured. And they failed to have any understanding of the significance of the bank or why Malloy would be going to any bank at all. It was very troubling and raised more questions than it answered. What seemed clear was that the Russians knew Rick was in East Germany, and they seemed to know what he was doing. They were probably hot on his trail, if they did not already have him. The Allied team knew Rick's capabilities well, and had real concern about his ability to elude the East Germans and Russians once they got a fix on him. They had discussed all along the notion that Rick Malloy's only real chance for success was if he could stay undetected and not attract the kind of attention it now looked like he was getting. The situation looked very bad, and the collective spirits of the men involved with the operation were sinking by the hour. The last report for the day was due in over an hour ago, and the fact that it was late heightened tension in the room.

As the hour got later, Captain Smith approached Major Jimmy Whitcombe. "Major, with your permission, sir, I think we should begin to think about scrubbing this mission and getting Malloy out of there while he is still alive and has not been captured and forced to talk." Captain Smith was pacing in the makeshift command center which had been Jimmy Whitcombe's office.

"Captain, you've been under fire of the enemy and seen men killed at close range. Why so squeamish on this?" asked Whitcombe. "So far as we know, Malloy is fine, and even assuming the worst, he would likely get life in minimum-security prison. Hell, they ain't gonna hang the man...are they? Besides, as for his telling the Russians anything--well, he doesn't know anything much to give up to them, now does he?"

The questions were not very reassuring to anyone present. "Sir," responded Smith, "they most certainly will torture him--or more likely, use drugs to get information out of Malloy, and once they have done that, they will discard him like yesterday's rubbish."

Whitcombe looked up, pulled down his reading glasses and said "Captain, I know that. I just don't care to dwell on it. We all knew the danger when we started out on this mission, and it hasn't changed much since then. How many times did you give an order back in France that you knew was going to get somebody killed? I assume you didn't enjoy it then, either...but you did it."

Whitcombe's diatribe was cut off by the ringing of a phone. Smith picked it up, and finding that it was last report of the day coming in, he handed the phone to the ranking officer in the room, Major Jimmy Whitcombe. Whitcombe put the phone to his ear and listened, interrupting the deafening silence only occasionally with remarks like "I see," and "I understand." He hung up the phone and turned to Smith. "Good news and some bad. The good is that your boy gave 'em the slip, it would appear. They thought they had him at the bank, but he was long gone by the time they arrived. They found and have staked out his rooming house, but he has not shown up all day and its starting to look like he knew they would be coming and gave 'em a red herring. No sign of him anywhere."

"And the bad news in that is what?" asked one of the junior officers in the room.

"Let me guess," said Captain Smith. "They know what he looks like and have an all-points search out for him."

"That's about right," agreed Whitcombe. "Except that rumor has it that they have assigned one of their best undercover agents to lead the case, and it's a woman, whatever that means."

"Hmmm," thought Smith out loud, "interesting. Can you get any more information about this woman agent? I have a real bad feeling about this one."

CHAPTER THIRTEEN

Malloy worked hard preparing his plan. He sat in his room for several hours with paper and pencil, mapping out and then revising his plan to get to Weissensee and enter a building he had never seen before. He was a scientist and an engineer and was thorough and logical. But he was still new at this spy stuff and was very unaware of just how to do things. He missed having Smith alongside to guide him and help him think of the appropriate tactics he might need to employ. He also thought how much he had come to trust Captain Smith in the few short weeks he had known him--maybe more than any person he knew on earth, except for Anna. He thought of Anna and dreamed of being back in Boston for a few minutes and had to put her out of his mind to focus on the job at hand.

He was alone and in a hurry and would do the best he could. He broke each step of the plan into parts and examined each move he would make, every person he would interact with, and every tool or prop he might need to use over the course of the plan. Then he looked at each step individually for flaws and ways to improve it. He turned a very simple task into a detailed, scripted plan that afforded him the maximum protection in reaching the house in Weissensee undetected.

Based on his plan, he should be able to reach the address in Weissensee by 3 p.m. if he started right after lunch, although it was less than a half hour away if he went there directly. With any luck, he would have completed this part of his search by nightfall. At least that was the plan.

Rick understood that things might not go as planned and had prepared several contingencies, asking himself over and over "What would Captain Smith do in a situation like this?" In preparing to leave, he packed all of his essential gear to take with him. He had been in this inn for two nights, and knowing for sure that the East Germans were hunting him, he felt it was probably time to move on. He left a toothbrush and comb out on the desk in his room so it would be apparent that he was intending to return, in case anyone came into the room looking for him. Following his plan, he stopped at the front desk and asked the manager to look out for a friend who was planning to meet him later that evening. This was not at all true, but it clearly gave the impression to the hotel manager that Rick Malloy would be back that evening. If he came back, it would be no big issue that the friend did not show up. But if the secret police were to locate this inn, then they would also assume that he was returning and would stake out the wrong location. Rick was pleased that his plan included a number of these failsafe checks that might be very helpful and at least had no downside risk.

His next move further went to confuse anyone trying to track him, as he asked the manager to call him a taxi and gave the manager a false destination address that would be his starting point for the trip north, but not his destination. Taxis were a luxury item that most guests in a small inn like this, in East Berlin, could not afford, and it would therefore draw attention in itself. Rick had considered this and knew that if looked into, it would be misleading at least. Rick took the taxi southwest to the stated destination and then walked several blocks to a trolley line and took the trolley northeast toward Weissensee. He got off in a congested shopping area about a half-mile south of the address on Grunestrasse and finally found another taxi at a waiting stand. Having studied public maps of the area, he asked the taxi driver to take him to a small market area that would likely require driving down Grunestrasse. He thought it would be prudent to have a look at this address and the surrounding neighborhood before walking right up to the building. His plan had checks and balances, failsafes and counter measures. He felt sure it would be impossible to follow him to the house on Grunestrasse.

The taxi rounded the bend onto Grunestrasse and Rick began counting down addresses to find #143. Starting with #228 on the left he focused on the right side of the car for the odd numbers and looked for the specific address. Rick was puzzled and excited. This neighborhood was residential as he had thought, in fact it was full of large mansions, packed in a bit tightly, but mansions nonetheless. It would be very unlikely that any manufacturing had been done here, and although the vault box could have been as much as seventy-five years old, most of these mansions looked even older. No, there was something very interesting about this address.

The taxi continued along the street and the house at 143 Grunestrasse came into view. A large boxy mansion with a mansard roof with a large porch supported by ornate columns out front, this structure was at least one hundred years old and certainly was no manufacturing building. The lawn was a mess; the gate and fencing had fallen down, and the exterior was in need of repair. In fact, it looked as if no one lived here or had for a couple of years. Some windows appeared broken or boarded. This was not the only house on the street that had fallen into disrepair, and honestly it did not stand out as special as compared to many of the other houses on the street. The taxi went on past and Rick began to think about what the address engraved inside the safe-deposit box could possibly have been other than a clue to the contents of the box.

Rick stared out of the window and pondered the possibilities until the driver turned around and pointed out that they had reached the market, and unless Rick wanted to go elsewhere, he should pay up and get out. Rick paid and stepped out of the cab, and found a bench to sit on for a minute. "Let's lay out all of the possibilities" he thought out loud. "It could be real, in which case I am close to finding the location of some information about a project I believe probably does not exist. Or it could be a mistake, either with the engraving on the box, or with my memory of the address I saw. Or, God forbid, it could be a trap."

These were the obvious alternatives, each of which had a few variations on the theme. There was only one sure way to find out. But first, he wanted to change his look a bit more. Rick Malloy went into the market area and found a small stall selling second-hand clothing. Actually, as he looked at the dingy, worn-out things for sale, he thought it was more of a disposal area for clothes that had already had a long life, not a legitimate store for allowing unused items to get new use. He bought an old used fedora hat and a beat-up walking cane, and he was now ready to go.

Malloy began walking back down the street toward the mansion at 143 Grunestrasse. About six houses away, he saw a thick hedge with an iron fence and decided that he should stash his personal effects, including his other clothes, money, and toiletries, which were all contained in his small canvas bag--things he would not need in order to search the house. Also, it was just prudent to be able to move freely and quickly, in case he was mistaken about the house at 143 Grunestrasse. As he put his personal effects in the bag, he stopped for a second to decide whether he should also put in his MIT school ring and the watch he loved so much. He first thought that this was overkill, but his mind asked what Captain Smith would do, and that made the decision easy. He placed his belongings, including his wallet, the SIG-Sauer automatic, his multiple sets of identification papers, his toiletries and appearance kit, money, watch, and school ring in the bag he had been carrying and put it deep into the hedge, behind the fence, well out of sight. No one would find it without his help. He had planned his appearance to not attract attention, and it forced him to move cautiously. He pulled the hat down over his brow, and stooped a bit, and used the cane to assist him in his walk. He looked about like any other elderly man on a stroll in the afternoon with no place to go to in a hurry. He deliberately limped just a bit to play the part, and it was actually easier to limp with the cane than to walk upright in a convincing fashion.

Rick continued down the street to the mansion and stopped across the street in front of it. He had looked around for a trap and had seen nothing. No real traffic, just an occasional car going by. No odd foot traffic either. There was nothing across the street, no parked cars anywhere nearby, and no one around who seemed interested in him or out of place. Everything seemed ordinary and normal, and that was the problem--it looked too good. He sat down on the curb, much like an elderly man who needed to stop for a rest in front of the mansion, and thought, *If this is a trap, I will drive them crazy sitting out here.* He chuckled to himself. *Or they have already driven me crazy for suspecting a trap.*

He sat for over ten minutes, until he could not take it any longer. Satisfying himself that the house was not being watched, he abandoned his plan to continue walking all the way down the street and decided to approach the house from the rear. He was sure that this house was empty and that he alone was looking for it. Based on how he had learned of the house and how he had planned, nothing else was conceivable. He carefully walked up the side yard, around the house. He peered into the windows, but saw no light and no movement. Quietly approaching the rickety back door, he looked around and stepped up and lightly knocked. There was no answer, nor did Rick expect one. He was also relieved to not sense any danger or movement from the inside, and so he turned the handle and opened the door.

Judging from the dust, dirt, and absence of furnishings in this great old house, he estimated that no one had lived here since before the war ended. He entered cautiously into the back foyer and turned to go into the living room. As he turned the corner into the room he heard the words in German, "Ist good to see you again, meine darling. We have been expecting you for some time."

The female senior East German field agent was speaking to Rick Malloy. The combination of the sound of Anna's voice and the sight of his true love from back in Cambridge standing in an East German secret police uniform was beyond comprehension and was astounding beyond anything Rick Malloy was prepared for. Never mind that he was dumbfounded by the presence of anyone at all in the house, but Anna, his Anna? Unthinkable.

He stammered a few phrases, finishing none of them: "How did you get.... What are you doing ....You knew all along...?" ending in "Oh my God."The impact of his lover, Anna Sturm, being in the house took a few seconds to sink in. She had been on assignment the whole time. She had never loved him, he slowly realized, but needed to be close to him because she knew from an informant in London that the Americans would call him to action for this mission. She had used him, and she had been called back to Germany to track and find him. He was devastated. He was just not prepared for this.

On either side of Anna were a pair of secret police goons, both of whom reached out and grabbed Rick Malloy by the arms and proceeded to tie his hands. The remaining two agents kept their revolvers trained on Rick as if they truly believed that he was a dangerous spy who might perform some miraculous feat and take them all by surprise. And in the middle of it all was Anna, his true love Anna. It was a crushing blow that in some way dulled the reality that the East German secret police had just apprehended him for espionage.

Captain Smith's jaw dropped as he read the dossier prepared on short notice about the female East German agent. Her name was Anna Sturm, and he recalled that it was the same first name as Rick Malloy's girlfriend. He could not remember the last name. She was about the right age, spoke several languages, and had blonde hair and blue eyes and was about the same height, at least based on Smith's recollection. *Coincidence? Hell no*, Smith thought. He knew that Malloy was in serious trouble and that he was completely unprepared for this. He alerted the major and started to make plans to go in after Rick Malloy. He would have to find him before the Russians and East Germans did. He hoped he was not too late.

The East German agents had tied Rick's hands behind his back and walked him out of the back of the house to a car parked in a nearby driveway, and put him in the car. As this was going on, Anna had started to explain that she had hoped it was not Rick mixed up in this mess. She talked to him in English, maybe out of some lingering feelings and maybe so the other German agents could not understand her. It was not until she saw the pictures drawn of him based on descriptions from the bank that she really believed it was Rick. She knew from the bank description and sketches that they were both just agents for different nations and that she not only must do her job, but must do it better than Rick Malloy. She said that she actually thought she might love him when they were back in Boston, but having lied to her about his leaving and realizing that he really was simply a spy for the West, she could never love him. He stood in front of her, dumbfounded as he listened to her. She even explained that these men around her had thought he was a great agent because he had been so lucky and their incompetence had allowed him to get this far. And she finished with the explanation of how she was waiting for him in this house. She too had gone back to the bank and asked the vault attendant to recreate everything Rick had done. And when she stuck her head in the safe-deposit box and saw the address, she knew where she would find her American, Rick Malloy. East German senior field agent Anna Sturm was very proud of herself indeed, for today she had captured the elusive American master spy, whom so many others had been unable to apprehend.

Malloy, tied up in the small back seat of an old beat-up pre-war DKW sedan, was flanked on one side by one of the guards, with the other guard sitting on the front seat with a pistol pointed at him. A third goon drove the car and Anna, and the final East German man followed in the other car. Malloy did not know where they would take him, but he guessed he would get to see the secret police HQ and be shown off to Anna's superiors before he was pumped for information. After that, depending on what he said and how things went, he might be allowed to live, or he would be executed as a spy.

After about twenty-five minutes of driving back into the central city from Wiessensee, as the sun was going down, the black sedan pulled up at the rear of a nondescript office building on a side street and stopped. This was not the busy side of the building, but was the side few ever saw, or wanted to see, he thought. It was the Haupt Polizei office, secret police headquarters in Berlin and the nerve center for all of East Germany. With guns trained on him both near and far, he was helped out of the car and ushered inside and up a set of back stairs, down a corridor and into an interrogation room. It was going to be a long night, thought Rick.

Within a few minutes, the door opened and Anna walked in with two older agents whom Rick had not seen before. He assumed they were her superiors, and they scoffed as they looked at Rick, and spoke amongst themselves about Americans and the incompetence of the West. They confirmed that Malloy would be "interviewed" immediately and then they turned and left the room. Indeed, it would be a long night.

Captain Smith had secured permission from Major Whitcombe and from London to go into East Germany to retrieve Rick Malloy, based on the news that Rick's girlfriend, Anna, had been an East German agent all along. The logical assumption was that his mission was already compromised and he was in personal danger. Smith was in a hurry. He knew he had no time to waste and he had a lot to do to get ready. His current plan was to enter the East the following morning with the worker traffic so that he would stand a better chance of not being spotted by paid "watchers" who hung around the various obvious crossing areas looking for anyone and anything suspicious. Unfortunately for Smith, he looked American and his German was only barely adequate, so he would be an easy spot in a sparse group. Captain Smith left the Berlin HQ and went back to the barracks to get ready. He would return in the morning for the latest news prior to crossing into the East.

At 6 a.m. the following morning, Captain William Smith returned to the makeshift HQ in Berlin, got a cup of coffee, and went to the communications room to get any late news. The expressions on the radioman's face told him it was not going to be good news. He listened as the news out of East Berlin was told to him. "Last night at about midnight we got word from an informer that Malloy had been caught by the East Germans in Weissensee, north of the city, and he had been arrested and taken to headquarters for questioning," relayed the communications officer. "It has since been confirmed by another operative who added that the woman you mentioned was seen taking him into the secret police headquarters. Looks like you were correct to be concerned," he finished.

Smith was stunned and sad. He had invested a lot in Rick Malloy, in time, effort, and emotion. He knew that this was the end of the mission, and there was nothing that could be done for Malloy, and the fact that this was true hurt all the more. It was as if he were watching

Malloy drown from a distance and could do nothing but watch him go under. The US government would not even admit that Malloy was working for the US, let alone ask for his return or any clemency. His fate was sealed, and he would probably have to be lucky to merely spend the rest of his life in prison and not be shot.

While he stood pondering the events and Malloy's dismal future, he was summoned by Major Whitcombe. Whitcombe who had been informed of the circumstances and wanted to start wrapping this mission up. It was over, and nothing more could be done to help Malloy. In fact, any admission of his existence would endanger him more. So a concerted cover-up of the mission would now be put in place, as agreed at the outset in planning, in the event things went wrong. The first point was a debrief on what Malloy knew and would be able to tell the East Germans and Russians about the mission and the US capabilities. It was going to be a long day, thought Captain Smith, but not half as long as Rick Malloy's day would be. He turned away and went up to the briefing room to meet with Whitcombe and the army intelligence team.

Rick Malloy was interrogated most of the night. Tied to a chair and locked in a small room with dim lights and a window which he was sure had people on the other side watching his reaction, he had been asked the same questions over and over about his knowledge of American atomic secrets and the United States pursuit of the German atomic bomb program. Rick came to the conclusion early in the process that he really did not know very much that would be useful to the Russians or East Germans, and he did not know whether that was a good thing or a very bad thing.

After nearly nine hours of questioning and sitting around in between sessions, early in the morning of his fifth day back in Germany, Rick Malloy was exhausted and scared and emotionally drained, and in custody of the East German secret police. They had questioned him in German mostly, but had also asked some of the same questions again in English, no doubt to see if they would get the same answers. Anna was long gone, and he had been in the hands of professional interrogators. They had asked about his childhood, his father and mother, his studies and work at MIT, and his contribution to the Hiroshima and Nagasaki bombs. Anna had been able to tell them what to ask about and where to probe. And of course they wanted to focus on what the Americans knew about the German atomic program, and how far they were in uncovering any German secrets. They gave him precious little information about what they knew, and Rick Malloy had little information to add to it. The interrogators were clearly disappointed in how little Malloy knew, and based on the thoroughness on the interview, they were surprised that he had no information of any real value. Finally, in the early morning of the 15th of August, Rick was led out of the small interrogation room. He figured that he would be taken to a holding cell to wait for further processing. He knew that there would be no trial, no attorneys, and no due process in the American sense of the words. Rick sensed that the Russians might want to keep him around, either in hopes that he might be useful in a trade, or maybe to embarrass the Americans if the opportunity presented itself. At least, he hoped that was the case.

Rick Malloy soon realized that he was only partially correct in assuming that the East Germans and Russians wanted him alive and healthy. In fact, they were just not done with him yet. He was taken from the interrogations room in the secret police headquarters downstairs to the cold, dank basement, to another small room. He was blindfolded and told to lie on a table. With his hands still tied and two strong guards holding his arms, he had little opportunity to do otherwise. Immediately he was tied to the table--a surgical table, he guessed, as his mind started to race and he conjured up all the things they might do to him. Rick could hear people coming in and going out, and the rearranging of furniture, or maybe equipment. But he could see nothing, and there was very little talk that he could fully understand. After about a half an hour or so he felt the sleeve of his shirt pulled up and the pinch of a needle into his arm. He wondered what they would do with his body when they were done with him. He expected the worst and knew that the use of these debilitating so-called "truth" drugs, used to see if he knew more than he was telling them, might kill him or at least make him very sick. Five minutes later, he lost consciousness.

CHAPTER FOURTEEN

AUGUST, 1946

Back in London, the combined army intelligence and MI-6 teams had been notified by Berlin about the capture of their third agent, Rick Malloy, by the East German secret police. The mission had been immediately suspended pending the usual post-operation review that would be scheduled in a couple of weeks. In Berlin, the whole mission had begun to look like a disaster and everyone, from Captain Smith up to Major Whitcombe, recognized this was not going to be a bright spot on their career service record. The facts were sobering: one agent confirmed dead before the mission ever really got underway, a second agent removed from service due to serious illness which may have been induced by the enemy, and the third agent captured and presumed killed by the East Germans after interrogation.

Although it had been only a few days since Malloy's capture and no one knew for certain if he was dead or alive, Captain Smith could see officers and staff who had worked on the team starting to distance themselves from the mission. No one wanted to admit to the apparent failure or think about the fate of the American Rick Malloy. Officially, there would be no admission of his existence, much less any inquiry about his condition or potential release. Rick Malloy had been on his own, and the Allies were not about to admit that he was operating as an undercover agent. And besides, the odds were good that he was already dead.

Major Whitecombe, never the sentimental type, had gone back to his duties almost immediately. He had no strong bond with Malloy, and he had rationalized that this was still war and that this type of outcome came with the job, a sad but acceptable risk. Captain Smith, still in Berlin, requested a couple of weeks of leave to refresh and get on with his life and career. He had gotten to know Rick Malloy and liked him. He had trained the man and was responsible for recruiting, planning, and sending Malloy on this mission. He remembered the warnings from the elite French underground trainers who cautioned that Rick Malloy lacked the temperament and training to succeed in the mission, and he blamed himself for pushing the matter forward to its inevitable conclusion. Smith had decided that a change in scenery was needed and had made plans to accompany a group of friends who also had leave, on their trip down to Salzburg, Austria, adjacent to the American occupation zone. This would give him time to relax and get the whole mess out of his mind, he hoped.

Rick Malloy had indeed been injected with scopolamine, a drug pioneered by the Nazis, that would reduce his senses and allow him to tell more about what he knew and about the mission and the Allies' search for German atomic weapons plans. Rick was enough of a scientist to understand that truth serums were not foolproof. He also knew that an overdose was often lethal and usually very painful. The fact that he knew so very little about the American weapons program not only likely saved his life, but it made the secret police interrogators believe he was using some extraordinary combination of training and will-power to fight the drugs. Refusing to believe that he could have been brought into such a mission having so few facts, they again started to put forward that he was a top American agent and would be valuable to them at some future time. This man must be a superbly trained master spy, and as such he could be used to embarrass the Allies at the appropriate time. It was their excuse for not getting better information out of Rick Malloy, never mind that he did not have it to give up. He would not be deliberately overdosed and left to die. At least, not yet.

Unfortunately, the side effects of these "truth" drugs were known to be terrible, with delusions, delirium, and paralysis spells for days and a temporary dementia that kept most people from walking or even standing up easily. Malloy was alive, but very ill. If he ever completely recovered all of his senses it would take weeks, and often people subjected to this form of interrogation would have flashbacks and delusions for years following their interrogation. Some never recovered at all. Rick Malloy had been young and strong and of sound mind a few days earlier--now he was haggard, weak, and nearly insane.

Rick had been taken at night from the secret police headquarters to a nearby Soviet-built prison compound with minor medical facilities to be watched and to regain his strength. It was in the small suburb of Hohenschoenhausen and the camp went by that name, but was also known as NKVD Special Camp #3. Orders indicated that as soon as he was able, he would be transferred to the maximum-security Nazi-built Sachsenhausen prison camp, now called NKVD Special Camp #7. It was a place reserved for the most dangerous criminals in East Germany. This was the place the Russian NKVD had kept intact for Nazi war criminals either to live out their life sentences, or to be executed. In contrast, the holding compound where Rick was sent was a much smaller detention camp just east of Berlin that had been built to hold political prisoners, minor dissenters to the Russian occupation, and small-time criminals that did not justify the expense of maximum security. Reopened in 1945 by the Russians as soon as they occupied Berlin, it was used by the East Germans and Russians to keep political prisoners, dissidents, and Communist enemies at bay. The fact that they were not Nazis did not make them any less dangerous to the Communists. Hohenschoenhausen was slightly cleaner, and as a result of the type of inmates there, it was clearly more minimum security. Bars, cells, and armed guards were all in place, to be sure, but there were fewer of them, and more lax regulations. About half of the inmates were awaiting transfer to somewhere else, and the remaining half were low risk, mostly older men who would be of little use on a work farm, but had been judged unsafe to be released back into the population. No trial, no due process, no chance at anything resembling justice.

Rick Malloy woke up and could begin to focus his eyes on his surroundings for the first time in early September, some two weeks following the last interrogation His existence had been meager, as he had not been able to keep food down and had thrown up in his cell daily for the last week. He had often been incontinent and had not been able to get to the open latrine in the cell many times. This had resulted in the guards hosing him down on a regular basis. That was disorienting in itself, and it left him wet and cold. He had lost twenty pounds and looked like a dying man. But these were only a part of his worries. Although he was still very ill and he had a hard time focusing or concentrating for any length of time, he began to start understanding what had happened to him, where he was, and to start thinking about his next moves.

Few of the guards or medical staff, such as they were, ever spoke directly to him except to issue directions about eating, getting changed, and going to the latrine (when he was able) and so forth. No conversations or pleasantries at all. Even so, he had picked up enough from listening to the conversations of the guards and surrounding inmates to know that he was in a recovery area, waiting for final transfer to someplace far more dangerous. He also understood that the sooner he recovered, the sooner he would be transferred, and from what he could gather, that prisoners who were subjected to his type interrogation and that survived at all, stayed in about 6-8 weeks before transfer. Guessing that he would not be able to fake his illness or fool the guards for very long, he figured he had about four weeks to come up with some kind of plan. That said, he was still very weak and often dizzy, and had a hard time keeping any kind of nourishment down.

As he lay on the floor in his cell, he had a lot to think about. He wondered what the army intelligence and MI-6 knew--and if they understood what had happened, would they try to do anything to help him? He knew deep down inside that they could not and they would not lift a finger. But mostly he thought about Anna. How had he made such a bad judgment of character? How could she say the things she had said to him back in Cambridge and then turn out to be a spy, and a liar, and his enemy? He had truly fallen in love with this woman, and it really hurt to find out that the person he was living for was possibly the one who would cause his death. It was so improbable, but it was a fact and he just kept coming back to their relationship in Cambridge and then the image of her waiting for him to enter the house on Grunestrasse. It gave him a headache, and so he would have to close his eyes and sleep to keep it from hurting.

The layout of the facility was such that the medical ward where Rick Malloy was being held was situated in a central compound between the wing holding the political and social detainees and the wing housing real criminals who were awaiting transfers to other prisons. The long-term prisoners resided on one side and the short-timers passing through were being held on the other. As with most prisons, the long-term prisoners, who had demonstrated that they could be trusted and had records of good behavior, were "allowed" to clean and perform routine maintenance on the facilities. It was mopping, cleaning the open latrines, or washing clothes in large tubs--far from anything rewarding, thought Rick. And although he was pretty sure they were not being paid, at least it broke up the terminal boredom and provided some sense of hope and purpose for these typically older men who likely had little to look forward to on a daily basis in their lives. Rick wondered if he would look as defeated and worn-down as they did after he had spent ten years in prison, and feared the answer was yes. The men said little as they passed by Rick's cell area, but it was interesting to watch them and wonder what they had been imprisoned for in the first place. Every now and again one would say "hi" to him, and as the days passed they began to talk a bit more.

After another two weeks Rick Malloy was starting to feel a bit more normal. The dizziness and vomiting had subsided and his appetite had returned. Unfortunately, the food he was being fed was not very appetizing. Bread and weak soups were the standard fare, and meat of any kind was notably absent. This forced diet also had the effect of creating diarrhea and stomach cramps on occasion for Malloy, as he was truly unaccustomed to this kind of food by itself.

Malloy had also started to work on a plan to escape. He realized that unless he made good on an escape from this prison, he would have to contend with a maximum- security facility which would be a lot harder to get out of (if not impossible). He had observed several prison transfers and noticed that the condition of the prisoner made a large difference in the level of security provided during the transfer. Large, healthy men who were belligerent and vocal got a lot of attention: multiple guards, leg irons, and handcuffs. However, the more frail and meek inmates would typically get a single guard and only handcuffs. Rick guessed that the transfer was either by car or small panel van and that the only additional person involved would be a driver. He decided to make himself as frail and meek looking as possible, if not still sick, in hopes of getting a small and less secure transfer. It would be during the transfer that he would have to figure out how to over power the guard and driver and then get away.

Malloy started to think back to Captain Smith and again asked himself, "What would Smith do in these circumstances?" This led Rick to a couple of thoughts: he needed the element of surprise on his side, maybe a diversion, and he needed a weapon. He also needed to find the right opportunity. For the escape to work, he felt that he needed the guard to come to him, preferably unarmed. That would require having something of interest that the guard would physically take from him, while at the same time Malloy would appear to present little threat, such that the guards either relaxed a bit or maybe even approached Malloy unarmed. Rick was pretty sure he could act weak and ill enough to deceive the guard, but he had no idea what he would use for bait to lure him up close. He also had no ideas about getting a weapon, and was not at all confident he could overpower a trained guard with his hands cuffed, especially in his condition.

As the six-week mark approached, Malloy was seen by a prison doctor and it was determined that he would be well enough for the transfer from Hohenschoenhausen to the Sachsenhausen Camp in three days. He was viewed as far weaker than most, a surprising conclusion for the doctor, who felt that being an american Agent and relatively young, this prisoner should have been more healthy. But the diagnosis stuck, and Rick was judged a low risk and an easy transfer. Perfect.

Later in the afternoon during his fifth or sixth week in confinement, he was not sure, one of the older prisoners, while mopping the floor, stopped at Rick Malloy's cell and began asking him questions. Rick was surprised and cautious, suspecting that the East Germans had put this prisoner up to it, but Rick became more curious than suspicious, because the questions were not about atomic bombs and the questioner appeared truly interested and concerned. The inmate asked where Rick came from, if he had left any family behind, what he had been doing before he was arrested, what America was like and so on. It was harmless banter, Rick thought, and certainly nothing the secret police would care about. And if the questions had had a point, Rick had not been able to find it. It just seemed like a nosy prisoner who wanted to get any interesting news before the new prisoner was transferred out. Malloy was glad to oblige and told about the status of

Berlin and the world as he had seen it on the outside only three weeks earlier. He had also talked about his youth in Germany and his move to America to avoid the Nazis. The things he was careful not to talk about were his father or his wealth, for he could not see how this was going to help him and might make a bad thing much worse.

With one day to go until his transfer, Rick had refined his plan, but he still had no weapon and no exact plan for how to obtain one. In the late morning, one of the older inmates was again mopping the floor and he stopped to speak with Rick Malloy for a minute. As if he had read Rick's mind, he began to talk to Rick about his only real opportunity for escape. Rick was not sure why but this stranger seemed to care about him and want to help. He suggested that Rick make his move before he got to to the NKVD maximum security camp at Sachsenhausen, and he offered to obtain a weapon-- not much, but maybe a handmade knife of sorts. And lastly, he told Rick that he or a friend would return in the morning with this weapon. Rick was amazed, but very cautious. Were the secret police testing him, or was this the real thing? And even if it were real, why would this unknown inmate approach him and make such an offer? Shouldn't he have been suspicious of Rick Malloy being a plant? It could be a trap, and he was not about to fall for it, so he nodded and kept his mouth shut. It was about all he could think to do. There were lots of good questions, but no answers at all.

It had been close to two months since the American had been captured and interrogated at the East German secret police headquarters, and life had returned to normal for all of the officers, agents, and staff except senior field agent Anna Sturm. She had, in fact, been reassigned after wrapping up her most famous case, and she had earned and been awarded a small promotion. She was also somewhat torn between the pride in her professional accomplishments and her personal feelings for Rick Malloy. She had done her job well and been congratulated and been proud, but she could not shake the notion that she had walked away from one of the best things to ever enter her life. It was a hollow victory at best, but it was the choice she had made, and she would have to live with it. Besides, Rick Malloy was untouchable now. He was beyond her reach even if she had been able to bring herself to reach out to him. He was being held in Hohenschoenhausen until he was well enough to be transferred, and once deemed able, he was scheduled for transfer to the maximum security Russian NKVD Camp, Sachsenhausen. If history were any indicator of the future, he would likely die in that internment camp within a few years. His only hope was a trade for some Russian or East German agent, which might not ever happen. And since the West surely assumed that he was already dead, it was not a high probability that Rick Malloy would ever see the outside world again.

The enemy agent in West Berlin, the mole who had been feeding information to the East Germans and Russians about the operation, had reported in that the Americans and Brits had shut down the mission and were conducting a postmortem in a few days to put the matter to rest and move on. There was no fourth agent being sent in and the matter was not being further pursued. With the shut-down of the mission, this particular informant was no longer close to any useful top brass, but they would continue to monitor the situation. The official word in London was that there probably had been no Nazi atomic weapons secrets and that there would be no more attempts to search for them. Based on this information, Anna was pretty sure that the case was closed, and she would never see Rick Malloy again.

The morning came on the 5th of October with a clear bright sky, cool at dawn and a bit of dew on the grass outside around the prison compound. Rick Malloy was up early, in part because he could not sleep thinking about the day ahead, and in part because he wanted to put his plan into motion before the guards got to him. He deliberately made himself look disheveled and did a good job of messing up his hair. He was not allowed to have a razor, and shaving was allowed only once a week for the prisoners, so he also looked much like a vagrant. He acted out the part, being a little distant and weak--just enough so the guards found him pathetic, but not enough that they manhandled him. He made a point of eating his breakfast for strength and because if things went well he might be on the run and unable to get food easily. He had been told to be ready to depart for transport at noon, and based on his understanding of the process from listening to other detainees figured that the trip would take about 2-3 hours. His plan depended on that time.

Rick was preparing himself when he noticed that two prisoners had come toward his cell. They had been brought in by a guard who searched them briefly and looked closely at what appeared to be a small box or book that one inmate was holding--Rick could not tell exactly what it was. The guard had not come up to the cell itself, staying back a bit, but watching for any trouble. One prisoner he recognized immediately as the prisoner who had visited him a day earlier. The other, who looked vaguely familiar, was a disheveled older man, who appeared to be in his late sixties, although he might have been younger and just worn out from prison. He carried himself upright in a way that indicated, at least to Rick, that he was a very proud person, even in prison.

The familiar prisoner spoke to Rick. "I have brought someone special to meet with you, and I have brought you a gift which we think you will find useful for your upcoming trip."

With that, he handed Rick a book, which Rick took and looked at. It was a small leather-bound compilation of Grimm's fairy tales that was more than just familiar to him, as he had enjoyed reading these as a child and often read a story before going to bed. Oddly, this looked a lot like the very same book he had read as a child, right down to the torn hardcover. "Look in the book," whispered the other, older man to Rick. Rick opened the book and thumbed through the pages.

"I know this book," he said. "I read it many times as a child."

The new prisoner standing next to the man who gave Rick the book started to smile and said, "Where did you read it, my young friend?"

Rick was surprised by the question and puzzled by the tone of his voice, but answered, "I would read it before going to bed, often with my father, back long before the war." Rick was fumbling through the book a bit, when he looked inside the hard cover and to his amazement saw that written on the flyleaf of the book were the words: "To my son Eric, Happy Birthday, 1925." And though it had been many years since he had seen his father's handwriting, he instantly recognized this as his father's hand.

As the surprise of seeing a book, that appeared to come from his childhood, began to seep in, the older prisoner turned to the other man and said, "You may leave us alone for a few minutes now." Then, turning his attention back to Rick he said, "Yes, that is correct. I would often read these stories to Eric and later he would read them to me before going to bed."

Rick Malloy, born Eric von Malloy, looked up into the eyes of this new prisoner. "You, you are saying that you are my father? That is not possible. No, he is dead, I am sure, isn't he? But this book ....Is it really you?" The slow realization that he was standing in the presence of his own father, whom he had believed to have been dead for over six years, was hard to grasp.

"I was not sure it would be you either, my son," his father, the prisoner, stated. "I brought this book that I have kept the last thirteen years to see if it was possible that this could be my son, but...." His father started crying, and could not speak. Rick was in shock and the older prisoner started to get worried that the guard would come over and interrupt things. "Please examine the book again, paying particular attention to the spine of the book, Herr von Malloy," he said.

Rick tried to focus, looking at the book and at the spine of the book. He had noticed that it had been torn a bit and that the hard cover also had a tear in it. Then he saw it, a small steel rod had been inserted into the spine in a way that would make it hard to detect unless you knew to look for it. He pulled the rod out and it was a handmade knife, pointed at one end, slightly wider through the blade, and blunt at the other end. Not a perfect weapon, but better than anything he had come up with and certainly good enough for the job he had planned.

"Leave it in the book until you need it," counseled his father, holding out his hand to get Rick's attention. Heinrich von Malloy was still weeping, but he kept himself erect, noble and proud. "I have dreamed about this for over twelve years," he said. "But I never had any reason to think it would come true. It is a miracle."

The guard signaled that time was up and that whatever was going on must stop. Rick was still in shock, and his father was as well. The older prisoner stepped forward to the cell and took over the conversation. "I am a longtime friend of your family and have been in prison with your father the past eight years. I know what you will be thinking, but listen to me. First, we got your father to take the name of a dying inmate six years ago, fearing that if people knew they had a former noble industrialist in prison, that they might use him or kill him. His name is now Rheinhold Schmidt. Now, you must make good your escape. If you do not, then all that we have done is for nothing, and there will be nothing that you can ever do for your father. Do you understand?"

Rick realized that he had already started to think that he would try not to leave his father behind, but in fact, he had no choice--the secret police would decide their fate, not Rick Malloy. He could not speak, but he nodded. Heinrich von Malloy, his father, raised his head back up, wiped the tears from his eyes, and stuck out his hand to his son. It was not like German nobility to get sentimental.

"Good luck, my son. Should you be successful, get out of the country and do not return. Have a good life."

Rick grabbed his hand and kissed it, and fought to hold back his emotions. "Father, I will escape, and I will return for you. I do not know how or when, but you may count on this," Rick replied.

The guard, who had been impatiently observing this meeting from a distance, came over and interrupted. "It is enough time. Give him the book, as you wished. You must return to your cells."

Rick held up the book, showing the guard that he had it, and the two prisoners were escorted away. Rick slumped into the corner of his cell and cried. His father was alive.

CHAPTER FIFTEEN

Rick sat in his cell with his mind racing for the next hour. His father was alive, and he was right here in this very same holding compound! He had not seen him in over thirteen years, since he and his mother had left for America, and it had been nearly five years since the confirmed reports of his father dying in prison. There were so many unanswered questions, things he wanted to ask his father, and so many things he wanted to tell his father. He could not imagine leaving his father in this prison, but as noon approached, he realized that he had no alternative than to try to escape and then deal with his father in prison from the outside. If he ended up in the maximum-security prison, he could do nothing for his father, and he would likely be there a long time--maybe too long to be of any use to himself or his father. The one thing he knew was that he was going to be transferred out of this facility in less than an hour. Nothing good would come of trying to stop that. So he tried to focus on the immediate issues. He was preparing himself for the journey, acting frail, disoriented, and weak, and a bit senile and crazy, but not enough to cause canceling the transfer. And he hugged his book of fairy tales.

The guards came promptly at noon--typical German efficiency, even if it was communist-controlled East Germany. Two guards came to Rick's cell and led him out. He was handcuffed, but as he had hoped, due to his apparent frail and weak nature, they did not put shackles on his legs — why would they? He appeared to be unstable just standing; who was he going to outrun? They were probably more worried about his falling or tripping than his escaping. They searched him thoroughly, but that was not too difficult with the loose-fitting clothes they had given him to wear in prison. They looked at his book and quickly thumbed through the pages. He told them about the kind man that had given it to him when he heard it was his favorite book, and they let him continue to hug it. He painted a pretty pathetic picture of a weak, neurotic inmate who would surely give them no trouble at all. He shuffled along; handcuffed but not leg shackled, he was led out the way he was brought in nearly seven weeks earlier. In the open area in the compound, there was a beat-up black van and he was put in the back on a wooden seat, facing to the rear. A driver and one guard accompanied him. *Perfect*, he thought. The guard sat next to him on the wooden seat with a pistol leveled at him, just in case. Per his plan, as they were about to leave, he let the driver know he needed to go to the bathroom, and then recanted and said he was probably okay for the trip. The guard looked annoyed, but then relieved when told that the moment had passed.

The van stopped between the first and second set of gates and two security guards came out of the guardhouse and quickly and efficiently searched the car. The gates behind them closed as they signaled the tower, and the outside gate was opened for the van to drive out. They were on their way.

Rick could see as they drove away that this was a minimum-security facility. There were few guards, and aside from a some high walls, a lack of windows, and a little barbed wire, it could be a factory complex. He suspected that he had been held in the more secure part of the prison and that many of the prisoners were not kept alone in single cells, but lived in far less secure quarters with three or four inmates in each cell block area. That would be where his father was being kept. It would not be too hard to break into Hohenschoenhausen prison, he thought. Getting out with his father might be a bit different.

His mind was already working on a plan to get his father out when he realized that they had been on the road about thirty minutes. The van was now out of the industrial area and into the countryside north-east of the city of Berlin, into Panketal, where country houses were spaced further apart. This was the area he had been waiting for. In another 10-15 minutes they would head east and come into another urban area, and he would have missed the opportunity. He motioned to the guard and said that he had to go to the bathroom. The guard shrugged and indicated that he did not care and that the van would not stop. Rick squirmed and said that he needed to stop now, or he would have to go in his pants. The guard said no again and seemed very annoyed. Rick made the decision he had to force action and began to make himself urinate in his pants. He again motioned to the guard, and the guard observed the growing wet spot in his prisoner's pants. The guard became clearly angry and hit Rick Malloy in the stomach with the butt of his pistol. Rick bent over in pain, his stomach really in agony, but also he made it look worse than it had been. The guard was disgusted as he signaled the driver to stop the van.

The driver pulled the van over to the side of the road in an open area with only a few trees and a creek and a wide field between the road and any place where Rick Malloy could hide or escape to. The woods were 300-400 yards away. It was a lousy location for Rick--a good choice by the driver. The guard signaled for Malloy to get out of the van, and Rick carefully slipped the pointed homemade knife out of the book before setting the book down and stepping out of the van. The long, poorly fitting sleeves of his prison overalls had made con-cealing his efforts easier, and he was still bent over in pain, which also helped hide his motions. He slowly and deliberately got out of the van, emphasizing his frailty in the process. The guard led him to the side of the road and stood back. It was not what Rick expected, and he was not close enough at this point to attack his captors. So he stood by the side of the road and pissed on the ground. He made it last as long as he could, to keep up the charade of having to go badly.

When he was done and had put himself in order, the guard came over. The time had arrived for Rick Malloy. He had the homemade knife in his left hand and switched it to his right hand. He focused on the training he had received back in France. He remembered the hand-to-hand combat instructions from the ex-Deuxième operatives, and he remembered his hesitation. He could not hesitate this time. His life and the life of his father depended on his actions. As the guard moved up next to him, he pretended to lose his balance and stumble. The guard, believing the frail inmate would fall to the ground moved to steady Malloy. With a single deft motion Rick Malloy stood up, spun the guard around so that he was facing away from him, and holding the guard he plunged the knife into his neck. The astonished guard spit blood from his mouth and dropped to the ground, but as he did he pulled out his Tokarev TT-33 pistol and fired into Rick Malloy's leg. It stung, but the adrenalin was flowing and he hardly felt the immediate pain. Rick wrenched the gun from the badly injured guard's hand and dived down behind the van so that the driver could not get off a clean shot. He crawled around the side of the van as the driver who had jumped out of the van at the first sign of commotion searched for a position to shoot at the escapee, Rick Malloy.

Rick reached under the van, crouching next to the ground, and shot the driver in the foot. The man screamed and hobbled on one foot, tripped, and fell to the ground. Rick leapt across the hood of the van and shot the driver twice in the chest. The driver slumped on the ground and Rick stood up, walked over, and kicked his gun out of his hand. He went back to the guard he had stabbed and could see that this man was in poor condition, having lost a lot of blood and being close to losing consciousness. This man was not a threat any more and would be lucky to stay alive. It was over in an instant, and Rick had escaped his captors. He now looked down and saw that his leg was bleeding badly. The bullet had gone through the meat of his leg and not hit bone, but there was a lot of blood and it was beginning to really hurt. He tore the sleeve off the driver's uniform and used it to bandage his wound. He could use a doctor and medical treatment, but knowing that he was not going to get it, he was pretty sure that unless he got badly infected he would probably recover over time. He would clean the wound when he got a chance, but he needed to keep moving.

Quickly, Rick rummaged through the two men's clothes, finding the keys to the handcuffs and freeing himself. Rick pulled the two guards off to the side of the road into a ditch. One was dead and the other dying, and as Rick Malloy was pulling these men out of the roadway, he was once again pleased by his performance and ability to escape his captors, and horrified that he had killed two men in the process. He took their identification, clothes, money, and personal effects and put these on the seat next to him in the van. You never know what you will need. And he now had two Russian pistols available to him if needed, and a little extra ammo. He was amazed at his good fortune that no other car had come by, but then, cars in East Germany were not plentiful. And honestly, unless they had arrived in the 20 seconds during the shooting, they would have no reason to suspect anything abnormal. He also knew that in less than an hour the prison would note that the transport van was late and send out a search party. He hoped to get to someplace where he would be safe before the van was missed and a search put out for it. He climbed in and turned the van around. Rick started driving southeast, back toward the holding compound and the city of Berlin. He would have to ditch the van within the hour, so he drove it toward Mitte Berlin where it would not be easily noticed and might even be hard to find.

Rick drove back into the heart of the city of East Berlin and left the van on a side street, near the central train station and the crossover point where he could most easily get out of the East and back to safety in the West. He wanted the secret police to think that he had escaped to the West, but he had no intention of doing that. He knew that he could not return without his father and that he could not help him from the West.

Rick Malloy, injured by the bullet wound in his leg, left the van and walked back into the central section of East Berlin. He had put the guard's shirt on and used the belt from the driver to disguise his prison outfit a bit. He had wrapped up the remaining clothes he had stolen from the guards, bloody though they were, and taken their money to use on the above ground tram, heading north, back toward the house in Weissensee.

At 3 p.m. the prison managers at the Sachsenhausen NKVD max-imum-security prison camp recognized that there was a problem with the daily transfer from the Hohenschoenhausen work camp. The rou-tine transfer of an American prisoner had not arrived and was signifi-cantly behind schedule. Nothing major was immediately assumed. A search was ordered and sent out along the route, looking for engine trouble or a flat tire. There was no reason to assume foul play at this point. However, no trace was found of the van or its passengers. It took several hours before a serious problem was assumed, primarily because it was not immediately believed that the frail American could have caused trouble, much less escaped. It was likely a mistake, the van had become lost and had been delayed, it was not assumed to be a prison break. However, by nightfall the location of the van had not been determined and the secret police had been informed that the American spy, who was sick, very weak and not believed to be able to take care of himself on his own, had disappeared, along with the two guards transferring him. Oh, they had disappeared along with the van they were driving in, along with two handguns. It was a nightmare. The question unanswered was whether he escaped by himself, or with the help of other American spies. He was not believed to have been able to act alone, so the possibility of a larger set of problems was immediately considered.

The secret police were apoplectic. Having captured this American and interrogated him, to no avail, they had handed him over to the state's penal system for detention and incarceration as a dangerous spy. They were now being informed that the American had outwitted them all and escaped, probably to gain freedom in the West. They all looked like incompetent fools. Surely heads would roll for this incredible breach of duty, but right now the question was what had happened and where was the American and the two guards. They did not vanish into thin air! A detailed search was now ordered as a highest priority and all East German agents in the Berlin metro area were alerted and pulled back onto the case. All available officers were put out on the street with a description of the van and the American. Agents in West Berlin were put on alert to find Malloy as well, for if he escaped, surely he would try to get out to the West. The legend of the master spy, Rick Malloy, was also resurrected. He was labelled extremely dangerous--shoot on sight. And the hunt was on again.

This all-hands call, of course, included Anna Sturm. She had finished her day of routine paperwork in her office and had gone home for dinner and glass of wine before going to bed. She had had a few uneventful weeks of easy duty since the year-long assignment which had taken her to America and ended up back in East Berlin with the capture of the American, Rick Malloy. She had needed some down time as well, for she had had misgivings about her role in seducing him, and then hunting him down. She also had tried to put the whole episode out of her mind, as she knew that his fate was not to be a pretty one as soon as he was captured. The drugs administered during interrogation, the relentless questioning, followed by isolation in the work camp and then life in a maximum-security prison camp--it was not going to be an easy existence for the man she had become very close to.

Anna recognized that she still loathed the West, the Allies, and especially the Americans, wallowing in their self-righteous victory and living a shamefully decadent existence while her home country had been destroyed and innocent people were killed, maimed, homeless, and impoverished. She believed that the Communists would rebuild the Germany she knew as a child, and she would never forgive the Allies for destroying it. She did not care for Hitler or the National Socialists, but she remembered the fire bombings and the massive destruction of her homeland. It was this caring for Rick Malloy and hatred for the country he represented that created the emotional dilemma for her.

At 7 p.m. there was a knock on her door, and upon inquiring who it was and learning that it was a staff agent for the East German secret police that had a message for her, she opened the door and let the young agent in. She did not have her own telephone --it was a luxury she could not afford, but she also knew that to be sent a note at this hour meant that something important had happened. The young agent handed her a note. She unfolded the note and read the message; her face turned white, and her mouth dropped open.

Rick Malloy had escaped and probably had returned to the West. The van had been found parked near the Brandenburg Gate crossover area. It had spots of blood inside and outside, and the bodies of the two prison guards had also been located in a ditch by the side of the road along the route the van was to take. The American spy who had been on a mission to find Nazi secret weapons was now a murderer as well. Gefahrlichsten, or "Most dangerous man alive" was his new designation, and he had become the highest priority of the Russians and the East German police. All agents were ordered to report immediately. And Anna Sturm had been called back in to assist in the manhunt.

October 6th started as a particularly quiet Sunday for the Allied Intelligence team in Berlin. Life had returned to normal for the team, who had been supporting the Allied espionage effort in the East. The agent, Rick Malloy, had been missing for almost two months, was known to have been captured and based on his capture, and having no further information on his situation, he had been presumed to have been tortured and was also presumed dead. The postmortem on the operation, held several weeks earlier, had determined that Rick Malloy really knew very little in the way of top secrets. In fact, it was amazing how little he really knew about the American atomic weapons program. As such, his interrogation would have two likely results: first, he was able tell his captors almost nothing, and second, they would undoubtedly push him further and likely destroy his mind in an effort to get at information that he simply did not have. Even assuming that he was not executed for espionage or treason (he was a former German national, after all) he was surely now in prison and likely to be so weakened and feeble that he could easily succumb to influenza, or some other disease. No, Rick Malloy was either dead now, or soon to be. The only outstanding point was why the East Germans and Russians had not used the incident for propaganda and made the execution publicly humiliating for the Allies.

It was against this backdrop that Captain Smith had finally given up hope and sought reassignment, feeling that he needed to get out of Berlin. He had lost interest in army intelligence and needed a change. Nonetheless, he was still a creature of habit, and so he spent his Sunday nights at the officers' club, as he had done for the year-plus that he had been assigned in Berlin. He and several friends had gathered for their weekly dinner at the officers' club when he heard the news. It was incredible news, and it was the best news Smith had gotten since hearing that the war had ended. The information had come from a reliable informer in the East who had friends high in the secret police organization. It was brief but definitive: "American operative, Malloy, yesterday, escaped from East German custody during a transfer and a manhunt for his capture has been organized." Reading a bit further, it said: "Two guards killed in the escape have resulted in 'shoot on sight' orders."

Captain Smith, usually not at a loss for words, was speechless. His dinner companions were curious as to what his take on the situation was. "I don't have clue what is going on, but I just knew this was not over. Now we need to help that poor bastard, before he really does get himself killed. Get Major Whitcombe up to speed and ask if I can meet with him ASAP!"

CHAPTER SIXTEEN

Rick Malloy had taken the trolley northeast from Mitte, the central section of Berlin, through Prenzlauer Berg to Weissensee, gotten off and hailed a taxi to take him back to the square a few blocks away from the house on Grunestrasse. He paid using the money he had removed from the guards' clothes and got out of the taxi carefully, looking around for anything suspicious. There was nothing to see, and rather than stand around looking conspicuous, he immediately began walking. It was a typical late-afternoon crowd milling around. There were people going nowhere and people in a hurry to get someplace, but no one who remotely resembled secret police.

He was nearly back to the house at 143 Grunestrasse where he had been caught nearly five weeks earlier. He had not come back to see the house or continue his mission, he told himself. He had decided earlier in the day, before his escape, that if he got away he would not be a hero, and since he had always been a bit skeptical that there even were any Nazi secrets, he had come to the conclusion that getting killed over this was a bad idea. No, he had come back to get his clothes, money, and personal effects, which he had left in the small canvas bag behind a fence in some bushes before he had walked into the trap. But he was having second thoughts. At the same time that he was traveling back into Berlin earlier in the day, he had also considered that finishing out the mission might give him some leverage, and depending on what he found, it might be useful for freeing his father. Rick was very conflicted about his current position, but as he had already cheated death once, he was not eager to jump back in.

Malloy continued down the street carefully, approaching the wall where he had stored his belongings. He slipped behind the wall and was pleased to see that his small travel bag was exactly where he had left it and appeared to not have been disturbed. The canvas bag had even kept his belongings from the weather over the past several weeks. He quickly gathered up the bag and continued down the street. He walked past 143 Grunestrasse and looked over at it as he continued by the house on the far side of the street. He could not help but wonder what, if anything, the address in the bank safe-deposit box might have meant. He found himself drawn to the house like some powerful magnet. It loomed as a very large and very real puzzle and it was not in his nature to put down a half-read book or walk away from a half finished puzzle. However, he also had never previously encountered so potentially dangerous a puzzle, either.

As he stood pondering his next actions, he began to realize and accept that if he was going to go in, that now was the time to do it, before the East Germans started looking for him. It had been nearly six hours since his escape, and so he was pretty sure that the secret police had figured out that he was missing by now, but he was also fairly confident that they had not figured out what happened, would not have gotten organized and certainly would not have started searching yet. And until they found the van and the guards' bodies, they would focus on the area between the work camp and the prison. If he was going to go into the house, now was the time to do it.

As he stood and sized up the situation, he yet again asked, "What would Captain Smith do?" He smiled, realizing that it had been a couple of months since he had had the opportunity to use that line of thinking. He was pretty sure that Smith would carry out the mission. No, he was positive about that. And as he thought about it, he realized that he could not just walk away from the house without satisfying at least his curiosity. Whether it coincided with his mission, a plan to secure the release of his father, or just a scientist's desire for the truth, he turned toward the house and walked up the steps, around to the back of the house, and toward the door. It was nearing dusk, but he looked carefully for footprints in the yard that might indicate that someone had been there recently. He found none. Although the door was locked, he was easily able to break in and gain entry into the house. And much to his reassurance, this time the house was empty.

Rick was not at all sure what he was looking for, but having had several weeks in the prison holding cell to think about what might have been important in that house, he had assumed that if the East Germans had found what was there, they probably would not have interrogated him as long as they had. Based on this thinking, he reasoned that it was most likely still there (of course, there was the possibility that they found the information/clue and it was useless or that there was no clue, but.... He did not focus on these possibilities). He also thought about the only lead he had, the address inside the engraved safe-deposit box. Working on the belief that there was something to be found, the engraving was clearly the clue, as the box itself had not been made or sold at this address, and so the engraving of the address had to have greater meaning. He had decided that the name and location of the engraving inside the box were probably not put in the rear corner of the box by accident, and that whatever he was looking for was probably located in the right rear portion of the basement of the house, roughly in the same place as in the box. It all still seemed like a long shot, but it was all he could come up with. Rick had thought about the name inside the box as well, and it was not lost on Rick Malloy that the company's name was Keller, meaning cellar or basement. Nothing else made any sense. And even if it was wrong, it was too obvious to ignore.

He found the stairs to the basement and descended to the bottom floor of the house. It was very dark, with light coming in only through small windows high in the walls that were just barely at ground level. He fumbled around as he moved toward the bottom of the stairs until his eyes adjusted and he got his bearings, and then began to look for the back part of the house. The boiler and electrical area were located in the back, and Rick wondered if that would be a good place to start. It was hard to see well, and he could not help thinking that this was a dangerous waste of time. But his imagination drove him on. He had to look at the rear back corner of the basement, and so he began searching for some something that would confirm that he was not on a colossal wild goose chase.

Agent Anna Sturm had arrived at secret police headquarters within a half hour of being told of the amazing and bold escape of the American, Rick Malloy. Already, the entire main station was at high alert and there was a buzz all around the place. She briefly met with her superiors and listened incredulously as she was informed about what had apparently happened on the routine transfer. Her prior lover, a man she was so sure she knew and was sure did not have the instinct for aggression, who was perceived to be so weakened from the drugs and probably no longer fully in control of his faculties--that man had overpowered and killed two trained guards, stolen the van, and left it near the Brandenburg Gate to return to the West side of Berlin.

"Are we sure that he has escaped into the West?" she asked.

"Nothing else would make any sense," a more junior officer responded.

"But we have no confirmation yet from any agents in the Allied zone that he has been recovered?" Anna pushed.

"No," was the terse response. "They appear to not even yet be aware that he has escaped. But it is early!"

"Then, until we know differently, we must consider that he has stayed in our country and that he is here for some reason, no doubt the unfinished business. I am as amazed as anyone of us that this man that we believed was so docile and one who would not take this effort seriously, has turned out to be a capable adversary and spy. But under the circumstances, I think we have to assume that these are the facts until we know for certain that this is not the case."

She spoke with conviction and commitment, but Anna Sturm was worried. She recognized that either she had misjudged Rick Malloy, or something had happened to him to turn him into a lethal opponent. She was sure she had not misjudged him, and so she was concerned about what could have turned him into a killer and determined spy. This was not some special training, not his latent nature, and not his commitment to the cause. He was not the type to have a "cause," and by all accounts he had had potential for only two weeks or less of training. And she felt sure, having known him for several months, that it was not in his nature. It was something else that had happened in the past two months and she needed to find out what that was. Whatever it was, maybe it could be used to recapture Malloy?

The US army intelligence office in Berlin had been largely shut down for the day by 6 p.m. and therefore had not gotten the message yet, but in London the brass were all buzzing about the news. Agents had reported by wireless that the Russians and East Germans were in a lather over the escape of the American, Rick Malloy. For the first few hours there was cautious optimism and some outright disbelief. It was an unconfirmed rumor and not considered reliable until two other informants reported similar stories, making the message clear. Somehow, some way, Rick Malloy was alive and had escaped. The first question became "Where is Malloy and what is he doing?" According to reports, he must have been free for nearly five hours, yet there was no information on his surfacing in the West, or any information on his whereabouts in the East. He had escaped and then disappeared. A messenger was dispatched to find, update, and re-engage Captain William Smith immediately.

MI-6 and US intelligence operatives were put on alert to find Malloy and assist in rescuing him in any way possible. There were no immediate orders for the reactivation of the cancelled project, but the implications were far-reaching. Major Whitcombe was contacted directly by London and he was issued orders to reinstate Captain Smith. Based on this, Whitcombe himself had issued orders for Smith and the original project team to report immediately in Berlin. The search for Nazi atomic plans just might be back on.

Still barely daylight, the shadows were cast by the light coming through the cellar half-windows. It was not much light, and it played tricks on Rick Malloy's eyes, but he had no good alternatives, and as his eyes adjusted he was able to slowly find his way around. He moved around in the basement, first near the stairs, then toward the far corner, the right rear lower portion of the house, the same location that the engraving had been in the safe-deposit box. There was a lot of old junk in the basement, nothing that looked even remotely relevant, but if he had to go through it and examine it all, it would take hours, and he felt sure that he did not have that luxury. Malloy worked his way along the back wall of the house, looking for the information, or at least some clues that would complete his quest. He wondered whether he was looking for a box of papers or a set of mechanical drawings or draft designs. He had no idea what to expect. Should he look for a safe or a trunk or a box or what? How would these papers be wrapped up? He assumed that the thing he was looking for was a group of scientific documents, but there again, he was not sure. He had also considered a couple of other alternatives, including the nagging possibility that there was nothing to be found at all.

As he approached the corner, he found no boxes or papers or bags or anything he could imagine was useful to his mission. He saw water pipes overhead and the furnace area with the coal-fired furnace and coal pit and the mechanical coal screw that fed the furnace, but not a clue at all on the floor anywhere. He was surprised to find so little in the area. It had been cleared out within a 5-6 foot area and this made him wonder about the possibility that the East Germans had already found the box or whatever was there. He was losing his optimism about the likelihood of finding anything useful when he saw some writing on the wall. It was a large paper label that spelled out the proper use of the coal filler chute and the amount of coal that the bin would hold during a refill. It was not directly relevant to the issues at hand, but it sparked a thought that Rick Malloy had not considered--maybe this was not the final clue or the destination which held Nazi secrets, but was just further instructions, some more directions to the scientific papers, and not the papers themselves. It seemed so obvious, but he had been focused on the house in Weissenssee being the end of his quest, not a stop along the way.

This spontaneous thought changed his perspective entirely. If what he was looking for was only another clue, the location of the clue inside the safe-deposit box, if it was indeed relevant, would indicate that the next clue would be located on the wall, not on the floor or near the wall. He had not really considered this possibility, deciding somewhat arbitrarily that he must be looking for documents that would be in boxes near the wall, but sitting on the floor—however, he had found no such boxes. With the thought that he was not looking for boxes or documents, but another clue or set of directions, the walls became relevant again. He changed on what and where his attention had been focused from the floor area to the walls. This was not easy either, as the light made the search nearly impossible. If he had time to go purchase a flashlight he would have a better chance, he thought, but he knew that his return to the house was risky enough, and he had no intention of spending a minute more here than required. He ran his hand along the back wall to the corner and started working his way slowly forward, looking high and low on the wall to find any clue or direction.

Exactly 4 feet out from the corner Malloy saw the small, bright red Reichs Eagle stenciled on the wall with a few small words painted on the stone foundation below it in blue paint. The lettering could not have been more than 2 by 3 inches in total. Had he not noticed the bright red eagle he would surely have missed the words, for the blue against the stone and cement wall foundation was very hard to see in the low light. The pit in his stomach moved to a lump in his throat. His pulse quickened as he stared at the wall. There was so little information, but what he saw held such enormous potential. There was no swastika, but the red eagle used by the Nazis made it seem possible that this was related to the information he was looking for.

He wondered aloud: "Is this really the clue at 143 Grunestrasse?" He wanted to think it was. This small discovery at least confirmed his thoughts about the safe-deposit box and started to soften his lingering doubts that he might be on a mission that was "much ado about nothing." Whether the end result was to be all it had been built up to be or not, he was clearly on the trail of something which had been purposely placed and it seemed likely that he was following a set of clues that had been laid out for someone to find and follow. The words were clear and legible, even if they did not immediately make a lot of sense. And even though they raised more questions than they answered, he memorized the two-line message, and then in what he thought was a stroke of brilliance, he smudged the words so that it would be very hard to read them and he scratched the red painted eagle off the wall with a coin from his pocket. If the East Germans had not already seen the words "Friedrich Anlauer," followed by a second line: "Weisskirche" on the wall already, Rick Malloy was now sure that they never would. He had no idea where or who Friedrich Anlauer was or what or where Weisskirche was, except that this word meant white chapel in German.

It was well after 6 p.m. by the time Rick Malloy went back upstairs and carefully left the house. Rick changed into different clothes from his bag and took the guards' clothes with him to dispose of somewhere else. He re-shut and locked the door he had pushed in to make sure that it would not appear that he had returned. He was confident that the East German police would show up sooner or later, so he left out of the back of the house and continued out of the rear.

Rick Malloy needed to find a place to hide, and he needed to plan his next move. It had been a very long day, and the wound on his leg was throbbing.

CHAPTER SEVENTEEN

In the center of Berlin it was early evening and Agent Anna Sturm, sitting in her office, was contemplating what to do first. She thought about the escape and the man she thought she knew and wondered what he would do next. She knew that Rick was an intelligent and educated man and assumed that he would not make stupid mistakes. But she also was very sure that he was not a trained master spy and that he might do something predictable. The first priority was to cover the obvious. The secret police sent teams of agents out to cover likely spots where he would show up, including the three primary crossover points to the West. He would likely not attempt to swim across the Spree river, either in the north part of the city or in Freidrichshain to the south, and so they would concentrate on the center section of the city where the river was not along the demarcation line.

The East Germans assigned men to the main train station, the Bank, and the house on Grunestrasse. And all contacts in the West were alerted to be on the lookout for Malloy surfacing in West Berlin as well. Her superiors thought it foolish to waste manpower on East Berlin locations, as they were sure that he certainly had returned to the West, but she reminded them that he had undoubtedly been in East Berlin on a mission and that mission was incomplete. Rick Malloy had been at each location for a reason, including the house on Grunestrasse, and he certainly did not accomplish whatever it was he went there for before he was apprehended.

Nearly two hours later, at 9 p.m., a report from the team at the house indicated that someone had entered and left the house. Based on the imprints left in dust powder that had been placed on the floor in the kitchen and hall areas several weeks earlier to monitor anyone coming in to or going from the house, they were sure it was Malloy. The shoe print found had a pattern that was consistent with the imprint made by a prison inmate's shoe. Most importantly, it was pretty clear that the person had come in, gone directly to the basement, returned upstairs, and left. He appeared to know what he was looking for and did not wander around upstairs in the house.

Anna Sturm was partially reassured by the simple and obvious trick of getting evidence with a light dusting of dark talcum powder. Not only did it show that it was Rick who had returned to the house, but it confirmed for her that he was the amateur she had thought he was. *Even a novice professional would have noted the use of talcum powder*, she thought. She was both angry not to have caught him there and curious about what he was looking for in the basement. They had searched the house thoroughly over a month ago when they first caught Malloy, but since they did not know what they were looking for, she knew that they did not stand much of a chance. And they surely did not search the basement with the care that the rest of the house received, her thinking continued. She was puzzled that Rick Malloy had not told them about the basement during questioning and that the drugs had not worked on him. An average person should have given up this information quickly. Even an expertly trained agent would have succumbed to the relentless questioning and drugs. But Rick Malloy did not. How could that be? After a few seconds, her mind came back to the task at hand: Malloy in that basement. What was he after down there, and did he find it? If not, what might he do next, and if so, what would his next moves be? She needed to get ahead of him.

Anna Sturm, East German secret police agent, called for a car to take her to the house on Grunestrasse to examine the basement herself. As she was leaving, she overhead one of her superiors, the captain who had previously been very vocal in declaring how positive he was that Malloy had crossed over into the West. This bureaucratic fool was now taking credit for discovery of Malloy's footprints in the abandoned mansion. She shook her head and continued on to the waiting car.

October in Berlin was not a time to sleep outside. The temperature could drop to nearly freezing at night and it was often windy and rainy. It could be done by an experienced person with adequate clothes and cover, but Rick had neither the experience nor the clothes. Staying outside had its own set of risks, but walking into an unknown place when all of East Berlin was searching for you was a sure way to get caught. Malloy needed a place to go and stay for a while, where he could blend in with the locals and plan his next move. He knew that trying to get a room at an inn immediately would not be safe, and every border guard and policeman would have his picture and be on the lookout for him. He needed a plan to confuse his enemies and buy himself some time to search for Weisskirche--or white chapel, wherever that might be--so he took a few minutes as he walked, to develop his next moves.

Tomorrow might be a better day to look for a place to stay. Tonight he would keep moving, try to keep warm, and hopefully give his pursuers a headache that would take days to get over. He had a plan to get them wondering about him and keep them off balance until he could get back his own balance. Captain Smith had told him to make sure that he controlled events, not let the enemy take control and then have to react to them. Make them play your game, never play theirs. He thought Smith would approve of his plans for the coming night.

In spite of the pain in his leg that throbbed incessantly, Rick walked several miles away from the big house on Grunestrasse, finally catching a tram back toward central East Berlin. He continued toward the west of the Main City center to a working-class community he had visited as a child. He selected a weinstube that looked about right-- not too upscale and not too dumpy--and began his plan to confuse the police, who would soon be searching for him. He took most of his clothes and his wallet and wrapped them in his canvas bag and went around the back of the Weinstube. He found a small area where they would be safe and hid them very carefully. He returned to the front door, entered, and picked out a table. He was very hungry by now, as he had not eaten since leaving prison early in the day. Having taken out of his bag just enough money to pay for dinner, he sat at his table and and ordered schnitzel and spaetzle, a typical meat and noodles meal, and a bottle of the local riesling, a white wine. It was a sweeter wine, not something he liked, but it was something a worker would have with his meal. He then sat back and watched patrons come and go as he ate and drank and drank some more.

Rick needed to eat slowly, as his stomach was not used to rich food--or any decent food, for that matter--and getting sick was not in his plan. He was getting comfortable, yet still a bit apprehensive. His clothes were working class, but a bit dirty. He would not stand out unless you were looking exactly for him. He had made no attempt to change his general appearance yet, so if the East German police were going to be looking for him, an exact description would be easy to match up. Actually, he was counting on it.

After several glasses of wine, he deliberately spilled his glass and fumbled a bit in trying to clean it up. The waitress rushed over to help, and Rick stammered out an obnoxious sexual advance and she took off in a hurry to get reinforcements. Rick acted quite a bit drunk, although he was not at all, and he fumbled in his pocket for money to pay his tab. The waitress returned with the bartender, a burly hulk of a man who was clearly in no mood to put up with some transient worker making rude advances to his staff. He was prepared for a fight, but Rick again acted meek and very drunk, unable or unwilling to protect himself. To ensure the outcome he wanted, Rick protested that it was the waitress who had, in fact, been coming on to him. He looked and sounded like a man very drunk with liquor, and the bartender had heard all he wanted to hear.

Before Rick could finish the story, the bartender grabbed him by the arm, pulled him up from the table, and dragged him to the door. He continued to drag Rick Malloy outside and Rick let him puff up his chest and demonstrate his physical prowess out through the front door. As the bartender pushed him into the alley next to the Weinstube, it was time for Malloy to end the charade and make sure the big man would remember him. Rick stood straight up, deftly took hold of the large bartender's hand, and bent it over backwards into an extremely painful position, just as he had been taught by the French Deuxième agents about two months ago. Then, with a swift chop of his free arm, with his fingers bent over at the knuckles, he hit the mid-torso of the man, right below the ribcage, knocking the air from his lungs and causing the bartender to fall to his knees, gasping for air. He had only meant to knock the wind out of the big guy, but he was acting on adrenaline and thought he might have broken a few of the man's ribs. The large bartender was now on his knees, holding his chest, and trying to gain his breath. Not the plan, but this guy would heal fast enough.

Rick then uttered in English, "Sorry about this," to make sure the bartender would not forget him, and finished the man off with a full-force kick to the groin which completely immobilized the bartender, now down on all fours. Although Rick really did not want to hurt the man, he needed to make sure that he called the police and reported the incident. Rick now moved quickly away and continued around to the back, gathering his things before he proceeded on to a different part of the city. In the morning he would have to find a place to change his looks, change his clothes, and find a secure place to hide out while he figured out what to do next. But first, he had one more step in his plan. If his estimates were correct, when he was done, he would be safe for at least a couple of days.

The call came in to police headquarters at 11 p.m. about a disturbance involving a man who resembled the missing prisoner. It was from a small restaurant in the southeast section of East Berlin. The secret police were already on full alert, and Anna Sturm was out at the house on Grunestrasse, searching the basement. The basement search had turned up nothing important after over an hour of going through every box and piece of old furniture. Not a clue.

An agent was dispatched immediately to tell her of the sighting of Malloy. She left the team at the house with clear instructions. "Find what it was that Malloy was looking for or keep looking until you do." Then she was out of the door in a huff with two of her henchmen to arrive at the scene of the Weinstube in the central part of the city.

The restaurant bartender had come back into the restaurant, doubled over and obviously shaken, and so the owner had sent a busboy to the local police. This had resulted in the normal response of a pair of officers coming to the scene to see what had happened and act accordingly. They suspected that this was no ordinary event based on the bartender's tale, and so they contacted the secret police headquarters. It had all taken less than three hours from the time Rick had left the bar until Anna Sturm arrived. When Anna arrived, there were nearly a dozen cars or motorcycles and twenty city and secret police in and around the building. She listened to the bartender tell the story of the intoxicated man who kicked him in the groin while being thrown out, listened to the description of this man, and finally she interrupted.

"If it is indeed the American we seek--and based on this description, I suspect it is--you may be lucky to be alive." She continued, "You say he was drunk?"

The bartender pointed out the waitress and she recounted the events leading up to the bartender getting involved. They showed her the bottle of wine nearly empty and where he had sat. They described his appearance, his clothes, and the way he spoke and acted. It was very curious to her, and while it seemed impossible of the Rick Malloy she knew, it seemed equally improbable that a trained American spy would be so obvious, not to mention drunk. It just did not add up, whether it was the Malloy she thought she knew or a trained American spy. Was Malloy so out of his element, or was he trying to deceive her? She was not at all sure what Rick was up to or even if he was fully in control of his faculties. He had been put through an interrogation that turned many people into sniveling idiots. And the last report on him was one of a weak and disoriented man leaving the prison only with the help of two guards. It was very troubling.

She stayed until after 1 a.m. at the wine bar listening to recounts of various patrons who had witnessed the incident, and the more she heard the less it made any sense. The man was apparently drunk, he had been dragged out of the restaurant by the bartender, who was twice his size and strength, yet the bartender returned to the restaurant essentially beaten up by this man. Of course, the bartender told a bit different story of a crazy drunk patron who got off a lucky shot, but either way, it was not logical that a bartender who had bounced a hundred different men out of the establishment in the past would get stopped cold by a smaller man who was drunk, unless he was only appearing to be a drunk. And although that did not sound like Rick Malloy, apparently it was.

It was late, and there was nothing more to learn at the Weinstube. Anna Sturm went back to headquarters. The incident at the restaurant raised many questions, and answered few, except that Rick Malloy was still in East Berlin and may or may not be fully in control of himself. At 2 a.m., asleep in her office, the attractive secret police officer was awakened by the men returning from the search of the house on Grunestrasse. They had knocked on her door and then entered to find her slumped over her wooden desk, hair disheveled and looking like she needed a real night's sleep. The search had indeed been thorough, and had produced twenty-seven items that might have been touched or used by Malloy in the basement. Fingerprints had been found on numerous objects, and it was possible to track his footsteps through the basement for the most part, or at least to determine where he had gone. Focus on the northwest corner had yielded nothing, and it appeared that he picked nothing up and removed nothing of any size (like a box). The only interesting points were his fingerprints on the label to the coal chute and again on the wall near a smudge of red and blue paint. It appeared that there had been words there at one time, but it was not possible to read anymore. The officers searching the basement felt that this was not what Malloy was seeking, and that if he found something, it was very small, and he had probably taken whatever it was he came for with him. Or it had not been there in the first place. Anna Sturm ordered the men back to the house to continue the search and to find out what the red and blue paint said, or meant, or where it came from.

"Find me answers, or you will find yourselves in a gulag in Siberia," she ordered. "We cannot allow this man to succeed. Do you understand?" The men nodded their heads in agreement and went out of the office.

The fifteen or so Berlin-based agents assigned to watch the various likely places for Malloy to show up had produced nothing and it seemed like this American was able to move about in East Berlin at will and able to taunt the East German police with impunity. It was angering senior officers and political types within East Germany and in Moscow, but, equally, it was driving Anna Sturm crazy.

East of the central Mitte section of Berlin, at a little after midnight, Rick Malloy walked up to the desk and checked into a small Gasthaus. He had picked it very carefully, hanging around outside at a distance watching to see that he had selected the correct place. He was making sure that the small inn had been visited by the police, and notified of a missing prison inmate, an American prison escapee. Again, Rick made no attempt to hide his appearance or identity. And again he had worn the same old clothes and hidden his other clothes to perpetuate the belief that he had nothing else in his possession. The proprietor examined the identification papers Rick gave him, one of the ones stolen from the guards, and he gave Rick the key to Room 12, upstairs, at the end of the hall.

Rick decided not to use one of the sets of papers provided by Captain Smith, as he might need these later, and the guards' papers had no photographs, so he could use theirs. As he checked in, Rick acted very weak, maybe a bit drunk or maybe a bit dull-witted, and definitely incoherent. His act surprised the innkeeper enough to make him pay close attention to this man as he checked him in. *On the other hand*, thought the innkeeper, *this guy is paying cash for the room, so what is the harm? There will be plenty of time to call the police later, after this guy has paid and gone to his room. I'm not confronting him; that's police business.*

So, he took the payment and handed Rick a key. After Rick had gone up the stairs and disappeared out of sight, the innkeeper had called out to his son, and told him to get the police and let them know that a strange man matching the description of the escaped prison fugitive had just checked in to a room.

It was after 3 a.m. when Anna Sturm was alerted that the local police had located the escaped American agent and that a raid on the inn where the American had checked in was planned for 5 a.m. She was elated but exhausted. And she was even more puzzled by the repeated and obvious actions of Rick Malloy. He was smarter than this, she had thought. But never mind; she would soon be able to question him herself and see if he was either not mentally sound, or merely the very poorly trained American agent she thought he was. He had shown no great competence in leaving behind a trail at the house on Grunestrasse, and it was becoming clear that he had fumbled badly at the restaurant. It seemed more and more likely that he had just been lucky and that his luck was about to run out. Again, Anna joined the team to go to the Gasthaus with the local police, and having had almost no sleep, she left the police station.

The team of nearly ten secret police and local police assembled in the small welcome area in the Gasthaus. According to the proprietor, no one had left or come downstairs since this man had checked in. After some quick questioning, Anna knew that it was Malloy who had checked in to the room. The layout of the rooms was reviewed, men were sent to the back of the inn and one was positioned on the roof. Other police were positioned outside, and an agent was sent into the building across the street and assigned to keep his rifle trained on the window of Room 12. There was no escape, and although there were no reports of the American using or threatening use of a firearm, they were not taking any chances.

Anna Sturm went up the stairs with two other secret police senior officers and they positioned themselves outside the door to Room 12, on either side. Then she knocked on the door loudly and called out in English, "Herr Rick Malloy, we have your room surrounded, and there is no possibility of escape. Please open the door slowly, exit with your hands up, and you will not be hurt." There was no answer, so she tried again, "Rick Malloy, if you resist arrest you will be shot. You are wanted in connection with the murder of two prison guards. You must give yourself up to remain alive." And yet Room 12 remained quiet.

After several minutes and some consultation, Anna stood back, and one of the large officers accompanying her kicked in the door and the team stormed into the room. It was chaotic in the dark, but no shots were fired, no one was injured, and when the lights were turned on in Room 12, it was empty. Rick Malloy was no longer in there. He had come and he had gone.

It was after 6 a.m., and Anna Sturm needed rest. She was now convinced that Malloy was not fully in control of his senses. He might even freeze to death out in the night cold, but he would not be a predictable man to track. This line of reasoning led the police to call off the search, and they ordered a regrouping of the team for the following day, in the afternoon. Since he was not acting like a trained agent, they were more likely to catch Malloy by accident than on purpose with some grand plan.

Rick Malloy had never intended to check in. He was pretty sure that the innkeeper would contact the police, and that they would arrive long before morning. He had paid for the room, pretending to be disoriented and to accidentally utter a word or two in English, gone up to his room, opened and shut the door, and then walked out the back door of the Gasthaus. Rick had thought about this plan for several hours and he now felt sure that the police had no idea where to look for him or how to get ahead of him. They would need some time to regroup and come up with another plan. He would have time to change his appearance dramatically and find a place to disappear for a while. He had thought about the East German police and hoped he was driving them crazy. And he had wondered if Anna Sturm was one of those pursuing him.

Malloy had walked down the street back toward central East Berlin, and after several miles he had gone into a large beer hall that was nearing closing time, and gone straight to the restroom. He picked this establishment because he knew it would be crowded and should have a large bathroom with more than one toilet. No one would notice or pay any attention to him. He went into a toilet stall, locked the door, and pulled out a small mirror and his scissors from his bag and proceeded to cut his hair short. A cheap haircut was in keeping with his new identity. It would be ugly for a few weeks, but it would completely change his appearance. He also pulled out the hair dye he had been carrying in his bag and went on to color his hair and eyebrows grey, a most unflattering color, but also far from the brown coloring they had been before. He used a razor to change his hairline yet again, a trick he had used before and that would now make him look much older. Finally, he plucked some of his eyebrows around the edges to create a thinner look. He changed out of the clothes he had been wearing and into a pair of much lighter-colored pants than the ones he had been in all day. He had only one coat and would have to wait to change this until the next day. When he was finished, he looked years older and nothing like the Rick Malloy the police were chasing. He looked like one of thousands of working-class men who roamed the streets of Berlin in search of work. Even Anna Sturm would have a hard time recognizing him now, Malloy thought. He slipped out of the back of the beer hall and walked off into the night. The Rick Malloy being sought by the East German police no longer existed.

Chapter Eighteen

Rick Malloy carefully walked the narrow back streets of the old Bohemian part of the city for the remainder of the night. It was easy to be inconspicuous in this part of the city until after 2 a.m. when bars closed and the drunks and stragglers got off the streets. Then he had to be careful until dawn, when people came back out onto the streets again. He was cautious not to go into obvious open places, and several times when a random car came by or someone walked nearby, he stepped in a doorway to hide his face, keep warm, and rest. Less than twelve hours earlier, he had been in the custody of the East German secret police, believed dead by his own Allied intelligence team in West Berlin, and had never come close to deliberately killing anyone. Until eighteen hours ago he had believed his father was dead. It was a whirlwind day that was coming to an end with Rick Malloy on the run in East Berlin, hiding in dark niches from people who would surely kill him on sight.

Fortunately, only once did a police officer walk down the street where he was, and Rick had crammed himself into an alley behind a drainpipe to keep out of sight. He had not been noticed. His hands and feet were numb and cold in the late-night air, and the side of his leg throbbed from the bullet wound, but this was not the time to focus on the pain. When it was daylight, he would join a group of old homeless men who hung out down along the river and he would try to blend in. That morning, after a tiring night of staying on the move, he hid his remaining money and his clothes in order to get some sleep in the late autumn sun without fear of being robbed by the men around him. He was fairly sure that the secret police would take some time to catch up with him now. And he needed the rest.

Later, in the afternoon of that day, Malloy awoke in the grass on the banks of the River Spree that ran through East Berlin. He was still very tired and it was not good sleep, but it was some needed rest and he felt much better than he had felt when he lay down at 8:00 that morning. His leg was sore and swollen and needed medical attention, but he knew he could not approach a doctor in the East, and he could not risk going into the West now. When he got a chance, he would wash and bandage the gunshot wound he got when he wrestled with the guard the day before, but he could do little more. It was time to think about what he would do next. He needed another plan, a plan to find Weisskirche. But most of all, he wanted to get his father out of prison.

Rick Malloy had had little time to think about anything in his prison cell. He had not been all that clear of mind up until the last few days. Then he became completely absorbed by his plan for escape and then sidetracked by the discovery of his father. Finding his father was wonderful--and yet, it was an overwhelming distraction to his mission and thinking about one was detrimental to the other. Having to escape and then kill two guards in the process was far from anything he had ever thought could happen, and he knew he was really not trained for this type of work. But his love for his father and his desire to stay alive had been a powerful motivator. And he had received some training, even if it was during a brief two-week period. So now he lay on the bank of the river, thought about his mission, the name Friedrich

Anlauer, and the clue called Weisskirche. He looked for meaning, both hidden and obvious. Was it so easy as looking for a white church? And if so, there were probably more than fifteen churches in Berlin that used the word Weisskirche in at least part of their name, and maybe another 30-35 that were literally just white churches. Rick wondered how many of those buildings had been destroyed during the war, and how that might change his search. On the other hand, it could be a code name that had significance to the Nazi SS, but to no one else. Or it could be something in between, a name of a place that was not a church at all, but commonly called Weisskirche. These were the obvious options, but there were undoubtedly others that he had not yet thought of. If he had to search every location it could take weeks and the chances of getting caught were higher, especially if the East German secret police found and could read the writing on the wall in the basement of Grunenstrasse. He hoped they had not.

He could surely use some help from London about now, he thought. But he knew that there had been concern about a leak in the intelligence unit in London. His experiences over the past several weeks had strengthened that belief. And unless the team had been left intact, whom would he contact? It had been several weeks since they had last heard from him, and if they had heard anything coming out of East Berlin, they probably knew that he was captured and believed he was dead or in prison. No, he would have to be very careful in depending on help from the West right now.

In West Berlin, and in London, the MI-6 and US army intelligence offices had become a flurry of activity. The mission that had been scrubbed six weeks earlier when Rick Malloy was captured was now alive again. Captain William Smith had been recalled and was already back at headquarters in West Berlin. He was meeting with Colonel Whitcombe and several trained field agents who had been assigned to monitor and give assistance if possible.

"Do we know the current status of the subject?" asked one of the senior agents.

Captain Smith, agitated by the tone of the agent's query, immediately spat back, "Dammit, his name is Rick Malloy, and he is one of our own, and you will...."

Smith was interrupted by Jimmy Whitcombe, senior officer at the meeting, who took charge. "Now, everyone, take it easy. We all want the same thing and we are all on the same side here. Smith, what is the recent intelligence on our most fortunate Mr. Malloy?"

Smith sat back a bit in his seat and looked down at the papers he had in front of him. "It seems a bit confusing, but what we have been able to confirm is that after interrogation and monitoring in the East Berlin secret police facility and then being sent to Hohenschonhausen prison for several weeks, Malloy was being transferred from that low security prison, that has mostly political prisoners, probably to the NKVD #7 maximum-security prison, which was called Sachsenhausen by the Nazis. During the transfer, he escaped and is currently at large in the East. How he escaped and where he has gone is not known, but one source indicates that two guards were killed during his escape."

Whitcombe's eyebrows went up. "A shackled, weak prisoner overpowers two armed and trained guards, kills them, and escapes without a trace? This does not sound like the relatively passive and untrained man we sent in, now does it? Could it be a trick?" He paused and then continued, "To get us to expose our network in the East?"

One of the intelligence agents who had been studying the intelligence reports and radio traffic coming out of East Berlin said, "It does not appear that this is the case. The Russians and East Germans appear to be genuinely trying to catch him and there are a lot of signs that they are very concerned about him."

Whitcombe interrupted, "What do you make of the fact that he has not come out into the West yet?" Major Whitcombe looked at

Captain Smith for the answer.

"I can only speculate, sir," Smith began. "He surely knows that the Russians are watching all crossing points and probably have orders to shoot on sight. Also, he is dedicated and understands what is at stake on his mission. It is just possible that he is intent on finishing it.

"And we have to consider that it is also possible that he is injured or not fully in control of his faculties and is not able to get out on his own," chimed in one of the new field agents.

"But we are just guessing," finished Smith.

"Then let's stop guessing and find out what the hell is going on in East Berlin!" bellowed Major Whitcombe. "I've been ordered by London to fully reactivate the team and this mission until we sort this thing out. All leaves are cancelled, and we are on 24- hour, round-the-clock alert. Clear?"

It was indeed perfectly clear, and Captain Smith had not felt this kind of energy in a long time. Malloy was alive, and the mission was back on.

Back on the riverbank in East Berlin, Rick Malloy was formulating his plan. He needed shelter and he needed information about Weisskirche. He thought he might find both in West Berlin, but he did not know whom he could trust, and he was worried that there was an insider in London. He also knew that while he could get no help in East Berlin, West Berlin was surrounded on all sides by the Russians and infiltrated throughout by East German secret police and informants, so it was not exactly friendly turf either. He would be shot dead just as quickly in the West if found as he would be in the East. He could not use any known safe houses in the West either, as the East might know about them and be on him before he could get any rest. Rick understood that he was alone in East Berlin and would have to stay there until it was time to leave Germany for good. But Malloy had been trained by some of the best, he was one of the brightest, and he had a powerful reason to see this mission through--his father.

He sat on the bank of the river as he thought up the right plan, the backup plans, and alternate scenarios based on things that might change or go wrong. He sat and thought, and watched people and the boats go by. If he could just come up with a way to safely contact Captain Smith and get some intelligence help without letting the East Germans know what he was doing, then he might be able to get out of this mess alive, and with his father as well. He just had to think like Smith and develop the right plan.

East German secret police HQ was also abuzz that afternoon. After having killed two trained guards who were taking him to a long-term prison, and having escaped, the American agent, Rick Malloy, had popped up three times in different places and given the impression that he was slightly insane and extremely dangerous. He had not left the East Berlin sector as most thought he would, and the last word from informants in the West was that he had made no contact with them either. It was very strange, and his actions defied attempts to predict his next moves. Orders had gone out to all of the nineteen crossing points into West Berlin and to agents operating in the West. Anna Sturm had personally overseen distribution of an old photo of Rick with a description and likely disguises to district police captains and border supervisors. All hotels, inns, and guesthouses in the city were being notified to report anyone new checking in. The American would not escape, and it would be much harder for him to hide. The East German Police had started reporting back to the Russian NKVD agents based in Berlin as a result of this American agent, Rick Malloy's escape. This was a development none of the East Germans liked, but was a result of their own perceived ineptitude. The report that the situation was under control fell on deaf ears, for the fact was that Malloy had made them look foolish, and he had still not been caught.

It did not take long for the Russians to act. The importance of the issue was even reported to have Stalin's personal attention and the failure to resolve it was dangerous to all involved. This led to the announcement that assistance would be arriving in Berlin, courtesy of the Russian government. Moscow was sending the assistant deputy of internal security of the Russian intelligence service, Igor Taimov himself. A ruthless communist and trusted adviser of Beria, Stalin's hand-picked head of the Russian secret police, the NKVD, he was a no-nonsense autocrat who thought little of the Germans, East or West, and loathed the Americans most of all. He had praised agent Anna Sturm in public, but privately he did not believe this was work for women. Taimov arrived with an entourage of Russian agents, storming into the secret police headquarters and announcing that he was now in charge. He took over part of the building for his men and immediately set about getting up to speed on actions to date. He made it clear that he would be making the decisions and authorizing all activities. He met with Anna and the other senior officers briefly, and then his team settled in to take command of the overall effort. He would use Anna Sturm and anyone else as was needed to get the job done, but that was all the courtesy he would extend to anyone.

After reviewing several briefs and the prepared material about Malloy, Taimov called a meeting and announced that they would be setting up several traps to lure and capture this inexperienced but lucky American agent. He refused to accept the possibility that Rick Malloy was a master spy, but rather he believed the American agent was in over his head and his luck was about to run out. He would reach out to their agents in Berlin and London who had been so valuable in the past in relaying US intelligence and MI-6 activities. The combination of inside information and an irresistible trap would secure the capture of this American. From now on, the ruthless Russian NKGV would be calling the shots and giving the orders. The East German secret police were no longer in charge of this operation.

Rick had now been lying by the river all day, developing plans and then playing them out in his head. His first order of business was contacting the West for help and letting them in on his plans. A major part of this was making sure that if there was a leak in the Allies' area, in Berlin or in London, that the East Germans did not get an understanding of his plans--or at least controlling what was leaked and using that to his benefit. And that meant confirming that there was a leak and understanding how to deal with it.

He had remembered that there were two US intelligence contact points in East Berlin provided to him by Smith, and he could remember the location for at least one of them. He was still a bit fuzzy and had forgotten the details of one completely, but was positive about the location of another. He did not trust any of them at this point, but knew that if he told one contact that he was sending the same message through several contacts to make sure it got through, he would be pretty sure that the message would be delivered intact. To do otherwise would risk the contact exposing themselves as a double agent. He had remembered the one contact only because the location was a place he had visited often as a child. Based on this memory he had come up with a plan to use the one known contact given to him by Captain Smith. He would deliver an emergency message that would specify a meeting time and location. Smith alone would understand and know the correct location, but he would need to give each and every member of the team a different location and time to isolate the leak...if there was one.

The contact was a dead drop contact, meaning that Malloy was to leave and pick up messages at a specified location, but would never see or meet the contact or speak with the contact in person. He carefully walked into the heart of the city and delivered his message late in the afternoon, and then he left the area. He had picked up his clothes and money and once again sought to change his appearance a little bit. He purchased a pair of cheap eyeglasses to further alter his look. He had purchased a worker's hat and a different coat to keep warm. He did not shave his face and his scruffy unshaven face after only two days also made him look very different from the Rick Malloy that the East German police would be seeking. And he bought some tincture of iodine at an apothecary for his leg. It was a common disinfectant that would hopefully stop any infection.

Having changed his appearance he needed to look for shelter for the night. He decided to seek shelter in a small residential area, 3-4 miles south of Mitte, the city center, near Rummelsburg, where he would be less conspicuous, and he started to look for a carriage house. After walking through several likely streets he found a garage that had been left open that appeared to have an attic. He watched for a couple of hours from a wooded area across the street and then carefully entered the building. He checked it out and found that the back of the garage area had a loft with a ladder and was only used for storage and probably not used on a daily basis. It would be perfect for a day or so; then he would have to move again to avoid being caught.

It was getting late in the night and Rick was hungry, but he knew that the police were surely on a manhunt and it would be safer tomorrow than it was right now. Besides, until he better understood this garage loft, its owner and use, he dared not do too much up in the attic for fear of being discovered. Oh, and he was exhausted. He needed rest more than food. He climbed the ladder up into the loft, sat down, and looked at his leg in the dim light of nearby streetlamps. It was swollen and infected, and it hurt. But he was lucky. The bullet had missed the bone and not severed a tendon, and it had passed through and exited his leg. He got out the tincture of iodine antiseptic he now had in his kit and poured some on the wound. It stung like he had stabbed himself with a knife, but he recalled that his father always used to say that the sting proved it was working. If so, it was really working. He bandaged the wound with some of the tattered clothes he had worn the prior day and he prepared for some rest. Rick was very pleased with himself as he lay down to sleep--after all, he had found a somewhat warmer, somewhat safer place to get some rest. He was sure Captain Smith would approve.

Early in the morning in Berlin, the US intelligence office was abuzz. Rumor had it that the escaped agent, Rick Malloy, had communicated with one of the East Berlin contacts. The message had been received through normal channels, delivered by a courier who passed through the various checkpoints on a daily basis. The message was marked as urgent and top priority, so it was delivered sealed and unopened to the ranking officer on site, Major James Whitcombe. After reading the message Whitcombe had summoned Captain Smith to his office. "Smith, I need you to read this. After all, it's addressed to you." He handed the note to Smith who read it to himself:

"To my old friend, Smith, Berlin (I hope)

Still on case, have some clues, but could use assistance. Fear you have a leak and I have a plan to address. Please let out news of your meeting me in the East in three days. Provide different location to each and watch for who shows up where. Then please meet me in four days at the Gasthaus zum Alpen, near the Brandenburg Gate at 5 p.m. Ask for Herr Schmidt at Bar if you do not see me. I will contact you if it looks clear. Otherwise, you should go back home." It was signed, "Your Cambridge friend."

"Well, Major, he appears to be back with a vengeance," said Smith.

Major Whitcombe was direct. "Is he nuts, or is he right? Is there a mole in our operation?"

Smith responded, "We have wondered about this for months, only due to how close the East Germans seem to have always been to our own actions. The only time they were not ahead of us was when Malloy was alone in the East. So, yes, I think there is a good chance we have a leak in our system, sir."

"Then, dammit, let's flush the bastard out and get this mission back on track. Smith, are you still up to going into the East? You do speak some German, I hope?"

"Yes, sir, I'll be just fine."

Captain Smith had a lot to do in the remaining three days. As a practical matter, he was marginally conversational in the German language--he did not speak German all that well. He was lucky that his experience in German bars had given him some confidence that he could go into a Gasthaus to meet Malloy. Fortunately, unless he was linked to Malloy, getting caught in the East would result in his just being taken back to the West, and at worst being traded for some East German the Allies had caught. So until he met up with Malloy, he was not in a lot of danger. After that--well, it wasn't worth dwelling on, and he had plenty to do. He had to leak phony information to about twelve different intelligence staff and agents who had been involved in the operation, and none could know that the others had the information, especially that each actually would have slightly different information.

He liked Malloy's plan, but he decided to modify it a bit to make it simpler. Rick's plan had the false meetings spread out over the two days prior to the actual meeting between Malloy and Smith on the third day. The captain's altered plan was going to do them all on the same day, so that there was less chance of staff learning what was going on and ruining the plan, and also providing an extra day to set things up and let the information leak back to the East. Each person who could possibly be the leak would have a different time or location and a set of separate agents would have to be brought in to see who showed up and where. He could not change the meeting with Malloy, but would have preferred to get a message back to Malloy telling him it was all set up and inform him of the changes. There would be some serious late nights coming up.

CHAPTER NINETEEN

OCTOBER, 1946

Rick Malloy slept in the garage attic. He had never been a heavy snorer, and his stay in the East German prison camp confirmed that on more than one occasion. Several times guards had opened his cell and poked him just to make sure he was alive because he was not making enough noise. Now he lay down on the attic floor and put his jacket up under his head for a pillow and to muffle any heavy breathing/snoring noise. And so he slept until early morning.

When Malloy awoke, he was more alert and a lot better rested, but now hungry and cold. He lay on the floor of the garage loft in the darkness as the sun started to come up and thought about the last few days and his mission. He had plenty of time to just lie there and think, as he knew that he would not be meeting Captain Smith for three more days and if things did not go well he would not meet at all. Reflecting on what had transpired over the past several days amazed even Rick.

Rick Malloy could not shake the feeling that Friedrich Anlauer and Weisskirche might not be just a person in a white church at all, but he knew that this was the obvious and logical starting point, and he could not ignore that fact. Searching for the name seemed less likely to bear fruit than searching for a location. He did not have the resources to trace a person in East Berlin and had no idea where to start. Rick wanted to send the information to London and give MI-6 a chance to figure it out, but he reasoned that if there was a mole and they got hold of this information, he would be handing the Russians his clues--too dangerous. So he would focus on looking for something called Weisskirche, "white church" or "white chapel." And as a practical matter, unless the East German police found the writing in the basement at Grunestrasse, they would not be searching for him in churches anyway—so it might be a safer place to start. Malloy devised a basic plan to systematically check the churches in the north of the city center. His logic was that Weisskirche was most likely to be in this area based on his assessment that the secret information had been transported from the north of the city to begin with, and also because he was less likely to run into the police in this area because he had not created any sightings of himself up there. This area was less industrial in its buildings and so had not received the pounding that central Berlin had during the war. Why not start in the most logical and easiest places until he could meet with Captain Smith and think of something better? He had a couple of days and might be able to get lucky and find something.

His idea was to speak with the priest at each church about the burials and memorials and any structural changes that had taken place during the war. He was not sure about the reference on the wall to "Friedrich Anlauer" above the word "Weisskirche," but he suspected it could be the name of the person who placed the information at Weisskirche--or a priest, or Nazi, or scientist, or a prior owner of the house on Grunestrasse. The name meant nothing to him, but it surely meant something to someone. Whoever knew what the name meant might well understand the mission, and that could be dangerous. This name was one of many things about which he just did not know what to do. For his visit to each church, his cover story was that he was looking for his father, and fearing that his father had died, he would ask the priest to look through the records for funerals or burials made at the very end of the war. He would lie convincingly and mention that in his last letter, postmarked from Berlin, his father had mentioned "Weisskirche."

About 10 a.m., Rick got going and carefully exited the garage, making sure that no one noticed his departure. He bought some lunch at a food stand along the river and set out in the early afternoon. He moved carefully on foot to the north of the city center as planned and randomly selected a first church to start. He found this first white church, and after some awkward introductions, he met with the priest. The meeting went pretty well for his first attempt, and his story seemed credible enough, and so his conversation with the priest was very productive. He learned what he needed within a half hour. Based on what he heard, he felt sure this was not the right place. He was not sure what to ask at first, and the conversation had been a bit awkward at times. He did, however, pick up detail about the church's history, which was useful and would allow him to be even more convincing at the next church.

Rick had not been a very religious person after moving with his mother to America, and his believing for years that his father had been murdered had reinforced the lack of need for structured religion. With his background, he knew little about the ceremonies that took place in churches, the difference between different types of churches, and so on. And church history, which governed much of the ceremonies and differences between denominations were a complete enigma to him.

The priest had gladly pointed Rick to the nearest next white church, and he moved on. This first church had been taken out of commission early in the war for political reasons--it had served a largely Polish congregation. And although it had been used as a hospital late in the war, this building was only slightly damaged and had only recently been reinstated as an active church. Although a white church, it was unlikely that this was the Weisskirche he was looking for.

Rick moved on several blocks to the church recommended by the first priest and met the church steward, because this church's priest was away, and he repeated his request. This was a smaller city building that had been clearly damaged during the war but had already begun being restored. It was flanked by other buildings on both sides, and the courtyards in front and out back were small. Rick surveyed the property before entering the building to understand as much as he could before encountering the steward. He could see that this particular church had no burial capability and no land for a cemetery. It did not seem old enough to have a crypt below the building, but he would find this out quickly enough. He wondered if this would affect the credibility of his cover story about looking for his father's grave. This was going to be a quick stop that did not fit what he thought he was looking for, and so Rick listened, thanked the steward, and moved on. He was directed toward another white church and left.

He visited six churches the remainder of the first day, taking about thirty minutes on average at each to get from one church to the next, and about forty-five minutes waiting or talking with church officials to see if they would be able to help him. He asked about things related to the search for his father, but he also asked about what happeneed to the church during the war, and especially at the end of the war. He really needed to see if there was anything unusual that might make this church the one he was looking for. None of these churches was a likely potential, for one reason or another. One had been closed and ransacked early in the war, and three were still so badly damaged by the bombings in late 1944 and early 1945 that it did not seem reasonable that in the last days of April 1945 that anything would have been hidden there. Besides, most of the area in and around these churches had been excavated to some extent since the war as a start toward rebuilding. Not much was left to uncover. A couple had lost or destroyed records, so they were not helpful relative to his purported reason for being there--that being his search to find his father. This was a minor complication, as it could have ended the conversation prematurely, but Rick Malloy had refined his story and was able to keep the dialogue going long enough to learn about the church's fate during the last days of the war. One priest told him that he was the fifth person that year that had approached his church in search of their family members. Rick had been pleased that he had been able to be so convincing, but he was disappointed that he had not gotten lucky to find the right Weisskirche.

At the end of each conversation, he had asked for a recommendation for the next white church, and each had been able to easily direct him to another white church within several blocks or a half-mile. Based on the estimates of the priests he had spoken with, there could be as many as sixty buildings in the East Berlin area that would need to be visited, and nearly as many more in the West Berlin area, a thought he had not even contemplated. Rick started thinking that this could take days or maybe even weeks, time he probably did not have. An army of East German police could cover the territory in hours, but one American on the run and being sought by authorities might never find what he was looking for. And that reminded him that he did not know exactly what he was looking for. He had reasoned that the church would need to have been viable at the end of the war and hoped that he would "know it when he saw it." He had decided to hold back on the Freidrich Anlauer part of the clue, in part because he assumed it would not be relevant until he found Weisskirche, and in part because he was not sure what it meant and it may confuse his cover story. And he was the only person who had this clue—it might be best to keep it that way for now.

He was getting hungry and tired. His leg hurt, and he was not at all sure that the clues he was tracking down were relevant. He was even much less sure that he would find any secret atomic bomb plans, even if he found the mysterious Weisskirche. Malloy bought some food at an open-air market as they were closing and headed back into the

Bohemian part of the city. As it became dark, he became more invisible and he could move around with less fear of being stopped and questioned. At this point the only things he had in common with the Malloy the East Germans were seeking was being male and the right height. His beard had grown in a bit and his hairline had been shaved back. His hair was short and a different color. Anna herself would not recognize him, he thought. "Anna," he said under his breath. It still hurt him. She had seemed so perfect. He had come to believe he loved her, only to find that she was using him and that he had been assigned to her as her job. He wondered if she had ever cared. He knew that Anna Sturm had lied to him, hunted him down, trapped him, and sent him to torturous interrogation and at least life in prison, if not worse. And no doubt she was hunting for him right now and her East German secret police would shoot him on sight if they found him. No, he had no illusions that she would have a change of heart and come back to him; he just was having trouble reconciling the Anna in Cambridge with the Anna in East Berlin. He kept walking and thinking, and he kept an eye out for anyone looking at him or following him.

Malloy returned to the garage attic again that evening after dark. He had not yet seen anyone entering or leaving the adjacent home, but had seen a light on inside the house the prior night. He would need to be on the lookout for the owner and to see the number of people who lived in the house and what were their ages, so he would know what he might be up against. He needed to understand whether they were likely to come up into the attic and who might confront him if they did. Malloy sat on the floor up in this garage attic and ate his bread and cheese and wondered what was happening in the outside world. He had not seen or spoken English in over a month and not spoken to a friend in just as long.

At about 8 p.m., a car pulled up in front of the house and two people got out. It looked like a beat up pre-war DKW car, the type that common people aspired to own in the late 1930s--not a wealthy person or government car, but someone well off enough to own a car at all. Rick remembered that the name DKW came from the German words for steam-powered vehicle, "Dampf KraftWagen," which he had always found an interesting choice for a modern car company. Rick noted that the two passengers were a middle-aged driver and an elderly man that appeared to be in his late 60s or early 70s. The driver got out and helped the older man to the door of the house attached to the garage.

From the angle of view that Rick had he could not see them actually enter the house, but he could hear some of their words. The driver acted in a way that led Rick to conclude that he was the son, and it appeared that they had spent the day away from the house and were returning. After a few words at the door, the older man went inside and the driver returned to his car and drove away. Rick Malloy seemed very relieved to see that the person who was in the house would not be a threat to him and probably was not much of a threat to come up into the garage loft area at all. Further, knowing that there was no car in the garage and they had come home in another car, he felt he could assume that they did not park a car here and would have no real reason to come into the garage, much less the attic above it. Rick thought, *Maybe I can stay here a few nights longer.* Rick Malloy lay back on the loft floor and tried to get some sleep.

The night was still young, and there was a flurry of activity for the East German secret police. Igor Taimov, the Russian who had taken over the operation, had settled in as head of the manhunt for the American agent and he was already showing his true character when all efforts had shown virtually no progress after thirty-six hours of searching. Over forty potential leads had been tracked down, and none had been accurate. Some were sightings that had been false, and many had been tips that Rick Malloy had been to this place or that place that needed to be checked out. None could be confirmed, and he was nowhere to be found. A police artist had taken Malloy's picture and drawn several variations in hair color, hairline, and beard, but they were confusing and would not make it easier to find Malloy. What they did do was to create a large number of false identifications. This frustrated Taimov, who knew that in East Berlin, part of a city of nearly two million people and spread out over fifty square miles, it would take dumb luck or Malloy's stupidity to arrest the American agent.

Igor Taimov called in the senior East German secret police agents, including Anna Sturm, and he berated them for their incompetence and simple-minded thinking. He walked them through each of the nearly forty reports, noting how each one had been false or inconclusive and how much effort had been exerted on short notice to investigate. He made it clear that in his opinion this could go on forever and never find Malloy, the American. But if a trap could be set, a compelling trap that Rick Malloy could not resist, then they could prepare for and capture the American agent. Based on his assessment of the situation, that compelling trap could be set only by someone Malloy cared for deeply. And based on his review of the files, that meant Anna Sturm. Anna was repulsed by the idea and annoyed by Taimov's obvious use of her as a decoy. She did not object to being the one to lure Rick Malloy out and capture him--in fact, she believed all along that she was the only one who knew him well enough to catch him. But she loathed the Russian and his ordering her to do it. She recognized that if successful, he would take all the credit, and if unsuccessful, she would be the scapegoat. But she had made her choices and she was a professional who would do as ordered by her superiors. And all of her superiors were scared to death of Igor Taimov. She knew that she would help set the trap.

In West Berlin, Allied intelligence was also hard at work. Captain Smith had begun to execute the plan to let it leak that he would be meeting with Rick Malloy in two days. Actually, he would not meet until the third day, but this was the plan suggested by Rick to flush out any potential leak. He had used two other members of the staff whom he trusted with his life to spread the message, and they had carefully crafted a different place or a different time for each person who had any potential to be a leak. The message had been delivered casually to these individuals in a way that sounded more like an unimportant statement rather than a security breach. The info was non-technical, but adequately specific in location and time. One identified agent was told that there was a plan for Malloy to be met at the Ostbahnhof (east train station) at about dinnertime. Another staff member was told that the meet was at a different location at noon. Yet another heard that there may be an attempt to get Malloy out of the East by meeting near the Brandenburg gate in late afternoon, and so on it went. In all, eleven locations or times were given out to specific individuals and each told immediately afterwards that they had been told in error and not to mention this to anyone lest they all get in trouble.

By 8 p.m., the plan had been set in motion. The next step was to see if the East Germans would fall for it, and if so, who would it point to. There were a few new members of the team that could not have leaked information previously, so they had been excluded, but all possible team members were on the list. Captain Smith had been reluctant to include the ranking US army general in Berlin or Major Whitcombe in the plan, but then realized that this was a one-shot deal, so he included them as well. Besides, General Grimes, back in England, had repeated his order to find the mole if there was one. He ordered him to ferret out the leak at all costs, so Smith assumed that he should not be constrained by rank. So even Major General Irwin Johnston had been given the wrong info, and he was also set up and tested just like everyone else close to the team.

The message arrived on Taimov's desk at 11 a.m. the following morning. Malloy would be met at 4 p.m. tomorrow at a Gasthaus near the Ostbahnhof, the main train station in East Berlin. The transmission had been verified and it had come from the informant in Berlin who had been so accurate in the past. There was no cause to question whether it was accurate this time, but Taimov was a cautious man. He had sought verification and asked how sure the agent was of this information. The answer had come back that it was to be considered "A" quality, priority "1," referring to the source who had given the information to the informant and the manner in which the information was obtained. It was accurate and was believed very real by the agent. Now Igor Taimov felt he had the information he needed to end this nonsense and show the East Germans how to apprehend a criminal like the American Malloy. He would show these incompetent East Germans some Russian effectiveness and in the process reinforce that East Berlin was just another outpost of the Soviet world, not the center. Orders for this mission came from Moscow now. Igor Taimov developed the plan and prepared for informing his team of agents and secret police. This American, Rick Malloy, was his now.

CHAPTER TWENTY

OCTOBER, 1946

Over the next few days, while Malloy was waiting for Captain Smith to show up, he kept searching for Weisskirche, the white church. He had visited ten churches the second day and about as many on the third. This would make twenty-six in total so far, and based on his estimates, he then would have visited nearly all the obvious potential churches in the East Berlin city area that he could identify. There were a few more he would cover the fourth day, the day after he would meet with Smith, but already he was not hopeful. By his estimates, he had found no clues and felt no encouragement. He had seen small and large churches, ones in perfect condition and those bombed into rubble. He had visited big active parishes and small dormant ones, and about everything in between. Through his meetings with priests and ministers, he had identified most if not all the churches in East Berlin with the name Weisskirche and several that were just churches painted white. And he looked into a location where he had been told that there had once been a church, but it was long gone and there was no sign of anything remotely useful there, either. He was having his doubts about the message on the wall at the house at Grunestrasse. Was it intended for some other purpose? Was it a hoax? Was he interpreting it erroneously? Who or what was Friedrich Anlauer, and how was this related to Weisskirche? These thoughts kept running through his head and he just could not stop them.

It was the end of the day, and Malloy was returning from the northern part of the city to his garage attic in the residential neighborhood to the south that he had used for the last four days. He was passing near the Ostbahnhof, which was only a block away. His mind was preoccupied and he was daydreaming a bit, not paying as much attention to his surroundings as he should have been. He knew this area well from his youth; he knew where he was going, and so he was on auto-pilot, just moving forward to get to the next destination. He did not notice that the streets were a bit empty in the direction of the station, and that there were a lot fewer people wandering around at this time of day than there normally would have been. He should have seen that something was not right. At that time of day, the streets should have been crowded with workers heading home, but they were not. There was some activity, but it was lighter than usual and people walking seemed very deliberate, almost cautious.

As Rick continued to approach the station, he started to focus on his surroundings, and he too began to see that something was not as it should be. It started to worry him that this could have been the case for several minutes. At first, he wondered if he was being followed, but he concluded that this was not the case. He was not in a hurry, so he slowed his pace and then decided to stop and get a handle on what seemed different. He stepped into a doorway and stood in the shadows to be able to watch the area without being conspicuous about it. His instincts had told him there was danger, but it was very subtle, not at all obvious. He looked carefully up and down the street and began to realize that there were several other men standing around and they were all dressed in a similar fashion. As he looked at these men, he began to realize that these were most likely East German secret police, and they seemed to be waiting or on the lookout for something. Could it really be Rick Malloy they sought? Had he wandered into their clever trap by accident? How could they have known he was coming, when he did not know himself?

His mind began to race, and his heart pounded, but he stayed put and observed what was going on. From his position he was largely out of sight and he hunched over a bit to make it look more like he had been there for a long time and was not going anywhere soon. He watched the men to determine what they we up to, but it was not clear. The men seemed to be occasionally looking in the same direction, and based on their attention, Rick concluded that the object of their interest was a Gasthaus down the street, near the Ostbahnhof. *This is not good*, he thought. Even if they were not looking for him, this was a bad place to be, and he needed to get out of there as soon as he could. But he had wandered into the area, and continuing on or turning back would be very conspicuous at this point. He surveyed the doorway he was in and found that the door behind him was locked and there were several doorbells--to apartments upstairs, no doubt. He thought about ringing the doorbells, but that had its risks as well. He would wait.

He would have to stay put and hope not to draw any attention to himself. He looked down the street to try and see if there was anything else he should be aware of. He could see people moving around, but he focused on those who were seemingly staying in the same place or moving to keep from being obvious, but not really going anywhere. It took a few minutes to identify about eight individuals who were apparently waiting to see who went into or came out of the Gasthaus near the Ostbahnhof. As he scoped out each of the people to gain any insight he could, his eyes focused on two people who were also standing in a doorway about 200 yards further down the street. They seemed intent on watching the entrance to the Gasthaus as well. It was a man in a trench coat, or possibly a military-type winter coat, and a woman who seemed professional. The man seemed to be in charge.

As Rick stared at these two people, something seemed familiar. Rick looked hard at them and believed that he knew one of the people and as he realized what he was seeing, his heart leapt up into his throat.

"It's Anna," he blurted out to no one around him. "Oh, my God, it's Anna." And in seeing her standing with this other man who also had the demeanor and dress of an officer, he realized it was indeed Rick Malloy they were after. He had stupidly walked right into his own trap.

The Russian, Taimov, was no fool. He had planned to have every angle covered in apprehending the American agent, Rick Malloy. He established plainclothes agents at several locations around the Gasthaus where the meeting would take place, in addition to planting people in the Gasthaus building itself. He assigned Anna Sturm to a location across from the Gasthaus to identify Malloy and alert other agents and police to move in. He would himself accompany her, for if successful he wanted to be right there on site for the capture and make sure he took the credit. And if it did not work out as planned, he wanted the young East German female agent front and center to take blame for the failure. He would either get Malloy or get a scapegoat.

It was nearly 4 p.m., and Taimov had his dozen or so agents in place for the arrest. He wanted badly to make an example of this American, and this was the only reason he had not issued shoot on sight orders to the agents and officers. He wanted a public arrest and he would then use this occasion to rub the East Germans' noses in their own incompetence. He would show them Russian superiority.

But something seemed wrong. Malloy should have arrived by now and had not shown up in the Gasthaus. And it was close to 4 p.m. and there seemed to be no American agent coming to meet Malloy in sight. If the American agent who had been reported to be coming to meet this Rick Malloy was going to be on time, he should be coming at any moment. Taimov was getting anxious and he was not the type to sit around and be patient. But he would have to wait a bit longer.

Back in West Berlin intelligence headquarters, Captain Smith was alerted by a message from MI-6, whose informant had found out that the East German police had been made aware of a meeting and had taken the bait. Rick Malloy's plan to identify the mole was working. But as information came in about the time and location that the East German police had for the meeting, he was shocked at the implication this had regarding the apparent source of the leak. He had no reason to suspect any one of the staff or officers that had been given the information, and he had hoped the source would prove to be elsewhere. But the source of the leak, based on the information he had distributed, shocked even Smith. All of these people were career army and they were all American-born, with no known connection to East Germany. It just made no sense. He had believed that none of the people in the US Army could be traitors, and he was at a loss to explain why or how the meeting information had been leaked to the East Germans. It not only made no sense, he now wondered how to approach and arrest one of the most senior US army officers in West Berlin. But facts were facts, and so he called for two MPs and waited for them to arrive. Then he asked that the building be sealed and no one be allowed to leave until they got to the bottom of the leak.

"US Army Major General Irwin Johnston? Could it really be a two-star general?" Smith thought out loud.

Smith and the two military police walked upstairs to the general's office and after explaining to the general's assistant out front that the general could indeed be interrupted, they went into the general's office. Smith was not sure how to approach the situation and decided to just lay out what his plan had been and then explain what had happened. This was not how he would have normally handled things, but then it was a decorated general he was arresting, after all. If true, this would be headlines around the globe, so he decided to be a bit more cautious than he might otherwise have been. He would measure the general's reaction and then sort out where it went from there. He explained to General Johnston that the MPs were standard procedure during a "sting" operation, and although the general was not buying it, he told Smith to sit down and explain what was going on. Captain Smith remained standing, but proceeded to walk the general through the entire operation from the time they had reactivated the group based on finding that Rick Malloy was still alive and had escaped the East German police. He described the attempt to catch an informant who appeared to be sending information to the East Germans from inside Allied army intelligence headquarters, most likely from this building in Berlin. Then Smith explained the process of having multiple times and locations and that based on this information, that the only person alive who had been given the meeting time and place of 4 p.m. at the Gasthaus next to the Ostbahnhof was General Johnston himself. The note was given to the general and he was later told to destroy it and forget about the accidental mention. And then Smith sat down and watched for the general's reaction.

The general was clearly shaken. He was surprised, thought Smith; he either had done something inadvertently, or he did not think he would be caught. Captain Smith was not sure yet.

General Johnston cleared his throat and said, "So, I take it that I must be the informant? I must be the mole?" Smith nodded in agreement. The general leaned back in his chair and took a deep breath. He took a full ten seconds before he responded. "London did tell you to find the mole, didn't they? Well, most interesting. I cannot explain how this has happened, but I can tell you that I did not contact anyone or divulge the information you provided me to anyone. However, I think I understand your predicament, and I think until this gets cleared up you'll have to place me under arrest, to give integrity to the process." He leaned forward and looked straight into Captain Smith's eyes and he seemed to genuinely be asking for help. "You will not eliminate the mole by locking me up, but you may be able to find the person better if they think they are in the clear. I will do anything asked of me to clear my name, but I strongly suggest that you not assume just yet that I am the leak."

With that, the general stood up and presented himself to the MPs for arrest. This was not what Captain Smith expected, and based on what he had seen, he believed the general. Something was wrong, just plain wrong. But if the general had not been the source of the leak, who had been, and how? Smith thought immediately of the administrative assistant to the general who sat out front of his office and who was often privy to the same information the general saw. Smith had not thought to check out the assistant--it just had not occurred to him to spend a lot of effort on the general or his staff. Clearly, he had been wrong. Since he had specifically instructed the general not to show the note to anyone and then to destroy it, he could not figure out how anyone else but the general could get the information to pass on to the enemy. It was puzzling, but in believing the general was sincere, he felt an obligation to try to sort this out. He turned and asked the MPs if he could speak with general alone for a few minutes. The MPs protested for a second, then realizing that there was no other way out of the office and asking the general and Captain Smith to relinquish their weapons, they indicated that they would stand outside the door.

The door shut, and Smith turned to the general. "Who else has access to your office, General?"

The general was hesitant, which did not make Smith feel better about his answer. "No one should be in my office except official staff," he replied.

Smith probed a bit more. "General, you were delivered a note from me with the place and time of the meeting written on it. Did you destroy that note?" The reply that the general did burn the paper as was procedure did not help the situation. "General, I want to believe that you are not the mole, but there is a mole and they used information that only you and I possessed, so something does not add up. Let's walk through your every move from the second you received the note to the time you destroyed it."

The general and Smith sat down and the general started to walk through the minutes that passed between receiving and destroying the note. The general had committed the place and time of the meeting to memory and slipped the note under the blotter on his desk to put it out of sight. His phone had rung, and as he needed two hands to burn the note, he hid the note until he could destroy it. There had been less than thirty minutes in between his receiving the note and his destroying it. During that time, he had taken the phone call but had no visitors to the office, and the note had not been visible and no one could have seen it or known it was there but the general himself. Smith started to question him about who else was in or around his office when he received the information about the meeting, but the general interrupted him.

"I also recall going to the bathroom during that period, which I remember because it was not my usual schedule--it was a bit earlier than my usual time to visit the facilities.

Smith chuckled to himself, thinking that the general was a real creature of habit. "Why were you earlier than usual?"

"Well, the coffee was good and my assistant kept bringing me a fresh cup, and...." The general's eyes lit up as he stopped in mid-sentence. Smith could also see what the general had realized. "Damn," the general continued. "Robert kept bringing me coffee, and he would know my habits better than anyone. He would know that I kept important papers under my blotter, and he would have had access while I was in the bathroom. Damn, and I like that boy."

The assistant had had access and opportunity, thought Smith, but what was his motive?

Two hours later the assistant, Robert, had been arrested and after very little questioning, had confessed to passing information to the East Germans. He was American-born, a requirement in the intelligence service for this sensitive work, but he had married a German girl right after the end of the war, while stationed in Berlin, only last year. And the East German police had wasted no time in using this as leverage. He had provided them occasional information in exchange for better treatment of his aging mother-in-law, who lived in a small town east of Berlin. It was not an uncommon situation in these times, and one that Allied intelligence worked hard to screen against. But this one had gotten through, and it had cost the mission dearly. The assistant had not had access to all of the mission's information, but had access to enough information to give the East Germans a good fix on American plans and to be one step ahead.

Captain Smith was relieved that the general was not the source of the leak and also that the general was complimentary of how he had handled the situation. It could have been a disaster, but instead had turned out fairly well. And to top it off, they had apprehended the mole in the organization. That is, unless there were other informants still out there. Captain Smith did not want to even think about that possibility. It had been a long day, and now Smith could start to relax a bit. He wondered what Rick Malloy was doing about now.

Rick Malloy had been lucky to see Anna Sturm before she had seen him, and he knew it. Had he walked another 200 yards he would have walked right by her. He wondered if she would have recognized him instantly, or would it take a few seconds? He felt somewhat comfortable that the other agents would not recognize him with his rough beard and his hair cut and dyed as it was and deliberately hunching over to look about three inches shorter than the person they were looking for. But he had no comfort that he could fool his ex-lover, Anna. She would notice his walk, his mannerisms, and his look. If she had seen him first, he knew that he would have been apprehended. Rick started to formulate his way out of this mess. The obvious retreat was to go through the door behind him, but it was locked and breaking in would alert the secret police to look in his direction and investigate. He wanted to head away from Anna Sturm and the Gasthaus, and that meant going back in the direction he had come from. He did not know what had changed and who might be waiting in that direction, and worried that he would be trapped. So he decided that he would wait and see, and so he turned back to watching Anna.

Nothing much happened, and it was driving Rick crazy. The East Germans and Russians stayed put and only occasionally moved about, likely to be somewhat less conspicuous. Anna Sturm and the man next to her appeared increasingly agitated. It was nearly 4:15 p.m. and Rick had been standing over twenty-five minutes, way too long. A few civilians walked down the street past the Gasthaus, and anyone even close to looking like an American was closely scrutinized and in some cases followed and stopped. After nearly ten more minutes of standing, Rick was getting concerned. He studied the street leading away from Anna and the Gasthaus and saw that there was only one agent to walk past to get to the end of the block and round the corner, out of sight. Of course, that assumed that there were no more agents around the corner. As Rick was sizing up the situation, he saw one of the men point in his direction and motion the nearest officer to investigate. The other officer shrugged, but started moving slowly in Rick's direction. He was about 150 yards away, but would be next to Rick in about a minute at current speed. Rick's hand was forced, and he had to act now.

He turned and faced the doorway and began ringing the doorbells, all of them. Nothing happened. Returning to look at the approaching agent, he saw that the agent had closed about half of the distance, and time was running out. Rick's brain was full of thoughts about being captured, having to fight with this agent, the potential torture he would be put through if captured, possibly dying, and he thought of his father and of Anna Sturm. It was enough to give a normal person a headache, but this was not the time for that. Rick turned back to the door, and pushed, but it would not budge. He again pressed the door-bells repeatedly. Nothing. He turned and saw the agent only about 100 feet back. Time was all but gone. Rick started preparing himself to greet the agent and then attack him. Rick had no weapon but his hands, but he would likely have the element of surprise if he played it right. Suddenly, the door behind him opened and a middle-aged man stuck his head out complaining that whoever was ringing the doorbell better stop it.

Rick spun around and grabbed the man by the lapels of his coat, pushed him back into the entry hall, and shut the door behind him. The man began to protest, and Rick slapped his face and put his hand over the man's mouth. He told him to be quiet. The man was startled, but he had no idea what was happening. And so he did not keep quiet. He started to yell, and this made Rick jump into action. He was already under stress and not in the mood for explaining to this building tenant. He turned the man around, put his arm around his neck, and told him that if he did not shut up he would break his neck. The man squirmed and Rick applied more pressure. The man stopped squirming and got quiet, but Rick did not let up, and after a few more seconds the man went limp and Rick let him slump to the floor. He was not dead, but he had passed out.

About the same time, Rick Malloy heard the agent outside reach the door. The agent tried the door handle, which was locked, and then called for the door to be opened. He demanded that the door be opened, and then as Rick had done just minutes earlier, he started pressing all the door buzzers. Rick's first reaction was to run. He was sure that there was a rear entry into an alley that he could use to es-cape. But in the instant he had to think about it, he also realized that there might be someone waiting in the alley, or the agent might be able to get help and corner him in the alley before he could get away.

He decided on a different course of action. He pulled the coat off the man lying on the floor and put it on. Then he pulled the man down the hall and around the corner, out of sight. He went back to the door, acting like an elderly tenant, and he opened it and let the East German agent in. The agent reached out and grabbed Rick and pushed him up against the wall, a lot like Rick had just done to the tenant a minute earlier. Malloy acted like an old man; he fell back against the wall and cowered down a bit. He pointed up the stairs and said in German, "A young man rushed in a minute earlier and he ran up the stairs." Rick added that the man who ran up the stairs said something in English and was very agitated as he ran away.

The agent looked Rick over for a second, drew out a gun, told him to stay put, and headed up the stairs himself. Rick acted very surprised and backed farther away. He sat down on the stairs as if he were tired and had been there before the agent came in, and watched as the man went up the staircase carefully. Rick waited a few seconds after the agent disappeared out of sight, and then he got up and walked quickly to the back of the building, opened the back door, and looked out. There was no one in the alley, so he walked out and disappeared into the early evening dark. Rick Malloy had stumbled into the trap and escaped from the clutches of the East Germans and Russians a second time.

CHAPTER TWENTY ONE

OCTOBER, 1946

B ack at East German secret police headquarters, the accusations and questions that had come from the failed stakeout were difficult to sort through. Taimov had accused the East Germans, particularly Anna Sturm, of extreme incompetence, for letting the American be alerted to the trap and then to slip away. The East Germans had countered this charge with their own claim that this was his plan and he had decided rashly to act on the informant's information without adequate preparation or positive confirmation of the facts. To make matters worse, it was not certain that Malloy had actually been in the area, although most agreed that based on the description given by the old man found on the floor in the apartment building, and the fact that the East German agent was told (presumably by Malloy himself) that a man ran upstairs speaking English, it was very likely that Rick Malloy had been the person who had come to the Gasthaus for the meeting as planned, and something else had gone wrong. Somehow this Malloy had sensed a trap, and Malloy and the American who would be there to meet him both escaped.

Compounding the confusion was their inability to contact their informant back in West Berlin to see if something had gone wrong, or learn if the plans had changed, or whatever else might have happened. No one had seen the other American who was supposed to meet Malloy, which only added to the concern over what had happened. It was a real puzzle and the unanswered questions were troubling. The East Germans were once again convinced of Malloy's expertise as an agent, Anna Sturm was surprised by the series of events and frustrated by the accusations of incompetence, and Igor Taimov was furious and self-righteous.

Rick Malloy returned to the attic in the garage in Rummelsburg after dark and lay there trying to figure out what had happened. What he understood was that a trap had been set to catch him, and it had nearly succeeded. Maybe the East Germans had better inside information than anyone suspected. He wondered if they now knew what he looked like as well. Did they set the trap for him intentionally and he had been lucky to escape, or had he just been in the wrong place at the wrong time? He had no idea what the facts were. What he did not understand was that Captain Smith had moved the timetable for the sting by one day and that was why it occurred at a different time than Rick had expected. Rick was also not aware that the mole had been captured. What he also did not know and what made him worry was just how much the East Germans knew about his movements and his mission. Realizing that he must be wanted for the murder of the two guards, he was sure that he was actively being hunted and that if found he would be treated harshly at best, shot on sight at worst.

Malloy wanted to call off the meeting with Captain Smith. It seemed too dangerous, based on what he had seen earlier that day. But he knew that he could not get a message to Smith in time to stop him from coming to the meeting place, and the only way to warn him was in person. Rick spent the night tossing and turning on the hard floor, wondering what the next day would bring. It was much-needed sleep, just not good sleep.

He awoke earlier than usual. He heard voices coming toward the garage, and the noise had startled him. Was it the police, the elderly homeowner, or someone else? Still half asleep, his mind started to race. The voices were male, but one sounded younger than he would have expected. It was certainly not that of the old man he had seen enter the house a few nights earlier. The voices were approaching the door to the garage. Rick began to listen to understand what was happening, but he had missed the beginning of the conversation. Suddenly, the door to the garage opened and two men were standing in the entrance. Based on Rick's guess, it was probably the son of the older man, and the elderly man himself whom Rick had seen several nights earlier. Rick held his breath--he was trapped. If they saw him, he would have to run or fight. He was not eager to do either.

Rick stayed still and was very quiet. He tried to watch through the floor cracks to see what was happening. The younger man was looking for something in the garage. Rick looked around and was pretty sure that there was nothing in the attic he would be looking for, so he watched quietly, and very carefully. After several minutes the man gave up his search with a sigh and threw up his hands and both men walked out of the garage. As they left, Rick breathed a sigh of relief, but Rick also knew that leaving the building he would have to be more cautious than he had been on previous occasions. He got up and gathered his things and got ready to leave the building. Unlike the previous three days where he slipped out of the front door and around the side of the building to get to the street, today Rick went to a side window, carefully opened it, and climbed out. He wanted to leave no chance of being seen by the son or anyone else as he departed; this hideout would be finished if he was seen. After climbing out, he shut the window from the outside and proceeded through some bushes to get access to the street. Rick was headed back into East Berlin city center to continue his search for Weisskirche.

According to his plan, he was not supposed to be meeting Captain Smith until 5 p.m. at a busy Weinstube near the Brandenburg Gate, so he had all day to search several more churches. Rick Malloy had identified seven more churches to be visited that day, based on information received from his visits to other parishes and the tips from people in these churches. He proceeded from the first white church to a second and then a third. Like the two dozen or so before, he heard interesting stories about the war and the use of the church and many tales about the people and the hardships they endured during Allied bombings and at the hands of the Russians as the war came to an end, but nothing that was remotely useful for his search. No one was very helpful or even encouraging in his stated quest--that being to find his father, lost in the war. Although it was just a cover for his real mission, Rick had learned a lot about the thousands of people looking to reunite their families and even after more than a year after the end of the war, there were still a lot of questions about what happened as the war came to an end. It was sad and tragic, but it was also not Rick's real reason for being in Berlin. He moved on.

At the fourth church he visited, which was a white church called Kirchegarten, the Garden Church, due to the small plot of land adjacent to it that had been used for almost a century before the war as a community garden. He sat with the priest and listened to his stories about how the parishioners had spent time during and after the war repairing and keeping the building up and how it had been very difficult without a benefactor, or "patron saint" as he called them, to provide funding for the renovations required as a result of the war. Certainly, by the time Allied bombs started routinely dropping on Berlin in 1944 there were no funds available or any sympathy from the Nazis in command for the rebuilding of any churches. The elderly priest was clearly moved by his own recounting of the hardships his flock endured, including those that perished in the process and the enormous waste of effort to rebuild something that should never have been damaged in the first place. He made it clear that he felt real hostility toward the Allies for their relentless attack on the city, and he surely hated the Russians and the way they had ruthlessly taken over control of life once they had occupied Berlin.

The priest then started talking about an older established church that did get funding and care from the Nazis right up until the very end, even though it was not even in the immediate bombing area. Called St. Estephe for over a hundred years, it had been adopted by several members of the Nazi high command as a place they would use for their family worship, and as a result, many of the original parishioners had stopped attending, some even coming to his church instead. Rick listened politely, but his mind was wandering. He was thinking that this was just another interesting story that had no bearing on his mission, and although he wished to be polite to the old priest, he was done here and was ready to move on to the last three churches on his list.

But the old priest was not done yet. He continued, "During the twelve-year reign of the Third Reich, St. Estephe was painted and renamed because the staff officers of the Wehrmacht's Edelweiss division, who attended with their families, preferred a German name to a name that they felt sounded French in origin. Did you know that this Edelweiss division was a group of elite paratroopers closely affiliated to the SS?" he continued. "They were a part of Hitler's elite corps. They started out as the 1st Mountain Division, and were the best of the best, the smartest, strongest, the best athletes, the best trained and the best equipped. It started as an honor to have been assigned to this division and early in the war they were the best. They were one of the first divisions into Poland, and they were among the first divisions to march into Paris. They escorted Hitler when he marched down the Champs-Élysées and under the Arc de Triomphe." The priest almost seemed proud as he spoke. Then his voice changed. "Two years later, with the overall Wehrmacht failure at Stalingrad, the division had lost its luster and spent most of the rest of the war in Yugoslavia and

Greece. Hitler, however, finally brought them back north to prepare to defend against the final impending Allied assault."

Rick had gone from polite boredom to wanting to interrupt the priest, but he held back. The priest kept on, "The church they had chosen to take over wasn't even a white building, but these arrogant men had decided that white was pure and they would only attend a church named White Chapel. So, they had it painted white and they called it Weisskirche. There was no one to stop them, so they just painted it. Immediately after the war the paint was stripped off and it was returned to its pre-war appearance by the original congregation. Few if any would ever refer to it as Weisskirche again." The priest proceeded to recount how this brownstone chapel, for most of its life called St. Estephe, had gotten attention that no other churches in Berlin received because these Nazis attended services there until the very end of the war. He went on, "It was said that a detachment of troops guarded the chapel to the last man as the Russians took over the city. It was very odd, but immediately after the fall of Berlin the church's name was restored and life moved on."

Rick had been daydreaming and had missed some of the story, but his ears perked up when he heard the word Weisskirche and he was suddenly a most attentive listener. The priest might have thought it strange, but he continued to tell his story, and Rick began to ask questions about this St. Estephe. Rick was nearly bursting from this amazing revelation. Might he have just stumbled across the answer and found Weisskirche? It sounded so promising, but he knew that he had had this feeling before over the past few days, and it had led to nothing. He now listened intently and worked to contain his excitement.

Rick spent another fifteen minutes with the priest and thanked him profusely for his help. For his part, the cleric was not exactly sure how he had been so helpful, but he was glad to find that this visitor had enjoyed his company for an hour or so and hoped that he had been somewhat useful. Malloy even made a special donation, the equivalent of $100 in Reichsmarks, a very large sum in these times, which was graciously accepted. Rick was nearly a half-mile from St. Estephe, but he could not contain himself. He took off in a fast jog toward the old church once called Weisskirche. He slowed down as he approached and started to realize that the location of the church, on the corner of two well-traveled boulevards, was one he had walked by at least a half dozen times. As he got closer, he looked up at the brown façade of the building, its single spire, and noted that it also did not have any land or space for burial plots. It seemed so unlikely to Rick Malloy, but then it also seemed so possible.

Rick stood across from the church and surveyed what he saw. It was an old baroque building--dark stone exterior with large wooden doors, and the stained glass was still largely intact. The steeple was as it had been for over 200 years. The roof was missing a few slate shingles, but probably did not leak and might have been that way for decades. It had somehow survived the Nazis, the American and British bombings, and the Russians' attack on the city. Granted, it was not in the city center and was in a more residential area that had no military significance, but many of the buildings nearby had been severely damaged and a few totally destroyed. It was amazing that now that he knew it had been painted white and the paint stripped recently, he could easily discern areas where the white paint was still intact. Rick walked around the building as best he could, looking for any clues and signs that this was the Weisskirche he sought.

There was nothing that indicated that this was the special church. It had no obvious markings and no land for a cemetery for hiding or burial of important papers in a grave. He approached carefully. *Could it be a trap?* he wondered. Rick entered the building and asked to speak with the parish priest. After about ten minutes waiting, a somewhat younger priest than Rick expected came out and sat down in the pew next to Rick Malloy. Rick told his usual story about seeking his father, and mentioned the story told to him by the previous church's priest about this church being called Weisskirche. This young cleric freely admitted the past of this building and told the story in greater detail, including the names of some of the senior Wehrmacht officers who were regulars and patrons of the parish. Rick did not recognize any of the names, but he was not surprised by that fact. He listened to the whole story and sized up the priest in the process. As he listened to the story, he learned that this priest had only been at the church since the war. This holy man replaced the man who comforted Nazis and who had been dismissed by the old congregation. Rick slowly concluded that he could trust the man and that he was no ex-Nazi and was not a Communist sympathizer, either.

After nearly an hour of talking, Rick finally decided that it was safe to ask the priest about Friedrich Anlauer. He told the priest that he had read the name somewhere and did not know who the person was or what it had to do with churches. He started to go on, but the priest interrupted him. Rick was surprised at his response. The priest smiled and told Rick that Friedrich Anlauer was a devoted follower of the famous reformer, Martin Luther. He had lived in the area surrounding Berlin in the mid-sixteenth century. He was also an early reformer of the church who made a lot of enemies due to his disrupting the graft and corruption that was rampant in the church in this era. He did not have the fame to support his campaign to end the corruption, bribes, and unfair church taxes that were strangling the lower classes, and he was an easy target for the wealthy bishops and clergy that were very upset by his teachings. The priest explained that according to history, Anlauer had been brutally murdered in 1544 and his remains were taken to the small town of Emmen about thirty miles outside of Berlin and placed in an unmarked grave so that he could not be made into a martyr.

Rick was surprised to hear about this little-known theologian, but he was also disappointed to learn that he had never set foot in this church and was not buried in it. *Was there no connection between this man and Weisskirche, and if not, could this possibly be the right place?* he thought.

But Rick was also curious that this man of God knew so much about this little known reformer who died over 400 years earlier. Rick asked the priest how he knew so much about this reformer, and he was relieved and elated at the answer.

The priest pointed to the annex behind the alter and the large carved marble tomb to the side of the alter and said, "That is our Friederich Anlauer. This church felt a kinship with his cause, and about one hundred years ago the church adopted him and placed this marble sarcophagus as a memorial, here in the church. His real remains were buried anonymously, and I guess our parishioners of that time felt he deserved better than that."

Rick's eyes opened wide and he looked in the direction of the large marble sarcophagus. "Can I look at it?" Rick and the priest got up and walked over to the carved marble tomb. It was huge, and very heavy. "What is in it?" Rick asked innocently.

The priest answered without missing a beat. "I am told that it was opened by the Nazis late in the war. I guess they got curious as well. But as far as I know, the thing was and still is empty. But since the top must weigh two hundred kilograms, no one has opened it again to my knowledge. Why do you ask?"

Rick said he had no special reason for asking, but that he was just curious about a sarcophagus meant to contain nothing. He could not say what he was thinking.

Rick asked the priest what time it was, and realizing it was getting late in the day, he wanted to get to the meeting point for his rendezvous with Captain Smith. He wanted to be prepared for a potential trap and be early enough to check things out in advance. He thanked the priest for the information and the tour of the sanctuary and left. He had about an hour to get to the meeting point and it was at least a thirty-minute walk. He could spend no more time here and he was certain what his next step should be--Rick Malloy just had to look inside the sarcophagus.

Chapter Twenty Two

The meeting place was less than a mile from where Rick had nearly been caught the day before, but of course Captain Smith was not aware of this. He had been on the other side of the city, in West Berlin, dealing with the uncovering of a mole, and so he had no knowledge that it had been a close call for Malloy. Smith had been briefed earlier that day about what to look for, and he had studied and practiced several typical German phrases, such as asking directions and ordering food and seeking simple help. He spoke a little German as a result of having been in Germany for nearly two years, but he would never be able to pass for a native and his accent would be recognized as that of an American if he had to engage in any significant conversation. So he had worked on acting a bit stupid and bowing a bit, as if to indicate he was an injured war veteran or was not altogether well. He would make his way slowly and deliberately to the meeting to avoid drawing much attention.

He had also made the decision on his own to remove his military uniform as well as his ID tags (dog tags) and to put on civilian clothes and walk alone into East Berlin. This was strictly forbidden by US military code and intelligence procedures because if he were apprehended he could be treated as a spy, not as an American soldier. He knew this, but also felt that he had no chance of meeting Rick Malloy any other way. Smith's one exception to being a true civilian was that he had tucked his .45 automatic into his pants, in the back, under his shirt and jacket. Heck, he did not normally carry the thing around in West Berlin, so it felt very strange to be carrying it now, and in this concealed manner.

So, dressed as a worker in civilian clothing, he slipped through to the East on Invalidenstrasse and then would approach the Brandenburg Gate area from the East. No one would be looking for someone coming from that direction, and this area was known to be an easier place to cross into the East. The harder part would come later--trying to get out. He noted how East Berlin had already fallen way behind the West in reconstructing the buildings from the war. Some of the rubble had been removed and many windows replaced, but most destroyed buildings had not been rebuilt yet and in some cases where rebuilding had occurred, the replacements were tacky, hastily constructed, and out of place next to ornate 80-year-old structures.

He continued to walk at a normal pace and melded into the crowd pretty well. Although possible, it would be hard for someone to spot him as an American or even as not belonging. As he approached the general area for the meeting, he stopped and observed the movement of others and the buildings and his surroundings. He would move forward a block or so, and repeat the process. He slowly became comfortable that no one was watching him and that he was not being followed, but as he came to the small restaurant where he would meet Malloy, he turned away, walked back down the block, and sat on a bench for five minutes. He sat, a bit slumped, but looking very comfortable so as to not draw attention as he watched keenly and looked for any abnormal activity. He was fifteen minutes early, and although he did not see anything out of place and could not find anyone following or even interested in him, he also did not see Rick Malloy, and that bothered him. Surely, Malloy would be on time, he thought. As the meeting time approached, he got up and meandered over to the restaurant and went inside.

Rick Malloy had already had an eventful day, but he was excited to get to the wine bar and link up with the Western world. He had not talked to anyone in English in a long time, and strangely he was very eager to speak in his adopted tongue. He had run from the church that had been called Weisskirche and had arrived nearly half an hour early. He approached carefully, based on his experience from the prior day, but no one was in sight. He was somewhat more comfortable that this was not one of the locations Captain Smith would have used as a trap to catch the mole. Rick decided to check out the back of the restaurant and found that he could even enter from the rear. He was pleased with the choice of rendezvous locations, and with that thought in his mind, he walked in through the rear door and took a table in a corner in the back of the bar area. Rick inspected carefully all of the patrons in the bar. There were about fifteen people in the place, and after a few minutes' observation, he was comfortable that there was no trap there and that all of the customers were legitimate. He hoped he was right.

He ordered a stein of beer and sat back and watched the world go by. After about twenty minutes, he saw a man come in and look around a bit and then walk up to the bar. For a second, he was alarmed because he thought the man looked familiar, but then he realized that it had been a while since he had seen Captain Smith. He waited until Smith looked in his direction and nodded to catch his eye. It took a second for Smith to recognize Rick Malloy, with the changed hairline and hair color. He did, after all, look very different, as well.

Captain William Smith walked over and with a big smile reached out and shook hands with Rick Malloy, the man believed dead two weeks earlier, and on whom the hopes of the Allies depended to find and recover the Nazi atomic bomb secrets. It was so incredible that he was alive and free that Smith just stood and stared for a second or two. Rick called the waiter over and ordered another beer for Captain Smith. They began to talk, very quietly, in English.

Smith told the story about how they had feared Malloy was dead, causing Major Whitcombe to shut down the operation. He continued through to their hearing that he had escaped, which caused the team to be reactivated. He then relayed the capture of the mole the prior day. Rick was pleased to hear that the mole had been caught and was glad to understand that it was not some sophisticated espionage effort .

Malloy then began to recount his past adventures, including his experience entering East Berlin, his discovery at the bank, capture at the house on Grunestrasse by his girlfriend Anna, his incarceration and questioning, his torture, imprisonment, meeting his father, his escape, his return to Grunestrasse to find the writing in the basement, and finally his search for Weisskirche. It took him over two hours to tell the whole story, with his tale ending with the supposedly empty tomb of Friedrich Anlauer in the church previously known as Weisskirche.

Captain Smith sat transfixed, listening to the story. He was amazed at what he heard, and hearing that Malloy might have actually found the missing papers was almost too much to contain. They ordered dinner and ate and caught up until nearly 11 p.m., and Rick began to think about the garage attic where he had been staying. It might not be safe anymore, he thought, and if Smith was a noisy sleeper, it could be very dangerous to go back there tonight. As midnight and closing of the café approached, Rick leaned over and told Smith that he should act very tired and a bit drunk so they could ask the café owner for a bed for the night. Rick got up and proceeded over to the owner and thanking him for a great night on the town, explained that his friend had missed his ride back home and they needed a place to stay the night. They would gladly pay for a room, if the man had any accomodations. At first the bartender-owner was a bit hesitant, but when he realized that he could make a bit of easy extra money, he offered an empty store room in the back of the café in which he could set up a few blankets for Rick and his friend. It was not going to be luxurious, he made clear, but getting a room at an inn at midnight would be nearly impossible. Rick had offered 50 Reichmarks for the night, a significant overpayment for such accommodations, and this had convinced the man to let them stay.

Rick went back to Smith, and they sat and talked some more as the staff closed up the restaurant and cleaned up for the night. Both Malloy and Smith were very tired and so when they were shown to their room, they wrapped themselves in blankets and lay down to get some needed rest. Within minutes Malloy knew that he had made the right decision, as Captain Smith was snoring loudly and making more noise than would have been prudent in the garage attic.

The café owner and his family lived upstairs in the building, as was often the case in small family-run restaurants. Two of his daughters had been waitresses and another relative was involved in food preparation. They retired upstairs, as they did nightly, but based on their schedule they typically sat up for a little while to unwind from the day before going to bed. The owner, talking to his wife, explained the two guests staying below and the extra profits obtained from two blankets and use of the store room. He was very pleased with himself, but she was less excited.

"What do you know of these men?" she asked.

"Nothing at all, and I do not care to," he replied.

"And you think it wise to leave these two unknown men alone" she continued.

"Well, they are already asleep and the liquor is all locked up and the beer is put away. They will cause no trouble," he asserted.

"If there is trouble, you will wish you had let the police know about these two before it happens," the owner's wife reminded him. "I think you should go right now to the police and let them know that you have sheltered two men for the night. We may all get in trouble if you do not."

The owner shrugged it off, but his wife would not let it rest. After another ten minutes of discussion on the subject, the owner relented. "I will not go out at nearly 2 a.m. to tell an empty police station that I lucked into some easy money giving shelter to two travelers who missed their train. But, if it will make you happy, I will get up early in the morning and report this to the station down the street, before the guests wake up. Does that make you happy?"

His wife begrudgingly agreed that this was the best course of action, and that this was probably better than creating a stir in the middle of the night over nothing.

The East German Police and Russian NKVD operatives were anxious. They had not found Rick Malloy or the American with the trap, and their mole had gone silent. It looked like the operation was going very badly, and for Igor Taimov this was absolutely unacceptable. But the canvassing of the city had produced nothing, and they had no leads. During the prior day, the team that had been assigned to go over the house at Grunestrasse had completed their results and had come back with three possible things Rick Malloy could have been looking for or found.

Since it was known that tracks left in the house led to the basement, they had focused all of their efforts on the areas Malloy appeared to have looked at himself. The first two leads were weak, the first being that a book in the basement seemed to be missing from a box. It might have been picked up and replaced or moved to another box, but the dust in the box seemed to indicate that someone had moved the box, disturbing the books inside. Whether it was Malloy was difficult to discern, as no fingerprints or detectable smudges were found on the box itself. And if so, the book was gone, providing no clue anyway. The second clue was the switch for the furnace, which, based on a review of fingerprints, had been handled by the American, and there were typical words associated with the warnings for the furnace surrounding that switch--nothing very useful.

The third area, which seemed most promising, was a red paint smudge on the wall, and the footprints below that indicated that someone, presumably Malloy, had spent some time looking at this part of the wall. The smudge made it impossible to read the words exactly, and the top line was completely illegible, but with some difficulty and a lot of time analyzing the smudge, they could make out the word weiss and the last letters "he," but no more. *Something white or white something*, thought Taimov.

Anna Sturm was summoned to the makeshift command center and asked to add her thoughts. The team had come up with eleven words or groups of words that were about the correct length and started with "weiss" and ended with "he." Most seemed irrelevant, and some required more than two words and provided no insight. They were ignored. One word stood out, at least as being a real word, but what could it mean? Weisskirche? After some staring at the word and thinking about the meaning of the word Anna came up with quite an astute idea.

"We need to understand if this is really a clue and if it is, then what the clue means, correct?" Anna continued before anyone could reply to the rhetorical question. "Assuming that there was a clue in the basement in the first place, then we must assume that Rick Malloy now has it and is acting on that clue as we sit here. So, we can verify that this is the clue and understand its meaning by determining if Malloy has been searching for this Weisskirche as well, right?"

Taimov picked up her line of reasoning quickly. He chimed in, "If Malloy is searching for Weisskirche, we can be sure that this is the clue."

"Yes, and by going to several white churches in the city, we should be able to quickly know if this is the case," Anna Sturm put forward. "At the very least, we can eliminate this possibility very fast."

Taimov ordered four agents to go out to the churches in the immediate area around the police headquarters and see if they could find any enquiries recently that might match the description of Rick Malloy. It was early in the day, and they should have some answers before noon. Even though the young female East German agent had come up with the idea, Taimov was still somewhat pleased that he was now making progress. He could always take credit for it later.

At about 5:00 in the morning, Rick Malloy was awakened by the sound of someone leaving the restaurant by the back door, next to the store room. At first he though nothing of it, but as he listened and thought, he decided that the person leaving was trying to be very quiet, really trying to sneak out undetected. It was one thing to be considerate of the two guests, and initially Rick had attributed the quiet exit to this politeness, but as he lay and thought, he more and more realized that this was not consideration, but trying to leave the building without being noticed.

"But why?" Rick thought out loud. The restaurant did not serve breakfast and would not open until 11 a.m. Deliveries would not start for another two hours. "Unless they have something to hide from two guests such as ourselves, and aside from the obvious, contacting the police, I cannot think what that might be."

Rick began to be alarmed. The person--Rick assumed it was the owner, but was not sure--had been gone over fifteen minutes, and it was now almost daylight. He woke up Captain Smith and told him what he had heard, and they agreed that the safe action was to get out of the place immediately. They gathered their things and also very cautiously and quietly exited through the rear entrance. They stopped several blocks away in a park area and picked a bushy area which protected them somewhat while allowing them line of sight back down the street toward the area of the restaurant to see if Malloy had been right or if he had been overly paranoid.

It was now nearly 7 a.m., and as they sat in the cool of the morning they started to talk about their plans for checking the sarcophagus of Friedrich Anlauer. Before they made much progress, the morning quiet was broken with the noise of several rushing police cars, all heading toward the restaurant, lights flashing, but without sirens. It seemed like every available officer was rushing to the location. Realizing that they were still very close by, they decided it was time to move on. They got up and left the area in a hurry.

Just before 7 a.m., a report came in to East German secret police headquarters that a restaurant owner had reported in at 6 a.m. that he had given shelter to two men. The local police station had considered that they might be the Americans, one possibly the sought-after Rick Malloy. Agents had rushed to the scene, but the two people, whoever they were, had fled and were nowhere to be found. But the owner was able to provide a good description of both men, and police sketches would be available by noon.

At 11 a.m., three of the agents sent to see if Malloy had been searching for white churches had returned from canvassing churches in their assigned areas, and all three reported that within the last few days a man had enquired about his father at all of the churches named or possibly described as Weisskirche that they had contacted. Based on that description, it had surely been the same man at each church. And based on the description given by the owner of the Weinstube, it was surely one of the men who had stayed in the bar the prior night.

Although it was not positive confirmation, it seemed very likely that they had found the secret clue from the house on Grunestrasse, that being Weisskirche, and had found Rick Malloy still in East Berlin and now knew what he looked like and where he was going. Igor Taimov was very happy with himself. He was starting to have a very good morning.

Chapter Twenty Three

Rick Malloy and Captain Smith had avoided a close call, but they really did not know how close it was or how many people in East Berlin were now on the lookout for the Americans. They had to assume that the information had been passed back to East Berlin police headquarters, but they could not know that the Russian NKVD and East German secret police were on the case as well. Having just arrived in East Berlin, Captain Smith had no understanding of what was going on, and Malloy was just not trained to identify who was pursuing them. They were unaware of the magnitude of their problem as Taimov and the NKVD closed in on them. On the other hand, the East Germans and Russians did not understand that the leak from US intelligence HQ had been plugged and as a result, that the inside information on their movements would not be coming anymore.

What Malloy and Smith did understand was that they needed to find out what was in the sarcophagus, and they did not have a moment to waste. And while they could not know that the East Germans and Russians had discovered the clue of Weisskirche and were closing in, it would be foolish not to assume that they might have found something and be close on their heels. Given what was known and the fact that it was still mid-day in Berlin, they needed a plan to inspect the contents of the tomb as soon as possible without alarming the priest and without letting the East German police know what they were up to. This was a problem, because the church was in active use and held services daily. Smith and Malloy walked back across Berlin toward the church and sat on a bench, diagonally across the street, almost out of sight. They studied the situation and they began to develop a plan.

Smith asked Malloy questions, and together they pieced together an approach. Malloy had met the Weisskirche priest and sized him up. They discussed whether to let the priest know about their mission. Based on his observations drawn from spending over an hour with the man, Rick believed that the priest was no ex-Nazi or Communist sympathizer. He was a lifelong man of God, and he would surely be a pacifist if given a chance. Rick believed that if the priest understood, he would probably prefer that the Allies have these military secrets instead of the Russians. Captain Smith felt that the priest was a risk that could potentially create major problems for them if he knew their plan. Therefore, he should not be made aware. Smith was equally sure that if the priest thought that defying the authorities would put his congregation in danger, he would turn the two of them in without hesitation. And in the worst case, what the priest did not know could not be tortured out of him by the East Germans.

Rick was less dispassionate. "We could create a new story for the priest that would not reveal the true intent of our mission, but would secure his cooperation. What if we offer him money?" Smith had entered East Berlin with about 25,000 Reichsmarks and Malloy still had almost 10,000 more Reichsmarks on him--a lot of money between them. They discussed approaching the priest with a donation in exchange for allowing them a look inside the sarcophagus. But this would raise questions they did not want to answer. They also agreed that they might need these funds to get out of Berlin later. Should the sarcophagus be empty, they would have spent the money for nothing.

After all, once given to the priest they could hardly ask for it to be returned just because they did not find what they hoped for. Having discussed all the pros and cons and thinking through each alternative, they continued to work through their plans until they were satisfied.

In the end, they agreed on stealth. They would enter the church later that day, after the last service was completed, open the tomb, and reseal it before leaving. Assuming that there was something in the tomb, they would remove it from the sarcophagus and take it with them. It sounded so easy.

The East Germans and Russians were now in frantic pursuit. Teams had reported back in after having canvassed all the white churches and all churches named Weisskirche in the greater Berlin area. They had found that Rick Malloy, now widely regarded as an American master spy, had been to almost all of them and had consistently indicated that he was looking for his father. The same story was repeated over and over. Igor Taimov had read all the reports and files and he knew that it was well documented that his father was dead, having been arrested, imprisoned and having died in prison. He was forced to wonder whether this was a cover for his real search, or had Malloy lost his mind?

Did Malloy know something about his father that no one else knew? And how was this relevant to the search for Nazi atomic bomb secrets? Could it be that the first two agents sent were decoys for the real master spy, Rick Malloy, who, together with his father, who had been missing and assumed dead, were an expert team brought together to steal these secrets out of East Berlin? Taimov posited these theories to whoever was in the room.

Preposterous rubbish, thought Anna Sturm as she listened to Igor Taimov pontificate about what might be going on. But she did enjoy listening to this imbecile Russian act as if this nonsense could be true and then pat himself on the back for seeing this as a possibility. She alone understood that Malloy was no master spy and that Rick was not really looking for his father. It was all wasted energy and detracted from the real effort to find the American before he found any secret papers. But Anna knew that Rick was ahead of them in his search for the Nazi documents. He had found out about Weisskirche first, but it was not clear that he had found the correct white chapel yet. And it was not clear what "Weisskirche" really meant. It was an assumption that it would hold important documents, but it could be just another clue, or be off track completely. What she did know was that Rick Malloy did not have the resources that Anna Sturm had available to narrow the search to the right church. With her access to information and manpower, maybe she could regain the edge and get ahead of Malloy in finding the secrets. Anna ordered a search of records to identify all churches frequented by high-ranking Nazi leaders late in the war and sent a pair of agents off to bring this information back as soon as possible. It was already 3 p.m., and every minute counted to her.

As dusk approached, at 5:30 p.m., Malloy and Captain Smith began to enter the church once called Weisskirche. The last person had left and the priest had come out and shut the door. They approached the building carefully, pulled open the door, and entered. Malloy had never been a church person and was surprised to find that the door to the building had not been locked, but Captain Smith was a devout Catholic and he understood that a house of God would be left open until later in the evening. Both were happy to see that no one appeared to be inside--not a parishioner, priest, sexton, or altar boy; no one. It was good fortune indeed, but they wondered how long it would last. Smith walked carefully into the church, and even after all of his military training, he could not bring himself to just walk by the altar. Malloy was really surprised when Captain Smith briefly stopped and kneeled. It just seemed a bit odd under the circumstances. So while Smith stopped, knelt, and made the sign of the cross, Malloy surveyed the premises to see who else might be in the building. They then proceeded to move behind the main sanctuary to the sarcophagus of Freiderich Anlauer. Malloy went back, checked, and then locked the front and two side doors while Smith looked around and kept watch. There were only three exits to the building, and they were far apart. If someone knocked and appeared to be coming in, they could exit through one of the other doors to escape.

Having secured the doors, they moved to the sarcophagus and started to examine it and determine how they would open it. The top had a small lip that would help somewhat in lifting it, but it probably weighed 200 kilos or 450 pounds. Minutes ticked by as they looked for something to use as a pry bar. A metal leg of a broken table was found in the basement and they returned upstairs and began work to remove the top. At first it was slow going to get the table leg wedged into the case of the sarcophagus, but after several minutes they had the top raised an inch and were positioned to push the top to the side and look inside. Both men strained to push the large stone top to the side, and after moving it a few inches they stopped to peer into the case. It was dark and they had no flashlight, but as they peered in, it was certain that it was not empty. There was something in there, and although it was not easy to see, it was clear that it was large and covered in canvas. And it did not look like a bunch of papers, either. Captain Bill Smith started worrying that there might be human remains inside and that he was defiling a real tomb in a church, and although he was on a mission and could reconcile with that, it was not what they were after. Malloy reminded him that the priest had said that the sarcophagus had been inspected as recently as several years ago, and it was empty.

"Whatever is in here was put here very recently," Rick insisted. Still the tension and concern were very real.

They continued to pry the top off, and as the light began to enter the sarcophagus they could see that there was a large pile in the center covered in canvas cloth, and a metal box at the near end. They created just enough space to get the metal box out first, and Captain Smith placed it on the floor. Malloy took the top off of the box and inside was a yellow cloth wrapped bundle of papers with a red eagle and swastika on the outside. The prospect that they had found the missing documents created palpable tension and both men were silent but excited.

"While I take a look to see whether this is what we are searching for, why don't you see what else is in there," Malloy said quietly to Smith. Rick began to carefully unwrap the papers and inspect them. It was difficult at first to see if these were the sought-after papers, but after a minute or two Malloy was at least sure that they were technical papers that dealt with high-level physics. He recognized instantly the shorthand handwriting of noted scientist Werner Heisenberg, who had been reported to be working on the Nazi atomic project in Peenemunde, late in 1944, when the project was moved due to Allied bombings. He would not take the time now to examine them because he was going to take the papers anyway and should have plenty of time later. But his heart was racing; as improbable as it had seemed a few days earlier, it looked like they had indeed recovered the missing Nazi atomic bomb research papers.

Malloy rewrapped the documents and set them on the ground. As he looked up at Captain Smith, who had been removing the canvas from the mound in the center of the sarcophagus, he saw a large smile that he had never seen on Smith's face before. It was as if the man had seen something lovely inside the tomb, and Malloy stood up to see what it was. With the tarp removed, you could not miss the shiny refection that emanated from inside the darkened sarcophagus and as his eyes focused, his brain began to race. It was gold. It was bars of Nazi gold, to be precise. Gold bullion, and there was a modest pile of it. There were six layers of eight bars in each layer, each layer stacked perpendicular to the one below. Smith picked up a bar and handed it to Rick Malloy. It must have weighed thirty pounds, maybe a bit more. Rick started thinking, *Thirty pounds equals nearly 500 ounces each, and 48 bars. My God, there was almost 24,000 ounces of gold.* At $30 per ounce in 1946, this was about $750,000 in gold. At a time when few people, even in America, made more than a few thousand dollars a year, this was an absolute fortune.

What Malloy and Smith could not know was that this gold had been embezzled by Himmler for his own personal use and placed in the sarcophagus at the same time the papers were put there, and with Himmler's suicide at the end of the war, not only was its location not known, its very existence was not known.

Malloy and Smith wasted no time in taking the gold out of the sarcophagus, but 1500 pounds of gold could not easily or quickly be transported. They could carry no more than two bars each without looking conspicuous and this would mean twelve trips for both of them in and back out of the church. That would be far too danger-ous. They had already been in the church almost two hours, and they were aware that sooner or later someone would show up. If those people could find this church, they would likely know about Friedrich Anlauer and look in the sarcophagus. They decided to move the trea-sure to a different place in the church that would allow them to come back and more easily retrieve it at a later time, or at least keep it away from the Russians.

They chose to move the gold bars to a closet near the front parlor area. There was an older, large ceremonial armoire being stored in the closet that they pulled away from the wall. Smith punched a hole in the wall with the metal leg they had used to pry open the sarcophagus. They placed the gold back, out of sight, down in the wall cavity and covered it with the old canvas. Then, they put the chest back, in front of the wall that now held the bullion, and then piled some mops and brooms, also already in the closet, next to this to make it look like it nothing new or special had happened in this area. As they were finishing up, they heard footsteps and then a hand on the door at the front of the church. From the voice it was clear to Rick Malloy that this was the church priest, but what was of concern was that he was not alone. There were several other voices in the background. The priest seemed clearly surprised that the door was locked from the inside and began to explain to whomever he was with that the door was never locked. After all, it was a house of worship, and there was nothing to steal inside. Malloy and Smith could only imagine the conversation that followed as they heard men pushing on the door to force it open. The two Americans took off in a run out of the rear entrance with the papers under Rick's arm and each man carrying two of the bars of the gold with them. They were not moving very fast with sixty pounds each and a box of papers, but they were out into the dark and had escaped the building without being seen. There had not been time to replace the top of the sarcophagus, so it was left partially open. There would be no mistaking who had been here or what they were after.

Anna Sturm's hunch had paid off. There were four churches identified that had been attended regularly by high-ranking Nazi officers. In three hours they had found that only one had not already been visited earlier in the day by the secret police, and that this church was neither painted white nor currently called Weisskirche. Initially the tie to Wiesskirche seemed broken, until one of the older officers in the secret police, who had served in the Wehrmacht, pointed out that the SS had called this church Weisskirche. With this revelation, Taimov jumped back into the lead and took command. He ordered a team to accompany him to the church, and included Anna Sturm, even though he still did not particularly like or trust her.

They arrived, and finding the doors locked, went next door to the priest's home, the Rectory, and got him to accompany them. After only a minute of inquiry, they found that Rick Malloy had also been to this church and that he had stayed and talked longer than at other churches. The priest did not mention Friedrich Anlauer; however, he did confirm the story about searching for his father. They brought the priest to the church front door to find it still locked. The priest was puzzled as it was locked from the inside and he could not unlock it with his key. Two large men came to the front and began pounding on the door and after only a minute or so the door gave way and they entered the church, guns drawn, looking for trouble. But there was no one there.

It did not take long for the secret police and Russian agents to see the sarcophagus, with its top half off. They gathered around, peered inside and Igor Taimov stamped his feet and pounded his fist on the stone top. The priest now piped up that he recalled that the man they described, this Malloy, was very interested in Friedrich Anlauer and was excited to hear that his sarcophagus was here in this church. He had not thought much of it at the time, but then he had also been sure that the sarcophagus had been empty. The priest pointed out that he had left the church after 5 p.m. mass, and this was only about two hours ago. Taimov looked at the priest, at Anna Sturm, and then stomped out of the church.

Anna Sturm was herself surprised. Once again, Rick Malloy had been one step ahead of them. She was still positive that he was not a serious or experienced agent, but he had been able to escape and evade and keep ahead of her and the East German police and Russian NKVD for over a week. In a strange city he did not know except from his distant youth, he had eluded their entire combined police forces, had found Weisskirche first, he knew about Anlauer when they did not and he got there first, and it appeared that he had gotten away, maybe with the Nazi secret atomic bomb documents. If it had not been so frustrating, she would actually have admired him. Under the circumstances, she was confused and angry.

Rick Malloy and Captain Smith exited, moving as fast as they could, and kept going. They knew that they could not get out of East Berlin that night, and they needed time to examine the documents. They could not use the same trick of seeking refuge in a Gasthaus that they had used the night before--the police would be smarter this time. Assuming that the people knocking on the door back at the church were East German police, then they would be in a frantic search by now. They needed time and did not have many options. They agreed to head for the garage attic where Malloy had stayed for three nights. It was not ideal, but it was the best Rick could think of, and it was a lot safer than starting from scratch or staying outside or trying a public inn or guesthouse. They were careful as they walked south into the residential part of the city, first east, then south, through Freiderichshain, pausing several times as they observed intersections, other people walking, and making sure that they were safe to move on. It took over two hours to walk the four miles from Weisskirche, to the Rummelsburg section of East Berlin, but they finally reached the small house with the adjacent garage in the suburb southeast of central Berlin. The main garage doors were closed, but not locked. They carefully inspected the area and then went in and climbed up into the attic. Rick Malloy was pleased to observe that nothing appeared to have changed or have been touched since he was last there. He needed some rest, so Captain Smith agreed to take the first watch. They would switch after four hours so that each could get some sleep, but someone would still be alert to any potential problems.

The situation had grown critical for Igor Taimov. He had spoken directly to Beria, who had spoken to Stalin himself. The secrets must not leave the Russian sector of Berlin. All crossover and border checkpoints to the Western part of the city were to be put on full alert and Beria himself ordered extra security forces to be placed in a ring around the isolated West Berlin until the two Americans were found and the documents recovered. By morning, the city would be virtually sealed off from any chance of easily getting away into West Berlin.

CHAPTER TWENTY FOUR

The night passed without incident for Malloy and Captain Smith in the garage attic. Each had stood watch while the other slept. Both men were physically and emotionally tired and the sleep was needed and welcome. In the early morning Malloy, who had taken the second watch, woke Smith. They needed to make sure that they had retrieved the right documents. It was a strange position to be in, as Rick Malloy noted, for they had nowhere else to look if these were not the right papers, and they were being chased by the East Germans and Russians, who certainly believed that they had the secret papers, whether they really were the right documents or not. They opened the yellow cloth packet marked with the red Reich's eagle and began to more closely examine the bundle of documents taken the night before from the sarcophagus. The light was not very good anywhere in the garage, but they needed to be careful about going out into the open unless they had to, so Captain Smith stood watch for someone coming up toward the garage by peeking out of the door and listening for any footsteps approaching. Malloy sat at the bottom of the ladder that led up into the loft. In this position, at this time of day, rays of light came through the small window and he could read more easily. Malloy had used this window to exit the garage a few days earlier, and it looked out onto a narrow walk bordered by overgrown bushes. He would also be able to hear someone approaching down the walk easily and then get out of sight.

The documents in the packet that Malloy had examined back in the church were cover materials, letters and documents describing the information contained within the bundle at a high level, including project authorizations, contact information, and the like that was pretty useless over a year after the end of Nazi Germany. These provided no substantive information or technical insight into materials or construction techniques, but did indicate the importance of the documents that would be contained in the packet. They also led Rick to believe that the materials were authentic, that the subject matter was advanced physics, and that the intent was military in nature. He set these aside and found a series of folders in the packet, including sets of documentation, technical white papers, explanations of theory, and schematic blueprints. The papers were still neat and had not appeared to age much at all. They were clearly labeled for easy use and understanding. Had these been delivered to scientists in a Nazi research laboratory, they would have been able to get to work with minimal delay. Malloy first looked at the schematics, as they would quickly indicate the nature of the project. The drawings were precise and detailed and he could tell immediately that these were intended to be payloads for rockets, or missiles. Although the device looked to be too large for any known missiles available at the end of the war, the rocket section was labeled "A9." Malloy had been briefed by Allied scientists now working with Werhner Von Braun that there were at least twelve designs developed, named A1 through A12, but Rick was not famnliar with the technical aspects of each succeeding version. Of course, the well-known version, the V2 rocket (which had actually been called the A4 by the Nazis, or 4th version of the "Aggregat" series of rockets) had been used to attack London and Holland late in the war. There was only a little additional information on the rocket, but the information was footnoted as having come from Kummersdorf, the special projects Wehrmacht facility where initial development and testing of the engines for the V2 rockets took place. Rick also knew that the rocket program had been moved to Peenemunde in 1939 to test and perfect the guidance system, and when the program was completed, it moved again to Nordhausen for production in 1944.

Comparing what he understood with what he saw in front of him, these papers were certainly the "real deal." The remainder of the drawings focused on the payload, the explosive device itself. Based on the limited information provided to him by the American scientists prepping him at the start of the mission, the device was indeed much smaller than he expected, far smaller than the US-developed version, and so it would be easier to transport and to launch. The US atom bombs had to be dropped from a plane and were much too large to be launched from any existing rocket.

Malloy moved on to the technical specifications and documentation. He scanned the documents for key words such as plutonium or uranium. He did not see these and at first, and it concerned him. Were these not the right documents? How could any serious discourse on an atomic device not include uranium or plutonium? But as he read more carefully, he noted the references to fusion materials. The atomic bombs he was aware of were fission devices, not fusion. He did not know a lot about the details of the US atomic bomb program at all, as had been confirmed in his interrogation by the East German secret police. But from what he did understand, the United States had focused heavy elements to create a nuclear fission reaction using Uranium238 and Plutonium235, while these German documents referred to far lighter elements and materials. These papers referred to using deuterium oxide to stabilize and create tritium, materials many scientists believed might be suitable for creating an atomic fusion reaction.

Rick understood that deuterium oxide was a material often called heavy water due to its having a higher density than normal water and being essentially ^2H_2O or D_2O. His physics background allowed him to see the connection easily. He had also been briefed about the source of these materials and knew that the materials used to make this "heavy water" were to be derived from a fertilizer plant in Norway. In 1943, a daring land based raid on the facility had knocked it out of action and a subsequent bombing raid finally destroyed the plant and it was no longer able to provide Hitler with these raw materials for his super weapons, the ultimate weapon based on "schweres wasser"--heavy water.

The question that could not be answered at the end of the war was how much atomic-bomb-capable material had been produced, and how far along was their engineering effort to create a "Super," or H-bomb. Based on what Malloy found in the documents, the physics principles were somewhat different from his understanding of the American approach, but that did not concern him much at all, and based on what he saw, the device should work, at least in principle. There were several technical issues unresolved in the papers, such as how to detonate a fusion device, but the idea of a fusion reaction seemed sound. And there appeared to be information on quantities needed and quantities available in Germany at the time. This was important information for the Western Allies.

Malloy read and analyzed and cross-referenced what he saw to what he had studied and had learned about America's atomic devices. After about two hours, he was convinced that they had indeed found the missing Nazi documents, the ones many thought were nonexistent and others believed lost with the destruction of Berlin. Captain Smith was mesmerized by Malloy's description of how this deuterium oxide, this heavy water, was forced to accommodate another extra proton, and thereby became tritium, which was then extremely unstable. It could theoretically be used to create a fusion- reaction bomb by massing enough of the unstable material and then by creating an event that caused the materials to melt together rapidly, maybe by something like a very large explosion. Malloy knew that the American bombs using plutonium and uranium also used an explosion to trigger their atomic reaction. He observed that the Nazi bomb plans used the slightly less unstable material, the heavy water, and surrounded it with multiple explosive devices that would be timed to detonate concurrently to create intense heat and fuse the unstable materials to release unthinkable amounts of energy. The numbers he found in the documentation were stupendous, beyond belief, but also empirically seemed correct.

He did not profess to have a definitive understanding of the difference between these two approaches, but it was clear from his understanding of the physics that this Nazi device had the potential to be far more potent than even the most massive American atomic weapons. Malloy reflected on the experiments that he was just barely aware of back in the United States and the research he knew about to explore using hydrogen as the primary material in a fusion device instead of uranium/plutonium in a fission bomb. Hydrogen was the primary component in water, the essence of heavy water. Based on Rick's assessment of the plans before him, this appeared to be just such a device, and it looked to be one thousand times more potent than the current US atomic bomb. It was scary and yet exciting, and understanding what they had in their possession made both Malloy and Captain Smith nervous. The responsibility was astounding and terrifying. And just to top it off, they alone knew the location of three-quarters of a million dollars in Nazi gold bullion.

US intelligence headquarters in West Berlin had been on alert, waiting for news for two days, since Captain Smith had ventured through to East Berlin. The communications room was also listening in on East German radio traffic, with little success. On the second morning, it was observed by spotters stationed near the major crossing areas that the East German guards at the numerous crossing zones into the West part of the city were increased and all access points in or out were under far greater surveillance. MI-6 sources in the East had reported that the secret police were in full-alert mode and that the Russian NKVD were believed to be in Berlin and had taken an active role. The conclusion was that the Americans had not been caught, and based on the increased activity, it was possible that they had discovered the Nazi secrets and were trying to get out. There was certainly an all-out search underway, and though there was no obvious safe place to hide, the two Americans had not yet been found. The US intelligence team had heard nothing from Malloy or Captain Smith for well over twenty-four hours and had no way to assist them. The tension was intense, and so the team focused on developing potential exit strategies and plans to get the two men out.

The East German police had called in all their available manpower. Men from the surrounding areas had been brought in and deployed to locate and apprehend the American spies. Teams had begun a building-by-building search, fanning out from the last known point, which was Weisskirche. Pictures of Rick Malloy, based on the description provided by the priest, had been drawn and handed out to all officers and patrolmen, and the key intersections had been staffed with spotters who were told to stay put and keep a lookout until the spies were found.

With all of this in place, Igor Taimov might have felt that the situation was well in hand, but he knew that he had something even bigger to worry about. The American spy had kept ahead of them for days. They did not know anything about the other American who had joined Malloy, and the descriptions from the proprietor at the Gasthaus had not been helpful. The man had spoken some German, but whether he was American or German was not known. He was average height and weight, and had a hat that made his hair color hard to determine. No eye color was observed, and his clothes were nondescript. The family of the Gasthaus owner had not had much to add to this, leaving the sketch artist with nothing to go on. They had lost contact with their mole inside US army intelligence HQ and had to assume that the man had been caught. This also meant they had no inside information on the whereabouts and plans of the Allied team. Other informants in the west were not in a position to gain information or to help.

To make matters worse, much worse, Lavrenty Beria himself was being sent to East Berlin by Stalin, and he would be arriving within 48 hours by plane. Beria, the enigmatic leader of the NKVD through the great purge in Russia, was credited with ruthlessly killing tens of thousands of his countrymen and deporting thousands more to Siberia to labor camps. By the end of the Second World War, The Great Patriotic War for Russia, Beria had been elevated to the level of deputy prime minister, and Stalin had put him in charge of obtaining atomic weapons capability, at any and all costs. He had led the Soviets in identifying and arresting dozens of German scientists at the end of the war and then having them deported, along with their families, to the newly built and expanding atomic weapons research site at Novaya Zemlya, an island up on the Arctic Circle, adjacent to the Barents Sea. Beria had launched several spy missions to obtain US atomic weapons secrets, but he was now convinced that his best opportunity to get a jump on the Americans might be the secret papers from the laboratory at Faschgarten.

It had not been said, but was well understood by Igor Taimov, that it was critical to capture the Americans and have them ready for Beria when he arrived. If he were able to do this, he would assure his future and advance his position in the NKVD. If not, his career was in danger and quite possibly his life. This meant that within the next day he had to resolve this matter. And although it would be a great thing to present two live spies to Beria, he was perfectly content to display their dead bodies if that would assure that he caught them in time. The secret Nazi documents might or might not have to be recovered, because it was more important that the Allies not recover the documents than that he recover them. In fact, with both spies dead he could search for a while and declare that they had not been found and might not exist. This was nearly as good as catching the spies, after all, if the documents even do exist, they would certainly not have these documents on them and may not divulge their location if caught. So, Taimov issued the command to shoot on sight, and although Anna Sturm did not like it, he had the command sent out to all operatives in the field. He had not slept in two days and he needed a few hours' rest, so he left his makeshift office and went to his hotel room for a few hours of shuteye.

Malloy had concluded that the papers he examined were the genuine secret Nazi atomic bomb documents they had been searching for, and that made his mind shift back to the issue of his father. He and Captain Smith sat in the garage attic and talked quietly to each other about the alternatives, plans, and options. Malloy was appreciative of Smith's kind understanding about his father, and his offer to help in any sane way, but Captain Smith had also made it clear that it would be difficult to get both of them and the documents out to the West. By adding a quarter ton or more of gold into the mix, it became nearly impossible. By including his father, a prisoner in a political refugee prison camp, into the equation, the odds of getting out alive became very long indeed.

They decided that they needed to get out to the West as soon as possible, but just returning, hard as that would be, would not be safe in itself. The East Germans and NKVD would pursue them to the ends of the earth. And the secret documents created a second problem that must be dealt with--the Allies must have them, but it would be good if the Russians did not know it, and better if the Russians believed that they had recovered them. Their plan would need to be very special. They needed something else, and for that, they would need help from the Allied intelligence agencies, which meant that they needed to get a message out to them. Malloy knew that Smith had a limited vocabulary in German, but they agreed that he was probably less easily recognizable to anyone on the lookout for the Americans. He also knew the locations of agents in East Berlin and how to contact them to get the message out. And traveling alone would not be expected, either. As they had done several times before, they needed to develop their plan for escape. They did not really need the gold in the church, but having some of it could serve multiple purposes, including being used to stop bullets when stacked in the trunk of a car. It might also be useful for buying freedom for Malloy's dad, and of course, if caught, it might provide some leverage. So Rick would need to return to Weisskirche.

They began to formulate a plan that would accomplish as many of their objectives as possible. They needed decoy plans and alternatives in case things did not go as expected. They needed to think about the Nazi atomic plans, the gold, Rick's father, and maybe most importantly, themselves. They needed to anticipate the moves of the East Germans and their reactions to Malloy and Smith's own moves, and although they were not aware of the Russian level of involvement, they had to assume that there would be an all out search to keep them from escaping to the West. They needed targeted help from the West, specifically, a diversion and escape coordinated with army intelligence. It would need to be a really good plan.

After several hours of developing and refining their escape plan, they were satisfied that it was the best they could do. The largest concern was that US army intelligence could not, or would not, put it in place in time. But it was time for Smith and Malloy to start putting their mission into action. They parted company to each embark on their part of the plan, and as agreed, Rick gave Captain Smith his watch and the MIT ring he had worn for several years. It was an important part of their plan to have their worldly belongings together in one place, so Captain Smith put Malloy's things along with his own, wrapped in a piece of brown paper found on the floor in the garage, in his pocket. After noon, Captain Smith headed north back into the central part of the city to contact a relay operative and set up assistance from the West in executing their plan. Based on his discussion with Malloy, whose experience and suggestions he had come to admire, he would walk five or six blocks on one tangent, then pause for a few minutes and continue in a little different direction toward his goal. He had a schedule, but was in no particular hurry.

Late in the afternoon he reached his goal, the workshop of a carpenter who had often provided information to Allied intelligence after the war and acted as a relay when it was needed. He was one of the most reliable couriers they had used since the end of the war. Smith had to wait about thirty minutes for the man to return from an errand, and so he looked around a bit. He knew little about woodworking, but he assumed that in these modern times, the man would have lathes and drills and planing tools required to build furniture. But what he found in the small shop was hand tools--chisels, various handsaws and mitre boxes, and even hand drills. It was clear that this man was a craftsman, not a mass producer of cheap items. A few partially completed pieces showed the detail and quality and painstaking work that was done to complete his furniture. As he surveyed the shop, the owner, the relay, appeared back from his errand. He had never met Smith in person, although they had spoken once by telephone and exchanged notes several times. The man was cautious and they reviewed the last time they had communicated, several weeks earlier, to establish that this was indeed Captain Smith of US army intelligence who was in his shop.

Having gotten through the formalities, the operative began to tell Smith about the extraordinary efforts going on in the city to catch the two American spies: random searches, checkpoint stops along major routes, increased train station and border checkpoint guards, and serious involvement of the Russians in apprehending Smith and Malloy. The operative did not know what Malloy and Smith's mission was and did not care to know--he feared he knew too much already, and meeting Smith in person did not help with that. Captain Smith gave him explicit instructions to be relayed to US intelligence in West Berlin. These instructions would be critical to their escape from East Germany alive, and so even the smallest detail must be relayed perfectly, and the intelligence team then had to act on the information immediately and exactly as given. Timing would be critical to success.

Just as the operative did not wish to know more than he had to, Smith did not ask how the operative would transmit his information. It would be interesting, but dangerous for the operative if Captain Smith were to know and later be captured. He did ask when the information would be received and was told that US army command in Berlin would have the message before midnight tonight. Smith handed the man Rick Malloy's and his own watch, ring, and personal items, which were also to be delivered to Allied Intelligence in the West as part of the plan. There was little time for pleasantries, so after this he left by the rear entrance and started back into the city returning from his destination.

The tension in East German secret police headquarters had grown to a fever pitch. Taimov had returned to the office after five hours' rest. He and his men were completely in charge and directing every movement. Bad news or even no news was greeted with insults about incompetence, and threats of potential dismissal. The two Americans had disappeared during the night and they had not been seen since being spotted and nearly caught at the church the night before. Did the West have hiding places in East Berlin?

"Impossible, we know that this is not so!" stammered the head East German officer in the bureau.

"Then, how is it that the Americans can hide from you so easily?" bellowed Taimov.

"I do not know," came the weak reply. And so it went.

Taimov had ordered every available officer into the hunt and cancelled traffic duties to increase the manpower on the search. He had concentrated his men near all of the crossing points into West Berlin, and based on the distance it would take to get to the border with West Germany or even Austria, he believed that they would not risk traveling on open roads during the day where they could be spotted and easily trapped. All roads leading out from the outskirts of the city to the south and west had checkpoints, and orders were to stop every car leaving the Berlin city area and search it. This applied to the Autobahn as well, and already the traffic jams were causing problems of their own. And yet nothing had turned up, and no one had seen the Americans in over twelve hours. Taimov knew that Beria would arrive the following evening and he felt the pressure continue to build. He called for Anna Sturm to come to his office.

"Yes?" Agent Sturm said coldly as she came into the makeshift office Taimov had set up for himself.

"Sit down, Anna Sturm," commanded Igor Taimov. She took a seat across from his desk, but you could feel the tension between them. There were no pleasantries, and Taimov made no pretense of hiding his dislike for Anna. "Let me be very clear, Ms. Sturm. If we do not find your young American friend by tomorrow night, neither of our careers will be worth much. The difference will be that I will return to Moscow without the promotion I deserve, while in your case, I will personally see to it that you will be sent to perform guard duty in a gulag. I do not know if you have any ability to help catch these spies, but I suggest that you put forth every possible effort. No, let me be even more clear--I demand that you get out there and find these bastards, or I will personally see you sent to Siberia. Now go!"

Taimov had gotten red in the face as he leaned over the desk screaming at Anna Sturm. Sturm was angry herself, but she knew he was not kidding, and this was not the time to argue about who had

268

done what. Still, she could not sit back and take this without any re-
tort. She got up, looked Taimov directly in the eye, and as she left the
room she turned away from him and said, "I have performed my mission exactly as instructed. You let him escape and you cannot seem to
catch him. Now, I must bail you out of this as well?"

She stormed out and slammed the door before he could respond.

Taimov got even more contorted in the face and screamed after
her, "Find those bastards!" and then he sat back down in his chair and
stared at the ceiling. It would be a long day if the spies were not found.

CHAPTER TWENTY FIVE

OCTOBER, 1946

After hiding the secret Nazi papers and the four gold bars they brought from the church under an empty burlap sack in the back of the loft, Rick Malloy set off to complete his part of the plan about fifteen minutes after Captain Smith left the garage. As had Smith just a bit earlier, he slipped out of the side window and made his way through the bushes to the street. It may have been unnecessary, but being cautious just made sense. He headed back toward the church. He knew that he must stay away from major boulevards and intersections that might have secret police on the lookout, and he planned his route to use side streets and stay far away from any crossing areas into West Berlin. He was sure that these would be carefully watched.

He also knew he needed to change his looks one last time. With careful consideration, he found a small Weinstube and he went in and found a seat in a corner, ordered a glass of white wine, and after sitting a few minutes and reading the paper, eating bread and drinking his wine, he paid his tab and went into the bathroom. It was still early in the day and he would probably be able to be alone, undisturbed in the bathroom, for quite a while. As before, he got out his small grooming kit, the one he had carried with him since he entered the East. Rick shaved his beard stubble, but left the mustache and chin area unshaved and again shaved back his hairline even more to change his look as much as possible. He got out his hair dyes and mixed them in the sink. He took his light grey colored hair and dyed it dark brown, almost black. In all, it took about twenty minutes to redefine his look significantly. He exited quietly, without drawing much attention to the fact that he was very different in leaving than he had looked in entering the wine bar. No one paid much attention as he left the bar.

His next stop was to obtain another pair of reading glasses, for he no longer had the pair he had used when he entered Berlin. He was able to do this easily at a pharmacy just a few blocks further down the street. These were not needed for reading, but again, it changed his look just a bit and would tend to age him to the casual observer. He knew of an open-air market and there he looked around until he found a very sturdy two-wheeled cart--somewhat like the type typically used by elderly to carry their groceries home from the market, but one that was a bit more sturdy. He haggled over the price and then ended up overpaying for the cart, after trying to borrow it and then trying to rent it, but he felt that this would raise less suspicion than just offering to buy it right off. He purchased some bread and cheese and gathered several large brown cloth bags and put it all on his rolling cart to disguise it somewhat. In all, he looked pretty much like an old man returning from grocery shopping, exactly the image he wished to present.

He continued carefully toward the church called Weisskirche and sat down the street and observed. He ate some cheese and bread and watched carefully for who was doing what in the area. He waited about twenty minutes, then moved his location and sat and ate a little more. After nearly an hour, he was satisfied that there was no obvious police detail watching the building, and only one person who seemed suspicious. This man seemed to just hang about, and based on what Rick had observed, he was either a sexton who worked at the church and was on a long break, or he was a clever police agent assigned to watch the building for the return of the Americans. Either way, this man would have to be dealt with, although Rick Malloy had already decided that he was not about to kill someone over a bunch of gold bars. He did think that he would have to render the man unconscious in order for him to complete his mission. He also decided to use his cart and his old man look to get up close and then he would decide how to handle the man wandering around near the church.

He hunched over and shuffled up to the man but just could not tell if he was a janitor--or sexton, as he had learned that they were often called--or an East German agent. Malloy had little practice in these matters, and he had no weapon in his possession. He had not brought a gun and would not shoot the man if he had one. He had his two weeks' instruction in hand-to-hand combat, but had had little real experience. He would hope to rely on the element of surprise. He moved slowly toward the church, pushing his cart. The man who had been milling around in the area in front of the church moved to greet him as he approached the side entrance. As the man got closer, he spoke out to Rick and asked him if he was a member of this church, and Rick interpreted from this that the man was not the sexton for he would surely know many of the older parishioners and at least know that he had never seen Rick. This caused Rick to assume that this man was a plainclothes officer working for the secret police, watching the building. It was likely that he was not a seasoned agent, having been assigned to sit around all day, so Rick reasoned that he was likely a reassigned local policeman, someone more accustomed to directing traffic, someone who would hesitate before using force, someone Rick could deal with. But Rick was still not a trained mercenary himself and he wanted to be sure before he attacked this man; he decided he would allow one more test.

He kept his head down and slowed, but did not turn around. He responded in street German, "I am just attending afternoon confession with the reverend," assuming that the sexton should know that this was not a Catholic Church and thus would not have confession, and that a reverend would not hear confession anyway. If the man did not object, then Malloy felt sure he knew whom he was dealing with. The man continued to approach but said nothing to indicate he knew Malloy had said something odd, and Malloy had decided that he would have to subdue this man by force and prepared for the task. Rick pretended to not know the agent was coming up behind him, but as the man reached out to grab Rick by the arm, Rick reached up and grabbed the man's hand, and once again bent it down painfully, and turned the man around. Then he grabbed the man around the neck and as hard as he was able, he gave him a chop to the back of the neck. It was partially effective, causing the man to crumple to the ground in a heap, but while the man was in pain, he was not unconscious. Rick panicked and kicked the man hard in the side of the head, and he then slumped into unconsciousness. At least he hoped it was just unconsciousness.

Rick dragged him into the bushes next to the side entrance to the church. He took the shirt off the secret police agent and ripped it into long strips. Then he tied his hands and feet and gagged the man so he could not move or cry out for help when he woke up. It had all happened in less than five minutes, but as Rick completed tying up the agent, he was pleased at how he was able to catch him by surprise and disable him, even if it wasn't a textbook-clean performance.

Malloy carefully walked up to the side door and went in to the church. He knew it pretty well by now, and he moved quickly to the front anteroom that had the closet containing the large armoire chest. He opened the door and looked inside the closet. The chest was still in place, and clearly neither the East German secret police nor the priest had found the hole in the wall hiding the treasure behind it. Rick was pleased that the church was empty, but he also knew that this could change quickly. He pulled the chest forward, reached into the hole in the wall, and removed the canvas covering that had been hiding the gold. He carefully removed each bar and put it into the cart as quickly as he could, placing them carefully in the brown paper sacks. He had suspected that the cart would not handle the load and quickly realized that they would not be able to take all of the bars of gold with them. He and Smith had calculated the weight of the entire load, and based on this they had come up with a contingency plan that would leave the remaining gold behind to use as leverage if it was needed, either in case something went wrong with their plans, or to use to get his father out of prison.

He moved twelve of the 44 remaining bars into the cart, and at about 360 pounds it was severely taxing the capabilities of the device meant to carry about 150 pounds. He would need to be careful transporting it so as not to break the overloaded two-wheeler. He took out one additional bar and set it aside, leaving the remaining thirty-one bars of gold in the wall behind the closet and after once again covering the gold with the canvas cloth, he pushed the chest back into place. Unless someone moved the chest, reached into the hole in the wall, and then removed the canvas, this gold would sit undetected for a long time. Malloy was counting on this. He carefully wrapped the paper bags around the gold in his cart so that nothing was visible and the entire cart looked like it was just full of very heavy groceries. He took the one last bar back into the sanctuary of the church, went up to the altar, and placed the bar behind the large crucifix. It was out of sight to the public, but would be clearly visible to the priest when preparing for a service.

He wrote a brief note: "Thank you, Father. Sorry for violating Friedrich Anlauer's memorial. I hope you will find this useful," signed, "Rick Malloy." He placed the note under the bar of gold and returned to his cart. He left the church through the same side door by which he entered and checked to see how the man he had tied up less than an hour earlier was doing. Rick was glad that he had not regained consciousness, but he was also worried that he had kicked the man too hard. Nonetheless, he had already thrown a man from a train and killed two guards, and he needed to move on.

Malloy headed carefully back toward the garage lair he had used for the last several days. It might have looked strange for a young man to be pushing such a heavy grocery cart, but having worked to alter his look, he was also hunched over a bit, taking it slowly, and with his disheveled clothes and demeanor he presented himself as an older man returning home from grocery shopping. He followed his careful route, retracing the steps he used to approach the church. Berlin was a big city and he was glad that even with all the secret police that must be on the search for them, none were to be found on the back streets he had chosen. Rick had planned to arrive back at the garage after dark and being the fall, he was approaching the garage loft about dusk, right on schedule. He noted that the lights were on in the house, and so he was very careful in approaching. In order to get the gold into the attic, he had to open the garage doors a little bit, and so he waited a few minutes until it was fully dark, and then he entered cautiously. He had completed his task and now only had to wait for Captain Smith to return.

Smith had delivered the plans and message to the operative in the north of the city with a fair amount of ease. It was a long walk, and on several occasions he altered his route when he saw something suspicious up ahead, just to be sure. He stopped in a market and bought some food and a bottle of wine for the two men to eat and drink, and he occasionally would stop and sit on a bench to make sure he was not being followed. He was not stopped, and being very sure that he had not been followed, he finally completed his route back south to the garage. Having completed his mission for the day, the success of their escape was now in the hands of Allied intelligence in London and West Berlin. He returned about an hour after Malloy, and both men marveled at the gold that they had now stacked in the attic as they ate the cured meat and cheese and drank cheap wine.

At 10:00 that night, the US army command received the message from Captain Smith and it nearly sent the top brass over the edge. On the one hand, it was a stupendous victory, as it appeared that the American team believed that they had recovered amazing Nazi documents that might significantly help the US atomic bomb program. On the other hand, the escape plan detailed in the message was so outrageous that it was hard to consider seriously. At first, there was the thought that it was not possible and therefore would not be attempted. Worse yet, it seemed risky to the participants, including Smith and Malloy. However, the alternatives were few. Knowing that the two Americans could not be reached in order to be alerted to any change in plans at this point made further consideration of the proposed plan absolutely necessary.

The man put in charge, Colonel James Whitcombe, started to see the cleverness of the plan, and based on his warming up to the idea a bit, stopped trying to deny that it would work and started to organize a team to see if it could be made to happen. He contacted London and received the initial go-ahead for the rescue mission. It would take a lot of political juice to get this set up in only eighteen hours, but understanding the potential value of the Nazi atomic secrets and how desperately the East Germans were searching for the two Americans, there was no question that every effort would be made and the resources expended. Besides, Jimmy Whitcombe had no love for the senior brass, or for that matter, for any bureaucracy; he enjoyed stirring things up a bit. So, pending official approval of the plan, Whitcombe moved forward to make it happen. As requested, the colonel authorized a small jump trainer plane that could be fitted out to land in a field, and sent out a call for a pilot who was willing to take on this dangerous mission. He sent a messenger to the military hospital to retrieve the other things requested by Captain Smith, but it made him shake his head just thinking about it. The team stayed at it all night, obtaining clearances, identifying and locating the requested materials, and preparing for the upcoming day.

By morning, the plan was just about pulled together precisely as requested, although no one was yet comfortable that the plan would even work. Never mind that it had not been fully authorized for a "Go" by London yet. No airplane pilots were qualified for the exact work required so a call had been put out to a nearby army airborne regiment for a paratrooper who might have some flying experience. They were lucky to find a lieutenant who had previously been in pilot training, and he had volunteered for the assignment. He would report for duty by 0700 hours and be able to practice landing, take-off, and flying the trainer plane for about five hours before having to stop, so that ground crew and agents briefed on the mission could prepare the aircraft properly for the rescue attempt. According to the plan, the plane must be ready to take off right before dusk, and completion of the mission be achieved before sundown. Ultimate success depended on getting the job done at dusk when it was difficult to see too far, but before it was too dark to see anything clearly. The timing was important to achieving the desired result, although full details of the escape plan were kept close by Major Whitcombe and were not fully known to most Allied intelligence operatives for fear of any leak that might jeopardize the entire plan. Only Colonel Whitcombe and General Johnston fully understood the nature of the mission, and the general was informed only in order to gain clearance for the mission.

Anna Sturm had been pursuing every possibility she could come up with. She had sent a team to Rick Malloy's old ancestral home East of the city center and found that the building was in ruins and no one had been in it in years. Hitler had confiscated all of the family's property over a decade earlier and then done nothing with it. He had given it to a general who had been killed during the Russian campaign, and as a result the grounds had really never been used or even occupied. The cost of fixing the place back up had led to no one wanting the home. Anna had no direct informant contacts in Allied intelligence at this point, but she did have several well-placed people on Allied military posts and so she leaned on these people to get her information. It had taken all night and a part of the morning, but finally she had heard from one informant who worked at the Allied airfield at Tempelhof, in West Berlin.

When the news came, it was just what she needed. It was reported that a small, unarmed aircraft, usually used for surveillance or paratroop training, had been requisitioned and called on for duty later that day. The order had come from a very high-ranking officer, which was not typical of standard operation, certainly not for this type of aircraft. Practice sessions of some sort were being conducted that morning and while there was no information at all about the flight plan or the intended destination, that in itself was of great significance. It was believed by the informant that the plane would be used later that day, but with no flight plan, it was impossible to tell.

Anna had the break she needed. She alerted her superiors first so that the pig, Taimov, could not claim credit for her excellent work; then she went to Taimov himself with the information. Igor Taimov was already in a horrible mood, knowing that Lavrenty Beria would be flying in late in the day and that unless they were able to apprehend the Americans, it would be an awful situation. He listened intently to her report on the informant's description of the timing, the secrecy and the type of plane, and he actually began to smile.

"So, the Americans think they can fly in low, swoop down and pick up their spies and get out before we can react, eh?" he spat out indignantly. "This is good work, Anna Sturm. I still do not approve of you, but it is good work. It is the break that we need. Now work with my team to see to it that this plane that must be planning to enter our sovereign airspace does not succeed in its mission."

Then before Anna could get much of a word in, Taimov got up and left the room, stepping into the main vestibule of the headquarters and announcing that he had obtained accurate and reliable information about the spies and they would be setting a trap to capture them later this evening. Anna Sturm was again furious with this obnoxious Russian ass.

Based on the leaked information, The Russians and East Germans identified exactly fourteen open areas large enough to land a small plane and take off again within five kilometers of the border around West Berlin. It would be foolish for the Americans to fly deep into Soviet or East German airspace--this would not provide reasonable odds for success and would provoke a very public and humiliating explanation that the Allies would prefer to avoid. No, thought Anna Sturm, Rick Malloy would be at one of these open areas tomorrow night to fly out of East Germany for good, and she would be there to stop him. The Russian-led team she was now a part of began to draw up plans for troop deployments at each field. The fields would be ringed with machine guns and some would have anti-aircraft guns on site as well. But this would take some time, and they had only a few hours now before the American mission was likely scheduled to commence. They had to hurry.

It was mid-morning on the day they expected to escape from East Germany, and Rick Malloy and Captain Smith were painfully aware that their plan of escape required split-second timing and luck. They also knew that this was their last day in the garage. In the morning they were hungry, and neither man had had a bath in several days. They decided to drop in on their benefactor, the older man who owned the house, and take advantage of his home for this last day. Rick went around the back of the house while Captain Smith, who had his .45

automatic at the ready, rang the doorbell. The elderly man answered the door and was shocked to be pushed back into his own house by an American holding a pistol. He tried to scream something in German about not being a Nazi, but he was terrified and not very coherent. Smith did not understand his German well anyway.

Rick came in the back way, having jimmied the lock, and he assured the old man that they had no intention of harming him. They were just hungry and needed to take refuge in his home for a while. If he cooperated they would reward him well, and if not, then it could be more painful than anyone wanted. They tied the man up so that they did not have to worry about his doing something silly, and sat him on the sofa in his living room. To assure the old man they were sincere, Rick Malloy placed 2,000 Reichsmarks in his lap, a decent sum of money, even with the post-war inflation. He made it clear that the man would get to keep the money and never have to tell anyone where he got it if he cooperated. After a few minutes the man was breathing normally and actually wanted to talk about the war and his attempts to try to repel the Russians in the final days, as well as his service in the First World War.

Rick got the man some water and asked if he was on any medications that he needed to take, while Captain Smith washed up in the man's bathroom. Afterwards they switched places, and Malloy cleaned up as best he could without having any clean clothes to put on. Then they went through the man's kitchen and made some sandwiches using what was available in his icebox and cupboard.

After they were cleaned up and had eaten, Captain Smith left to complete the next stage of their plan. They needed a car for their travel plans later that night. They had discussed at length what type of car would be best and Rick, who knew little about cars, relied on Captain Smith, a self-professed car nut, to tell him what type of car would be needed. They decided on a large car that was sturdy in build, had a powerful motor, and might afford some level of protection in case they were fired upon on their escape route. This limited them to either an expensive but sturdy Mercedes, which would be ideal, but hard to find in East Berlin, or an older Horsch or Auto Union sedan, which would be easier to locate, but not as sturdy. These auto manufacturers had tried to emulate Mercedes prior to the war by building big, luxury sedans, thus meeting the criteria of large, heavy, and powerful. These large sedans had heavy-duty metal frames, solid oak coach work supports, and extra-thick exterior sheet metal that would slow or deflect small arms fire. The car needed a large trunk area and ability to carry the weight of the gold and the extra protection they would add to the car. Malloy knew the Berlin area from his childhood, and so he directed Smith to a neighborhood not too far from where he had grown up, where this type of auto might more likely be found.

Captain Smith returned several hours later, about 3 p.m., driving a large black Horsch sedan. He had stolen the car after hot-wiring the vehicle and he had then driven it off without incident or detection by its owner. At Rick Malloy's insistence, he had left 5,000 Reichsmarks in an envelope in the home's mailbox to cover the loss of the car. Smith, immediately upon arrival back at the house, went to work reinforcing the car to withstand bullets by stacking thick oak boards onto the back seat that he got out of the old man's garage. They easily would stop any small arms fire and probably stop a machine gun if it were at a distance. He hoped that if required, it would be adequate. But then he also hoped there were no machine guns fired at the car in the first place. Anything larger than that, and he did not care to think about it.

He then placed these same boards in the driver's door area up to the door sill and stacked them upright behind the seat to protect the driver. Smith would drive, and he would not be able to enter the car through the door, but could still climb over from the passengers side of the car. After doing the same on the passenger side door, Smith loaded the sixteen bars of gold into the trunk and stacked them to protect the gas tank from gunfire. It was no armored car and far from perfect, but they were more secure in this way than almost any thing else they could think of.

It was nearly 5 p.m., and it was time for them to leave and begin to put their escape plan into motion. Rick untied the old man, who became a bit afraid when Rick then retied one hand to the stove in the kitchen. The man would be able to untie this hand in only a few minutes, but by then the Americans would be gone and the man would not be able to tell the police which direction they had gone, because he could not see out to the front of his house from the kitchen where he was tied up. Besides, the man did not have a telephone and it would take an hour for him to report anything to the police if he worked hard at it. Both Malloy and Smith hoped the old man would count his money and not call the police at all.

Rick Malloy thanked the elderly man for his hospitality and then ran out to the car in the driveway and got into the back seat. He would stay low so that if seen there would appear to be one person in the car, not the two Americans being sought all over Berlin. And if seen, the one person visible would not be Malloy, whose face was known. Following their plan as they had laid it out they headed southeast, through Kopenick, following the Gosener Landstrasse, then heading back west into Eichwalde, slowly moving around the southest of the city of Berlin. Rick had a map and based on his memory of the area from years earlier they took side streets and avoided main intersections altogether. They were headed to their pre-arranged embarkation point, the place where they would attempt their cross over into West Berlin. If all went well, they would sleep in West Berlin that night.

Chapter Twenty Six

The American plan was moving into full gear as they approached 1800 hours, 6 p.m. Berlin time. The plane would take off from Tempelhof airport at 6:15 p.m. and should touch down approximately twenty minutes later, southwest of the West Berlin-American sector, and just a few hundred yards into the East, in a field in Johannisthal. According to the announced plan, the plane and pilot would have less than five minutes of wait time for the two Americans, then, with or without them, would take off and return to the American sector in West Berlin, landing back at the Tempelhoff airport. Total elapsed time would be less than an hour. It seemed so simple, but there was significant risk.

The paratrooper pilot had finished his practice earlier in the day and was in the briefing room preparing for the mission. He was being briefed by Major James Whitcombe himself, and as the plan unfolded he began to understand the true nature of the mission. He would be required to wear a parachute in case it was needed due to enemy fire, which was fully expected, and the plane would be carrying several containers of very strange cargo that made no sense until all the details of the mission were explained to him. As he understood the exact way the mission was intended to unfold and its top-secret nature, he also began to realize how dangerous it would be.

The plane was prepped by security-cleared personnel, and because only the pilot and the two top intelligence officers in Berlin understood the entire mission or knew what was in the cargo crates that had been loaded inside the plane, the plane was guarded closely, awaiting take-off. The pilot left the briefing room and was taken straight to the plane. After going through the pre-flight checklist he started up the engine and was cleared on to the runway. At almost exactly 6:15 p.m. he lifted off and banked a low left turn and headed south and east, toward East Berlin.

The Russians and East Germans had massed over a thousand combined troops and police and positioned them around the eastern border with West Berlin discreetly, but very efficiently. Nearly all of these troops were positioned in the fourteen identified potential landing areas and were setting up and preparing for the Americans by 5 p.m. They had orders to stop the exit from the East at any cost, and "shoot to kill" had been authorized. Anna Sturm had decided, based on her information, that Malloy would use the south of the city for his exit. She would position herself in that area in a car and be able to move to the specific field in only a few minutes, as soon as the plane was spotted.

Igor Taimov, not to be outdone, had moved his command post to the south as well and had established himself in a farmhouse adjacent to one of the more likely fields. He was extremely nervous as a result of knowing that Beria would be arriving from Moscow this very evening, and he had no idea what he would be able to report when the feared man arrived. He was taking no chances. To that end, he had called for air support to be ready if needed to assure that the American plane did not complete its mission. Two Russian Yakovlev Yak-1 fighter aircraft had been called on to be at the ready, in the air and waiting should the need arise. He had asked for the newer, faster Mikoyan-Gurevich aircraft, known as the MiG-3, but none were stationed close enough to provide the assistance he requested. He hoped neither would be required, but he would not be caught unprepared. No expense would be spared and no precaution not taken.

Rick Malloy and Captain Smith were only a couple of miles from the American sector, and safety, but had driven over fifteen miles and had taken nearly an hour to arrive at their destination. They had moved around several roadblocks by traveling slowly and turning off when they got into a roadblock area. Some of the roadblocks had not even been manned, as personnel were diverted to potential landing areas, but Smith and Malloy took no chances. It had added time and distance, but they had avoided confrontation that might have ruined their plans. They moved south of East Berlin proper, staying far enough away from the East/West border to avoid detection. Now having come to the small town of Teltow, south and a bit west of the main city center of Berlin, they were less than a kilometer from a usually lightly guarded crossing gate and freedom into the West. There were no houses in this pastoral area, and no vehicles passing by at this time of day. They parked their car out of sight, in a small wooded area next to a small park or field dotted with brush and small trees that no one seemed to be focused on. It seemed like a perfect area to land a small plane in, and the random trees and bushes would make landing and take-off easier to hide from view. They then rolled down the windows and listened for an airplane. Now all they could do was wait and hope for the best.

Back in US intelligence headquarters in West Berlin, Major Whitcombe and several high-ranking officers were monitoring the mission's progress from the situation room. A second ground team had been dispatched and was in place in the woods near the border area and adjacent to the landing zone. Their stated objective was to watch and report on what happened while the plane was over East German territory. They would observe but not be able to be of any assistance over the border without jeopardizing the mission. By now the US plane was traveling at a very low altitude and was moving along the border between the Russian and American sectors in Berlin. The mission called for this flight plan to create the deniability required when the Russians protested, as they surely would, when this was over. The idea was one of claiming that the plane was merely on a routine training mission and went off course temporarily. At 6:25 p.m. the pilot radioed that he was in position and after receiving a go ahead, relayed from Major Whitcombe, the plane turned south and headed toward a field just over the border. The plane flew by at treetop level once, and then banked hard and came back in for a landing in the field.

Rick Malloy and Captain Smith heard the plane fly over near where they were waiting and started to get ready. When they could hear that the engines had shut off, signaling that it had landed, they would start up the car and head off. The timing was critical. They only had a couple of minutes to reach the destination. The men shook hands and said a few kind words, but the tension was clear and they knew that the next several minutes would determine their fate and probably their lives.

Anna Sturm did not need to wait for the call, as she heard the plane as well. She immediately called for a car to race to the field where the plane was in the process of landing. Based on her map and the direction the sound was coming from, she had guessed very well and the plane was indeed coming to the South. The field that the Americans had selected was only a few kilometers away. She would be there in less than five minutes. Compared to the previous several days, when they had seemed a step behind the Americans, this time it looked like the tables had turned and they had the upper hand. They would have the field surrounded and there was no chance of Rick Malloy or the other American escaping.

She had every intention of apprehending Rick alive, but she understood that if Taimov got his way or if there was any resistance put up by Rick or the other American, a hail of gunfire would rain down on the plane and its occupants.

Anna Sturm and her team arrived at the road that passed by the field at about the same time as Igor Taimov and his group of Russian agents. They stayed out of sight, as did the other police officers and soldiers, numbering nearly a hundred, that were now stationed there watching as the airplane touched down and bounced across the field in front of them. The plane taxied through the field toward a wooded outcropping across from them and then the plane stopped, some 600-800 yards away from them.

Immediately the order was given to apprehend the plane, and so two trucks with armed men in them came out of the woods and started slowly heading toward the plane. It would be a matter of only two or three minutes until they were at the plane and even less before they were within shooting distance. Taimov had his binoculars out and was watching the proceedings carefully. The door on the far side of the plane opened and although he could see very little of what happened he could tell that there was some activity. After several seconds, he observed a man wearing a dark-green shirt, like that of an American army soldier, run from the tall grass behind the plane around to the near side and jump in the open door of the plane. A half minute later, also from tall grass behind the plane, a second man wearing a gray shirt and carrying a yellow satchel under his arm was seen running toward the plane and then jumped in. The trucks were almost within firing range of the plane, bouncing across the field as fast as they could reasonably travel. A few seconds passed and the plane started to rev its engines for taxi and take-off.

The plane began to move, and even though the distance was too great for the police and soldiers to be accurate, several shots rang out. First, a few shots were fired, meant to be a warning to the pilot to not attempt to take off. It was quickly clear that the pilot was not going to heed the warning shots, and so Taimov gave the order by radio to the pursuing trucks to disable the aircraft to prevent it from taking off. More consistent small-arms fire, followed a few seconds later by machine-gun fire, began to rain down on the moving airplane.

The plane was moving much faster now and approaching the end of the field. It turned around and started coming back toward the two trucks, and as it did it gained the speed needed for take-off. Faster and faster it moved as it approached the trucks. The trucks turned to block take-off, and this also allowed the soldiers to take better aim. The plane came right at them, and as it got closer some of the men jumped from the trucks for fear of being directly hit straight on by the plane. At the last second, the pilot pulled up on the stick, launching the plane into the air and just over the top of the trucks, crashing one wheel of the landing gear into the roof of a truck, breaking the glass of the truck window and twisting the landing gear, damaging the take-off capability of the plane and eliminating a safe landing potential. The plane could be seen to have numerous bullet holes in the sides as it flew over the trucks, and although it floundered a bit after hitting the truck with its landing gear and dipped somewhat back toward the ground, it continued its take-off and started to gain altitude.

Only fifty feet off of the ground, the plane banked slightly toward the north and slowly started to gain altitude. The hail of bullets continued and gunfire was poured into the plane by the ground troops, although hitting a moving object with a shoulder-fired rifle was near impossible. The plane started to show smoke from the left side of the engine area, but it continued to climb. Taimov was already on the walkie-talkie and had ordered the two Russian fighter planes, already in the air and on standby, to shoot down the small American trainer plane immediately. He received a response that they would be on the location in less than twenty seconds, which would allow them to catch the aircraft before it reached the border.

The small plane was still under fire, as it climbed to 200 then 300 feet. It was clearly struggling to gain altitude, and it had not fully completed its turn toward the border yet. As Taimov watched through his binoculars, he wondered if the pilot and the other two Americans were hit and injured, as the plane might have had a better chance of making it if it had immediately moved straight toward the border. As the small plane now continued its gradual turn toward the US sector, the two Russian fighters appeared, each with its twin 7.62 mm machine guns firing as they streaked by. They were moving so much faster than the small, slow trainer plane; it was not clear that they even hit the plane with their bullets. Then, suddenly, the rear of the small plane exploded into flames and smoke, and then the tail section of the small aircraft started to fold up.

Igor Taimov and Anna Sturm and the entire force of East German and Russian pursuers watched through their binoculars as the plane faltered and they could see the pilot seem to leave his place in the cockpit of the plane and struggle to try to go back and help the two American spies who must be passengers sitting back in the rear section of the plane that was now on fire and falling apart. Then they saw the side door open and what looked like the pilot jump from the plane. Just after he jumped the entire plane burst into flames and then exploded, and it began to crash toward the ground. The right wing strut broke and with that the wing folded up and back. The plane ceased flight and was simply falling to the ground. It was clear that only one person had made it out of the plane and it looked like it was the pilot. They had not reached the border with the American sector, and Taimov was very sure that the plane would crash in Russian territory.

The pilot was not easy to follow as he fell from the skies. He was able to pull his parachute ripcord, and although the chute opened, the altitude was so low that Taimov wondered if the chute would slow his fall much before he hit ground. Given the short time that had elapsed, he suspected that only the pilot had a parachute on and properly fastened for use anyway. The pilot would also likley be killed, and that was too bad, as it would have been good to capture and interrogate this pilot. But he did not care much about this as he moved back to watching the aircraft slowly crash toward the ground. It was now engulfed in flames and black smoke and as it tumbled to Earth, and as it descended, it had also fallen back toward the Russian sector, assuring that the two Americans and their cargo would not be leaving East Berlin.

The plane crashed into a lightly wooded area not far from the field where it took off, having traveled less than a mile in total. The fighter aircraft had come back around, and based on the outcome of their first pass, they were released and would return to base. They radioed down to Taimov that the plane had burst into flames from their firing on it, a fact that was not so obvious to Taimov or anyone even casually watching. It seemed that the plane had caught fire before, but what was the sense of arguing, and what did it matter? As the plane hit the ground it exploded, signaling that the petrol tanks had caught fire on impact. Taimov feared that the secret documents had just gone up in smoke as well, but he was satisfied that the two Americans had not escaped, and he knew that the mission to capture the documents, at least as related to his career, was as much about keeping the Americans from getting the information as about using it in the Soviet Republic. Besides, he rationalized, they were likely not complete documents or the Nazis would have used them. He was also aware that his military was already working on developing an atomic weapon of its own, copying the designs stolen from the United States. So, all in all, he felt much better as he saw the smoke rising from the crashed airplane off in the distance.

Anna Sturm had watched from a car only about fifty yards away from Igor Taimov, and she had mixed feelings about how this had played out. She had no love for Americans and had come to grips with any feelings she had had for Rick Malloy, but she found herself somewhat disturbed about watching someone she knew so well burn to death in a plane crash. She started to hope that the men had died of gunshot wounds prior to the plane crash, but that was small consolation as well. She gathered herself professionally and walked over to Igor Taimov, NKVD senior agent in charge and coldly congratulated him on successfully completing his mission.

He looked at her a bit strangely at first and after a moment's reflection, he softened a bit and said, "Thank you agent Sturm, that is very kind. Your experience and assistance were very important in this operation. However, I think we should sift through the aircraft wreckage and make sure that in fact we have finally apprehended the elusive Mr. Malloy and the other American spy." He then ordered several of his staff to take him over to the wrecked plane.

Anna Sturm asked to go along and got in the car with Taimov. They drove for about five minutes to get as close to the wreckage as possible. They got out and walked toward the wrecked and still-smoldering parts of the airplane. Parts of the aircraft were spread across two hundred yards around the main fuselage. Only ten minutes after the crash, most of the flames had died down, with just a few areas still burning actively. The Russian NKVD men had spread out to look for human remains and the evidence came back very quickly. A yell from one agent rang out and several men ran over to examine a badly burned body, or at least a torso and head. The man had a ruined watch and American soldier dog tags. The tags indicated that the man's name was Captain William Smith, U.S. army intelligence, and showed his military ID number. There were a few more minutes of searching and another yell came that announced that a yellow pouch had been recovered. It was partially burned, but many of the papers were still completely intact and completely legible. The packet was somewhat thinner than Taimov had expected, but he did not care; he had now not only eliminated the Americans, but he had recovered the Nazi secrets in the bargain. The fact that this pouch had the red swastika and Nazi Eagle was considered a major success for Igor Taimov.

He was now starting to feel very good about the way things were turning out, but he wanted confirmation that Rick Malloy had been on the plane. Another ten minutes passed as men searched through the wreckage and surrounding woods. No complete body had been found, and it was becoming clear that one would not be found. A couple of legs were receovered, badly burned and severed from a body. Looking at the remains, which had parts of khaki pants and what was left of two feet with civilian shoes on them, it was clear that they came from someone different from the badly burned torso with dog tags. That was excellent, but not conclusive. And this presented a problem for Taimov that he did not wish to have and was not able to easily explain. He had clearly seen two different men climb into the aircraft with the pilot before it took off, and only one jumped out as the plane was shot down.

"Did Rick Malloy perish in the crash, or was he the person who got out of the aircraft, leaving the pilot as the second body recovered?" asked Anna Sturm, who was thinking the same thing as Taimov, out loud.

They had started to assist the agents performing the search when Anna Sturm was confronted with a grisly discovery. One of the search team members found an unattached arm in the bushes and directed the team to retrieve it. It appeared to be a left arm and had a ruined watch still on the wrist. Anna Sturm knew very well that Rick Malloy was proud of the very expensive Patek Phillippe watch that his father had given him, and seeing the watch and confirming the inscription on the back of the watch casing made her shiver a bit at the ultimate fate of the man she had come to know, love, hate, and pursue. This confirmed irrevocably for her and Igor Taimov that the two American spies had been on this plane and that they had finally been apprehended.

Over the next half hour additional body parts were found, including a badly burned severed right hand that had an MIT class ring, known to MIT grads as a "brass rat," and on it was engraved the graduation year of Rick Malloy. There was no inscription inside, but Anna Sturm by now knew that there would be no inscription, as Rick had none inside his ring. It was getting dark, and the team roped off the area and finished putting out the small fires. They were done here.

Anna Sturm felt a bit sad about the fate of Malloy, but she left satisfied that she had done her best for her country and had been better than the Americans. Igor Taimov rushed off to greet his superior officer, Lavrenty Beria, at the airport. He was thinking about a promotion.

On the other side of the border, in the American sector, Major Whitcombe had been listening to detailed reports from the team at the border near where the pick-up had been planned. This team was in constant contact back to the situation room by wireless radio. They observed the fly-over and the approach before the landing and heard the gunfire from less than a mile away. They saw the plane start to climb after take-off and then watched it burst into flames. They watched as the pilot bailed out, and although he was too low to open his chute fully and effectively for a safe landing, they saw him land alive in a bushy area only several hundred feet inside the American sector. They also saw that only the pilot jumped out of the plane; he was alone, with nothing in his hands, meaning that Captain Smith and Rick Malloy must have gone down with the plane, along with the Nazi atomic bomb documentation and plans.

The Allied team was shocked and in complete disbelief. They rushed to the aid of the pilot to find that he had been shot twice, in the arm and side of his body, and had been so weak that he had not broken his fall properly and as a result, had broken his leg. The man was a bloody mess and nearly unconscious from a combination of shock, blood loss, and pain. They did not have an ambulance onsite, so they put him in the back of a sedan and took him to the army hospital. Major Whitcombe ordered that he be put in seclusion and posted a guard on his room, for his protection.

Back in the situation room, at US intelligence headquarters in Berlin, officers and staff stood around and stared at each other. Not a word was said for several minutes. Major Whitcombe, realizing that this had the potential to disrupt morale in the American operation in West Berlin, finally stepped up and said, "Men, we all understood that this was a very risky assignment, and that this rescue was a long shot. Like you, I am disheartened by the outcome, but it appears that the documents this mission sought to recover have been destroyed and will not fall into enemy hands and as such we have succeeded in our efforts beyond our best hopes. Let's get back to our posts and try to put this one behind us. It is a win--not a perfect win, but a win none-theless. Please remember that this has been a top-secret operation and I expect no discussion internally as well as the obvious secrecy outside this room. None of this ever happened."

With that, Whitcombe got up and left the situation room. He went back to his office, sat in his chair, and stared at the telephone. It had been a very long day.

Chapter Twenty Seven

OCTOBER, 1946

Major James Whitcombe, ranking intelligence officer in the US West Berlin sector, sat in his office and waited for the day's incident report that he had requested as soon as it was available. Earlier in the evening, after the crash of the plane, he had told his staff that he wanted hourly reports on any unusual activity along the border between the Allies and the Russians in Berlin. He said he suspected a reprisal or some kind of retaliation on the part of the Russians as a result of the mission to rescue the two Americans, a mission that had seemed to go so horribly wrong earlier that evening. Given the nature of the mission, he would not admit to the East Germans that anyone was on the plane that went off course and was ruthlessly shot down, much less ask for return of the two men's bodies. He called his assistant into the office and directed him to find the paperwork for starting a "missing-in-action" report, the first step in the official army process to inform next of kin of a potential death in the line of duty when the body was not recovered. He would busy himself with paperwork as he waited for the upcoming incident report.

In the East, Deputy Prime Minister Lavrenty Beria had landed and was greeted by a smiling and relieved Igor Taimov at the military airfield just outside East Berlin. The two spoke for just a brief minute before getting in the car and heading to the house Taimov had prepared for the important head of Stalin's secret police.

"So, I was prepared to come down here for an unpleasant discussion, but it sounds like you are in order for congratulations, Comrade Taimov," started the great Beria.

"Thank you, sir. The mission was a challenge, but I never doubted for a second that we would prevail over the Americans," replied a relieved Taimov.

Back in East German secret police headquarters, Anna Sturm was wrapping up a few things before going home for some much-needed rest. As she typically did, she asked for a copy of the day's police activity report and began to glance at the numerous violations and crimes committed that day. There were the usual robberies and one mugging reported, as well as several domestic arguments and two unrelated murders being investigated. On a daily basis there were people apprehended trying to flee to the West with all of their belongings. This day was no exception as two families were stopped trying to leave the East sector.

"Why would anyone want to go live among those capitalist pigs?" she thought out loud for a second, and then kept on reading. In the early evening, there had been a strange event that caught her eye. Just ten kilometers from the field where the Americans were shot down, there had been a somewhat successful escape from the East by a single man driving a car that was reported as stolen. According to the report, it was at about the same time as all the commotion at the field was taking place. According to the reporting guards, the car approached the checkpoint at a normal pace, and as it came up on the guard station it accelerated and ran through the barricade, headed for the American sector. The guards shot at the man and the car repeatedly, and the guard tower opened fire with their machine gun and riddled the car with bullets as well. Surprisingly, the car did not stop or explode as might be expected and although at least one tire was shot out, the car kept going and would have crashed through the American barricade as well, except that the Americans raised their gate and let the car through.

None of this by itself was that extraordinary, and although the timing was convenient due to the plane incident that was going on at the same time, there was no reason to pay any great attention to this escape versus any of the thousands of others, thought Anna Sturm. Except for the hand-written note at the very bottom of the report by the officer in charge and on site that said: "It seemed as if the Americans were expecting this car."

Anna Sturm began to wonder if it was meaningful. She had seen Rick's ring and watch and knew that they were indeed authentic. And she had seen the yellow pouch with the swastika. But she had not seen the face of Rick Malloy, and as grotesque as that might have been to find in the wreckage, it would have provided the finality she wanted. She knew that Taimov would not be interested in this "coincidence" and would not want to even hint at the possibility that the Americans were still alive. And if the men had escaped, Anna Sturm likely could not catch them now anyway; they were gone. For a minute she pondered the logistics that would have been required to use the plane crash as a diversion and she quickly dismissed this as not being a reasonable possibility.

"The Americans are not that clever or that resourceful," she said to herself. No, there was no point in stirring up trouble that had no possible upside benefit and a lot of downside risk. She sighed, reached over and put the report in the trash can next to her desk, packed her things, and left the office for the night. It had been a long day and she needed a bath and some sleep. Besides, her career was about to take off with the promotion she would undoubtedly get from the completion of this critical and successful mission. She should be celebrating.

Major Whitcombe received the incident report update just before 22:00 hours. He knew what he was looking for and quickly found the report on an escape from the East sector that occurred at 18:35. The sergeant on duty was the senior officer at the checkpoint, and he reported that a large sedan, appearing to be driven by a single man, rammed through the East German checkpoint without stopping and continued on toward the American side. Guards on the East side opened fire on both the driver and the vehicle, in itself a fact that was very unusual in normal conditions. Normally, they would fire a warning shot or two, maybe try to shoot out the tires, but not rain bullets down on the car like they did this time. Much to his surprise, the car was successful in reaching the American side, and the American crossing guards allowed the car to pass into West Berlin as they had been instructed. The car in fact had two men in it; the second one was not easily visible, as he was hunched over in the back seat. The car was shot full of holes and the windows were shot out, but the men had braced the inside of the car with wood planking, which apparently kept them safe and protected, along with most of the car's mechanical parts. Also as instructed, they asked the men if they needed assistance and although it was clear that the driver had been shot and was bleeding, they turned down the assistance and were allowed to continue into the city of West Berlin, as instructed by superiors.

Whitcombe began to smile. "By God, they did it," he exclaimed. "Holy cow." He started to realize that in addition to a successful escape which included the two very much alive agents, these men undoubtedly had the real Nazi documents in their possession. He was elated, but he also recognized that he had no one to tell and no one to share the good news with. It had to be top secret, to protect the two men. He reflected back only 24 hours earlier on the plan that Malloy and Smith had sent to him and how outrageous it seemed. The logic was sound--the men must be believed to be dead and documents destroyed or recovered by the enemy, or they would be pursued forever. West Berlin would be no safer than East Berlin. The plan, of course, had been to have them appear to be killed in a very public diversion while they escaped quietly and without fanfare.

They felt sure that the Russians had enough spies and informants in West Berlin that suspicious activity at the airport would be picked up on immediately. Believing, as a result of their intelligence, that the Russians would be prepared, they also felt sure that the plane would be fired upon, and this led to the realization that an ordinary pilot would not be able to jump from the plane at low altitude and survive. They recruited a paratrooper who had decent flying experience, and they trained him to fly the mission and deliberately gave him an easy trainer plane. Colonel Whitcombe had ordered the military hospital to provide him with a full cadaver and several body parts, which had to include a left and right arm and legs. Combined with the jewelry and personal effects that Malloy and Captain Smith had provided, these bodies would become the two Americans, killed during their escape attempt. The plane had been filled with a several glass containers of aircraft fuel and the body parts were doused in the flammable liquid as well. The glass would shatter and be undetectable in the wreckage, whereas metal cans might be found and be suspicious. An igniter fuse was prepared for the pilot to activate as he exited the plane to ensure that the plane caught fire and then exploded. And Smith had provided a description of the yellow pouch with a red swastika so that Whitcombe could stuff useless documents into the fake pouch. Creating these useless documents was probably the hardest part of the mission, given that they only had eighteen hours in which to do it. They used some old captured Nazi weapons documents and had typists work all night adding false details. The documents were also doused with the fuel, in hopes that they would be at least partially destroyed in the crash as well. Whether they burned up or not, it would add authenticity to the event. It would take several days for someone to sort out that they contained low-level classified information about the Nazi V2 rocket program captured at the end of the war and little about atomic weapons at all. It was the best they could do on short notice.

Among the many tactical concerns was the possibility that there would be no Russian or East German presence at the landing site, in which case the plan would not work, as there would be no plausible explanation for the plane to crash and burn, thereby exposing the diversion. This was not what was needed, so they took steps to made sure that there were several intelligence leaks indicating that a small trainer plane was going to head south, toward the demarcation zone, on an unknown, last-minute mission. By not filing any flight plan, they were hoping to signal that this was an unusual flight and thereby attract attention from potential Russian informants. The other significant operational concern was exactly the opposite--that the Russians might be too well informed and too effective, leading them to be in exactly the right place and prepared to apprehend the plane when it landed. Should the pilot be apprehended alive, the operation would be exposed as a diversion.

To increase their odds, they chose a large field that would provide maneuvering room at a distance and some chance to stay away from gunfire until absolutely necessary. It would also provide a chance to take off successfully while making it look close. The paratrooper pilot himself had come up with the idea of stopping in tall grass and climbing out of the far side, nearest to the American sector, where the Russians were less likely to be waiting, and crawling through the grass away from the plane and then running back to the plane to present the image of two men boarding the plane. As it turned out, the Russian trucks advancing toward him let him know where the enemy was coming from and how to position the plane most effectively for this deception. He merely wore three shirts so that he could quickly remove one each time he got out of the plane, performing the process twice to make it look like two men ran and jumped into the plane, and before starting to take-off, he put his parachute on.

The plan had worked. Major Whitcombe reflected on the operation and its success, and he shook his head and smiled. It had been a very long day.

Rick Malloy and Captain Smith were sleeping in their safe house in West Berlin, having escaped through the barricade and driven on to the house. They had been lucky that the car had not been severely damaged by the hail of bullets, although it looked like a mess. Smith, driving in the front seat, had been shot in the upper arm and had gotten two large splinters in his left side as a result of bullets striking the oak planks. He had not thought of this possibility or he would have covered them with a blanket or something. Rick Malloy had had bits of oak, splinters, and glass rain down on him during the gunfire, while crossing the checkpoint, but he had not been injured. As they approached the checkpoint, his job was to hold a large, thick oak block up behind Captain Smith's head so that Smith could drive without being shot in the back of the head. It had largely worked, as the piece of oak had taken four bullets, any one of which might have been lethal. Unfortunately, one bullet came in at a sharp angle and hit Smith in the upper arm. It did not hit bone and although it bled a lot, it was a fairly clean wound that would heal.

Arriving at the safe house, Smith went in to tend to his arm and lie down while Malloy emptied the car of its valuables. First he took the yellow satchel inside and then came back and moved the bars of gold, two at a time, out of the trunk of the car and into the building. Then Malloy moved the car to a side street a long way from the safe house. He slowly and carefully walked back to the safe house to eat, sleep, and help patch up his friend, Captain William Smith.

Over the course of the following week the documents were delivered to US army intelligence headquarters in West Berlin, transferred to London and on to the United States for analysis by the scientists in Los Alamos working on the atomic weapons program. In a short period of time these documents would play a part in changing American thinking about atomic weapon design, confirming the work of Teller and Ulam, who had already postulated that a "Super" or H-Bomb would work, and it would cause a further shift from developing more powerful uranium and plutonium devices to developing the hydrogen bomb, roughly 1,000 times more powerful than the bombs used over Japan. Most importantly, the Russians were still trying to build atomic weapons based on the Fat Boy design, and were not able to leapfrog the US and not even working on hydrogen or heavy water devices. In a little less than five years, in 1951, the first hydrogen fusion bomb would be successfully tested by the USA, using deuterium/tritium, or heavy water.

Smith and Malloy were to be transferred out of Berlin and Europe separately, each using an alias. It took over a week for Smith to feel well enough to get around, much less travel. After he regained his strength, he visited one of the large branches of a Swiss bank in West Berlin and paid several years in advance for a safe-deposit box. He visited the box several times prior to leaving West Berlin to place items in the box, but no one other than Rick Malloy knew that the items were sixteen gold bars. They had agreed that the gold would be kept intact, unused, until a good use was found. It was to be donated to Holocaust survivor charities anonymously and not spent personally, and both felt that the US army was not a charity, so there was no mention of the gold in either man's debriefing, or in Smith's formal report on the mission's outcome.

Captain Smith was the first to exit Berlin. He and Rick Malloy promised to see each other often in the future and finally, in mid-November, 1946, said their goodbyes. William Smith was promoted to the rank of major and reassigned to provide training to new operatives back in the States. He would, in the following year, become a part of the new Central Intelligence Agency as it was formed in 1947. William Smith would retire from the CIA in 1967, as the war in Vietnam was in full swing. He lived in a modest home in the Virginia suburbs outside of Washington, DC, and filled his time volunteering at local charities and administering a small group who managed a charitable trust. As they had agreed, Smith had the Swiss bank convert the gold to currency and then it was donated to charities benefitting Holocaust survivors. In exchange for this, Malloy decided to set up and fund an honorarium, which, when invested for over thirty years, allowed Bill Smith to retire comfortably when he was ready, in 1987.

Rick Malloy stayed on in Berlin in the safe house, letting his hair grow back in and recovering from the entire ordeal. His primary motivation for staying, however, was that he wanted to assist in the release of his father from the East German prison camp. It took a few weeks to coordinate negotiations with the East for release of a specific prisoner from the work camp East of Berlin. At first the East Germans denied that the camp existed, and then when aerial photos were presented to them, they were suspicious about why this lone prisoner was being requested. The explanation stemmed from the truth, and the East Germans accepted that a relative had learned about their uncle being alive and held in this camp, and that they had political pull with the US army. After several days of negotiations, the old man was released to the West in exchange for two informants that had been caught and were being held by the British in their sector. The exchange took place and on December 21st, 1946, Rick Malloy watched from a distance as his father was walked out of East Berlin, a free man after over twelve years in prison. The older man was taken to US army intelligence headquarters for a routine debriefing and a physical, and that is where Rick was reunited with him. He wept as he saw his son waiting for him, and the reunion was touching for all who were present, none of whom knew who Rick Malloy really was or why his father had been in prison.

Epilogue

Neither Rick Malloy nor his dad had a home to go back to. They had to decide where they would go to live, as Rick could not go back to Cambridge, Massachusetts. Officially listed as killed in a plane crash in Berlin, for military purposes, Rick Malloy and his father were given new identities and passports. Because Rick had significant wealth back in the United States, the government arranged to have Rick's accounts transferred to numbered accounts that could be accessed under his new identity. The elder von Malloy would live on another sixteen years and came to know and love America, and even became a citizen of the United States. He visited his wife, and they remained friends, but did not reunite.

Rick Malloy and his dad settled in the Hanover, New Hampshire area, where Rick could teach physics at Dartmouth College and his dad would feel at home in an area where the terrain and weather were similar to his home country. Rick kept in touch with Colonel William Smith regularly and they remain good friends to this day. They even worked together a few times after this, but then that is another story.

In 1990, soon after the fall of the Berlin wall and reunification of Germany, an anonymous letter was received by the priest of a church in what had been East Berlin. The letter suggested looking behind the wall in a closet fronted by a large credenza in the front hall vestibule. Upon investigation, Thirty-one thirty-pound bars of Nazi gold, hidden for almost forty-five years, were recovered, with a street value at the time of well over six million dollars. An attractive finder's fee was paid to the church. and the remaining funds were delivered to Holocaust survivors' support organizations by the German government. This discovery set off a series of searches to recover Nazi gold for the benefit of survivors. And this led to numerous newspaper articles, and to the writing of this book.

With the reunificartion of Germany, Rick Malloy, retired, and at just over seventy years old at the time, was able to reclaim his real name and with the declassification of top secret post-war files a few years ago, he could finally tell his story.

And I was the lucky person to hear it first.

The End